Praise for

THE UNRULY PASSIONS OF EUGÉNIE R.

"Provocative. [A] poem of female desires: sexual, artistic, political, intellectual, maternal. And all of these unfold amid a richness of historical detail, rendered in elegant nineteenth-century-style prose that convincingly transports us beyond the date when Nana disappears, at the start of the Franco-Prussian War, through the siege of Paris and the fall of the Second Empire, to the hope-filled yet tragic Paris Commune and beyond."
— *New York Times Book Review*

"Second Empire Paris . . . is so richly and sensuously drawn one can almost feel it. . . . Perhaps if her contemporary, Emma Bovary, had possessed the ingenuity, wit, and tenacity of Eugénie R., Madame B. wouldn't have had to take that arsenic."
— Valerie Martin, author of *The Confessions of Edward Day*

"A lush dream filled with beauty and brutality. . . . A panoramic story of war and peace, love and betrayal, innocence and hard-won wisdom, told through the eyes of a compelling woman who kept me at her side through it all."
— Lauren Belfer, author of *A Fierce Radiance*

"Against a carefully re-cre̶̶̶̶d̶l̶̶̶̶̶̶̶̶̶̶̶̶̶e City of Lights during the 186c̶̶̶̶̶̶̶̶̶̶̶̶̶̶̶̶̶̶̶̶ng for Paris, DeSanti brings a t̶̶̶̶̶̶̶̶̶̶̶̶̶̶̶̶̶̶̶̶r the plight and passions of wor̶̶̶̶̶̶̶̶̶̶̶̶̶̶̶"
— Mireille Guiliano, ̶̶̶̶̶̶̶̶̶̶̶̶̶̶̶̶̶̶̶̶̶̶ *et Fat*

"Powerful. *The Unruly Passions of Eugénie R.* is epic fiction in the grand tradition of Dickens and Tolstoy. . . . It is impossible not to fall in love with [Eugénie] and with this magnificent novel, at once a page-turner of the highest order and a literary master-work."

— Howard Frank Mosher, author of *Walking to Gatlinburg*

"Lord! This is a great piece of work . . . [Eugénie Rigault] lives up in her head even as her boots are in the mud of desperation, and her loves and lovers have layers on layers — just as does the society DeSanti makes on the page. How beautifully this is written. How rare that is to discover on the page."

— Dorothy Allison, author of *Bastard Out Of Carolina*

"A magnificent novel in scope and achievement, powerfully written yet delicately evocative. DeSanti's undoubted literary skills bring the life and times to vivid life. Death does its worst, passion wears itself out, civilisation moves a notch forward, and with it, or because of it, female understanding of what it is to be a woman. A book to make you think."

— Fay Weldon, author of *Chalcot Crescent*

"There is much vivid, sensual writing of the dark underworld of 1860s Paris in this book of a girl seeking the man who abandoned her and the child she lost. With unflinching vision, the author portrays a perilous world where women can rely only on each other for a better life and one woman will never give up."

— Stephanie Cowell, author of *Claude & Camille: A Novel of Monet*

"There is nothing more magical than being transported right into the heart of another world, in this case, nineteenth-century Paris, the city of light at its most transformative moment, and its bordellos, the dark velvety centers of sex, sin, and political intrigue."

— Lynn Hunt, Eugen Weber Professor of Modern European History, UCLA

"Epic times make for epic books. *The Unruly Passions of Eugénie R.* is both sweeping in scope and painstaking in detail. Eugénie R.'s story, from naive goosegirl to resilient survivor, makes for wonderful, suspenseful reading, but tumultuous Paris is equally compelling, laid out here by DeSanti in all her grisly or gorgeous glory. If you love a novel that brings a place and time alive again, this one is for you. If you love a novel of character and adversity, again, here it is."

— Karen Joy Fowler, author of *The Jane Austen Book Club*

"Eugénie R. is every girl in a daguerreotype looking over her shoulder, every woman with a baby hurrying away from you down a gaslit street, and then, too, she is the first of her kind, a woman who stands at her own barricades and fights a France determined to render her silent. I lost myself wholeheartedly in her story, and would have followed her down any narrow alley, into any candlelit room, just to know what happened, to stay back there and to delay coming home."

— Sarah Blake, author of *The Postmistress*

THE UNRULY
PASSIONS

— OF —

EUGÉNIE R.

CAROLE DESANTI

Mariner Books
Houghton Mifflin Harcourt
BOSTON   NEW YORK

To my friends

First Mariner Books edition 2013
Copyright © 2012 by Carole DeSanti

For information about permission to reproduce selections from this book,
write to Permissions, Houghton Mifflin Harcourt Publishing Company,
215 Park Avenue South, New York, New York 10003.

www.hmhbooks.com

Library of Congress Cataloging-in-Publication Data
DeSanti, Carole.
The unruly passions of Eugénie R. / Carole DeSanti.
p. cm.
ISBN 978-0-547-55309-2   ISBN 978-0-547-84021-5 (pbk.)
1. Self-realization in women — Fiction. 2. France — History —
Second Empire, 1852–1870 — Fiction. I. Title.
PS3604.E7549U57 2012
813'.6 — dc22
2011016540

Book design by Brian Moore

Printed in the United States of America
DOC 10 9 8 7 6 5 4 3 2 1

The logic of passion is insistent.

— STENDHAL

PROLOGUE

PARIS, MAY 1871

This train, the *Aurore,* is a night train, headed south-south-west. A drape is secured across the window and behind it is a deep, quiet blackness. The compartment is a box with brass locks, rough-napped tapestry, and some silk fringe; fitted with a lamp. Here, one can remove one's gloves, take the knife from the boot; perhaps find again the textures of things, or one's own thoughts. Between one place and another, at last neither here nor there. It is a respite, a still rush of night air. Behind us: the roar of a city on the brink of burning.

An hour ago we stopped for dinner just outside the capital, at a café counter in a station where the French tricolor flag still flew, and it was strange to see it in place of the Commune's red, the defiant banners and colorful rags that had cropped up across the capital like spring poppies after a long winter.

We had a hasty meal, and then the entire body of passengers (Prussian officers included) climbed a low rise to see what we could. Whether, on the horizon, a dull red pyre lit the evening sky. Someone had a telescope, and silently, among strangers, we passed it from hand to hand. From this distance, no sign. The Prussians stood silent. They must certainly be marveling at a Paris again under siege, on the heels of what came before. If Paris burns, it will be the second

time in my life that I have left fires behind, flames that laid waste to
all I had known.

No sound but shuffling footsteps as we head back to the train.

Because I was a girl, and am now a woman, I have dreamed, some
nights. Dreams do their best to reset the soul, but it is heavy work.
Dawn, or noon, or whenever it is one pushes back the bed linens,
brings the pressing needs of the day. Those who do not dream, or
do not remember, are able with confidence to say, "I *think,* and so I
am," like the philosophers. I might once have said, "I *love,* and so
I *am,*" and then, love was lost to me along with a thousand other
things.

. . . How does a woman learn to doubt herself? When does it
happen, and why? Is it in her blood and bones from birth, does her
mother nurse her on it? Or is the alphabet learned later, then syllable by syllable a secret language between mind and heart, an argument between lovers? A night full of tears; by dawn, a heart gnawed
to pieces. Ah, but it conjures itself to life, doubt. Preys on the sleeping; is the infection of everything touched.

Sometimes it seems that she cannot answer a single question
about her life. *Why has it been thus? How did it come to be what it is?*
And how does she begin to speak when all that has been understood
has made any story too difficult to tell, when what is truly desired
is so far from possibility — when she has made herself cynical, and
before that, only guessed at what she knew? One's story is made of
gulfs and gaps; lies and arguments; the rise and fall of voices behind
walls, placards pasted up onto walls at night, torn down in a fury
and replaced. And then too — she has spent the days and weeks and
years . . . in giving way. When, at what hidden moment, was the
choice made; and what, in the end, did it yield?

I want to wake after the night's rocking journey south to be dazzled
by old white stone, the sunlight of late spring on the countryside
where I was born. A relaxation of vision, a widening, finally, of the
slits my eyes have become. Years pass, and one does not remember
what might lie beyond the Paris walls. If the train window's dark reflection could be lifted like a shade, would there be old walls, spread-

ing oaks, the arches and spires of villages? Or are we yet too near the city, its slaughtering yards and rubble heaps, places where the night soil is dumped and the capital's detritus is hauled to be picked over by ravens and urchins. Where the old women drag themselves, one-time boulevard girls rattling like stray stones. The grand *cocotte* who didn't safeguard her hoard when she might have, and now sews sandbags for the Commune's street barricades or serves the forts. All of a woman's appetites become fiercer as she drives herself to ruin—I have seen it a thousand times.

Underneath my ribs, heat flickers—a feeling secured by whalebones and laces but nevertheless a hot, tight orb of—*what?*—rises and smolders in my throat.

As I boarded, a group of off-duty soldiers staggered through the aisles—French government troops stationed outside Paris, now encroaching on the Commune's barricades and as ill-behaved as they were rumored to be. Searching out contraband, they said—*evidence of insurgency*—but they rifled through hand baggage, pulled cases off the racks, laughing and joking. Hunger rose from their bodies like the reek of cheap brandy. But I have knives in my eyes now, as well as in my boot; and I swayed through the cars unscathed, pressing my skirts through the narrow aisles.

I am in first class with the Prussians, but the lock is secure and I have no business with them. How I arrived here—in this compartment of blood, doubt, and collusion, all tacked together with elegant railway fittings and the black brocade of my going-away coat—is a question even I who lived it must ask. The *Aurore*'s whistle howls; we stop; then slowly pull out of an unlit station. Now we are well beyond the girdling Paris walls, the stones and mortar that Parisians call the *enceinte*.

Another train, another time. A girl, myself—a stranger now—one who took it upon herself to dare her destiny, and lost. I close my eyes against the roaring.

> *Horridas nostrae mentis purga tenebras.*
> Cleanse us of the horrible darknesses of our minds.

BOOK I

BETRAYAL

All that I have not dared say aloud,
I am going to set down on paper.

— MOGADOR, *Memoirs*

~ 1 ~

To Paris, 1861

THE TRAIN, NEARLY EMPTY when I boarded, had filled.
La Loupe, Chartres, Rambouillet, Versailles—each station a fresh roar of voices, a jostling of shoulders and parcels and luggage. The car smelled of damp wool and iron, musky
sweat and sour bodies; the windows were grimy with soot and
dusk. In the seat next to me, empty an hour ago, was a stranger
wearing the crumbs of his dinner—bread and Camembert. Once
inside the Porte Maillot the carriage halted suddenly, went black for
an instant of silence, a gasping intake of breath: *"Next, Saint-Lazare!"* We shuddered forward. I squeezed shut my eyes, *wishing it
all away?* And abruptly smacked my head against the rail on the
seat ahead, bone against iron; a wave of dizziness and emotion—
Wait, turn back the clock, is it all a terrible mistake? A charred, acrid
odor.

"PARIS!"

"They'll be unloading us directly from the station to the hospital
wards soon enough," muttered the stranger, brushing crumbs off
his waistcoat. "Just drop us off at La Salpêtrière!"

Paris. My aching brow. The bump was already beginning to swell
into an egg.

"*. . . A hat, you goose — gloves,*" Stephan had said, thrusting into my hands these unfamiliar items, companions to the soft silk of the dress I was wearing. *"You can't go about Paris bare-fisted and naked above the neck!"* Now the veil's decorative flecks swarmed before my eyes, an irritating nest of spots.

In the cab, scents of horse and leather, musky cologne in the chilly air; my breath misting the window. Sharp, rolling turn down an ancient alley with walls close enough to touch. A stairway too steep to climb, cut into stone; rusted iron loops for handholds and strips of cloth on a blackened beam for a door. I hung hard to a strap as the cab took a steep, winding descent.

"Passage Tivoli, rue Saint-Lazare!" came the shout, and I reached for my handbag. Fat, stuffed to bursting, the flimsy thing, but I counted out every last sou of the fare. The driver threw a curse behind me; I flushed hot under my veil. In my limited experience of travel, Stephan had paid, and undoubtedly tipped, the cabmen. Before that, it was the rutted market road to Mirande on the back of a mule, or we traveled on foot, and not very far.

Dusk had fallen. A double archway led to an arcade divided from the road by a gutter; suspended lanterns swayed above, with illuminated letters: HÔTELS: TIVOLI, NO. 1; LISIEUX, NO. 2; VAUCLUSE, NO. 3. Every surface was plastered with placards and signs — generations of ruined broadsheets and framed notices for SALONS. CHAMBRES. CABINETS. Gaslit signs, lozenge-shaped, glowed above the hotel entrances, and a dubious gust scattered debris into a corner. Stephan had said that rooms in Paris were in short supply.

The Tivoli was nearest, and from behind the desk, Madame evaluated the scrap of black velvet on my head and its drag of veil; ran her eye over my smooth, strangled fingers clutching the strings of my handbag. Her shawl had a fringe of jet beads that clicked like a patter of rain, or Maman's rosary when she tackled her penitence after months of neglect.

Silently, the required envelope crossed the counter, white against the pitted mahogany. Its edge was sharp, unsullied as fresh linen;

the seal, red wax like a drop of blood, once hot and now congealed. I had laughed, the afternoon Stephan dipped his pen, finished, and dusted the page. We weren't drinking champagne then, but tingling bubbles were still in our noses. *"You'll see how things are done in Paris!"*

Madame slipped a knife under the wax and, with great and slow deliberation, unfolded the document inside, a thick, milky sheet. Her eyes narrowed and her gaze slipped over the page; then from the page to me and back again—cataloguing qualities unknown, the way my cousin cast his eye over the beam of a measuring scale as he slit open the bellies of the ducks and geese to weigh their livers for *foie de canard, foie d'oie.* Now, Madame's eyes narrowed again with an *opinion,* the kind that is a known truth to the rest of the world. I had an impulse to turn and flee—but where?

"Haussmann is nearly on our doorstep with the tear-down boys," she said finally, with a solicitude purchased, perhaps, by Stephan's pen. "There's not a room left on the Passage, but you're lucky tonight, Mademoiselle Rigault. Yes? Very well then." She slid the envelope back across the desk; now it showed a pinkish stain where the wax had been. "Ladies' curfew at seven, sharp. No gentlemen above stairs. We have no improprieties *here.*" She gave me another beakish, penetrating look. "Candles twenty sous, gas is not piped all the way up." Outside, from the *bar à vin* across the Passage, came shouts and drunken, echoing laughter.

My throat ached; the lump on my brow throbbed; my belly gave a hollow stab and a rush of heat rose behind my eyes . . . Paris. *City of light, center of the World. Of civilization; of art.* It took several matches, cheap and smoldering, to ignite a taper that revealed the attributes of room 12 atop an interminable stair: a scrap of carpet worn down to the threads, walls spidered with cracks, and a sagging mattress on an iron bedstead. A wooden chair, a candle stand. Freezing, dusty with neglect; the very walls closing in with a reproach.

I wedged the back of the chair under the knob. Then after a while, lay stiffly on top of the bedcovers in my street clothes and under my cloak, listening to my heart pound and the blood surge in my ears; crashes and yelps from the alley below. Cold seeped up through the floorboards.

Of all the damp gloom and dusky shades I had so far encountered, the void next to me was the most disconcerting and lonely of all. But Stephan would know, as well as I, this gaping emptiness; my lover would be feeling my absence just as I felt his. Yes, I had gambled; exchanged all that had defined me in the world—a rustic life in a distant province (where anyone who had ever been to the capital at all was called a Parisien for life)—the rutted road and antique habits of church and village, the goose pens, the obligations of a daughter—for Stephan's kisses and his promises, murmured like silk to my neck and imprinted on every part of me, stamped into the wax of my being. Yes, I had contoured my life to his since Saint Martin's Day last November, with not much to show for it but a promise and some borrowed finery against the January winds—but still.

"Don't doubt me, Eugénie," he had said. *"Doubt, you know, is contagious."*

The last echo before I drifted under seemed to be the voice of my mother, Berthe, mocking behind my ear . . . *You think your eggs are on the fire when only the shells are left . . . !* An old country saying, never-turn-your-back. Maman felt closer, in that instant, than Stephan, though I had left her farther behind. And in the moment of collision between what I had imagined and the clamoring consequences of my real actions came the ache of foreknowledge, like the bump on my head, and the simultaneous etherizing of it deep within.

I woke to the sound of church bells; insistent, unstopping, pulling me from the shallow marooning shoals of a dream. Dirty light filtered in through the window; a wafer of ice lay on top of the water in the pitcher. *Paris.* Blackened stub of wick in a pool of wax; an aching head and skirts pulled up and rumpled as though I had been ravished by something unseen in the night. I reached up gingerly, felt the bump above my eyebrow, glanced toward the door. The chair was in place. Splash of icy water, skirts pressed smooth with the palms of my hands. No maid, no Léonie; no iron nor fire to warm it; certainly no pot on a silver tray outside the door of number 12.

From below, the dim clink and clatter of crockery held out the promise of hot coffee, at least, so I followed the sounds down to a dull, high-windowed room. Four men in coats and cravats pushed back their chairs; and a kitchen door exhaled a cloud of steam and the odor of spent coffee grounds. A sullen boy scraped down pink tablecloths, steering around bud vases containing fabric flowers, their stems stickily coiled with green tape. Madame had said nothing about breakfast. Was it included with the price of a room?

Over the coming days, I would learn that the help spoke no French; nor did most of the guests. As unaccompanied ladies never set foot there, my appearance on that morning set off a ripple of glances that sent me slinking out to a street cart, an old woman with a coffee urn, and a tin ladle meant for workmen. She too looked fish-eyed at my gloves and hat as the wind luffed up. A strangled giggle rose in my nose and I tossed back the bitter stuff. If Stephan were here, it would all be a terrific joke — all of this unfamiliarity would disappear in a puff of smoke. Meanwhile, I must make the best of it. With the black brew in my hollow guts, I fished out my *Nouveau Plan de la Ville de Paris 1860*, with its indigo-marbled covers. My key to the capital.

By hard frost of that year — now past — the goose-girl from a tiny village hugging the Pyrenees had tasted defiance, and with it what she found she preferred: afternoons in a library sprawled on a carpet thick with Turkish flowers; a stack of leather-bound volumes pulled from the shelves. Cream with chocolate, yolks of eggs; the meat of the bird and a lover's attentions. Instead of hoarding coals in a brazier and poking the ashes on a frigid morning, as the goose-girl had once done, she enjoyed fires laid by a maid (Léonie). All of it an extravagant taste of what had, in sixteen years of living, been skimmed off the top, plucked and gathered, measured and weighed; priced and packed and sold off down to the bones and renderings. My new life fit like a tailored bodice, a dressmaker's creation tossed my way after the original wearer had cast it off. Indeed, there were corsets dug out of the chests and armoires; petticoats, bonnets, and stockings; past-fashion dresses belonging to absent relatives. In short order I learned to delight in *foie d'oie* rather than sell it; and soon greeted the rural folk at the Saturday market, the flower girl and the bread man, and chattered of our domestic affairs to Léonie, who uttered only murmurs of assent.

My seventeenth birthday had passed just after the New Year. We had celebrated it in Stephan's bed — or rather his uncle's bed, to which we had made profound claim — dining on brandy plums, *foie d'oie*, roast chicken; market cheeses, crusty white bread. The carpets were littered with corks and bones and plum stones and *Bovary*, its binding splayed over a mound past due for the wash. Stephan had tossed it there.

"In Paris, you know, girls your age are not allowed to read *Bovary*."

"What do they read?"

"Works of moral improvement that encourage them to uphold the social order!"

He laughed and threw back the bedclothes. Drowsy and effervescent, I slipped into the warm furrow his body had left. The windows were fogged from the heat of the fire; Stephan shed his robe. Water slapped gently against the sides of the bath as he stepped in. The taste of *foie d'oie* and the musk of his flesh lingered on my tongue, a touch of salt; champagne tingled through my veins. Our sprig of Saint Nicholas mistletoe still dangled on the bedpost, its white berries now dried to husks. Outside, the gardens lay under a glittering sheen of frost, the last of the roses long gone; the lush foliage of the borders stripped of color. The day's diminishing light fell through the diamond panes of mullioned glass.

"Little goose, wake up! It's nearly nighttime." My lover parted the bed curtain and stood clothed. He picked up *Bovary*, passing his fingertips along the spine. Emma, as I had left her, was bankrupt with dresses, running from lover to lover. I slipped beneath the sea of linen, awash in a strange irritation. Stephan lounged on the edge of the bed, picked up a knife from the litter on the carpet, and began peeling a winter apple. That knife drew a line between us, as he ran the blade across the fruit's surface, flaying it of its rosy skin. Then he told me a story, better than *Bovary* because it was our own. It was set in Paris and there were parties, dances—masked balls in gardens. Ice skating on frozen lakes inside the city; fires with crackling wood and hot drinks with rum. Horse carriages along the streets, with bottles of champagne. We would fool them all, delight and convince them—*who?*—I did not ask.

He dropped the paring, an unbroken spiral, to the floor. Cut a thin, perfect slice to the core, a sliver like a new moon. An owl hooted, a gentle but worrying *hoo-hoo,* very near. Toast crumbs from our bed feast pressed uncomfortably into my flesh.

"So, we will be—married?" I ventured. We had discussed it on our long flight from my home province to the chateau—it was not so much a promise as simply an understanding, clear as the sky was blue, which it was, once we left the southwest's clouds and smoke.

"But we must avoid *Bovary* at all costs, don't you think? A stifling life, both of us miserable and bored."

I giggled. "It wouldn't be; you are nothing like Charles Bovary. A dull doctor."

"I'd rather not find out if marriage transforms me, then." Stephan assured me that Paris was nothing like a tiny, convention-bound provincial village; the capital was law unto itself. I hesitated—never having considered Tillac, the place I was born, in that light. I did not miss the odor of the goose pens, though.

"Why can't we just stay here? The days will lengthen soon. The ice will melt and we can plant a kitchen garden." Fingers in the dark soil newborn from the frost, sieving it to breadcrumb size, nestling tiny seeds—carrots, lettuces—tucking them in a moist, well-aired bed, and watching for the first pale green shoot. "I'd like to eat something besides *foie d'oie.* A radish." Its taste fresh and sharp, like a slap of spring wind . . . "And if not married we should be engaged." Stephan pulled himself up and gazed into my eyes, and with all the earnest belief that this slate-eyed scion—heir to difficulties I could only imagine—could muster, he summoned up what he could.

"I will be your protector. It is—you know, how things are arranged. In Paris." And then the heavy beat of wings and a flustered scuffling above our heads, and another wavering cry.

The next morning I left for the train with the sheaf of bank notes that Stephan had laid out on the library escritoire, a cache of borrowed gowns in my traveling bag, and visions of blue silk dresses. (*"Paris skirts are very wide."*) The bolt of fabric, another New Year's gift, did not fit into my luggage; we stood awkward, the cloth between us, and tears threatening. Finally Stephan promised to bring it with him when he came. "Our first stop shall be the dressmaker," he said, planting a kiss on my brow; rather more like a father, or an elder brother, and in fact—now that I considered it—in the very place that had been smacked and was now a bruise.

Flashing, blue-fledged hue of a teal; the last of the wild-breeding ducks to appear, fast and wary of hunters in the ponds and rain-filled ruts of southern France . . . the fowl's colored feathers appear in December, briefly against his mottled brown. After that, he molts, flightless.

In this world, a girl like me, brought up with her knees regularly pressed to the flagstones, the church's incense mingled with the pine-needle scent of the forest floor—the oldest daughter of ambitious parents—such a girl did not dare her destiny, her parentage, *everything*—and lose. The consequences of would be so catastrophic, so utterly beyond the imagination—even a rich, rebellious one like my own—that they did not, even for a moment, enter my waking thoughts. But I had begun, again, to dream.

I stepped past a used-book stall, its offerings stacked like slices of bread, moldy at the crust. English hymnals, cookery books, cheap novels, and *Bovary* in two volumes, bound together with a band advertising it as BANNED! CENSORED! Somewhere in those pages Emma was in midflight, but I had lost my appetite for her travails.

The streets spiraled inward and tightened toward Notre Dame and the city's beating heart; peddlers hawked chestnuts and tobacco, coffee and thread, paper and dried fishes, songbirds and window glass. Pyramids of dusty wine bottles. Passing the shops I saw signs of my lover everywhere, tying invisible strings between Stephan and what he loved: chestnuts in honey syrup; racked bottles in a wine shop; in a patisserie window, a tower of raspberry tarts. These stood out like flags, those of the nation to which I belonged. We had brought home just such oranges in a string bag; those brandied apricots in a bottle.

Now, choppy January currents ruffled the gray waters of the Seine. I nibbled chestnuts and sipped at another coffee, bitterer than the first. Nearby a gang of workers in blue *cottes* were packing up their spades and turning their horses. The wind picked up; I shivered under a paisley cashmere, borrowed warmth. Blisters already chafed under my boots, very nice kid ones that buttoned up the side, barely worn, recently white.

Back at the Hôtel Tivoli, with no knife to cut a loaf of bread, peel an apple, or pare a portion of sausage and cheese so as not to have to bite off chunks with my teeth like an animal — with no cup nor table at which to drink from it, I took out a thin sheet of paper from a fresh, new stationer's package. With a sharp-nibbed pen atop the shaky candle stand, I wrote, *Dear Stephan, I saw the Seine today, and a cart full of Seville oranges . . .*

In the wavery, pitted mirror of number 12 was a young woman, myself, certainly — dark hair and pale skin; not so badly off in her borrowed finery. The soft hair, the curve of cheek and shine of my eyes — violet-gray (a shade off Stephan's) — were as they had always been; but the calluses and rough edges of a faraway province had been buffed away in recent months by some chemistry of love and unaccustomed kinds of bathing. Staring, I willed blindness on myself; insistent, willful ignorance. The holes in the story I told myself, pinpricks of truth like the quills sticking through the mattress ticking of number 12, would become rips as long as those my petticoats would show in a few weeks' time. But doubt, smaller than a tiny seed, sown somewhere deep — had not yet sent its root tendril; had no thought, yet, of unfurling its leaf.

THE TRAP

ANY PAINTER'S DAUGHTER (and I was one, of course) knows that a picture requires constancy of place, climate, care, and conditions to maintain and protect its surface, to prevent its color from cracking and falling away. But to apply these principles to life — to shield it from the ebb and flow, the shifting and carrying on, the wearing away — this knowledge my mother, Berthe, did not pass on. She never explained what substance hours and days are made of; nor how time wears on the mind when one is in love. How a lover, once present, becomes a story you tell yourself — although I believe that she knew these things.

It was soon clear that the Tivoli was not a pleasant place to spend time. For one, the clerk who frequently replaced Madame at the desk pretended not to notice my presence, while I knew that he had. When he appeared I lowered my head as the sheep to the dog. Only once in the corridors had I seen a guest anything like myself — a blonde, pale-browed girl in indiscriminate garb — "neither fish nor fowl," as Maman would say, and not to flatter. The girl appeared only briefly; when I looked for her again she was gone. With my diminishing clutch of bank notes the initial charms of the capital were already, by the third day, wearing thin. Dingy swells of working girls coming and going, knots of beggars in the shadows of Notre

Dame, the tides of workmen with their spades; and unapproachably extravagant shops on the rue de la Paix — all were becoming tainted with vinegar, like wine going off. Omnibuses passed up and down the rue Saint-Lazare while I walked endlessly and without destination in shoes not meant for cobbles; in a veil that trapped the street dirt in my eyes. (My old sabots, woolen dress, and thick winter cloak would have stood up better to the conditions, but those things had vanished as though they never were.)

By the time dusk fell, the working girls in sparrow brown and the cinched and silk-clad shoppers alike disappeared behind gates and doors, the battered clang and the turn of latchkeys echoing behind them. I hurried to make it back to the hotel by curfew, with no idea of what would happen if I was late — would I be stopped by a gray-coated police officer, like those patrolling the perimeter of the Luxembourg Gardens? Scolded by Madame, thrown in prison, taken before a court? So every evening I returned helplessly to dwindling provisions laid in for this siege of waiting.

Across the street from the Tivoli, the crinoline shop's empty bells swayed, knocking dully against one another in the sharp gusts.

On day five, the baker on the farther end of the Passage Tivoli cut bread into squares and put the samples out in a basket. A woman at the counter (wrapped in a blue shawl too good for the dress underneath) moved her hand cautiously from basket to mouth and back again, slowly moving her jaw as though trying to make the chewing movements small and invisible. Out of kindness, the baker had turned his back.

And now I missed Stephan terribly. No response had come to four nights of notepaper beset with inky, faithful marks and envelopes stamped boldly with the hotel's address. Each morning, Madame sorted letters on the mahogany desk — her usual method was to extract some few and mysteriously disappear with them while I stared at the newspapers and waited for the shadow indicating her return. Eventually she proceeded to sort the mail into pigeonholes by guestroom, her bulk eclipsing the whole project. From no place in the lobby was it possible to discern whether an envelope had found its way into pigeonhole number 12, and so I was ignorant of my fate until the whole abysmal task was complete. Then, empty-handed and with a hole in my heart, I went out to walk.

Around the supper hour the lamps flared to life; my stomach pinged, and the trousered portion of the citizenry and those on their arms proceeded to conviviality and dinner. I lingered before a chalked board in front of the restaurant Trap a short way up the rue Saint-Lazare.

Potage aux Croutons

Spécialité du Jour: Fricandeau

Potage de Fantasie

Bouilli Ordinaire

Dessert: Tartes Sucrées

The parted curtains exhaled warmth and the scent of mussels and garlic; the *chink* of cutlery and the music of glassware floated out to the street. On one of these evenings, the barman appeared with a cloth flung over his shoulder.

"The *soupe du jour* is good tonight, the *boeuf à la mode* like butter. And some very nice oysters grilled in their shells." He nodded at a pile of bricks and rubble. "They won't cease over there, will they? Pulling people's houses down around their ears. The dust today was terrible. Why don't you come in? The wolves are kind at the Trap." When he squinted, creases feathered around his eyes, but he was not an old man.

But I shook my head and hurried back up the Passage.

By seven on the Friday of my first week in Paris, I was pacing my room and rationing candle ends—cheap, fast-burning tapers bought from a sundries shop. A bottle of spot remover, cheap stationery and broken pen nibs, and the remains of my own dinner, chocolate crumbs wrapped in paper, were crowded on the small candle stand. Like the worn-out carpet, flat pillows, and meager walls, life itself had thinned, and I dwelt on what, in the recent

months with Stephan, had been thick and fat: rugs and rose petals; framed pictures; pillows and featherbeds that were fluffed and
tucked into place every morning. Cream in coffee, the glistening
edge of the meat. Hours marked by chimes, heavy and honey-
laden, like dusty bottles of Sauternes in a cellar; not least, Stephan's
presence, around which I could wind my self and soul. It had begun to seem like a dream as I flopped onto the flat, prickly mattress and faced the ceiling cracks, seeking the connection between
these forking lines in the plaster and the events that had led me to
stare at them now. A plausible story to wrap around my situation.
Smuggled up from the lobby was the evening's entertainment, a
copy of *Paris Illustré*, with its society events, brief anecdotes, and
gossip.

From this source I learned that on the contract day of her marriage, Mademoiselle de Gr——'s engagement gifts from her equally
aristocratic fiancé, Monsieur de T——, included antique lace, an
ivory fan, a candy box inlaid with semiprecious stones, two cashmere shawls, and a purse of gold coins for charity . . . Also, that
residents of the rue Saint-Jacques would miss a familiar figure, a
tall gray-clad lady who had wandered the neighborhood carrying a
shredded umbrella and a zinc pail into which tourists dropped coins.
She had been found dead in her lodgings (asphyxiation by fumes
from a coal stove, a suicide). She was in such poverty that she made
her bed in a soap crate, but in a metal box inside her chimneypiece
was a fortune in bank notes, along with a letter asking that the funds
be used to fly her to the moon. Her one-time love had gone there already, she wrote—a soap magnate who had lost his fortune . . . And
that it was now possible to find twenty-nine varieties of mustard
in the capital, among them Red, Powdered, Flavored with Garlic,
with Capers, or Anchovies; with Lemon, Tarragon, Fines Herbes.
Truffled, prepared for the empress in honor of a marquise; Tomato,
Black, Green, Roman, and "For the Health"; this last, though prized
as a condiment, was also known for the treatment of—

Next to my ear I heard a sighing sizzle, and the last of the candle
ends snuffed out: then, silence. In the darkness, afterimages of the
newsprint floated.

EMPEROR EMPLOYS GAS IN PALACES,
DISAPPROVES OF ELECTRICAL LIGHTING INDOORS.

CONSTRUCTION WORK ON THE RUE DE RIVOLI TO PROCEED
AT NIGHT: FEMALE VIEWERS, ESPECIALLY FOREIGN
TOURISTS, WISE TO BE ESCORTED.

RENTS SOAR: LODGINGS IN PARIS IN SHORT SUPPLY.
ARTISTS AND STUDENTS REVOLT.

PLAGUES OF RATS AND LICE.

GREATER NUMBERS SEEN IN THE UNRULY FEMALE POPULATION;
MORALS BRIGADE TO ADD OFFICERS.

EMPRESS TO HOLD USUAL WINTER ENTERTAINMENTS.

What I had gleaned, these emptied-out evenings, was that an intricate web of law and social relations spread out over the capital like a giant net. From cradle cap to mourning veil, fashion, rumor, and gossip suggested what was good and bad, frowned on or approved. Columns and anecdotes hinted, critiqued, and applauded like great crowds pointing and chattering on every corner, making oblique references to the Code Civil. I knew about the Code Napoleon and how it had abolished a piecework of old feudal laws and practices, organized the legal system — but I wished that the rules of Paris — *"law unto itself!"* — had been spelled out. (Of course, if they had I would have been confronted with the fact that the Code Civil had also been written to organize out of society exactly the behavior that had thus far characterized my path — that is, passionate flight and a love affair with a man not my social equal — though of course, this was not how I viewed it at the time.) Instead, I could draw my conclusions only from the mysterious rules about hotel rooms, reports of old women who slept in soap crates, and the information that a poor girl whose virtue had been compromised might stick her arm full of darning needles and find a career as a hysteric at La Salpêtrière.

If Stephan were here we would have discussed it all, and he would have laughed and said that neither love nor money should drive you mad. But—where *was* Stephan? Why had he not arrived? I was about as equipped to manage Paris alone as to fly to the moon myself. A queasy wash of anxiety swung my feet to the floor.

Downstairs, the desk was unattended and the lobby empty but for a single man wearing a pince-nez. He glanced up from his papers, frowning as I headed past without looking to the left or right; and the hotel door swung wildly open, gale-force winds seizing it. The latch fell to; a gust caught my skirts at the mouth of the Passage.

The Trap's draperies billowed with a moist, fragrant breeze. At this hour, the early crowd had gone and had been replaced by a loud, convivial group. A hundred pairs of eyes flew in my direction and lit like beetles, as waiters in blue aprons carried zinc trays aloft, unloaded plates of food, uncorked bottles, poured, and bent to hear their customers over the din.

With a gesture of pleased surprise, the barman (whose name I learned was Claude) settled me at a small table in a corner. I did not know whether to remove my hat and gloves or where to look, so I just stared at the bread and butter, served on a saucer. The butter was pressed with the letters REST TRAP. A carafe appeared.

"*Bouilli ordinaire?*" I said; the most modest of the chalked offerings. Then waited, hands twisting in my lap; finally, with gloves on, lifting the veil to put each morsel between my lips, and nibbling. A few women were dining with companions at neighboring tables, and they were not eating with their gloves and veils in place.

When the barman reappeared he removed, with a flourish, the lid from a steaming copper pot. "*Potage de Fantasie,* mademoiselle," said Claude, ladling it into a generous white bowl. "Ham, a good cut of veal, yolk of eggs, sweet almonds. Last portion; I'm about to wipe it off the board." And he broke into a crinkled smile, refilling my glass. I lifted the spots from my eyes and spoon-by-spooned every last glorious speck, and at the end of the meal the bill read only *bouilli, vin.* Claude told me to come again when I liked, though he could not promise the *Fantasie,* and saw me to the door. So: glancing up and down the rue Saint-Lazare for gray-coated gendarmes (for it was they who enforced the Code and curfew) and seeing none, I half-ran all the way back to the Tivoli, getting in on the coattails of the pince-nez, who had a key.

"What about *soupe* tonight, but just a very plain one?" The next evening, the clock's hands again stood past six, my luck had not changed; once again I was hungry.

Claude smiled and gestured toward the bar, where a man was half-sprawled. "Look—he's not a bad fellow, likes his abs but he's no *bibard*, and doesn't need to be killing himself. He's been here since four. Get him into a cab for me and *soupe* is on the house."

Long, strong fingers wrapped loose around a glass; an immense length of leg in tight black trousers, great knobs of knees, an old pair of boots spattered with color. He had fine gold-brown hair and great calf's eyes too large for his face; an arm done up in a bandage made of a bar towel. Tall, gangly lope of a man.

Before him on the bar was an array of objects—a tall, narrow-necked green bottle with a flowery label; a pitcher of water and a bowl heaped with lumps of sugar; a small, spade-shaped filigree spoon, a glass. He poured a measure from the green bottle, balanced the spoon on the glass's rim; reached for the sugar bowl, but then knocked over the whole setup. Liquid pooled, a pale silvery green stain; ice slithered over the zinc. He swore and swiped at the mess.

"Pierre Chasseloup. He won't bite," Claude encouraged.

"'If a man be bitten or stung by a hornet, a scorpion, wormwood gives you a present cure.' That's from—well, at the moment I can't remember where it's from. But it's good for what's killing you."

"You've been bitten all right, Chasseloup," said Claude.

"Help a man get a drink, would you?" He turned in my direction. "Spanish wormwood, *Artemisia absinthium,* and Swiss herbs. You can't get this bottle in Paris and I won't have another drop spilled. Do you have a steady hand, mademoiselle? I have just been all day with medical men, but I am better off here. Two fingers of the green stuff—that's right—a lump on the spoon, my luckiest of evil spoons, pour water over—that's it—slowly, slowly! Let it trickle. Now, water well, but not too well. Claude, ice!"

He lifted the spoon from the glass's rim and took a delicate sip, closing his eyes and inhaling. "Now I have drunk an opal."

The drapes billowed again, blowing the cold and the cobbles through anise and beer, mussels and garlic; a waiter's starched apron flew up. My stomach clenched; it was six forty-five.

"Have you been in an accident?" I asked, looking at his arm.

"Without a doubt! A social accident, with Badinguet pulling the strings. How fast can we run the trains without knocking off too many in first class? And then, we poor souls don't even know what hit us. Dizziness—a numbness of the extremities—headaches, forgetfulness? Unusual behavior? Bouts of crying, waking in the night? What do you think? Is it a case of railway spine? This is what the medical men are interested in, to the extent that they can bill you for it . . . Paris is a powder keg. *'Abandon hope all ye who enter here. Through these gates you pass into the city of woe—'* To hell with a broken arm; I have Claude for that." He tipped up his glass, swallowed, and closed his eyes. "The entire railway concept is a wreck of human consciousness, of our conception of time. Barman, a glass for mademoiselle! Mademoiselle—?"

"Rigault." I supplied the name warily. "Who is Badinguet?"

"The lady's hotel has a curfew," said Claude. But he slid a glass down the bar.

" . . . Hotel?" Pierre Chasseloup looked at me for the first time. Heat rose in my cheeks.

"I have just arrived in Paris."

The man tipped a finger of absinthe into my glass and set up the spoon for sugar. I poured again and watched the liquid turned from green to cloudy white. Its scent was heady, thick with field flowers and weeds; licorice and mint and something sweet. The taste of it was bitterer than its scent and the liquid trickled down my throat like hot wax, all the way down my hollow interior. In the mirror over the bar, I saw a pale girl with tumbling dark hair, head to head with a stranger, and my hand went to my brow. My own injury (now dressed with a tincture from the pharmacy, including some concealing powder for the bruise) was still tender and aching.

"Badinguet is the carpenter who lent his trousers in order that this pretension-to-a-name, Louis Napoleon, could escape from his English jail cell, convince the peasantry of his glorious identicalness to his imperial uncle, sneak into Paris, and steal France after the economy had collapsed. Thus. 'Badinguet,' we say, to cut him back down to size. Are you here to model, Mademoiselle Rigault, did I see you on Monday on the rue Bonaparte? Your bones have an Italian proportion."

"No."

"Because I have to paint like a madman over the next few weeks."

"With a broken arm?" I eyed the dingy bar-towel bandage.

"With or without, like a journalist who must have the story out in the morning, whether or not it is true." He gave a short laugh. "So if you are not a model, are you a relation to that self-advertising brigand of the Left Bank cafés, Rigault? . . . No again? Names are portents. As for mine, the wolf is chasing me; and I must turn things around ere I perish in its teeth."

"Sir, I think that I might—need some air." The liquor was tightening around my head like a band of iron, blurring my vision. All of the silver and glass was catching sparks of hazy light, and I had to eat something or faint. Chasseloup slid his long body off the stool with a bouncing slide, as though his bones were made of India rubber, as perhaps they were, by then.

"Absinthe is best taken serially," he said. "Let's go." I glanced anxiously for Claude; the barman caught my eye and waved.

The street cobbles were wet, and the chill had seeped through to my skin by the time a cab pulled up, leaking a stream of gaseous heat from the brazier as the door swung open. Here it was, a ticket to Claude's *soupe*—or—what? Stephan's startled eyes rose before me.

"Climb in," Chasseloup said. "I'll take you—where will I take you? For a nightcap at the Gare du Nord?" He stood next to me, waiting.

"Hey," shouted the coachman, "that's my coal you're burning." In the warmth of the cab's brazier that drifted into the night air, through the lingering scent of absinthe, the artist's arm smelled of linseed oil and pigment, like raw earth. *Her* scents. Maman's — Berthe's. Like a warning, of a known place I should not like to visit again. Beguiling, sirenlike, but dangerous and full of betrayal. His coat, a shabby soft leather, pressed lightly against my arm.

"I can pay you three francs a sitting."

"No, I don't model."

"My studio is on the Impasse de la Bouteille. Look, I will even give you the omnibus fare in advance." He dug in his pocket. "No? Are you sure? And you really won't come with me to the Nord? . . . Go, then!" he said to the driver, and slammed the cab's door. "I can't afford the ride." He rocked back on his heels and swayed: an exaggerated dance of movement, a comment on it all, a joke, a bow, a form melting into the darkness.

It was past seven. No clock needed to say so, as not a female soul lingered on the street save two, gaily dressed, passing through the Passage to the Tivoli Gardens on the arms of their beaux; a gaggle of echoing laughter. Starving now, absinthe-queasy, I risked my luck a second time, ducking back under the Trap's drape. Collected my *soupe* from Claude at the end of the bar, the barman winking in complicity as I ignored the other inquiring eyes. What a game of cat and mouse! But my stomach didn't know the difference.

Madame was sitting by the desk in an armchair, knitting by gas lamp, when I made my way back to the Tivoli, loitering wretchedly in the shadows like a thief, just past the HÔTEL lozenge, until I could follow someone in. Tonight it was a man in a greatcoat, and he skirted me as though I carried the plague. Madame cast an ominous, judging glance over her clicking needles, and I wondered if tomorrow morning might be my last at the Tivoli. My thoughts flew inexplicably to the clerk, and the pale girl . . . Madame clicked away as I slunk past her and upstairs. Like an old *tricoteuse* at the guillotine, plying her skein as the heads fell, counting stitches. *Counting.*

3

CHASSELOUP

Is it the one you've been waiting for?" the clerk said softly, with his lingering, sticky glance. The Tivoli's lobby smelled of mildew and ancient horsehair. I'd just come in from the icy wind, from spending a few sous on hot chestnuts, a bar of chocolate, more postage stamps. Then my heart began to pound. A sliver of white had appeared in number 12's pigeonhole behind the mahogany; thin as the edge of a new moon. At last!

He reached for the envelope with an elaborate gesture, held it down with his thumb a moment too long. Leaned over to peer at the postmark. "From the baronet, perhaps? Monsieur de Chaveignes? . . . Why, you think we don't do our research, mademoiselle? But we must protect our establishment." I recalled Madame's scrutiny of Stephan's original document. The envelope now in my hand had a strange, foreign texture and many stamps. *Mlle. B*—the letters blurred. I passed it back across the desk.

"But this letter is not addressed to me at all! It's not mine."

"Oh! Well, we do have so few mademoiselles here," the clerk said, full of sly, barely veiled delight and—I grasped finally that my link with the outside world, to Stephan—to Stephan's return—depended on his ill intentions and the poisonous Madame. "My apologies, it is R—Rigault, isn't it? It's not for number 12 at all, but number 16. And you are vacating your room tomorrow, is that correct?"

I turned my back without answering.

According to the *Nouveau Plan de Paris 1860*, Pierre Chasseloup's studio on the Impasse de la Bouteille did not lie across the Seine, near the cafés and artists' haunts, but past Les Halles and uphill. Traveling there, the heels of my boots sank into the gaps between the cobbles as I traipsed past looming advertisements for fabric and chocolate. Giant stockinged legs marched across walls; vests and jackets drawn in silhouette paraded along like the vestments of ghosts. One window displayed linens and bed coverings; another, crinolines. The Impasse de la Bouteille itself was a tiny alleyway in a seedy central district, a gate at its mouth . . . NO. 53, HAT MAKER. I touched my own head apparel, the element of my dress that marked me out from the crowd and conferred its whiff of the gentlewoman's armoire, the veil a shred of the social net that I was about to fall through, probably before the fashions changed.

"Fill this from the pump, while you're down there!" The voice came from above, and down came a long cord with a key and a pail tied to the end of it. "Four *hundred* omnibuses have passed since I saw you last," said the painter when I arrived, dizzy and breathless, face to face with him at the threshold of the studio, with half a bucket of water. His arm in a bar towel splashed with color.

"You counted them?"

He laughed, and heat rose in my cheeks.

"I'm sorry, monsieur. But I walk where I'm going."

Behind him, the dull gray morning had turned pearly and glistening. A bird flew by, astonishingly, at eye level: the studio was made entirely of glass, a room built from windows, high above the city, looking like a great eye onto the heavens and rooftops; chimney pots exhaled smudges of smoke, and the thinnest branches of treetops made a filigree pattern against the sky. The February gloom filtered whitely through clouds; and something within me startled and awoke.

I stood dazzled by the light, numb and dizzy with hunger. To one side of the studio, a clothes rack sagged with silk bombazines, velvet-trimmed satin, dark suit coats; hats with plumes, crinolines, shawls striped and paisley; plain, short trousers and miniature petticoats. Despite its light, the studio was cold and my fingers and toes were numb. I blew on my fingertips. Chasseloup gestured to the screen.

"What do you want me to put on?"

"Nothing. Perhaps a drape."

"But—"

"This is a photographer's studio. The faithful citizens of Paris come to rent someone else's Sunday best and have their portraits taken. I, however, *paint*," Chasseloup said. "If you please, mademoiselle? It is this morning's light I am after."

Behind the screen was a teetering clutch of objects—horn and violin, silk flowers, a plaster Venus, apothecary bottles, columns of Greek design. A few sketches, nude figures without heads, were crumpled in a corner. Gooseflesh stood out on my arms; their soft fluff prickled and stood up. I bit my lip and undid my skirt with stiff fingers. A film of grit covered the floor, dusting the soles of my feet; tears threatened. Just because I had undressed for one man did not mean I might do so for any comer, but perhaps, given the circumstances, given the fact that I had to earn something to wait for my protector where we had agreed—

A faint impatient rustling from across the studio. "I am an *artist*, mademoiselle, not a rapist. Are you coming?"

"One minute." I grappled with a piece of drapery, hugging it around me.

"The cloth, please?"

"I—I have modeled only for my mother, and . . . sorry, I'm—"

"Ah, so you have modeled. Keep the drapery then, for now."

He slung a chair on top of a wooden crate, took it down again, stared at the box from one corner of the room and then the other, rearranged panels against the windows, changing the angle of light. When I climbed onto the crate and stood as he indicated, the slats felt unsteady, like they might splinter and crack. After a few minutes my arms went numb and I began to count back from a hundred:

ninety-nine . . . ninety-eight . . . ninety-seven . . . clenching my lip; fingers and toes going blue; blood stopped in the veins. All around was sky. My mind whitened.

How I had once loved the colors in Berthe's paint box: cinnabar, lapis, viridian, gold leaf. And her tools: pigment-grinding stones, a tiny mortar and pestle, and, fanned out in the box's lid, brushes two or three hairs wide, for painting miniatures. A small oval palette, and her high-keyed attention humming the air. Her art supplies had arrived in stamped packages from Paris, along with parcels of lacy underclothes.

Every two years, in the latest days of winter, when the earth had barely thawed and we planned our kitchen garden, Maman's paintings were ready to ship north, just like the crates of foie gras had been sent the previous autumn. She stayed up at night writing letters, streams of black ink ribboning across parchment; her hair falling from its pins. Sanded and ready for envelopes, the letters lay across the rough planks of our dining table, crisp emissaries ready for the long march. I was enlisted to read out the Salon regulations about measurements, mounts, crates, the date by which the paintings must arrive. It was a testing situation, the subject of much anxiety. The roads out of Tillac were barely more than potholed tracks, and a mule with a crate on its back would be challenged by unsettled weather, wolves, thieves, rain . . . And Berthe's connection to the capital of the art world was tenuous at best. Her ambition was encouraged by her teacher at Auch, who remembered (with the haziness of passing years) back to the past century, when any number of women had painted for the Paris Salon. And my father would have carried crates to the capital on his own back if he had thought it would make her happy.

Her paintings must, and would, be judged in Paris. The outcome mattered terribly to her, and thus to us all. And so we waited. Through the weeks, the months, the summer. Finally, Papa would rush across the square from the *mairie*, holding the envelope with the Paris stamps. From the time when I was very young, I learned that this event was the one to be dreaded. This, and afterward, when Berthe shut herself away and the house went dead between its walls.

When I was seven, I stood by her bed with the bleeding pan. Later, concocted broths and gruels, kept an eye on sharp things — goose quills and knives. Later, when the crate itself came back, battered and splintered, Papa carried it back across the square in his arms like it was a dead child.

And then, it all began again. New sketches; vows of improvement. The gathering of materials, trips to Auch to order supplies, furious days of painting; eventually the arrival of the envelope of regulations for the next Salon; the gilding and crating, the letter writing, the wait. Berthe's last crate had been packed with more than the usual care and contained paintings that my mother had been working on for a long time, always revising, making small amendments. The submission was a group of miniature family portraits on ivory, including my stern *grandpère* with his round glasses; my *grandmère* with a string of jet beads, each smaller than a poppy seed, at her throat; and a picture of our kitchen garden under past year's frost. I loved that piece: every withered leaf and fallen flower etched in fairy ice, while a clutch of tiny birds gathered in a corner to peck amid the seeds and berries.

That year, the letter — opaque and implacable — arrived in May, the month of birdsong that I have always since associated with weeping and the stony silence of the world's refusal.

I had gone to her, knocking on her locked door. The flickering *caleu* lamps were all lit and my mother sat before the mirror in her underdress and camisole. In the glass her pale face was dark-haloed by her hair; her neck, ivory, gleaming. She had a shawl embroidered with roses — red and gold and purple, amid winding green thorns; it was spread on her lap. The room smelled of the eau de vie my uncles drank, as though a bottle had spilled. She turned to me absently, as though she had forgotten who I was; and I realized that the odor came from her, was on her breath and her skin; I breathed and took a step back.

"How lovely the colors are," she said, almost to herself. "See how they gleam in the lamplight? Ah — if only to capture that. Before the impression fades."

Later, alone in my room, I entreated the heavens to let my mother paint as she wished; to grant her her triumph, her redemption and, somehow, my own.

But my mother put away her paints and ivories. She dragged out her rosary and began to attend the village church, which she had held in some contempt; took longer trips to Auch, to my grandfather's house; but ceased speaking of her old teacher. My mother, who had sat behind her magnifier by the hour, who had laughed away the gossips and mocked the villagers' adages *("You think your eggs are on the fire!")* — who in a certain mood took out her rings, her lace, her silver candlesticks, legacy of her Auscitain blood, and said to me, *"Someday these too will be yours — "* That Berthe disappeared; and another took her place, tight-lipped and with a temper like the wind.

The next year my brother, Charles Jean-Louis, was born. His infant boy body, wrapped and bowered with linens, was upheld over the baptismal font, cupped in the palms of the curé while the bells pealed and I shifted from foot to foot in splintered sabots. Berthe stood, and kneeled: her back straight as a rod. My uncles came and we had meat on the table for a week, salt and potatoes and wine. But the weight of things had changed. Tables and chairs came unmoored; cups and plates hovered over the tabletop or crashed to the floor. Winds grabbed the shutters and banged them against the stone no matter how many times they were secured. My occupations now consisted of sweeping up and standing by; shelling beans and feeding fowl, helping the wet nurse and the *bonne*, swiping cloths at the baby's soil. This was to go on (Berthe said the words as though she had a mouthful of dust) *until such time as I should marry.*

My father, the next spring, won what he had so long desired, his seat at the *mairie*. But there was less air between us all; we walked in circles around one another. And I learned to loathe "art," or at least what was done in its name.

My throat caught, and thickened. My soul, unmoored, came back to rest; toes tingling against the slatted wood once again; my arms aching in their uncomfortable position. From a few paces away, Chasseloup rustled behind his easel. Why was I here, *why was I here at all? Twenty, nineteen . . . seventeen,* I counted . . . At fifteen, boots clattered on the stairs; at ten, the door of the studio swung open. A tall man in a long dark coat stepped in. Behind him was a woman in a full black skirt, with a black lace mantilla covering her face. I smelled smoke, a whiff of tobacco, perfume.

Maman——? I gasped. It so looked like her. And in that moment, I forgave her almost everything.

Chasseloup leapt up and threw his pencil across the room; it hit the wall and fell to the floor with a clatter. "What are you doing? Really, Vollard——"

The man in the doorway started to laugh. He let his cigarette fall to the floor, stubbed it out with the toe of his boot.

"Chasseloup. I'm glad to see you working."

The woman threw off her veil and shawl and strode around the studio, peering out the windows, pulling up cloths that covered, as I now saw, various cameras and lenses and instruments. She was younger than Berthe, with a sharp eye, and it was because of her presence that I retreated behind the screen and scrabbled into my clothes.

"I have just today found my model."

"Excellent," said the woman, who had circled back around. She was frank in her manner, and now I could not imagine how, even for a moment, my mother—silent or double-tongued—had come to mind.

The men stared at the easel. "You'll need an acceptance this season, Chasseloup, or you'll be wearing striped trousers yourself. Standing with a tripod in front of Notre Dame, taking *cartes de visite.* Do you think you'll be ready? As for the jury I'm nearly certain to secure a couple of the critics, maybe Théophile and Fleury—so really—unless you'd rather be putting down Moslems in Algiers for Badinguet and your father——"

Chasseloup was cradling his bad arm with the other. He looked up when I came out from behind the screen, his glance bleak, as it had been at the Trap.

"Lovely," said the woman. "I've not seen her before."

"Chasseloup," said the other man, musing at the easel, "have you seen Courbet's studies for *The Dreamer?* This new Gabrielle he found is a miracle."

"Tilt your head just so, mademoiselle? To the right, three-quarters profile."

"She's a good subject. Who is she?"

"Damned if I know," said the painter.

"Call it *An Unknown Girl*, then," said the woman.

"It will be *called* nothing, and will *be* nothing, until it is begun and finished. And unless you want her to look like a dressmaker's dummy I will start with the body *beneath* the drape. Mademoiselle, will you come back tomorrow and leave your modesty at your *hotel?*"

"Hotel?" said Vollard drily.

The artist shrugged and turned away. Vollard removed a clip of bills from beneath his vest, thumbed a stack of them, and passed them silently in my direction. He paused. "How long will it take, Chasseloup?" But the wolf only growled and stared out at the chimney pots.

A sickish, giddy nausea scattered my thoughts as I walked all the way back to the Tivoli, Vollard's money wadded against my bodice lacings. At the desk, I informed Madame that I would require my room for a few days more and passed most of them over to her.

Upstairs in number 12, my scant belongings — combs, spent quills, a few candles, the bottle of spot remover — looked lonely and cold. From outside, the bells of Notre Dame de Lorette began to ring: three . . . four . . . five. *Five.* Idly, I picked up the bottle of cleaning fluid. It was made of blue glass and contained a milky, strong-smelling liquid. In fact, I had used it only once, for mud on my hems — not the purpose for which it had been purchased. My underthings, when I had taken them off and laid them on a chair behind the screen in the artist's studio, were as white as they could be when the laundry was missed. But——something was wrong. *What?* Notre Dame de Lorette pulled like an irate mother, like a headache, like thunder rolling across the mountains. Then, as the bells pealed out, insistent and gray, I began, for the second time that day, to count: days, this time——for a different reason.

4

A PRESENT CURE

LATER I WALKED a long way, across the Pont Neuf to the Luxembourg Gardens, the only spot in Paris that for me held any consolation. Trees branched bare to the sky in the silvery late-afternoon light; their fallen leaves still strewn, damp and blackened, on the ground. Stone urns held frozen sticks that had been flowers, and iron chairs were lined alongside the fountain. At its head stood a sculpture of white stone: a woman arched in her lover's arms, her face turned upward into his embrace. The light shifted, a shaft of wintry light-against-light: dove gray, pink, bluish. Nearby an old couple dozed in two chairs, pooled in the circle of pale sun. Winter light, light of Saint Nicholas's Day; the pure clear light that had diffused through diamond panes. With a finger of my being, I reached for my lover; cautious, beseeching. Like the vine torn from its supporting wall, I wavered. Drew my knees up to my chest and hugged them, rocking slowly, forward and back, on the iron chair. *How does a woman learn to doubt herself? By way of which events, what consequences?*

In the eye of my memory, I traveled back to the place from which I had come. Watched, again, as a dark smudge expanded on the far horizon. Felt the dry, stiff breeze against my face, bringing it closer.

I squinted down; the smudge looked like Stephan. But it was not he — not yet.

The summer before I left Tillac had been one of wells gone dry, springs stopped to a trickle, and ponds showing their marshy bottoms. Berries shriveled on their stems; I had choked on the dust from the road and longed for the rains, for a change in the wind. It was unbearable, the blood-pounding sleepless nights; my body a giant, overbudded flower, begging to be ripped from the earth. I took down my hair and opened my shutters just to feel a breath of a breeze, humid and full, at night. When the rains came that year — *soon* — I would lean into the cold slap of wind. Lie out in the fields, and let the downpour pound me into the ground. To be pummeled, buffeted, flayed by hail, and the peals of the bells . . . poured out, finally, into the earth. *Released*.

On an early September morning when the storms were due to break, we did not hear the usual peal from Tillac's bell tower, but a hurried, clamorous tocsin. It was not the particular pattern of rings that announced a thunderhead, nor that for a birth, a death, a mass, or a summons to the church square, but an anxious and irregular clamor of the oldest and greatest of the bells, the one that had survived the Revolution. We shaded our eyes and turned; then squinted and stared. The heavens were grayish green, storm-charged, pregnant with rains but unyielding, settled on a sullen, torpid watch.

From the north, the direction of Nérac, a black smudge rose against the sky. It grew larger and darker; some said they could see plumes of flame. We stood and scanned the horizon, gauging the wind's speed and direction, then hurried our feet over the cracked and thirsty ruts. Goose-girl first and always, I hauled feed buckets across the yard from the boiling pots to the pens; chased down fowl and pinned their huge wings against my body, struggling to get them into neck-hole boxes. I had always been a careful *gaveuse*, trained by the fingertips of my aunt, who could calm a bird to stuff it with feed, and leave it preening. But that day my hands shook as I tried to stroke the boiled corn down soft, sinewy gullets; my fingers were damp and my nervousness set the birds squawking and nipping.

To slaughter, harvest, prepare; to sell the result — *foie d'oie, foie de canard,* the fattened livers of geese and ducks; and *confit,* the preserved meat of the fowl — this was the life of our province. To beat the storms, then return and prepare for the cold; to load our carts and return with fatter purses — to this end, every back was bent. That season we had been driven by the news from the north and from Mirande, of higher prices being paid for *foie d'oie* and *foie de canard.* But fire brought fear, and if the towns barred their walls and the markets closed, our fattened flocks would die, with their useless livers inside them.

. . . You see, we knew so little. Whether it was a lover's grudge that set the spark, a pipe carelessly dropped, or inflamed tempers, bad politics, revenge — once started, fire could spread with the winds, those rogue gusts that harried our days and nights. Fire brought fear after it: the settling of old scores. Over the course of the day, the smudge darkened, and the wind brought an acrid burning odor. *The harvest is past, the summer has ended, and we are not saved —*

I could still taste it in my throat, that smell.

The afternoon shadows had lengthened. The Luxembourg fountain no longer reflected the naked branches of overhanging trees; its pool was a dark rectangle. The woman still arched back in her lover's arms, frozen in stone, but time had not stopped with her; the hard little hands of the Paris clocks ticked on. The old couple had gone to their supper and the air held a gelatinous dusky chill.

My last summer in Tillac had brought a drought of affection, as well. When Berthe gave up Art, the great wheel of the days, months, and seasons turned against itself. Life lost its familiar rhythm, for a hopeless woman is more powerful than she knows. I, as her daughter, was to be comrade and first lieutenant of her suffering, enforcer of the new order: *If I cannot live, none after me shall live!*

So Papa took no happiness in his hard-won mayoralty; my aunt and cousin displayed no pride in their glossy, fattened flocks. And I — I kissed the black-haired boy who stood guard at the Tour de

Rabastens, the stone tower that watched over the western gate of our village.

The burned began to arrive by the Nérac road. Clothing charred; sticks of furniture on their backs. Sober adults and sooty-faced children with pale rivulets down their cheeks. They were starved, singed, and burned because they had stayed to try to smother the fires, to gather provisions or help neighbors, drive their flocks to farther fields. To bury their dead. Tillac's *mairie* and church were given over to lodge the burned until we could take no more. And then our walls too were closed.

With the harvest stalled, the birds remained bloated in their pens. Useless, with their fattened livers — *worth their weight in gold* — my cousin muttered, angry and helpless, as if the birds themselves were to blame. Stupid and oblivious, too heavy to move on their useless spindly legs, they preened themselves with their big orange beaks. As the feed progressed, they all grew too heavy to run. At last, burdened by their size, they just fluffed down on straw — flapping fighters turned into complaisant creatures. During their last days they could not even stand; just swiveled their necks and opened their beaks for the corn buckets, like children begging for sugar syrup.

"It is like the Fear, again," said my aunt, who could still remember. During the Revolution, there had been fires, and much else; and the local economy foundered; sans-culottes did not want to eat foie gras, the dish of kings.

My parents quarreled, that night the smoke was rolling in. Berthe said the mob would set upon us and wanted to safeguard us in Auch. Papa, who had grown up in the countryside, assured her that our roof was made of good, fireproof tile and that no one under a modern, prospering empire wanted to make belts from the guts of the well-off or set the tax office on fire. As Tillac's mayor, Papa would douse the flames with the logic of local prosperity — roof tiles, roads, and rails; our markets supplying foie gras for a flourishing empire. Berthe pressed her tongue between her teeth. In the morning, he rode off toward the smoke-darkened sky.

That autumn, my last in the place I was born, Berthe waited

by the window; Charles wailed; and Virginie, his wet nurse, gave suck. The feeding of the fowl did not reach its yearly finale; we did not — my aunt and cousin and I, our village neighbors — hover over the slaughtering table with our stones and scales. No *sanguettes* were fried up in bubbling grease. Affection, goodwill — did not return. And my father was not among those who returned to the safety of our village walls.

. . . My brave papa. Gone to the Lot province with his pistol, his sharpened quills, and steady hand — and I ready, myself, to burst into flame. Ferrying rags and embers to the church — small fire in an iron pot to warm the burned on nights that had suddenly turned cold. He did not return by the Nérac road, or by any road, my father. His body was borne back to the village in a cart.

And still, no rain.

Berthe looked neither to the left nor the right, but straight ahead, under a long mantilla of Spanish lace. Under it, her face was pale as an orchid. My uncles Charles and Louis were tall as towers, silk hats covering, then revealing, their egg-bald heads, which gleamed under the gray-green sky. They had come from Auch for my father's burial, cocking their pistols at the roadblocks, claiming their Auscitain right of passage. With colorful cravats and gold watch chains, they were a sight against the dry landscape, the dull-hued country garb. Their watches, whose shiny lids popped open, were an insult to those who told time by the sun, the color of the mountains, and the bells. The curé stood to the side as pallbearers lowered the casket. The weather had turned frigid; the crowd was thin.

My father's body had been found on the Agen road; the cause of his death uncertain, a subject for whispers among the black hoods on the town square. The slab was lifted over the tomb, slid into place with a hollow, scraping sound; unspoken questions stirred the air. My brother, Charles, whimpered and pulled at my skirts, and I lifted him into my arms.

Berthe's dress had devoured ten bolts of silk crepe; black gloves went up to her elbows. She had never played the part of the provincial wife, and never less so than on that day.

"Berthe has a lover in Auch."

"The boy hasn't a hair of her husband——!"

"No good from the start, was she, with her assuming ways? A curse, she was, to that family."

"And the daughter!"

My cheeks burned. The black-haired boy clutched his cap and stared at the dust.

Afterward, my mother was to take Charles and Virginie back to Auch with my uncles. My responsibility was to make myself useful: expedient to my aunt and cousin and the fattened and unbartered flocks; useful to the curé and the church and the burned. Useful to the fields and the ruts. *Useful to stone and straw.* My stomach was a rock, heavy with the confusion of the day. I hurried after Berthe, carrying Charles on my hip. She walked ahead, her back stiff in her widow's black.

"Maman?"

"You!" Her voice rattled me to the bone. "The whole village is talking."

"Berthe," began my uncle Charles, taking her by the arm. "It has been a difficult day." Louis took her other arm.

"Petite salope."

"Maman." I gasped. "You can't believe what they say about—that boy."

"The girl is just like her father, with his peasant blood," she said; and her voice was a thunderclap. That voice, the understanding— the confused questions—*had she not loved him, did she not love me——?*

I fell back, stunned; tears beginning; but I wiped them furiously, so the gossips would not see me weep. Once my mother had made up her mind—about which way the wind would blow, whether radishes would sprout in March, if a certain village girl had fallen, or if she herself would no longer paint for Paris—no appeal was possible.

The traveler arrived at Tillac's gates, a stranger from the north. The bells did not ring out a warning, Marie-Thérèse did not open her throat, and the tower guard allowed him entry, for he was expected. (From where? "Tours?" said one old villager. "No, it is *Tulle*," said another with certainty, lighting his pipe. "*Toulouse*," said a third, chewing on his pipe stem.)

Tillàc's makeshift duck-and-goose market had been set up amid cooking pots, straw beds, piles of bandages, and the Nérac refugees. The traveler, come to buy the fowl in a lot and ship them north under arms, had set up his ledger and fine-nibbed pens; his Paris ink and his weighing scale with brass weights — and when he smiled, he cut through Tillàc's gloomy skies.

"My aunt's birds have been fed with corn mixed with lavender," I said in French, as my aunt's interpreter. She had had slaughtered one of her beloveds and extracted the liver, pale and trembling, a glistening fatted treasure. Simmered it over a small fire with a bit of Armagnac. I bore it across the square in a clay bowl.

This traveler had never weighed a goose in his life, despite all his fancy accoutrements; nor had he any instinct to judge the prize inside. Sometimes the smallest and least likely revealed a liver that would save the winter. Until those feathered bellies were slit open, though, you could only guess whether the harvest would be thick or thin; the stones in the scale pan few or plenty. This stranger, bringing with him the heady perfume of cities, was just a messenger; what he knew about fattened livers was limited to what they would fetch in Paris. His errand was to buy them for less.

"*Walk with me,*" he said. He was a pillar, a birch; white as salt, supple in the buffeting winds. "Come and see where I'm keeping myself." Everyone knew that the stranger had declined our simple village hospitality — though after the fires, it was scarcely that — to make camp in the chateau outside Tillàc's walls. An old place, with its windows boarded and nailed shut, its lands leased out.

The sky turned from pink-streaked to lavender; then violet, then indigo. Gray to black; then stars. Bats flittered, tree frogs chirruped. The scent of smoke still lingered in the air. We passed the black-haired boy and I experienced a small, ignoble flicker of triumph. My sabots felt their way along the familiar ruts of the path; lights from a farmhouse flickered in the near distance. Heart in my mouth; battering against my ribs. Fabric of my dress pulling tight, the bodice too small—it was a girl's, and unfit for me now. The wind gusted in small bursts, carrying a cuckoo's call, the sound of laughter, a voice from somewhere else. Louder—as Gers winds go—setting up a roar in the trees, storming up and falling back. On summer days it blew away the flies and bees and beetles; and when it died, the insects buzzed again in your ears and resumed their lazy circles. Stephan was my storm, my wind gusting up on a still night.

My neighbors, tongue-tied and timid, their patois not understood, were suspicious of him, and so my role in the business became that of an interlocutress. For the moment, I was flush with youth and eloquence—the former mayor's eldest making good on her father's promise; Berthe's daughter with French on her tongue, able to guess at what this stranger didn't know. A girl who had risen beyond gossip and a black-haired boy.

"*Walk with me,*" he said, amid the ink pots and goose feathers and clay pots and spoons; his fine coat splotched with goose fat. He stepped past the sooty rags, the piles of straw. His nails were smooth manicured ovals, mine ragged-edged and dirty when he took my hand in his and turned it palm up . . . "*Travels, I think. Broken hearts. Not a destiny of the goose yard, I don't believe . . .*"

"And what does yours say?" I asked. A wild, ticklish, intoxicating laugh bubbled up and the seething whirl began; soon we were both choking with laughter, giggling and rolling in the pine needles and dust. Little bits of quartz from the soil jabbed into my back through my thin dress and, breathless, we rolled apart. *His knee, bony and hard, could split me; his body arc and cover; faces flushed—lips that just brushed; scalding, ticklish, unbearable . . .*

"*Mine is a palm of narrow escapes.*"

In the evenings, at my father's table, I counted out the money, and my neighbors were shy with gratitude—though later, I believe, they told the story a different way. Mornings, I threw open the shutters and the scent that came across the Pyrenees was rich, fragrant with loam, perfumed with mysterious currents. And some-

thing in me had wakened and was rising fast, an errant planet in the
autumn sky, past the tears and scraping of Papa's gravestone and
my mother's rancid, bewildering scent, eau de vie and fury and perfume. It was a touch on my temple; an invisible kiss — some ghost
of my life-to-be; a wild, aching, deep-abiding yearning.

"Come with me . . ."

The village square was silent for once, its familiar bustle quelled
in the darkness before dawn as I hurried across, passing through
the gate and the Tillac walls. Our mule stood ready, cases already
strapped to his flanks. I climbed up and wrapped my arms around
Stephan's waist.

We rode past the forest edge, the stand of pines, branches heavy-
boughed and thick-needled. An hour's journey out, nearer the fires;
the trees were blackened spires, rising jagged against a bruised sky.
I tightened my arms; inhaled the scorched, befouled air.

Beyond the boundary of Gers province we dropped into the mists
of the Lot Valley, where the morning cool turned sunny as mid-
summer by noon; rows of vines sweltered in the sun, and old men
weighed bunches of grapes in their palms as they glanced at the sky.
We changed our mule for a horse at Quercy and wandered in the
market, where the summer peppers and fruits and salad greens were
passing into a fall harvest of orange pumpkins, mushrooms, and
beans; figs and braids of lavender-colored garlic. We stuffed ourselves with walnuts and later fell into a town banquet, a harvest celebration with a sheep roasting on a spit and small birds six to a stick,
so you crunched down their tiny bones. We had plenty of wine and
then a bed (or rather, two beds) at a whitewashed cottage that was a
roadside inn. We were shy with each other; Stephan took my hand,
so softly. Soon after that we were on a better road, a strange one;
and the beats of the hooves made me sleepy, child that I was — but
not for long.

We followed the flocks in the carts as far as Cahors, a two-day
journey, and by then they were just birds in crates — not my aunt's
fine-plumed flock that I had hand-fed, nor the Widow Nadaud's or

those of two-fingered Stanis. Their marks of distinction blended amid the rough-and-tumble negotiation that was the weighing and selling of them.

After that first hurried leg, we took the railroad spur from Agen, and Gascony gave itself up to territory unknown. At Limoges we boarded a coach, crossing the Vienne River to approach the ancient city at night, when the sky was red from the glow of the porcelain ovens my father had told me about. We did not stop there, but carried on by railway. Second class; Stephan's boot heels resting on a trunk as he told me about his family's chase of fortune and misfortune; speculations good and bad; tales of women and roulette and cinnamon and coffee; defections to the Americas and some recent luck under the empire. My own stories seemed small by comparison, but we had a common bond: a kinship with the defiant of our clans. We had only kissed, but already we traveled as one, as though we had done so for lifetimes. I did not ask myself what I was doing. I simply knew.

From the Tours platform we took a conveyance pulled by horse. It was past midnight and inky black when we arrived, the two of us creased and grainy-eyed, identically rumpled, like stained laundry rocked along in a cart. Bare curved outline of a drive; crunch of wheels on stone, an expanse of velvety blackness beyond . . . *"La Vrillette. The roof is falling in, the gardens overgrown, the gas is off, and the help has left, save a single girl. We are always in need of golden eggs in this family!"*

Tawny owls nested on the ledges and in the attics, he told me, and what was left in the cellar was vine rot. As for the books, they were soon to be packed up and sold by the kilogram to an empire businessman who wanted to flaunt a library of old leather spines.

A jolt, and our movement ceased; the scent of late roses swelling into the closed warmth of the carriage. The night air smelled like mown hay, flowers, and rushing water all mingled together.

Stephan levered his boot against the door; gravel crunched as he stepped down.

In the front hall, he fumbled for the gas lamps, cursed and plunged through the darkness, then returned with a dining-table candelabra. The chateau smelled of old silk and cork and wood, dusty velvet and polish; the air felt thick with ghosts. It was not quite a ruin; a fire had been laid in the bedchamber hearth and cast a flickering glow. In front of it stood an enormous tall-sided vessel, long and slipper-shaped, with a brazier at one end — a boat like that would soon sink, for it stood filled with water. Steam rose from the surface like fog over fields. I dipped in my hand, swirled my fingers through the silky warmth. What curious thing was this, and what absent soul had set the fire, carried enough water up a dark stair to float a small ship? Such bathing as I had ever known was a quick summer dousing in the river, or done quickly with a bristled brush and cold water in a trough, swiping beneath my chemise.

My traveling companion had shed his clothes and wrapped himself in a robe the color of wine, as familiar to him as my old goose-dress was to me. He shrugged it off in an easy movement, its folds puddling to the floor. A precarious laugh bubbled up in my throat — alarm, excitement, giddy disbelief. I dared not look, but did see in the shadows a lean and muscled whiteness there; then dark . . . He laughed and stepped over the tub's edge. I knew then, but not before, that I was to drown.

Oh — my arms around his waist on horseback, so close. And on board the coach, inside a locked box that smelled of cologne and leather and horsehair.

"Climb in," he said.

I inhaled the water's wild perfume; sucked in my breath and stepped over. My chemise floated up (pantaloons were unknown to me then), and the water went in up to my calves, knees, thighs — then tickling warmth reached all the way inside me and the careening laugh came again. Stephan stood, firm as a flagpole, raining droplets of bath water. I screwed my eyes tight and plunged. (*Allumette — bistoquette — colonne — goujon!* A match, a cue, a pillar, a pin, a worm, a wooden leg — street argot that I had yet to learn. How did I know there were so many of them in the world — male members — and how they liked to behave?)

"Lift your arms—you're not bathing in your chemise." Stephan turned me and undid my laces, plundered the soggy garment. Candlelight flickered over my flesh, and I gasped and pulled up my knees. Some girls my age had never seen their own navel, but I was not one of those. Still, I had to gasp for breath in these unfamiliar waters. My breasts floated, rosy with the warmth. Stephan reached around me and cupped a palm around each, softly pulling me to him; both of us awkward; he was not as sure as he seemed. I might have shivered and drawn away, but the warmth pulled like a string from the nether regions to my heart, and I leaned back, and rested.

"You've brought along half the mud clods of Gascony, I see," he murmured. Then with a cloth like a lion's rough tongue he scrubbed my back and belly. His palms, with the cloth, followed the curves of my body—breasts, waist, softness of belly . . . lips, then—warm and steamy, traveled where hands had never been, turning me at last toward his mouth.

"I'm hungry! Is there anything to eat?"

"*Foie d'oie* from your village and some very old champagne. Not a crumb of anything else until tomorrow, when we can send Léonie to market." He rose and stepped out of the bath, lifted me out in turn; settled us both on rugs in front of the fire. Lips buried in my neck; damp curls twisted between my fingers; we touched, kissed, leaned into each other for a very long time until our skin was warm and moist and waiting. The dark posts on each corner of the bed spiked up like trees and the filmy bed curtains surrounded us like fog. One could get lost in a bed like that, or fall from the height.

"You'll stay with me, then, little goose?"

What else, where else—in the world?

We broke into our stock of *foie d'oie,* what Stephan had held back from the shipment. The rosy brown *bloc* was flecked with gold, nearly melting in the warmth. Stephan cut into it with a penknife, raised the blade to my lips, but teasingly, pulling it a little distance away as though it might scald.

I took the blade from his hand and licked it, allowing the rosy morsel to grow moist on my tongue. The stuff tasted like salt tears, like the dusky flavor of rain on earth, or morning light slanting, dustily, through the forest. Sun on the fields, purple clouds over the Pyrenees. Something so terrible and familiar like my own bones and skin, the milk from my own breast—the stuff that made me, had made us all, in that rough corner of the world. I tasted, and tasted again, tears rising. I had hardly ever tasted it. He took the knife and dropped it to the floor, moving his body closer, seeking my mouth with his.

"The candles are burning, we mustn't fall asleep"—I slipped from bed to blow on the tapers, then licked my fingertips and extinguished an orange-glowing wick. The taste of smoke and tallow on my tongue, as I wet my fingers to put out each tip, joining the bouquet of salt and rain and goose fat.

"Don't worry so, *come*—"

We slipped between linens softer than spring grass, the heaven of our bodies pressed together: musk, licking flames, tangled sheets. Made love half-dreaming amid the damp linens until I fell into the void between flesh and nothingness, a refuge of sweat and perfume, where the certainty of flesh answered a surge of breath and blood and heart. It was a shimmering field, a breeze rippling across golden stalks.

And so that night I began to shed, hardly knowing it, the fur-matted, pond-bathed, forest-floor earthy roughness in which I had lived all my life. The old things I'd thrown off were like animal skins, dark and coarse, thrust down in a corner; a gentle humid ferment of the fields. While below, more deeply, but sunlike too; a pulsing arose, sure and steady, pressing from within . . . A window flung open; perfume of late summer roses, the last blooms of the year. Beneath him, I burst like a September rain cloud.

The pool, the trees, and the cold, voluptuous marble of the Luxembourg—it was all as it had been moments before. Too chilly now, too dark; time to go. A turning, then; a quickening deep inside me. Not hunger . . . not fear or cold, but something warm, fluttering, tingling, a touch like a sigh. Feathery, winging pulse.

———••———

Back at the Tivoli, no Stephan and no word of him, not that day or the next, nor the one after that. *No word . . .* When did I realize that there would never be a letter? That my erstwhile lover would not gallop through the Passage, or alight from a cab, nor would any of the other hundred imagined scenarios unfold?

The fairy eye has closed, my aunt used to say, when the forest fountains ceased granting our wishes. When luck ran out, or went rotten. There was a familiarity to it, this sense of loss. I searched my memory for omens of betrayal missed, ignored, shoved aside by an urgent heart, but the candles guttered out before I found any answers.

And in some sense, it did not matter, the whys and hows of it. But of course, love does not believe or understand that; love simply weeps; it is bereft. A deep current of movement, and from below, from some uncertain interior part of me, rose a question, an unsteadiness. For the barest moment, the wisp of a desire to reverse the course of events, those of the present moment but perhaps others as well; events from long ago. A crumbling wall, the music of glass shattering, falling onto a stone floor in a million tiny fragments. The tearing of old silk, blue and ivory; patterned crystal; the beating wings of a large bird; a man's body stretched full upon mine, his lips on my breast; a caress, melting away. *Such a long road. So tired.* Then uncertainty, and I fell a long, dark way.

Above the rooftops, the air was thin. Another day, one more sitting. One in which the coals that offered the atelier scant warmth burned down more than they were lit; and Chasseloup stared out at the buttes and smoked, a scarf wrapped round his neck. The studio's expansiveness had narrowed to a foggy, helpless anxiety; a state of arrest. From my position, standing on the wooden slats, I watched the progress of the day's light: dawn slowly grazing the wide surrounding sky, clouds wisping past windows. In some distant part of me, a bell clanged an alarmed tocsin, and yet I did not move.

Chasseloup accused me of standing as though all of my blood had drained from my veins. No position pleased him. "What do you think it is, this game, to work when you feel like it?" He retreated to the windows. I wrapped myself in a dusty length of cashmere from the rental rack and sat down on the box.

He rolled another cigarette, the twentieth of the day. Stared out through the north exposure, toward Montmartre, invisible behind the flat, sleeting sky. He flexed his fingers and sighed. "I'm sorry. It's not your fault."

I began to cry. Chasseloup swore at the falling sleet.

On the easel was a line, rough and dark, but graceful. The contour of a shoulder, stretch of leg, curve at the waist. A girl half-turned, looking over her shoulder. Brief reprieve; shaft of light in the dark tunnel of self-recrimination.

"That is a good line," I said, wiping my eyes with a handkerchief from the bins. "Berthe — my mother — taught me a strong line from a weak one."

Chasseloup flipped through the pages on the easel. He shook his head. "She studied?"

Tears, and the ghost of an emotion tightened my throat.

"Her teacher was an old painter. *Very* old." I smiled through my tears. "He hated Paris; he also thought there were too many railways here." Pierre's smoke curled upward; his eyelashes were so long, they lay against the curve of his cheek like a child's. That I was his *present cure*, like wormwood, and he mine, had pulled us together through the hours.

"You must be cold," he murmured. "Dress if you'd like. I am sorry to keep you." He let out a breath and leaned back. He was tired. More tired, today, than I. It would not be so difficult to slip my arms around his shoulders and feel his warmth; be of comfort if not of use. I drew in a breath.

"You just need to go on," I said. "I'll stay if you'd like."

The painter turned abruptly, looked at me where I stood, the length of cloth draped around my shoulders and falling. He adjusted the shades.

Was it just then, or a bit later . . . after the gaslights twinkled bluish on the street below us, that he turned. Pressed his face into the barely curved area of my belly, against the dusty pink shawl, folded me into him as though he had been doing so all along. And perhaps we had been holding each other, on a sightline across the studio, and it was not what was on the easel that had been important.

His scent of earth; of linseed oil and iron. Two hundred stairsteps into the sky I shed my shattered self, breathed in moments, one to the next. My present cure, the coiling, bone-melting green; his arms now around my body, ever warmer in a room full of windows, seven winding stories above the street. And so on a pile of rental dresses and Sunday suits, I made love to that part of him that wanted release; found the way to him with my lips, my hands, my belly and thighs. Amid all the draperies and boxes and columns and props, the smoke and days of futile effort, I passed the deadness, the empty spaces, what the green bottle forgot for him; what the white tablet could not remember; where he went when the work did not come. I understood that, in some part of me. And in his arms there — and later, in his bed, I let myself be comforted, a little, for all that had been lost.

~ 5 ~

LA LUNE

Down one flight from the atelier, in wedge-shaped maid's quarters off one end of the hall, was the place Chasseloup slept, hung his trousers, and heated a tiny stove. A window overlooked the balconies of other apartments; plants in pots and cloths hanging out to dry. Occasionally from the window you saw someone coming or going, a glimpse of skirt or a sleeve. The two rooms were so cramped that the door to the hall ran into the kitchen cupboard, which contained a bottle of vinegar, a soft potato, scraps of canvas, a bulging paper packet of sugar, and bits of drawing chalk. Coffee was dust at the bottom of a can; coal, silt at the bottom of the bin. The main room held a balding, velvet-upholstered divan for a bed; a writing desk; and a giant map of Paris tacked to the wall. It didn't matter; we spent every available hour in the atelier.

My key to number 12 had disappeared behind the Tivoli's desk for the last time, after I had bumped my small luggage down the stairs and flashed my eyes at Madame with the giddiness of a prisoner freed. She grimaced as though her joints were hurting her; as if the season had changed before she was ready for it. *She'd seen the likes of me a thousand times before*, she might have said. But still I sensed that I had made a narrow escape — so maybe Stephan's luck was with me still.

Chasseloup asked no questions. We lived from day to day, as was customary in such circumstances; that is, when Art rules, and crowds out everything else. After a week's effort, we sat across the table from each other, a bottle uncorked between us, half a loaf and a sausage. During that day's sitting Chasseloup had had me up on and down from the crate; altered the light — gone so far as to let me try on costumes from the photographer's racks, none of which ended up pleasing him. Vollard had stopped by to shake his head.

"So? What is the matter?" I took a blunt knife to our *saucisson*.

He hunched forward in his chair. Poured.

"I cannot — solve this problem in time for the Salon."

"But I have been absolutely obedient," I said, in an effort to lighten the mood.

"Or maybe it is just" — he reached over with a lingering caress — "that I am distracted."

I leaned back and felt his words trickle down, ominously.

"I will have to do a fish, a cheese, maybe a green bottle on a cool stretch of zinc — "

Chasseloup rocked back on his chair, folded his good arm around his thin frame. Those hungry, too-soft, full-moon eyes.

"Do you want me to leave, then?"

"No! I mean — "

He meant that it might be appropriate to study me, at rest and in the course of daily life. And besides, I took out the laundry and gave him courage; without the feminine influence life became primitive . . . Could we drink to that ? We did.

So the model-for-small-wages became a full-time *grisette*, maiden of the bed, hearth, and table; last of a vanishing breed. A feminine soul to believe in and serve the greater cause of Art, with a gay night or two thrown in. We went to little dark cafés where there was music and a bottle or two, and Pierre and his friends talked into the small hours.

Twenty years earlier, even ten, we might have seen a few more of these nights, talking philosophy until dawn; coffee from work-man's carts — as on my first mornings in Paris — but laughing with the cart sellers now; in a small herd of artists and young people, bubbles in our noses at sunrise and then blissfully, dizzily to bed just as the shops were opening, the cries of street merchants breaking the morning's calm. But it was late in the day for that. Pierre's friends didn't discuss "art for art's sake," or even argue its merits. Art was all for the judges now, because someone would be pushed forward and his work sold for a fortune, enough for flats and studios in the new Paris.

Rents were high and rising. Deal making was brisk. *"And women are expensive,"* muttered one of Chasseloup's painter-friends under his breath, to general laughter, although Pierre, stiffly standing on his principles, pretended not to understand.

"Ah, it was better when there was no money in it!" pleaded the grizzled elders. Awkward silences fell; dinner companions excused themselves and ducked out to go back to the studio. Salon competi-tion was commerce and winning was the work; deadlines and sched-ules and the lineup and the choice. Artists were hated for their med-als now — envied, and then copied.

Sometimes amid the swirl of conversation I thought about my mother: her naiveté, her shocking disadvantage. But it was the usual thing, one way of living slipping and slithering into the next; edges blurred and before you knew it, you were in another picture, an-other kind of story . . . I cared for him a little, Chasseloup, in all my besieged innocence. If I did not let thoughts stray too far; and did not think where we were heading — hurtling at a sober but gasping gallop, all of us together, and Paris too.

His moods set the pace of our days. I contoured myself to them, becoming the hands, the leg or the arm, the body studied or curled next to his on the divan. Went out for sausages and packets of cof-fee, accomplished tea or soup as the hour required; kept soaps and trouser buttons, paintbrushes and bed linens, what few there were. I listened; but did not ask how the work was going. Laid the fire, boiled water for coffee, and waited for the sound of boots clomping

down the stairs from the studio; each movement an act of staunch
belief in my role on our tiny stage. Sometimes he brought a newspaper or a long-necked green bottle, with some sketch or scrap of
canvas flapping around him like a sail. My arms went up around his
neck, stretching the length of his long body, all the way to his lips.
When he napped, I fished for change in his pockets for a soup bone,
a bunch of carrots, a few pieces of coal. Clattered as quietly as possible around our tiny plot of living.

We ate bites of things for meals. Sipped at the cup of *la fée verte*,
or usually (since absinthe was a luxury beverage for a household
unable to fill its coal bin) Chasseloup drank for inspiration and I
soaked in his licorice-and-linseed-scented wake. Overall, the arrangement seemed an improvement for us both. As the girl who
had not yet understood the breath of the future at her neck — one
who, until she woke up with frost on her nose and a basin full of ice,
never dreamed of winter's cold, much less how today's steps were
the footpath to tomorrow's road — I was content.

He began again to paint at night. This was lucky, for I was often
sick in the early mornings and had time alone in the hall privy.

One afternoon we climbed aboard an omnibus and rode to the Bois
de Boulogne, returning from half-frozen lakes and curving land-
scapes, pathways along which we threw breadcrumbs to the birds.
The lakes and cascades had been carved from the earth by giants
and filled like titanic bathing tubs, and as the sun lowered, the traffic
procession thickened even though it was the middle of winter. Big
barouches, light fiacres, medallion-crusted tilburies, all flagged with
color, mottoes, crests, and flowers, arrived for the hour of wealth on
parade. Chasseloup picked up a handful of pebbles, tossed them into
the water. A clutch of birds scattered, scudding off in all directions.

"God, this city is suffocation. It's a stinking cesspool. '*Qui paye y
va.*' He who pays has his way. Oh, and why not."

Chasseloup fell silent; I slipped my hand into his. We walked.

The streets of Paris were wide gutters sluicing mud and refuse;
urchins darted through the alleyways, and carriages spewed filth

on anyone on foot. Icy puddles lay in awkward places, along with mountains of earth and rubble. One building had been a lodging for medical students, but had been sold to some partners who knew the street was to be demolished. They raised the rents, stuck up some plaster, and opened a pleasure garden. When it was time for the city to tear it down, the tax men would assess it (a tax man was one of the partners) and they all walked away rich. Pierre said that the middle classes had been bought off with a cascade in the Bois, a few francs in the bank, and some thick drapes to pull across the windows, and this was why he was meant to paint for the Salon judges and no one else.

"I'm a hostage, one way or another," he said. I squeezed his hand, felt the callus where he held his brush, on the second finger.

"I don't mind eating a potato for supper," I said firmly.

"Hmmpf!" Chasseloup dropped my hand, headed into the tobacconist's; came out tucking a fat packet into his coat. "We can drink our dinner tonight. Tomorrow I'll go to the Mont de Piété, that great engine of Parisian commerce."

"Where?"

"The poor man's bank. The city pawnshop."

We shuffled up six flights in silence with no grocer's bags to weigh us down. Pierre said that bread cost too much in this district; forget about *vin ordinaire*. He rattled the key; inside the little pie-shaped room we were like birds stranded in the treetops, the untaught ones who let straw fall from their beaks as they flutter about, and there was the rent envelope underneath the door. Chasseloup scuffed it aside; opened the door to the cupboard and weighed the potato on his palm. His eyes were huge and liquid, his hair looked soft, like the brush between a cow's ears before you touched it and realized it was stiff. He weighed the potato and stared, then placed it on the narrow sideboard counter. Retrieved the remaining item in the larder, and broke the bottle's seal.

"I need some air. Need to breathe without Vollard bursting in, paint without photographer's tripods and *cartes de visite* on strings." (There was talk among Chasseloup's friends that painting would

soon be obsolete; the business of art would all go to the photographers.) Chasseloup took down the sugar, poured the green; set out
the water pitcher, his "lucky" spoon, a battered filigree.

My back ached and I put my hand there, feeling the desperate un-
dulation of these moods; the hunger of the man for what he wanted;
his furious need varnished over by an adherence to a strict set of
principles, a labyrinth for which there was no *Plan de Paris*. His
was a ranging, ferocious appetite and at the same time, its despair.
His claim upon me was dimly familiar. Different in its expression,
perhaps, but with no less urgency, or more . . . Had it come round
again, then, to this? The alarm at my center began to ring. I glanced
at the green bottle, nearly full. It could be a long night.

Chasseloup rolled a cigarette and folded his lean, tall self onto the
floor. Hustled a trunk from under the divan, flipped its brass locks.
The scent of camphor preceded a tossing up of trousers and coats,
well-cut and of good material; vests, cravats, and gloves; starched
and folded linens, a silk-faced overcoat, all very different from
Chasseloup's usual wardrobe.

"I didn't know you had these," I murmured, looking over his
shoulder.

"Like them, do you?"

"I don't care." It irritated me when Pierre pretended I had "aspirations," especially when I didn't utter a murmur about his strange
economies: our suppers of absinthe and potatoes. I slipped on my
cloak, made for the door. We had passed a butcher shop where I
might find a piece of bacon. A vegetable seller, maybe willing to part
with his beet tops.

That night I dreamed of a lady with a feather-plumed hat and a
man who wore a long dark coat. We stood together, the three of us,
before the doors of the lying-in hospital, that peaked-roof place of
gables and windows; it looked like La Maternité on the rue d'Enfer,
where poor women gave birth. The baby had survived; but she was
ill and fragile. Then the dream changed, the man was someone else.
The cord of misery, wrapped around the infant's neck, was cut; the
poison had come out of her. In the dream, I was crying, and when I
awoke, my cheeks were wet.

Chasseloup hadn't needed to say that he didn't want to be seen at the Mont de Piété the next morning, queuing with his trousers. He was still twisted under the sheets as I splashed my face, stirred up the coals, shook dust from the coffee tin into water from the pump—six flights down, and up again with the bucket. I bent and touched him, a tentative caress. Pressed my hand to his cheek, which was feverishly warm.

"I want to work today," he mumbled into my hair.

"I'll go, and bring home a soup bone."

"More than that, I hope. For all of that monkey suit."

"I won't take the coat. It's cold, you might need it." He pulled himself up, a mess of ruffled hair, his chest bare and full of creases.

"I will *not* wear a coat with silk facings and a collar."

"You *are* vain, aren't you," I said, sharper than usual. "You should wear it, and not care what they say." *Too much woman in him, Chasseloup,* whispered a voice behind my ear.

He groaned and sank his head back onto the pillow. "The madames will cluck like hens—a pretty-someone with an armful of gentleman's rags." I was so ignorant, still, that I didn't catch his meaning. But the way he looked at me, too close, made me catch my breath. Chasseloup always knew what he didn't know he knew. It was that, and his storms and calms, that shook me, brought me flying back.

"Make a good day of it. Please?" I said, bending down for a kiss. Then he pulled me back toward him, wrapped his long body around mine. The pale coffee water bubbled down to nothing, using all the fire we had.

Then, a bit later, it was cold, outside the narrow warmth of that bed.

"You'll need proof of Paris residence." Chasseloup scrabbled in a pile of dusty papers, and extracted a rent receipt—not a current one, as it wasn't paid up.

Then I had to be quick about it, for any luck with the queue.

The sky was still February-hard, not yet giving in to March, and I hurried, bag bumping against my knees. The Mont de Piété was across the city. On the rue de Rivoli, a shop window was hung with thick, jewel-colored fabrics. Russet and emerald, ruby and gold; striped silks. Two solid respectable figures in flaring woolen coats and sharp-heeled boots emerged with their packages. They left behind a cold whiff of perfume; stepped from the curb into a carriage.

The Mont was a crowded hubbub, the line snaking around the stone courtyard. The wait would not be short; by the look of it, several hours—with people carrying bundles and baggage like passengers boarding a train, only this time returning home with less than they'd had before. Characters of every sort were here—well-dressed and modest, ragged and tailored; doctor, sailor, seamstress, thief—I inched forward, first through the courtyard, then through the narrow door.

Inside, in a vast room hung with green-shaded lamps, a market in full sway. But this selling ground smelled of mildew, tarnish, and dust. The shelves behind the counters held tangles of white tags and strings: silver tea sets and stacks of cutlery, serving trays, candlesticks, violins, silver-backed hairbrushes, toilette sets, knob-topped claret and brandy bottles; and racks and racks of clothing. Toward the back was a horrible stack of mattresses, the stuffing falling out. Those in the line passed over watches, pulled wedding bands from their fingers, drew from their bags nested spoons tied with string. The clerk was brisk; barely glancing up before tying the tickets around the objects extracted from satchels and pockets, pulled from canvas bags and handed across the counter. The Mont, it seemed, was where everyone went who was in need of ready cash.

In my bag was Chasseloup's wardrobe and a few things of my own, as was only fair: a pair of cinnamon gloves, a jet hatpin, and that fine millinery product with its spotted veil that had become a joke, for the artistic set went defiantly hatless or wore scrappy, jaunty little things. The clerk counted out notes and coins, and I watched the hat, which had once lived in a bandbox in Stephan's sister's armoire, tagged and shoved down the line. Well—it would not be missed, not by me! So went my bravado. Just behind me, a woman reluctantly unclasped a small silver watch from her bodice. It was lovely, attached to a brooch with an enameled fleur-de-lis.

She stared at it, as if by doing so she could stop time from running out.

Chasseloup was in his shirtsleeves and a frayed pair of trousers, staring out at the buttes, smoking.

"You don't have to worry," I said, words pouring too fast downstream. "I have paid the arrears — enough to put them off." I brandished a long crusty baguette over my head like a sword. "The concierge nearly banged down the door this morning. You were asleep."

"You didn't. I hope you didn't."

"What else — why else did I go to the Mont?"

"For God's sake. And now what will they think?"

"What will who think? You are always full of people thinking." The words sounded more childish than I'd intended.

"Never mind. I'm working." Chasseloup stubbed out his cigarette and returned to his easel, arms folded.

Later our soup materialized like loaves and fishes, once there was coal, and heat, and my hands cutting every scrap from every bone, chopping and simmering. It was fragrant and steaming, and it was about time; we both needed some nourishment. Pierre's mood had not improved by the time his footfalls reached the door.

"To have the money all of a sudden, after being months in arrears, with you as the messenger? What do you think they — the landlord — will think?"

"That we are setting up a household, that you've pawned your trousers like a hundred others in this city."

"For God's sake. They think like brutes because they *are* brutes. The landlord is my father's spy; they want to cure me of 'corruption and Courbet.'" A dull silence fell . . . "All right. I thought you understood why I needed to pawn my trousers."

"So we can eat and pay the rent."

"No, I told you — "

"Told me what?"

"That I can't work in Paris; I need some air." He paused. "I'm sorry." He looked down, miserably, spooning his soup. "I have—well, I have only about three weeks to finish. I'm going to Croisset."

Oh, he was like the weather. And one never could predict what would come. I should have known by now—that Chasseloup would think of himself and I had wrapped my life around him, these past weeks. *Too much, too much around him.* It had been more of my keeping Chasseloup, these past weeks, than he me. Oh, I knew this—knew how a good line appeared, a promising streak of charcoal, and I knew how art had to consume everything, every scrap, how it swept through like fire, leaving nothing even for wolves to eat.

The next morning was a frantic chaos; hours in which nothing went well. Not the buckles on his baggage; the supplies he had intended to collect; the fact that he was feverish and jittery, his eyes worn out. I saw what it was like for him and was sorry; made tea and a boiled egg. He pulled me up for a kiss, nearly lifted me off the ground, but then he was absent, already elsewhere. We went together to the station. He'd be back in a few weeks; would write to the landlord from Croisset. Then, hoisting up bag, easel, big wooden paint box; half-finished canvas, a long cylinder balanced precariously atop everything—Chasseloup waved from the window, wan and pale and with light behind his eyes. Clanking echo of the turning key in the lock; belly suddenly tight like a gourd; heavier now, with its inner sea.

My situation was as old as the River Lot and just as fetid with the centuries' waste, but still there was no ready cure. For the next two days I rattled around in the triangular flat, pacing off the distance between Stephan and Chasseloup; Stephan, Chasseloup, and myself; the great gulf between Tillac and Paris in every respect; social, moral, geographic—my thoughts in furious tumult. Curfews, sidelong glances, and the clicking beads of Paris; the society newspapers and the mounds of earth in the streets all bled together, with the ill winds; with disappointment; with shame and contempt. Some in my condition, penitent or not, gave themselves up to bleach and boiling halls; the scurry of nuns' habits over stone and a wet lash to the wrists, in return for an anonymous bed when the time came.

Alone in that wedge in a tiny corner of the sky, I stared at the map of the capital, the scatter of clothing across the divan. Had I been too crediting, easily led by surfaces; indolent in my pleasures, insufficiently shrewd? Some truth-observing element within my Self seemed frozen; bound to a second, greater part oblivious to practical alternatives, the grave matter of life and what help might exist for it. Those two sides of my Self—the one that observed the world but could not act; the other that moved heedlessly, lacking a sense of the world's consequence, and the machinery to stave it off—these halves did not speak; possessed no common language; were incompatible residents in my woman's body. Some slippage, some muteness lay between; some fault or crack. That is what divided me and sealed my fate. I had, in that room, the first shuddering sensation of my own particular folly.

Then, was ill in the hall privy, with a sickness that did not soon abate. And within hours, the concierge's heavy knock informed me that despite the pawning of my hat, the cinnamon gloves, and the sop to the landlord, and whatever Chasseloup had written, my tenancy was not legal and the locks would be changed.

An icy rain was falling, the kind that stings fingers and cheeks and adds its chill to heartbreak. Letting go of the scent of bedclothes, the heat just left by a lover's body; the slap of wind was a reminder of the world's scant warmth. My reflection in shop windows showed a face barely recognizable, pale and puffy from too many meals of milk and white bread and sugared absinthe. I was hatless, *en cheveux*, like the artist's *grisette* I had pretended to be for a scant few weeks. But if one could not claim a lover in some dusty garret, hatlessness meant one thing only, which was not much different: a woman without resource.

I walked. Furious; the bag heavy and awkward. Vendors pushed their carts home; shops closed their doors. Here, then there, figures appeared under street lamps, first shadowy, then picked out by the light. A touch of rouge, a ragged glance, a smile that could shatter glass. Girls from a different world, one that allowed them some few hours on the street between gaslight and midnight. Anger drained and with it my energies as I walked, vaguely now, back to my old neighborhood, toward the Tivoli, edging into the dimness of rolled-up shop awnings; avoiding the lamps.

Rough voices, foreign; a whiff of the docks. They came up, slouched, one on either side of me, jostling as though we were in a crowd. One of them seized my elbow; I gasped and shook free, dragging my terrible bag over the cobbles. Haggard laughter behind, slapping feet. An omnibus came and I dodged in front of the horses; then cut a corner, zigzagging through streets until certain they were lost . . . and so was I. *Lost.* The gas lamps had stopped, and I leaned against a wall to catch my breath. I had missed the streets that led to Les Halles, the bright establishments that stayed open late. Enormous slanted red letters were painted on the bricks: DÉFENSE DE STATIONNER. No standing. And indeed, I could not. My legs felt rubbery, like they might bend and collapse.

Across the way was a church; an open gate to the side led to a tiny chapel. I pushed open its old, rusty-hinged door, not without glancing behind once more. SANCTUARY FOR ALL. OPEN FOR PRAYER. (The practice had not been mine, lately.) Heart pounding, I let my eyes adjust to the dim of the place. A gilt, open-armed Christ caught the dull flicker of the old-fashioned oil lamps. At the altar's foot stood silk roses in lurid pink. I slipped to my knees and rested my hot forehead against the wooden chair in front of me. The chapel smelled of old turnips and the crypt; floors scrubbed with greasy water; the wet, bleached knuckles of the boiling hall . . . I prayed now; I did pray. For succor, for mercy, to be able to stay there all night, to turn back the clock, for Stephan's return, for Pierre——? But a prayer for Chasseloup was lacking, just then . . . Had I not loved him much?

When I was very young, when our own roof was still made of thatch and not yet tile; in the autumn when the wind picked up and the skies darkened with the threat of a hailstorm, Berthe and I climbed down to the cellar. For me it was an adventure that involved everything known—the sky and trees; the house, her hand—my small one clenching hers; the smell of damp stone, worms, and dust.

Maman's hand would be soft and warm against my own, her face pale, dark tendrils of hair sticking to her brow. Ranged around us was our faithful harvest of cabbages and beets, apples and pears and chestnuts; preparations for winter. Outside, the bell ringer in his blue smock dropped his scythe at the door of the church; climbed the tower and threw his weight on the rope. Pealing slowly at first, then clanging and clanging as the storm rolled over. The bells an invocation; a prayer, an amulet; our tête-à-tête with the heavens.

When the skies cleared, we climbed up and walked out to the fields to see the hailstones, like moons and planets fallen from the sky. They made round holes in the soft black earth and I would gather as many as I could, bundle them into my skirts, and stack them in the kitchen garden as if preparing for a snowy cannonade. In our village, the bells had always rung the thunder past, pushed away the lightning bolts so they struck down harmlessly in open fields. Tillac had always been a fortunate place.

A tug at my sleeve. Odor of unwashed cloth, dampness, and onions; a swaying lamp lit a stained robe; the stubbled chin and the rough eyes of a priest. I was out of luck, I could smell it.

I hoisted my bag (had it been so heavy earlier?) and moved quickly, blindly; walked. Down that block, then another and another. An old woman, rocking from side to side, swerved before me for a while, muttering to herself. A necklace of keys — a hundred or more — swung from a cord around her neck, and when she stopped beneath a street lamp, it illuminated the big, gaudy red-and-white fabric flower petals stuck onto the front of her bodice. A lopsided grin. Which lock, which key? Perhaps she has tried them all . . .

Quiet. As it can only be, at that time of night; and I had reached the Seine, the ebb and suck of the current, dark and oily-cold against stone. Suddenly sober, as though I had not had a clear thought for months. The sky was a cold sea of stars and in it swam a full moon, high and bright. The wind caught briskly in my hair.

She was once part of earth, the moon. But earth turned too fast for the heaviness inside her. A bulge formed and earth began to list and wobble. Distressed, she did not slow but spun faster. Finally in a lopsided frenzy she pitched out this daughter in her and flung her far out into the sky. Staring up into that high cold heaven, I understood what had been writ large all around: I was now an exile. A pale body flung upward and cut off from the green and teeming life below. Hail from the storm; unsolicited and apart. A high, abandoned daughter. And *this* day, in the turning of the earth, was what all the previous months and weeks and days had led to, and all of my will could not stop the force of this orbit.

Thousands of girls entered Paris as I did, that year. Born somewhere else, blessed and cursed, they came from the four directions: from Brittany and Algiers, Moscow, London. By cart or train or mule or carriage or on foot, past fields, orchards, brick-and-stone-and-thatch villages, they followed their desire and need into the world and through the Paris walls. Hiked up skirts over the street debris; pulled meager shawls around their shoulders, and defiance and passion even closer, when the wind blew. Sooner or later, they began to search. For a place, a lover or a man to marry; a home or fortune; or just a bed and *soupe*. Magic in a blue bottle, like the fairy tale. So many searches began in Paris, and ended there, in those days at the height of the empire. And then the fun began — the real game of cat-and-mouse, the one you play for your life.

BOOK II

AN UNKNOWN GIRL

If they could be shown the future in a dream . . .
they would all recoil.

— MOGADOR, *Memoirs*

6

DEUX SOEURS

THE MAISON DES DEUX SOEURS was an old place, founded on a fear of vapors. Its original owner, himself a builder, had lived in the time of the real kings, and had planted the house in Paris's elegant heart, on former marshlands a stone's throw from the place des Vosges. The court's carriages had once passed under gates garlanded in carved stone; the streets of the Marais were filled with courtiers and theater banners, and a joyous mob of passersby went to and fro through the wide porte-cochères.

The house on the rue du Temple had not, originally, been built as a *maison de tolérance*. The old builder had intended it to be his own thick-walled fortress; a bulwark against the sins of his youth and a foothold on the future—a haven, eventually, for a wife and children. Because he had harbored weaknesses. He had wandered, in spite of himself, toward bruised vagabonds, outcasts, and the ill-done-by; the luckless in-betweens of the fairer sex. His own heart-softness ensnared him in dragging hems and hair falling in wisps; dreaming looks and warm currents of feeling; tongues turned slippery and fingers sly. More than anything he feared the pox; and at a certain point on life's compass, he became warier; even began to look with remorse on his past deeds.

Upon completion of any fine new structure, the plaster must dry and be purged of its sulfur stink and poisonous emanations. So (as was the custom then) the man let the place out to Madame X so the walls could be cured by musk and perfume, and a decent rent collected in the meantime. After six months, she and her flock moved on, and the place was emptied of the royal overflow from the Vosges square.

From the attic to the wine cellars, the builder found his walls whole and uncracked, but the saltpeter in the plaster had formed a porous, humid crust. The bedchambers in particular were pocked with virulent-looking boils, and his own fears seeped into the clean lines of the architecture. How strange that as one aged, the young replicated themselves; past ghosts (one of Madame X's girls, in particular) could materialize even from new walls. Then he began to fret that the mortar and plaster and wood, though they no longer stank, had retained agents of infection, a Madame X miasma; perhaps there was real poison in the walls and floors. Embarrassed that he could not purge his own building and live in it, as so many others lived within the walls he had constructed, he began to doubt himself into a feverish agitation that neither the priests nor the medics could cure.

So refinements were added: thick windows of smoked glass; alcoves off the smaller rooms; a dining hall large enough for a long, refectory-style table and rough bed stalls under the eaves. He fumigated with cinnabar, sealed the doors and windows: containing the contamination, the cesspools of desire; bottling infection. This good man cemented his relationships with the local authorities and the king's officers; imagined himself protector not only of the weaker sex, but also of religion and the city of Paris. Fear and desire, doubt and chaos and sweetness, would be closed up behind padlocks and smoky panes: clocked by the madames, regulated by the police, and checked by the doctors.

Like the generations of maids who dressed in black gowns and colored caps and aprons, descending its stairs by twos — the *maison* passed down its secrets. Deux Soeurs, as it was known (although the name appeared on no deed or document), reflected the world's double-sidedness. Its lowly activities stocked the larders and wine cellars of distant investors, even though it also paid dividends of infection and ruin. Through a succession of kings, until the mobs marched and the blade fell and the fashionable fled and grass grew up between the cobbles of the rue du Temple and pigeons pecked in the empty dust on the place de Vosges — Deux Soeurs stood irreproachable and blind-eyed, its patrons various but never few. Later, in the progressive age of machinery, its workings remained simple and old-fashioned — power derived not from steam or coal but from life's errors, the places where edges didn't quite meet, where the Code Napoleon went silent and Regulation picked up the tune. What was to be done with those who did not fit — the wayward or unmarriageable daughters, the straying wives, and the rivers of desire that ran in the veins of men? Wherever the warp, the fault line lay, whatever the insufficiency of the world — it was made of that, and the ways a female body contoured itself to fit it.

It was the violence of that idea — a rag stuck into the world's cracks — that made the assault on a person. But is the crack to be blamed, or the rag, or the hand that put it there? Life's exigencies and the old builder had created a lie at the very center of things, a place where flesh could be purchased as a surrogate for love, since love's demands were too great, too rigorous for our weak souls. Neither our circumstances, nor our character, were equal to what love asked of us.

On that cold night of exile, I made my way back from the Seine's banks toward the Mont de Piété. Settled against the stone steps of Notre Dame des Blancs Manteaux to sleep a little under the moon's eye, pulling skirt and bag well back into the shadows, succumbing to the cold's dangerous lull. Faint rustlings — rats, presumably — kept me from dropping deeper into sleep; and it was not long before a new sound interrupted the dark, the creaking of a gate, the swish of a skirt. Pointed toe of a boot, nudging. And a voice, light and girlish, touched with honey.

"*Hello?* You can't stay here, you know. The gray coats will come along any time now and it's a night for making salad if *I* know. The Brigade boys have to line their pockets with the city's lettuce!"

"I'm waiting for the pawnshop to open," I said drowsily.

"How about a bed with us tonight? Better than the basket to the Saint-Lazare prison, with a bounty on your head."

In the gas lamp's half-light, her hair, a glossy black sheet, fell unconfined to her shoulders; she was wasp-waisted, tensile. Her age might be twenty or twice that, and she spoke as if we shared a secret. "Didn't I see you a few days ago? Coming from the Mont? Don't worry, we have a remedy for that." Her patter of words like spinning pins of rain, and before I knew it, I was up and following her, her touch on my arm light but firm. On the rue du Temple, she paused before a building with a large number on it. The step was swept, lit with its own gas flares; it reminded me of a drawing I'd pored over in *Paris Illustré*, puzzled as to the caption's joke. "*No, the number you want is down the block!*" said a frock-coated man to a gawking group of tourists.

We passed the front gate, skirted the side of the building. Another door swung open to a jangle of keys, to a hand's breadth of gaslight; then she was behind me, deft as a thief in the night, and we were both inside.

It was warm. Not just the warmth of a candle flame, or a coal stove; this heat felt like a hundred logs in a hundred hearths. Warmth in which to bask, to melt. Buttery yellow light and the smell of drippings and bread, coffee grounds and wood smoke; a fire crackling in the hearth — the old kind of hearth, with hinged doors on the side for bread baking. We had entered a back door into a big kitchen, with a long trestle table cluttered with half-empty wine bottles, rinds of cheese, a wooden bowl of yellow pears and red apples spotted with brown, soft and sugary. The fire's heat crackled, loosened the bones, radiated to the corners of the room. My flesh, stiff from the cold, began to relax.

"Come along." She pulled me away, out of the gaslight and kitchen odors. The sudden change from being half-frozen to overly warm made my limbs soft and rubbery. "I'll need to find a place for you — we're past full tonight."

"Françoise." A voice lilted. "Oh, Françoise, what little bird have you caught for us?" A splash of color: azure, gold, cardinal red; a woman leaning from a doorway — red-gold hair loose and wavy; her skin pale, gold-dusted. Then gone, a tall shadow disappearing down a long hall.

"I can pay you for bed and board in the morning. When the Mont de Piété opens."

"Sure . . . but what then? Think the pawnshop will solve all your problems?"

A door opened and a gas jet flared; Françoise waved me into a kind of parlor, toward a sofa decked with pillows like lace-dipped petits fours. The room was stuffed with bric-a-brac, and a wide armoire spilled odds and ends — a haphazard assortment of lace and tulle, silk flowers and thin wraps festooned over knobs. Vacant, but with no evening chill, the whole labyrinth of chambers and corridors was heated from some vast, glowing core.

"Drop your things here, then. And you'll want something hot in your belly, on such an awful night?" She closed a roll-top desk and locked it with a key, companion to hundreds of others on a chain, then turned back with a silky expression.

I was loath to let it go, that grip on everything I possessed. Corset in red flannel, a camisole and collar in good stiff linen; two hair combs, a pair of stockings, two mended chemises; a petticoat in percale and drawers in the same; a better dress in cinnamon silk and one in fine-loomed wool; canvas ankle boots for spring. The bottle of cleaning fluid and one of freckle-removing milk (purchased out of vanity while I was modeling). A box of stationery; pen with a split nib and the indigo-marbled *Plan de Paris,* dog-eared, falling apart. Stephan's letter, its seal broken — my erstwhile protection. And, what was left of my *amour-propre.* My stomach growled; gave a pang.

"Supper first," said Françoise, seizing my arm with surprising strength.

"Fished you in off the street, did she? . . . What, are you deaf and mute, like he is?" The cook nodded toward a small, dark-faced boy, rocking on his haunches in front of the hearth. He was playing with a snare made of twine, the kind the village boys used to string up in branches, set with their lures to catch songbirds, marsh birds. Trapped, a bird's head would hang; wings flung open, cord neatly knotted around the neck.

"Françoise, you'll have to get the dogs in, the little poachers are white as ghosts from being all in the flour, and they leave footprints. And no sign of the cat; they feed her on cakes and cream. Rats in my kitchen, and the mouser eating petits fours."

She cut a slab of roast, a chunk of bread. Cheese and a slosh of wine in a china teacup. She crossed her arms across her ample waist and gave me a long look. I ate like a starved thing, a wild creature whose teeth rip at flesh.

Later, sleeping on that sofa in the parlor, I roused, wakeful, to bursts of laughter; dozed off again to the odor of cigar and perfume. An ebb tide of chatter, a river of activity flowed beyond the door and I drifted in and out of clamorous dreams, unable to tell the voices within from those outside. Eerie passages and twisting halls; rooms neither-here-nor-there, a labyrinth of a netherworld.

And in the morning, the rest happened quickly. Françoise's twitching fingers hustled me into a different dress, cheap silk, stained in spots and wanting pressing . . .

Out through yet another door, this one giving abruptly onto the cobbles, and into a waiting carriage. Françoise spoke over the rumble of the wheels; like a clock wound too tight, she emptied her words into the chilly air.

"Just look," she said. She dipped into her bag and extracted a small round mirror. I saw my pale skin, dark hair, and soft curve of chin. Eyes clear, despite the tumult within. "I know Madame Jouffroy will have you in; she has a nose for talent. But if she won't, Madame Trois will find a place for you." Her voice dropped and sweetened. "Listen: I'm saving you some trouble here." Her eyes dropped to my lap, to the gathered fabric of the dress, unpleasant against my skin. "Now — you must be firm and say you want to work for us. Otherwise I can't speak for the consequences. A prison cell till they get you sorted out, and you don't belong there, anyone can see that."

The carriage pulled up before the fortress looming palely over the rue des Fèves. Françoise hurried us across the courtyard, her skirts skimming over the flagstones and many-colored petticoats whipping about in the wind. A gate opened and at a word from my keeper we were ushered past a dozen or more citizens of Paris, men in workman's blue trousers, women with babies in their arms, a bird seller with a cage at her feet, a young woman or two, hatless and ungloved. Those awaiting an audience at the Paris Préfecture de Police. I would come to know it well.

M. NOËL read the nameplate in front of a young man with a polished mustache, his thick-fingered hand battened down on an ink pen. The sound of the nib across a dry page was a scuttling of leaves; the questions uttered as though from a conversation begun earlier, now resumed. The din of the place, the roar of a thousand voices echoed off marble, filtered through the cavernous room. On the wall above Noël hung an oily brown and varnished painting——a face from the papers, and here he was, the chief of police, in a portrait pitched at a slant as though he might drop like a blade. Françoise nudged my arm, and the mechanisms of a great machine, long-used and oiled with practice, ticked into place.

"How long in Paris? Residence, employment? Name and age, place of birth? Then, "Your palms, please."

I startled at his touch, the fingers sausage-thick, tobacco-stained, damp. He prodded my palms, one then the other, felt around my fingers and thumbs——the second time in half a year that a man had examined my palm to determine my future.

"You'll find them smooth as silk. This one's no blistered tin cutter or maid of all work. And no identity papers when she arrived, either," interjected Françoise.

"Mademoiselle, you have left your family and province to reside and be employed at the Maison des Deux Soeurs, rue du Temple, third arrondissment, Paris? You arrived at that address this morning and stated your intention?"

His eyes were blue and mild. "You are a long way from home."

"She wants to work," said Françoise, by way of assistance. Another voice, neither Noël's nor Françoise's, behind my ear, playful, mocking, clear as a bell: *"The mother says nothing, and the girl cannot speak up for herself!"* Françoise looked vexed and impatient; M. Noël's face was impassive, his pen for the moment stilled. "Is your father living? Your mother? . . . Any relative at all?"

"If you get into a scrape, wave it under someone's nose!" I'd laughed when Stephan had signed his name to that letter, but I could not produce it now.

Françoise and Noël were head to head, joking about something else; the pen scratching again, sputtering dry. Inkwells were scarce at the Préfecture these days; too few of them to take account of the river of girls who flowed through the place.

And my two Selves were silent, foreign to each other, too slow to catch up. My recent lovers, their influence and sometime-protection, were leaking wounds in separate chambers of my heart; their names stuck in my throat. Gascon stubbornness; that ignorance of sycophancy; a rustic muteness that knows so well how to survive in its element—a tongue to bargain and barter, to haggle over the qualities of a *foie d'oie* or supplicate the spirits at a running stream—that tongue could not speak. My back ached and I wished, so badly, to sit. (Was it a backache, merely the longing to rest, that finished the transaction?) Some emotion, like nausea, and the gulf widened. *The rutted road, Papa's body in a cart.* It would have to be another road, now. I saw it stretching before me, a sharp curve into blackness.

The paper, when it was finished, read:

Whereas the woman established as Eugénie R—, ex–department of the Gers, is charged with prostitution without being registered, it is consequently in the interest of public health . . . that she be submitted to the administrative regulations . . .

A flurry of administration: a babble of voices and Françoise's high-pitched laugh. The mood turned almost celebratory; a milling around of uniformed officers and men in dark suits. Françoise smiled to this official, then that one; fingertips cold against my hand as she steered a swift passage through the halls. How was I to have guessed that I had been arrested, convicted, subjected to an injurious penalty, all without judge, jury, or argument — and in the flick of an eyelash?

"All we've done, here, is to help you use what you've got to get what you need. Clean and legal, no more worries. And I don't know Nathalie Jouffroy if she doesn't find you to her taste. But I'd never've shown you without getting you on the books; I'd be out of a job! You'll thank me, you know."

A rank of benches filled with young women — most poor and disheveled, a few wearing hats and gloves, and our passage caused a fluster and commotion.

"Madame! May I see you?"

"Let me walk with you, madame, just to the door."

"I can work, madame, I can . . ."

Françoise quickened her step, pulling me by the arm. One poor soul went so far as to follow us and pluck at her shawl. "You know me, madame. You know me," she cried, and I started, and stared. Because she looked so like the young, pale-browed woman who had also been, briefly, at the Tivoli. Or perhaps I was mistaken. An officer stepped forward and seized her before I could be sure.

"My things, where are my *things?*" I was back in the bric-a-brac parlor, sobbing and furious, now dressed only in a camisole, the other garments having been peremptorily stripped.

"Calmez, calmez!" The woman who confronted me now had a broad Germanic brow, balmy, pale gray eyes; white-blonde hair piled on her head; and a voice as cool as a cloth dipped in water. She handed me a substantial square of linen, a man's handkerchief. From Françoise's rattling discourse I had surmised that my immediate destiny lay in the hands of this Madame Jouffroy who was now

towering over me and saying, drily, "Excellent . . . Our enterprising submistress has violated every statute in Paris bringing you in here. Do you want to tell me what kind of trouble you've gotten yourself into?"

She moved to the windows, slid open the draperies. The window-panes were colored glass: blue and gray, red and violet, like disarranged church windows. They let in a muted light, illuminating the bits and pieces of finery strewn about as well as her own attire, a kind of morning coat embroidered with birds.

"This is not a hotel and I will not have entrepreneurs incurring fines on my behalf. You can try to come up with a novelty, but these walls have seen it all. Well, whatever it is—let me tell you something. You are not the first and will not be the last. So? Difficulties with a man? And with money?"

Uneasily I folded my arms around my body; the flimsy shift was unpleasant. Madame Jouffroy's tone suggested that I was the perpetrator of my trouble and not its victim, an idea from which I jerked back like a hand that had touched a hot stove.

"All you innocents, you think that everyone in the world has your best interests at heart. Ah, and why not? A girl might fall in love, yes? Then one day she wakes up with the dogs at her heels. How many of these girls do you think there are? You, alone? Half a dozen, a hundred? I'll tell you: thousands.

"Oh, they will run after him, or run away from home to go begging in the streets, or go crying to Maman. Then the police catch them with nets and stock the prison cells; or they find comfort in the madhouses, which are stuffed full. Their children fill the hospice and staff the factories—there, have you stopped crying? See, you are not so badly off. And do you know the reason for all of this trouble?" I sniffed, and stared at her. The dusty, bookish odor was tickling my nose. "You do not know the world, and you do not know men."

The sneeze came, violently. The room smelled damp and inky; later I would come to understand it was the odor of a bank vault.

Madame Jouffroy went on. "So now, do you think you can wander Paris, trying your luck, without attracting the attention of the police?"

"No—I don't know what you mean!"

"Mogador was born right over there on the rue des Puits. No older than you when she was inscribed, went on the Register, and began her career at a tolerated house on this very street. But she kept her wits about her, played out her hand, and now she is the Comtesse de Chabrillan. Léonide LeBlanc was a stonebreaker's daughter from the Loiret. The man didn't break only stone; I saw the scars on her back. Now *she* needs a shovel to count her diamonds. This Mademoiselle Pearl who is so popular now—she was born Crouch in the isle of nowhere. She carried a *carte*, whether or not you want to believe it, and now she beds down at the Tuileries—or so they say. What do you think distinguishes the women who choose their lovers, name their price in Paris, and beat the Bourse by the month—from those who give away their advantages and wind up mad, dead, or both?"

"I don't know," I stammered, and sneezed again.

"Ignorance will not serve you in this world, my dear, and 'innocence' is a tool used to hammer healthy young women into unnatural shapes . . . Come here." She tipped my face up as though holding a kitten by the scruff of its neck. "You do not look like such an outlaw to me. *Un peu panné*, bedraggled and starved for too long, that's all. But the good Lord put us all here on this earth to learn the truth of one another; which always seems to find its way to the marketplace. And it is as good a place as any to start."

Beyond my veil of tears, I felt her theatricality, her certainty; her iron grip.

"But where is my bag, my—my clothes? I have a . . . a letter." My voice faltered as I made one last futile stand.

Nathalie Jouffroy turned again as she neared the door, spoke with slow emphasis. "Mademoiselle Rigault, this house is the most selective in Paris. Girls beg to be accepted; we turn away twenty a day, often more. If working here is your intention, as Françoise insists, you have achieved it. If it was not, still, you may have come to the right place. Certainly, mademoiselle, you should find something to your liking . . . Françoise" — her voice echoed down the long corridor — "see to her particulars." She closed the door behind her with a quiet click of the latch.

A row of empty bottles, champagne and Madeira, marched down the length of one wall; a long mirror with edges of chipped gilt and a crack running through its center was fixed on another. I had been shepherded up six flights to a slope-floored, slant-raftered attic made over into living quarters far less salubrious and decorative than the parlor downstairs. The place felt ancient, with the thick beams and heavy doors of a fortress. Cabbage-rose wallpaper, streaked with slashes of charcoal, was patched over ancient plaster; and on every available surface was a litter of combs and hairpins, pots of rouge, matches, playing cards, sticky glasses. A stove bubbled with heat, and the scuttle was brimming: even this drafty quarter was warm. A ragtag group was gathered; their voices rose in a babble; cigarette smoke coiled upward.

"*Girooonnnde.*" An arm caught me around the waist.

"*Chouette* . . . ," said another girl, and laughed, a sound as clear and hard as glass. Sinuous fingers crept up my arms, a dance of importunate, daring touches.

"*Journée gourd* . . . a good catch for Françoise, eh?" The last deep-throated and husky. Tiger-eyed, with red-gold hair. Another girl stood behind her, brushing it with long, slow strokes.

On the center table was a large plate with the remains of a yellow cake that looked to have been eaten by fistfuls. A girl with creamy skin reached back and broke off a piece, and put it to the lips of another, who lolled against her knees, eyes half-closed, her tawny curls dusted with crumbs. The others were in various stages of dress and makeup, with hair half-curled or twisted or pouffed under nets. One applied feathery blue lines to her temples with a brush, making veins like delicate branches; she held her hand steady and stared into a small mirror. Colored robes were tossed about, and little low-heeled slippers were scattered over the floor. On the table, as well, was a mortar and pestle, corked phials from a pharmacy, and small pieces of moldy, blackish sponge.

"Enough of that," said the girl who'd put her arm around my waist. "We've got no quinine, and these sponges are diseased. They look like they've been scrubbing the bottom of a boat."

"*This* is what they have on offer for protection around here?" said another girl, a plump blonde who'd been brought upstairs at the same time I had. But unlike me, she seemed to know the ropes.

"They like to keep the midwives in business."

"Angel makers, you mean," said a third.

"*Merde* on the sponges; it's like trying to keep black flies out of India with those. I'm handing out *préservatifs* from now on."

"That's what we did at Chevillat; things looked better over there, I'll tell you," said the blonde girl.

"*Michés* put them on?"

"Tell them they'll be pickled if they don't."

"Not here, maybe at Chevillat!" Laughter.

"They're all afraid of infecting their wives and their progeny, just need a bit of reminding."

"Yes, real estate will plunge into the sewer if their sons have the pox," said one of the girls who was eating cake.

"Yes, well, they'd rather the sewer, plenty of 'em."

"When your boyfriend gets his transfer out of the Brigade, what rotten luck!"

"Oh, your luck won't hold with him, the *fouille merde*."

"There's a new douche at the apothecary's; some girls like it. Someone's Hygienic Waters. It's in a tin with flowers."

"Hah — Jeannel's. He was in the Morals Brigade before he went into water."

" Now *that's* rich."

"Don't need to make him any richer. There's plenty of vinegar in the kitchen."

"Douche with wine and turpentine; nothing can survive that."

"Has Delphine come back? Françoise sent her lover to the rue Thérèse."

"Think she'll come clean?" asked another girl, small-boned and lovely, dragging on a cigarette.

"I wouldn't trust that bone-cracker," drawled the tiger-eyed one. "He's a murderer." A brief silence.

"The Dab will be here on Monday — tell *him* it's in the name of public health."

A bell clanged from the stairwell. Cigarettes were stubbed out and the group shook itself out and stood, as during a second-act intermission when the play is bad. It sounded again and the unruly band paraded down the stairs, a flurry of thin robes and satin slippers. None of their flimsy toilettes looked to have cost ten francs, and not one appeared as though she'd need a shovel to hoist her diamonds. The tall girl with red hair was last to crush her cigarette. Gave me a long stare as she drew a fluttering dressing gown around her shoulders. I followed the others as though being lowered by a rope.

And so it began. The price of ignorance paid, first, on tufted pouffes under chandeliers downstairs in the salons, where each client's "choice" was made. Then upstairs, in fancily named rooms with theatrical furnishings; on bed linens more staged than laundered; and, at intervals, at the long, scarred dining table where we gathered for meals, silently rising and sitting for Françoise and the two madames, at noon, six, midnight, and two in the morning. It was paid especially at dawn, when I dragged my tender, insulted body up a rope ladder that led up to a sleeping bunk in the attic quarters, tugged aside the curtain hanging on brass loops. This was the sole place of retreat; but even there, my pallet was shared with another girl who wedged her body next to mine. Later, where her head had rested, would be a tangle of hair, tufts of it, soft and dark. Like the first hair of an infant when it falls.

Crawling beneath that drape, pulling my knees to my chest, I listened to pigeons beat their wings and cluck and coo under the eaves. Willed myself back from oblivion. How, then, had it come to this? Was it the world's justice, its further transgression — or a colossal, evil joke? How was I to contour myself to this new, distorted logic?

To navigate blindly, hurtling ahead? For it was dark indeed, and my compass had failed.

Memory has strange ways. Downy-throated geese in their pens, the beating of wings . . . Chunks of pigment in Maman's palette box and the creamy weight of her dowry linens in the press. The uneven height of the stairsteps to Chasseloup's studio, the slant of the light from the windows. Even the battered spines and torn covers of love novels, the rapt expression of a girl sucking sweets and turning pages in an attic bunk—all of these leave imprints. But those other initiations, events of absent flesh passing over my own, are darker vessels over the river. For increasingly, my attention retreated inward to its own emptiness, its frozen emergency.

7

THE POINT OF THE HOOK

THE RHYTHMS OF LIFE at Deux Soeurs were not defined by nature. We worked until dawn, breakfasted, then slept until noon, when we rose from the dead to eat. Macaroni, potatoes, and pies; *matefaim* (a kind of fried dough) and roasts; wine and bread and viscous sauces weighted down our off-hours. My compatriots believed in minding the rules most of the time, stealing what they could, getting past the doctor — (called the Dab, after his loathsome instrument) and staying on the good side of Françoise. Hairnets at the table, gloves downstairs, rising and sitting and a facsimile of obedience to the madames; a schedule governed by bells and meals, by chits, by red marks and black marks collected in an old cracked-binding book. The place housed a collection of feminine spirits at odds with our keepers, collected here for a purpose but always ready to display a flagrant disregard for it. The Mignons, Ninettes, Blondines, Frisettes wore the shadow of the world on their flesh; the bruises from its fists and the marks of its teeth. They varnished over weaknesses, lacquered old sores. Hid this wound, sold what paid, tied off ruptures above the hemorrhage, and did what might (at some point) allow them to scramble up a rung or two; take half-measures toward better lives. Like flowery wallpaper peeling down in strips, or lacy hems dragged through the gutter, our sex took hard use here. *But just for now. Not for long, not me!* On Sunday, at a designated hour, they put on rented dresses at a stiff tariff and filed out to confess their sins. I watched them come and go.

After the first week, I was no longer inhabitant of my own skin but hovered some distance away; a vacancy of flesh and its ghost. Obscurely, amid the conversation that ebbed and sucked between the walls — often about ways and means to prevent pregnancies, or the various forces that could be marshaled to abort them — I had come to a new idea: that half-starvation, the filthy streams of the bedrooms, street gutters, excesses of coffee, and a too-sudden stagnation of love — this miasma had halted my body's rhythms, stopped its courses. Indeed, everthing else I had once known had been suspended, thinned down, or dried up. If a second life had indeed begun in this body, perhaps it had now fled. I could not tell anymore; could feel no flicker of life.

One of those mornings-that-were-not-mornings, a moody pall lingered in the attic quarters; a flurry of restless anxiety blew through the place like a shifty wind. Pots of powders, paints, and brushes were marshaled to the new task. The girl who slept next to me — she was called Lucette — was mixing kohl in a tiny pot, her hair hanging limp. The rest lined up for the mirror.

I had endured a sanitary examination after my registration at the Préfecture, but it had been superficial and cursory, as though my relatively innocuous status was understood, despite what the paperwork had to say. From what I had heard up in the attic quarters, the ordeal ahead would be different.

Lucette glanced me over. She had built a dark beauty mark on a flaking ulcer near her lip. "If you know what's good for you, don't ask questions, just get in and get out. It's not much, just a poke and a turn-around. Routine. *You've* got nothing to worry about . . . There, how's that?" Most of them, I knew, were only worried about being shipped off to the Saint-Lazare infirmary with the pox; the Dab wasn't looking for babies.

When my number was called, in my loose prisoner's garb I fol-

lowed the narrow-laced V of Françoise's back, her pencil-thin
nape under a heavy coil of hair. In the downstairs parlor, the
same one in which I'd slept, the drapes were drawn. The doctor
was young and a mumbler, not gentle; his coat, not quite black,
was spotted with grease. The cool leather of the examining couch
slid under me. Eyelids hot, I clamped shut my knees. He grunted;
it might have been half a laugh, and then the pain made me gasp
aloud.

Afterward, he was wiping his instrument with a dirty cloth and
shouting, *"Stand up! Stand up!"*

But if I did, I would lose control of everything at once, bowels
and guts together, and I rolled to one side and clamped my knees to
my chest. "Sir" — I gasped. "My courses have — "

"You can work. You'll have no trouble, not from me. Stand and
turn. Arms up. Very well. *Out.*"

In the hall, my rubbery limbs collapsed onto the Brussels carpet,
as tattered, half-formed notions flittered through my mind. *Release,
escape, rescue!* Ships set sail; trains clattered down the tracks, flags
waving aloft.

Then somehow I was back upstairs. Françoise's sharp features
hovered above, sugared over like candied fruit. She was shaking
my arm. Voices sang, somewhere, taunting like children playing in
the distance. The submistress was seizing me now, forcing me upright. The Dab's scrawl on a white sheet had marked me clean; fit to
sell again. *Routine.* The ritual examination would recur, I was told,
every week.

"Come on, a little of Madame B's hen *en cocotte,* a glass of wine,
and *la nausée* will pass?"

One thing, and one thing only was expected of us, the denizens of
Deux Soeurs; and the forces were marshaled to it with an efficiency
that not so many years later could be described as Prussian. The
madames knew what kept business going and supplied it for the easy
price of debt. Of the two, Madame Trois was hated; Madame Jouffroy admired and feared. Trois was the implacable, the enforcer of
rules; Jouffroy held the reins. It was she who chose and promoted

her "favorites" and mingled with some echelon of Paris high society (she was mentioned in the gossip columns, took a carriage to the Bois de Boulogne, betted at Longchamp, and took the waters at Biarritz). Jouffroy set the tone of the place; brought in the top-end business.

On the nether end—our end—for what seemed a few sous (but ended up being a pile of them) soft hands rubbed sweet oils into aching flesh; washed and brushed hair; pedicured, plucked, waxed, and polished. The establishment's chambermaids were a cadre of upright working girls whose jobs had been passed down through an aunt or a cousin; or whose mothers and grandmothers had served before them. They professed to envy us but perhaps did not, as they ran errands, fetched pins and baubles, droppers of tincture and phials of powder. They lied to Françoise and poured glasses of lemon water; flattered our attributes of hand or foot, lips or skin or hair; our skills, our great loveliness; our faked-up privileges. Cheered and stole—cakes and liquor, cigarettes from the salon boxes; and were exquisitely sensitive, all for a price. "Oh, mademoiselle—you need some tincture of arnica there; and how about a flower in your hair?" Evenings came and went according to an organization so old and so sturdy, a discipline so well-practiced and severe, that soon enough it seemed as though Deux Soeurs must set Paris's clocks, and the rest of the world was upside down.

Slowly, like a headache that will not retreat, I learned the twists and turns of the place. The two first-floor reception salons; the bedchambers off a central staircase for entertaining "guests." I became familiar with certain stretches of carpet runner, draperies that concealed false exits and secret entries (meant for those who eschewed public access) . . . actual doors to the outside that were barred and locked to us. Sitting alcoves were cozily furnished, dusted daily but never used; bronze nymphs reclined with greater comfort in their niches than we did in ours. Flowers stood majestically in their urns; briefly fresh; replaced as soon as they showed a tinge of brown. Along the many corridors, doors opened and closed to reveal a glimpse of trouser, a dangling set of cuffs.

The house had two reception rooms. In Salon Deux, for better-heeled clients, the furnishings were ornate with gilt, the rugs plush, the drapery several folds deep. Champagne sluiced from magnums; the chandeliers had crystal drops that the maids climbed ladders to polish. The clients there were men of government, business, and industry; they were judges and factory owners, lords of the realms of lace and ribbon, armchairs and ottomans, railways and racehorses; hand-picked for their silk-lined pockets, leather soles, and largesse of possibility. Each in his turn abandoned hat and umbrella or stick in the entryway and swung down the corridor leading to the house's deep interior.

Salon Trois, on the other hand, stood at the front of the house and was where we new recruits were stationed (and by way of Françoise's inscrutable system a rotation of others, which ensured variety—blondes and brunettes, dusky-skinned and fair; long-limbed and plump; vivacious and smiling, dreamy-eyed and wistful; the joker, the ingénue, the cynic, the blasé). The décor of Salon Trois was that of the bourgeois household, its sofas and drapes meant to make guests feel better off than they generally were. Its clients included half-formed spendthrifts from good and indifferent families, and it was the refuge of the wealthier students; the artistic and their hangers-on; young men light of pocket or green of seed; and the less important agents of the police. No customer was ever actually refused, unless unable to afford the ticket of entry. And it was here that I (wistful, brunette, of medium build) was tethered nightly to a sofa until chosen or called.

My compatriots, with few exceptions, saw through the ploys and deceptions exerted upon us; still, they did not want to act on what they knew, and would rather argue (slap, weep, pull hair, kiss, and make up) over pins and chocolates and chits above and beyond what their own five senses could tell them. Cake stealing, wild crushes; sudden maladies of mind and body like flashing storms; the making of mountains from trifling matters; spats and squabbles over hairpins; pecking orders, scapegoats. Whatever had landed each of us here had narrowed our eyes to slits. And then too, life was such that one would do anything to forget it even as it was happening. Trivia became an outlet for misery, tears passed through a needle's eye. I quickly learned, myself, not to think of certain things: when I did, terrible ideas seized and flattened me the way that heavy irons scorch cloth.

I was not, at that time, immune to shame.

Françoise's feet were small, clad in blue boots that laced up the calf and rested on a fat ottoman. What a strange creature she was: thin and blanched; anxious and jutting about with hair gathered up or falling; her eyes enormous pools. She quivered with intensity as she paraded up and down, affectations jangling like bracelets. The submistress exerted her tyrannies and then insisted she be pitied for her lot, sulky until coddled by those on whom she practiced her torments. This morning she wore a loose-fitting jumper with big pockets, cinched at the waist; her boots indicating that she might certainly go out and walk if she liked, or perhaps had just come in. Her hair was done up messily, as though mussed and tossed by the wind. The squat ottoman on which her boots rested was embroidered with a fish on a line, the point of a hook piercing its jaw. A drop of blood stood out, and its scales were etched in silver. I was beginning to understand the humor of the place, although I didn't laugh much.

I had been summoned to the "business" parlor, where Jouffroy and Trois hid out when they weren't on the floor, and the submistress held court on Saturday. It was the room in which I'd stayed, that first night. Françoise told me to sit. I was looking less peaked, she said, was I feeling better?

Yes, thank you. Conversations with the submistress made me feel as though my head was being held down under water. She turned back to the escritoire and fiddled with a fountain pen, one of the newly patented ones with its own ink resevoir inside.

Madame B's cooking agreed with me, then. Ah, well, she has always been the genius that kept the place running. Françoise herself was rail-thin, "a boy forever," as she often said. It left her unfit for the grand work we others accomplished, though rumor had it that Françoise had done a stint on the Register.

The parlor had a sweet, mothy odor of bank notes; the acrid tang of silver mingled with leaking gas that made me sneeze. I had peeked inside this room once, after a busy night, when bills and coins covered every surface like a gambler's counting table, and Madame Jouffroy and Madame Trois were draped over the divan, pleased and fresh as a summer's day. Today it looked like the business office of a lingerie merchant.

"You have made a good beginning—didn't I tell you that you would? The madames have noticed, you know, that you are often selected."

"Too often," I muttered.

Among the regulars in Salon Trois, each had her method. Olga angled for the most promising-appearing clients and made sure Françoise knew about it, as she had aspirations for Salon Deux. Tall Lucette, my pallet mate who pulled out her hair in her sleep, lived for her lover "outside"—the police officer who'd been assigned (unfortunately) to the Morals Brigade. She bided her time, dreaming of escape and erasure from the Register, a tidy domestic arrangement to call her own; she went by the rules and was thus favored by Émilie Trois. Two carefree, gray-eyed beauties who both went by the named Mignon pretended to be *cocottes* in training—at least that's how they saw it—competing with Olga and skimping on tips to the maids. Blonde Claudine had come over from Maison Chevillat. She looked like a juicy plum ready to burst, and kept up a flow of opinions on how things were run over there—easier access to *muffes*, the old rich men who spent a fortune, tipped, and left *gants d'amour*. (In Salon Trois we were not permitted *gants*, and tips were pooled.) Delphine, discussed on my first night, was still absent; her place taken by a succession of Belgians. And there was Banage, gamine and pointy-chinned, slight and strong as a cart horse. She was the mistress of colorful jokes, pointed humor about the clients, and she claimed no aspirations at all. Her brother was on the stage; she was supporting him until he made his name.

We played by the same rules, and there was a certain esprit de corps. It did not take long to determine the pecking order on any given night: if a girl wanted to pass or play, initiate the untested or bear up under the ugly. The least desirable (any obvious deficiency of face, form, or fortune) was passed to the newest aboard. This, at least, on nights when business was good, which it was generally. The basis of the invitation extended, the frisson of interest, appeared by sleight of hand (a stretch, a yawn, a turn of the head) to travel from customer to girl rather than the reverse, but in fact the merchandise came to life to play a part in the sale. If a guest stood dazzled or hesitant, uninitiated into the signals or unsure (as he might before a selection of goods at the Bazar de Hôtel de Ville), Françoise chose for him. If she was absent, he was "sent down the line" according to his qualities: the cut of a coat or the fall of the trousers, how a beard was trimmed.

"You have made an excellent choice, monsieur," Françoise would murmur, catching up to the scene, turning over one of the brass tags.

For each customer taken upstairs, we received a token, one marker apiece. Françoise kept track with sharp black strokes next to our numbers in her ledger, and at the end of the night, we compared our chits to her tallies and assigned tips to the maids. It was not untrue that I deferred when I could, with a careful disinterest or (apparent) absent-mindedness. Banage, slight as she was, seemed untouched by each trip, as if it were a Sunday turn around the Luxembourg, while I languished after the first tag was turned, and my knees shook on the stairs. I had not learned how not to take each encounter personally and I could see that this weakness would be a death sentence.

A skein of the submistress's inky hair slipped loose; Françoise fidgeted with a hairpin. "If I can give one small piece of advice, it is not fair play to slip the *passe* so often? You must build your resiliency. As it stands you have only a few *passes* against the debits. Now, you missed two nights after the Dab and I allowed you that, and not because Madame Trois was happy about it! But now you must make that up in addition—" She extracted a lined sheet, marked black and red. "Medical examination—bed and board before you began working—dress rentals, footwear, and jewelry—hair and makeup. Candles and soap. Street clothes for the trip to the Préfecture. Share of birthday gift for Madame Trois; we'll be celebrating next week. Tips. Masses."

"I don't attend Mass."

"Tithes are charged to your account regardless."

Françoise folded the page back into her book and closed it. "Beyond that." She hesitated. "More than once I have heard you are—"

What? Occasionally ill in the basin? Or I took a wrong turn, got lost in the labyrinth? Had I spoken needlessly with a client, missed a bell, expressed a like or dislike, exhibited a personal quality? We were not to laugh or cry; betray curiosity, boredom, emotion . . .

"Sympathetic to excess. You offered a handkerchief to Monsieur M—?"

"He had a head cold. I just rang for a maid." Really, it had seemed like the only thing to do, but the bells got mixed up and the handkerchief was delivered to the wrong room at an awkward moment; some other gentlemen had got wind of it and made a joke of him.

"Our guests prefer women to be cold, not to be reminded of their mothers or sisters. So. Stick to the clock. You must discipline yourself, Rigault. Oh, you'll be fine, you have qualities. You just need to learn to use them. How shall I put it? In this house, wealth is cultivated. Go by the ledger book. If you want to look after yourself."

Silence pooled between us; with a glimmer of a young Françoise who stood mutinous against her relations. (Gossip upstairs alluded to the very worst of histories for the submistress, spawned from a family of bankrupted lacemakers and petty criminals. She'd trumped the system and climbed on top of the pile—she was detested for that). A steely, slippery young woman who shipwrecked here, of all places; and had nailed herself to a plank in the roiling sea.

"All right," I said, surprised to be getting off so lightly, without a fine or a penalty, of which I had heard plenty, upstairs. Cautiously, I continued. "Françoise—something else."

"What is it?"

"The paper you said my mother signed. The document from the police investigation. I need to see it."

The submistress toyed with a strand of hair, swiveled to and fro in her chair. She raised a dark eyebrow and slid her hands into the pockets of her skirt.

"Of course. All this paperwork! What a headache. You have no idea. Well, I'm surprised you raise it, with other matters so much more pressing?" Françoise rose and went to the armoire, fishing and rummaging in its drawers and recesses, tossing about lacy underthings and whalebone, then back to the desk, where she scrabbled in pigeonholes and shifted piles of paper, all about to topple. "The doctor's report . . . Bringing on your menses, I mean. Better now than later, you know."

I looked down. The baleful fish eye on the embroidered ottoman stared up.

"Ah. Here we are." She was holding out a small bottle of brackish-looking liquid, spidery writing on its label: ERGOT, ABORTIFACIENT. "If this doesn't do the trick, we'll go for a visit to the midwife. Count yourself lucky. The madames could turn you out for this if they wanted to." I hesitated; she dropped the bottle in my lap.

"May I . . . see the paper?"

"Of course." She sighed again and rummaged through the pigeonholes for an eternity. Finally handed over a dense page of print stamped with a seal from the police and the city of Paris. My name had been written in — not whatever they happened to call me in the salons on any given night — and the date and place of my birth. At the end stood several important-looking scrawls of dark ink. A peculiar sensation crept over me and I stared at the woman across from me, her belladonna eyes glistening, for a fleeting moment wondering who she was, who was I — what was I doing here?

"This is not my mother's signature," I said. "I know it. I'm not one of your illiterates upstairs."

"I'm sorry that you are upset. It is — you know, it is what happens." I stared at her, then down at the paper, in a creeping blight of fear.

"Now, come. Whatever the situation is, you are going to need to think calmly. If your family can help you, well, you can post a letter today if you'd like. But I think you know, and I do, that they've washed their hands of this." She leaned forward. "Really."

My hands clenched in my lap. I shuddered in my skin as though to slough it off, vomit myself out of this body.

"A girl in your position needs a friend; don't think I don't understand. Just between the two of us, I'll send you up to the Josephine Room to rest a bit. Take it easy this afternoon, you know? Believe me, your situation's not so bad. Here, wait, I have something else"—she fished a second phial from a drawer. "A few drops of this. I take it myself for a headache. All right? Then the other. And it's chilly, wear a dressing gown through the halls."

The submistress pulled the bell rope, and a maid I didn't know, a violet cap from Salon Deux, appeared on cat's feet. At the door the submistress called after us, "You'll be better for tonight. It will be a gay evening; Madame Jouffroy has asked some of her special guests."

～ 8 ～

JOLIE

THE JOSEPHINE ROOM was white, gold, and coral; its furnishings a Bourbon mirage, the bed a rosy blister of satin. What new price would be extracted for this sojourn from the attic's dingy confines, I could only imagine—the Tivoli, with its drafty reproach and spidery cracks, was likely a bargain by comparison. The violet-capped maid left quickly, turning the key in the lock: business as usual. I started at the stoppered glass bottle of ergot; its message clear.

I palmed my belly; settled queasily into the armchair's faithless expanse. Pulling my dressing gown closer I felt a stab of longing for real clothing, the honest rough stuff of my old goose-dress; and a fleeting, murky anger. It was all too much, this jumble of need, coercion, and unwanted company. Françoise's headache potion was sweetish and flowery (digitalis, I think; Berthe had had it). The warmth and the potion leading me blessedly, fuzzily adrift under the pad of a giant's thumb, consciousness flattening and slipping away. I did not swallow the ergot.

. . . *Golden fields in September, and again in spring when the earth is soft; and green dots the black soil.*

Birds squalling, feathers flying. How they turned toward me, gabbling, mouths open. Slaughtered by Saint Martin's Day.

The smell of apples, slowly rotting on the ground, and fallen leaves.

Reaching, a color, a texture, a scent — what to hold on to? . . . Sliver of moon, hanging over the Paris skyline as a train hurtles down the tracks, through a long tunnel —

. . . Faint rustle, soft knock. Creak of hinges. Not the main door, but from some passageway behind. Murmur of a voice that did not wait for an answer. And then I was no longer alone.

"Are you all right?" she whispered. Lips warm and brushing; her hair falling like a heavy-tasseled drape. *"Come, lie down. You must be so tired."* I was, and did; and soon I didn't care why she was there; only that she stayed.

Next to me, she was a pale gleam of ivory, soft, known, yet strange. Spinning beneath the surface, very close; a hand, gentle but firm; perfumed breath against my cheek. What lapped against my own flesh was soft and loose as though nothing bound her; nothing familiar. Scarlet, crimson, ruby, blood red — like the center of an enormous rose; candlelight glimmered against soft draperies.

A gentle urging of fingertips brushed the bones of my hips, passed over my thighs and knees. She slipped her hands down my body, traced the curve of my neck; palmed the whisper of my belly's curve. As she touched I wakened to myself, curled; dared not move or breathe. A body's shift, then, down to the soles of my feet, pausing, just barely, at the rough places. My body was not mine; but it roused, nonetheless — as it had before, but not recently — and then she lay down with her arms around me, cupping me, no cloth between us. Slowly she retraced with her lips the places where her hands had been. Covered me with scent, every part of her smooth, polished; and at last urged me onto my back and pressed the length of her self against mine. Light; almost weightless even though everything about her seemed enormous; long-limbed. "Are you ready?" . . . Or I thought I heard that; words evanescing like drops into water. My thoughts, even, were wisps that vanished as quickly as they came, and all that remained was the cool of satin falling against my flesh, the soft cling of lips — nowhere, everywhere. I found the edge

of the bed and grasped it as if it were the side of a boat; I was rocking on the waves while something warm, flaring, bursts of green,
slashes of violet, flowerlike, bloomed within me. Sunlight on stones
from a crumbling wall. Wild bells of morning glories in a garden,
maroon and purple and white. The moan was mine, then the sob,
and hot tears; I reached for her again, my mouth searched for and
found her white breast, caught, gleaming against the crimson, in a
pale flare from the lamp.

"Would you like an orange?" Her fingers—long and tapered,
oddly (in this place) unmanicured—peeled away the skin, removed
the pith. The flesh of the fruit was red-tinged, each crescent flushed
like the harvest moon. She settled the sections on the plateau between her breasts—gold-spangled, brazen. A vine of her red-gold
hair trailed damply over my chest as I lay close. Breath falling in and
out. The juice was bright and sweet.

She rolled over, a heavy, graceful movement, extracted a cigarette from a silver case. Her back was long and her head dipped for
a moment between the shadow of her shoulder blades as the match
flared. She closed her eyes briefly as she inhaled; the smoke coiling up, blue. She smoked without speaking, letting the ash get very
long. The perfumed air was still and smoky.

"I saw you the first night, you know. But then I was away. As luck
would have it, I always seem to come back. So—are you making a
stay of it?"

"Is there a choice?"

She tipped the ash into her cupped palm and leaned up on an elbow, traced a fingertip along my cheek, lips, neck. Across my barely
rounded belly. "No ashtray." She laughed. "You're not a *prisoner.*"

"I have nothing to wear and all the doors are locked. Every day
she says I'm more in the red—" I stopped. Why did I think she was
trustworthy, this girl?

"As long as you don't owe, you can get out. Let me put it this
way: if you're smart about it and make it worth their while, you can
cut a deal that suits you."

"Is anyone else smart about it?"

She inhaled; tapped her ash again. "Bit of a dim crowd up there, wouldn't you say? Except for Banage."

"Well, it doesn't seem very likely, the way they keep the books."

"Oh, Françoise and her ledger." She gestured with the cigarette, making smoky curls. As if she had some magical way around the ironbound figures and chits.

"And now they have given me something to" — *stifle the infant seed, flailing in a curve of my womb* — "bring on my bleeding."

"Ah. Well, the madames cannot be accused of being sentimental about *that*. Or Françoise." She drew her long legs out of the bed-clothes and stretched; a lazy motion, soft and lithe, from the soles of her feet and up through her torso and neck, her whole physical length. Mocking self-possession came off her like the scent of musk and oranges and smoke; every curve of flesh, every inch and ounce of it, belonged to her. She gathered herself like a rich fabric, and the wildness of it — of her, her limitlessness — was frightening, arous-ing: I wanted it — *something* — *what?* The longing was sharp, so fierce and unknown. The rage against my captive status dissolved, and now . . . now I was groping my way back to that last moment, the one in which she had asked me if I would stay, as though it might matter to her.

When she turned quite slowly toward me again, with something like amusement, holding her handful of ash, the feeling shuddered and changed, bitter like the pith, longing-become-loathing and back again. Was she just cheap and coy, a spy of Françoise — ? And I saw, in a blinding flash, a lightning crack of vision in a dark landscape, how impossible it would all be, *worse than ever I could have imagined* — but this was nonsense because I could never have imagined — *this* — could not grasp hold of it, any of it, and how it changed, quick-silvery . . .

"How did you find me here?" I asked.

"A Bette-bird told me."

Bette was a Salon Deux chambermaid of high echelon; I only knew her from glimpses in the halls, as she escorted one important client or another.

"Why?"

"Why not? A broken heart in the Josephine Room is more interesting than another hand of cards with the Mignons. And Banage is
no fun this afternoon, she is like a rainy day."

"Who *are* you?"

"'Mademoiselle Something-or-Other, I think. Like all of us?"
She laughed, stuffed a pillow behind her back, lit another cigarette
lying down—it seemed as though she might always be lying down,
sprawling like a big cat in front of a fire—and studied me with half-
closed eyes. "What will you call yourself? You aren't a Mignon or a
Ninette, or anything-*ette*. Or an English Fanny. You're not fey and
sweet but proud and dark and a little Spanish. I will have to call you
after the woman on the postage stamp. The empress."

"Oh, don't! My name *is* Eugénie, like hers."

"I know it is."

"You'll make the others hate me, even more than they do now."

She just smiled, like a big cat. "Now, come. We have our worlds
to conquer. More than, I'd say." She reached under a pillow and
retrieved a man's pocket watch, gold and with decorative engraving
on the back, and flipped its cover. She sighed; her voice dropped so
low it was nearly a growl. "What, do you expect to eat and sleep for
nothing, around here?"

"I don't know!"

"If you don't, I'm sure someone can find an answer for you."

She stared at me as if about to ask a question, but then thought
better of it. "We can come back if you'd like, sometime . . . Would
you? I have a key to the passageway."

She knew she didn't have to ask. *She had startled me back among
the living.* Even now, color was seeping back into a landscape that
had become sepia-toned, like a *carte de visite.*

"Don't make fun of me, please don't." I turned toward her and
felt my fingers reach, as if by their own will, to touch her hair, a
tangle of scent and softness. A tremor moved through my body,
a spasm. She slipped on a gown and was halfway across the room
when she paused to open an armoire, pull out a robe, coral-colored
like the bed covering, like the orange peel left behind. She tossed it

in my direction and it slithered through my outstretched hands to the floor, like a puddle of oil.

"You can call me Jolie, if you'd like. Come on now, behave yourself." She slipped out the way she'd come in; and then the room was empty, as though the very air had been sucked from between its walls. Her timing was precise; seconds later a knock announced a different maid, shy and polite — maddeningly so, with hair skimmed back in a net and a spotless pink apron around her waist — and asked if mademoiselle required anything, and now, did she wish to be escorted downstairs?

Salon Deux was glittering, a velvet-festooned, sparkling cave. Bronze figurines arched against drapery; gaslight flickered from wall sconces, and tapers gleamed on the chandelier. On occasional tables, in silver bowls, lay stacks of small white cards, embossed in black: DEUX SOEURS. MAISON DE SOCIÉTÉ. 24 RUE DU TEMPLE. On this night, we were all mingled together; the doors between the two salons were open, linked by a corridor previously unknown to me, to make room for a larger party.

My feet in thin slippers slid over the plush, flowery carpet. Nathalie Jouffroy flitted through, cool in parrot green. Madame Trois, usually grayly severe, was tonight gleaming with sparkles like an old battleship lit for a coronation. Françoise was just behind her, an arrow in a dress the color of dried rose petals. She darted about, fixing bouquets, marshaling buckets of ice.

The women, my compatriots — the same hard-edged band who came and went, cursed and gossiped upstairs, ran their fingertips around the rim of the cake plate, and played cards — were silent and still as plaster, a living frieze of embroidered boots, tulle draped across bare shoulders, cascades of silky robes, eyes and lips composed like those in portraits. The madames and Françoise paced the room, making adjustments: a tuck here, the placement of a foot there, the drape of gauze against flesh, sunflower hair next to chocolate skin; a contrast of smiles and pouts. Émilie Trois had grown up in the theater; she knew what got the trousers walking through the door, the *quibuses* into seats. The curtain would rise, tonight, on perfection.

I felt feverish, submerged. I stared into the mirrors but did not find my own face: only a blur of pale skin against a pile of dark hair, a puff of aniline-dyed chiffon standing near the pointed dark leaves of a potted palm, where I had been placed under the acrid glimmer of a lamp.

Soon the drapes billowed and parted: heads ducked in, dark coats and ivory linen began to appear among the bright-colored gowns; mustaches and beards bent down to graze fair and dark heads, to brush rubied cheeks and lips. Champagne corks popped and all around was the fizz of bubbles; someone shoved a glass into my hand, this one filled with water colored with marrow. The din rose and the tempo picked up, and Jolie brushed past, or at least I thought she did, with a dark coat leaning toward her. When the tableau broke up I found my way to a sofa in the dimmest corner; suddenly exhausted. No one seemed to be watching, so I stretched full length upon it, rested my head on its arm, and closed my eyes.

"Mademoiselle! Are you with us?" *Shake, shake* — my arm shuttled to and fro by a dark arm, which was attached to an evening coat. Eventually a smooth-trimmed beard came into focus. "What spiteful fairy has cast her spell here? Why, I'd swear it is she, Pierre Chasseloup's mysterious model. The girl from nowhere, who knows no one—"

A familiar beard.

"Champagne?" he said, to someone I could not see. "Of course, champagne!" Then, "I have been turning over every cobble in Paris looking for you. That poor fool Chasseloup is beside himself."

Gustav Vollard looked around and settled himself next to me on the divan, crossing his legs and tipping back his glass. Leaning in. "So, tell me everything. The last I knew you were staying in a fleabag near the Tivoli Gardens."

∾ · 9 · ∾

SALON NEWS

A T THE CLOSE OF business—that is, dawn—my compatriots, still rouged and dressed in salon wear, tore into brioches, poured coffee, and gossiped. Breakfast was the only meal during which speaking at the table was allowed. The party had been a success: a well-known actor had attended; an acclaimed poet had stood on a tabletop and in the small hours delivered his epic based on the first Napoleon. The Russians had shouted him down and scattered pocketfuls of louis, setting off an orgy of coin tossing that ended only when someone began to set fire to franc notes. At six, a fleet of cabs still waited on the rue du Temple. Françoise was setting about organizing gentlemen's breakfasts; this at the hour usually reserved for digging stray coins from the folds of the sofas in Salon Trois. I had missed most of it. Sometime after seeing Vollard, I noticed Bette off to the side, refilling glasses. Desperate by then, I begged her to allow me upstairs. "It's the ergot," I muttered, figuring she knew everything. "Tell Françoise."

Alone, then, in the attic sleeping quarters while everyone worked the party below, I sat by the stove, poking at the ashes. The rows of cubbyholes for our pallets gaped emptily behind sagging curtains; double-decked like some evil coop, our tiny bolt holes overhanging the large central room. Mingled odors of scorched linen, tobacco,

burned hair, perfume, and soap lingered from the earlier toilette. A
love novel, its spine broken and stripped of its covers, lay open on
the card table where one of the Mignons had been reading it. The
girls liked this one. Passed it hand to hand.

On another slant-legged table, someone's embroidery had been
left behind: twists of red and yellow and blue silk dangled from a
wooden hoop. From the stove doors hung curling irons, and on the
grill, scattered pieces of burned cork. For once darkness reigned behind the bolted venetians, not that it made any difference what time
of day it was. Skitter of mice in the walls.

To Vollard I had poured out a raw and disordered tale. I didn't know
what to emphasize or suppress, and the man's attention kept straying to the phantasmagoria swirling around the room.

"What? Since *when?*" he kept asking — when *exactly* had I wound
up at the Préfecture de Police? Become *inscrit*, as though turned into
an object? "*After* you modeled for Chasseloup? You mean, sitting
for that poor sufferer was all that kept bed, board, and virtue intact
at the Hôtel Tivoli?" He laughed. I could see that he thought I'd
told a mouthful of lies. What were we, anyway, but liars and cheats,
wallet stealers, heart eaters, mendicants, and fakes? From what I'd
gleaned, most of the girls did slip and slide around when they'd hit
the Register; or, "outside," dropped the matter entirely, as convenience suited. My story ended with the requisite sooty tears pouring
down slabs of rouge, a scene that would have made a more gallant
knight than this one glance over his shoulder, and I sobbed in shame
at my own stupidity.

Even so, I came to my senses and begged. He'd paid my way
once, at the Tivoli when Chasseloup required my modeling services — would he help me again, settle up what I supposedly owed
to the *maison* — set me at liberty ? Vollard shifted uncomfortably,
looking for the champagne girl. Muttered something about certainly
not wanting to upset Nathalie — and at any rate, he had other news.

"So, our Chasseloup went away and painted like a lunatic — entirely in character, of course. On the last day he ran all the way
to the Palace of Industry with three paintings on his head. Pushed

through the crowd, with all of the rest of that horde who ply their brushes until the last minute and then rush the doors. But there you have it. He was accepted. And do you know it was not his damned plate of trout that carried the day? *An Unknown Girl* won third place! I gave a party; you would have come if either of us had seen a hair of your head. So wipe your nose and have a drink . . . our friend will have to be revived with salts if he hears about *this*. Quite the prude, for all of his artistic airs. Not a bone of his father in him . . . Or perhaps I shan't tell him at all!" He winked. One of the champagne maids finally circled back; she looked at me twice, and I knew that Françoise would be in this corner next. Vollard took two glasses.

"Don't give me that!" I said, and began to cry all over again. "It shall cost me I don't know what. We girls are drinking colored water."

"If you ask me, he *should* marry a girl who will scrape his palettes and cook his onions. But Papa doesn't want to pay for his paint boxes forever." Gustav drained his glass and stood. "*Salut*, then, my dear. Be brave." His back, dark and slim in coattails, retreated into the sea of color, into the bird wings of tulle and the fizz of drinks.

That I did not explode or disintegrate, after all of the evening's events, was my first astonishment. I had slept through the first breakfast bell and trickle of real daylight that filtered in through a high, tiny window. The attic quarters, usually a din of chatter and shrieks, were quiet; Lucette's place next to me on the pallet empty.

I swung a leg over the side and examined my thighs and calves; then each arm—cautious at first; afraid of what I might find—visible blackenings, blots, signs of decay; I touched gingerly for sensitive places. Some evidence of my body's further dissipation in the Josephine Room. (Though others wallowed in every known voluptuous act, I had absorbed the notion that anything resembling my own desire, respite, or pleasure was likely a punishable transgression.) But my arms and calves and breasts were exactly as they had always been; my belly gently rounded, flesh clear and white and supple as wax. My eyes, if anything, looked clearer in the glass, and for the first time in weeks I did not have to take hold of a slop pail and retch.

The second bell rang, distantly. Resting in the hollow where my pallet mate had been were four oranges, thick-fleshed and bright in a cracked kitchen bowl. A flush traveled from my knees and calves all the way to my fingertips as I touched one's dimpled rind, then split it with a fingernail, inhaled its bright, cool, astringent release . . . Have you ever been in prison, and smelled an orange? I pulled off a section, held it for a moment between my teeth. Then bit into the membrane, releasing its small flood of flowery juice, bright as the Spanish sun.

Before I went downstairs, I stashed the emptied ergot bottle under another pallet, not mine. Its contents had gone into a potted palm that was probably now not long for Salon Deux.

At the breakfast table I did not join the clamor and babble but instead read the newspapers that were tossed amid crumbs and coffee slops; Madame Jouffroy had decided the girls must be more up-to-date on current events, so Françoise had permission to place a selection of current broadsheets to the side of the breakfast room. (I have never looked at one since without remembering reading them on those bleary, ragged-edged mornings.) Devouring the words of those who enjoyed daylight and self-sovereignty; who wrote of daily affairs with careless privilege.

Apparently, it was spring outside.

I read:

The horse show has now departed from Paris's palace-for-showing-and-selling on the Champs-Élysées. Before the horses (who have left an equine odor behind them) were swine, sheep, and poultry; insects behind glass; flowers, cheeses, and *cartes de visite*. Now, to our drafty industrial palace stampede the artists at last. The paintings alone number in thousands, filling the walls to thirty feet. The organizing principle is that of the alphabet, a choice notable for its lack of originality. Yet all of Paris — not to mention tourists in droves — set up their ladders and peer through opera glasses to see. If you lack time and patience for such a display, and really intend only to admire the contours, the various shapes and sizes of Italian beauties, do not this year omit the demurely titled third-place winner, *An Unknown Girl*, by first-time exhibitor Pierre Chasseloup. —*Le Petit Parisien*

The peculiarity of *An Unknown Girl*, and possibly its appeal to view-ers—although the present opinion demurs—lies not in the blunt discursion on our present-day crisis of art. (At the left of the canvas, a trio of *cartes de visite* on a drying line reference the photographer's atelier; to the right of the figure stands the broken urn of Greek classicism.) It is the figure itself that arrests the eye: a woman of contemporary France, without question; her dress modern, though ambiguously so—M. Chasseloup is no avid chronicler of a lady's boudoir, and he has not indulged in an excess of fabric. The sitter appears to us not as the peasant of Courbet, nor the genteel sitter of Fantin-Latour, of whom there is more than a whiff in these brush strokes; in fact, the viewer does not know if she arises from town or province; educated or illiterate, if she is daughter, sister, *grisette*, or Madonna. Yet, as the murmurs and mutters in the crowd sur-rounding this piece attest, one is drawn back again and again to her particularity. The head and shoulders, so bravely confronting us, speak to us not as a portrait, but an evocation of our era: one in which our hearts ache with nostalgia, while all necks crane to-ward the future—possibly thence to be broken . . . One might even say Chasseloup has captured for us an innocence on the spinode of loss. —*Le Charivari*

This writer lies at the feet (though they are distressingly unseen) of *An Unknown Girl*, and makes his quarrel only with the judges, who have awarded this phenomenon of the Salon only a grudging third. First, we must have the identity of this *Unknown;* it is she who has wrung the hearts of this spring's Salon. —*Paris Illustré*

In the famous words of Couture (*Romans in the Decadence of the Empire*, 1847), *"Personality is the scourge of our time."* Chasseloup's model has defeated him; biography has trumped art, and we are in all the more danger for it. —*Félix Duport, "The Mosquito," Figaro*

It is an overtly social work. The dress of *An Unknown Girl*, pearl-colored and shadowed in absinthe, makes bilious reference to a social plague of our day. But does a painting say more when it moralizes at us? Only one thing is certain about M. Chasseloup's *Unknown Girl*, that is, that everyone is, for some reason, talking about it. —*La Gazette*

The final word on this is that it is a moderately good painting, and possibly even deserved its third as a work that both engaged the critics and spoke to the public. But the so-called investigation of the identity of the model is absurd. Once we insist upon hanging creative works on literal ropes, we are hangmen of Art. After all, why do paintings matter so to us? Not because their flesh-and-blood analogues may be stepping aboard an omnibus, or buying a loaf. —*Félix Duport, "The Mosquito," Figaro*

Jolie dragged a hand over her eyes. She was slouched on a chair in the Josephine Room, skirt hiked past her knees, looking as though she'd been pulled from bed and would rather still be there. I'd gone to some lengths to get her here — passing a note through Bette, because I hardly ever saw her upstairs, and never alone. Now I wasn't at all sure it had been a good idea.

"Look at these," I said, my voice shaking, holding out the clutch of papers I had taken, *Figaro, Gazette, Paris Illustré* — stuffed them under my pallet. "This painting they are writing about —"

Jolie stared at the clippings, first one and then the next, then said at last that I should just tell her what they said so it didn't take her all day to figure it out. Jolie had no idea what the Salon was and could care less. When I finished my explanation she said, "I don't know what those *michés* get up to on the Champs-Élysées. Art modeling's worse than the stage. After the show there's nothing in it. And these artists come around here all the time, adoring themselves. Think that a paint box gives them license for anything; they always want to draw you and not pay a sou. So, is he rich and old, this one?"

"No, poor and young."

"Ah. So you're just like those *stupides* upstairs, waiting for your boyfriend to come love you back?"

"No . . ."

"What, then? . . . You want out, and my help with it, I guess. You might think again, being such a favorite around here." Her voice was cold, or tired. Her face unreadable; tangles of hair, like fine-spun, wavy gold, shielded her eyes, the curve of her mouth; her eyes were shadowed.

"Hardly!"

"You have no idea, do you? You wonder why the others don't like you, but you've no idea what they've been through, most of them. While Françoise is giving you bottles and sending you up here for a rest cure, letting you slip the *passe*. Oh, I've heard. If you're not careful, you'll be traded at Brussels . . . And you don't want that, let me tell you, because this place is a palace compared to anywhere else." Jolie stared at the draperied window. Her voice trailed off and she pulled off her shawl, cheap silk in acid yellow. Underneath she had on a too-small camisole with thin black straps, tight across her shoulders and breasts, and a dark underskirt, ruched in tiers like a petticoat, faded and marked with cigarette burns. Even though the Josephine Room's hearth was unlit, the warmth of the whole house was extravagant enough for bare shoulders.

"So, why are they letting me off?"

"Françoise wants *mesdames* to think she can drag in the talent. Why do you think she trawls the Mont de Piété on her days off, watches the line, sees who hasn't picked up her pocket watch? She goes to the maternity hospital with dresses and hats too. Françoise just loves to hook them at La Maternité. First to the *tour* to hand off the brat to the Sisters of Charity. You are her acquisition, *chouette,* so she's in the mood to spoil you." Jolie got up and rummaged by the bedside for cigarettes, found one, and struck a match.

I considered this. "I thought they turned away dozens of girls every week."

"Not the ones they want, I suppose."

"I watered a plant with the ergot."

"Fine, then you can suffer the same fate." Jolie glowered. "Anyway, do you think you can get away with that? The Dab will catch you out."

"Already has. Now she says I must go to the midwife."

"You could say she's trying to spare you, Eugénie." A veil of hair fell over Jolie's eyes as she dragged on her smoke.

It was startling, to hear her speak my name; I would not have made a bet that she'd remember it. I took a breath. "That other girl never came back. Delphine?"

"They sent her to the angel maker, sure. But that's not the whole story. Nathalie was done with her around here." Jolie smoked until she burned her fingertips and tossed the butt into the cold hearth, shook out her hair, and ran her hands through it. "Look — I'm trying to help you. It's no good outside right now. Unless you think the painter will take care of you."

"I have my doubts."

"Well, then, what? Look, you're on the books now. You understand that, right?"

She stopped and stared at me, took stock of my actual state of ignorance — humiliating, provincial — all the same, I *didn't* know. She took a breath, gave a short laugh. "Listen. You are what they — the Register, the Morals Brigade, the Dabs, the madames — say you are. You aren't anyone else, in the city of Paris — well, even in all of France, I think, though I've never been anywhere else."

"There's nothing like this place where I came from, I can tell you that."

"Well, girls get traded away to Marseille and Toulon all the time. Lyon. Other places. You're on the books, registered, *inscrit* unless you can figure a way off, which is a good trick if you can do it." She paused briefly; elaborated. "First of all, if you bolt and leave a debt behind, they will put the Brigade boys on you straight away. You're playing into their hands, really, by doing that. It's how they break a girl down, a stint at Saint-Lazare, and if you get out alive, you come back with a warning — or Brussels."

I looked at her. Who was this Jolie creature? Trickster, prankster, comrade, spy? — So beautiful, with her tangled flame of hair and heavy-lidded eyes, in her strange costume. No wonder she had special privileges; they must all be half in love with her.

"But even if you work off what they say you owe, or get someone to pay it off, it's different 'outside.' The rules change." She ticked them off on her fingers.

"Carry a *carte* and produce it upon request. Health check and re-registration at the Préfecture every fifteen days. Walk only on certain streets, at certain hours. Stay away from windows, churches, and schools. No living in furnished rooms; you have to buy your own furniture, which puts you in hock and the chair and table men are all *souteneurs* — at least, I never met one who wasn't. If you go around the corner, say good morning to the baker, it might be 'procuring off location' — two charges against you. You are in and out of the lockup, and no leaving Paris unless a madame somewhere else sponsors you, so don't think of that. No women friends if they are also *inscrits*. But who else would be your friend? Other than your *souteneur,* and you can bet he'll be in the picture, robbing you blind in the name of 'protection.' Sitting here and talking, like we are doing, is breaking the law, if we're raided and caught — " She took a breath and turned aside. "Damn, I need another cigarette, and I'd better not steal anymore. Even Bette counts them." Jolie pushed her hands over her face; her nails were bitten. All the girls smoked as though a cigarette were a lifeline off a sinking ship.

In the end that was why girls preferred the houses, she said: for the company. "And everyone wants to come to a place like this. Look — " She flung her bare arm in a gesture that took in the whole room. "Satin on the bed. Four meals a day. Off hours, we sit around playing cards, and they handle the Dab and the police." She got up abruptly, hunted around the room, found half of someone's butt tossed into the hearth, crushed. She smoothed and lit it. Sucked in her smoke and exhaled; gray air drifting toward the dark cordoned drapes. Then she came closer, nestled near my feet; reached up and wrapped her arms around my knees — part caress, part the casual use of a convenient support. Warily, as though it might burn, I let my hand fall so it touched her hair, that tousled skein of soft-flaming thread. She smelled of cigarettes and bed linens.

"We should both get out of here," I murmured into her hair. Leaned into her; skin light as feathers. "Will you come?" She moved abruptly; pulled away.

"Where, to a cozy little somewhere? Haven't you been listening to a word I've said?"

"Feel," I said, and laid her palm, again, on my barely rounded belly. "I swear I just felt something."

"You're imagining it . . . can't feel anything." But she left her hand there, warm.

"I need to leave *soon*," I whispered. "Because I'm not going to lose the baby for — for *Françoise*. For — a place like this."

"Ssh . . ." We were quiet a moment, and Jolie shook out her great long limbs, went to the bed, and lounged across it like she lived there, beckoning me to join her. "We can . . . be together here. Here, it's easy. Not outside, you know. You know, don't you? Once after a raid, another girl and me — they locked us up, separated us, she didn't make it out. I can't forgive myself for that. And Nathalie, you know — she understands."

But there was a question in her voice; and lodged behind it somewhere, some kind of strangled hope. I slipped in beside her, and we touched each other lightly, with exquisite slowness, then lay tangled in the bedclothes until all the clocks in the house had stopped. Smoothing away her rough spots and jagged edges, the way my own had been when I had first felt myself cared for. She'd gotten under my skin, Jolie.

"*Merde*, what time is it, anyway? Past supper. Another one of Madame B's macaroni pies that could be used to fill the holes in the rue du Temple — "

"You still haven't answered. Will you come? I've got no one outside. Nothing."

Jolie sighed and kicked back the sheet. "I'm tired, you know?

. . . I've been out, I've been in. Been just about everywhere. Nearly got nabbed again, last time. I don't like the police, *chouette*. They're expensive."

"Where I come from they say, 'You think your eggs are on the fire, when only the shells are left.'"

"Meaning?"

"You think you've got something going on, but really they've robbed you behind your back. It's no good here, Jolie. Not really."

"We have to hurry or Françoise will take out her pocket watch. Or at least I do, those of us who care about making the month," she said. Bonus tokens, allotted monthly, were currency inside Deux Soeurs — if you amassed a few hundred, you were entitled to a silk chemise, a hair bauble, or some other treat. A protest rose and died in my throat; Jolie's head had disappeared under the bed. "Where is my slipper — ah, *merde!* Look what I just found under here." She started to laugh and, when I looked over, dangled a man's opera shoe, large, of yellowish snakeskin. "Now, how did this *miché* get out of here — hopping on one foot?"

"If that's the only way . . ."

"All right, all right, *chouette*. If you have to."

"You won't — help Françoise turn me in to the police?" I took a breath. "I mean — for all I know she sent you to me, before."

Jolie pushed back her hair and turned her head in surprise. "No," she said slowly, her voice a languid growl. "No, she didn't."

The way she said it might have kept me there forever.

Madame B, as it happened, harbored certain sympathies. The old cook understood how a girl might need a cold slap of night air, a taste of Paris rain on her face. She could turn her back without seeming to, when she was scrubbing the pots after midnight. And for a few sous the deaf-and-mute boy might hover hearthside, leave a key to the gate after he took out the slops and the trash. He might stash a sack of street clothes in the narrow alleyway where the king's *valets de chambre* once rubbed shoulders with the royal procurers . . . and shoes. Otherwise you wouldn't make it down the block — not after having walked on carpets for a month in slippers, those flimsy things frizzed with feathers or pocked with rhinestone.

Françoise would eventually take her night off. When? It was a fact that could be learned.

"And then — what about you?" I'd asked Jolie, my only friend. But once the plan was set, she drifted away. Curled up against Olga for cake and cigarettes, flirted with either of the Mignons or both; teased Bette and made her bring in sweets and almonds. She was forever in the center of some smirking knot of girls, with a bottle, sticky fingers, a cache of tobacco. My heart ached, and I tried to ignore it.

Then, on a night that was not so long in coming, just when the bell rang and everyone trooped downstairs, Jolie brushed by me and whispered, swift as a swallow skimming the glassy surface of a pond. The submistress was out; Madame Jouffroy was taking the waters; Madame Trois up to her ears because the Dab had called for the removal of some of our number, and she was several girls short just on the night that the police were in as guests. One of the girls called for removal was Lucette, my pallet mate. Her makeup job, the fake kohl beauty mark by her lip, had been discovered, and she was bundled away without even a chance to say goodbye . . . Everyone was in a tumult. Olga was whisked into Salon Deux and the Mignons were furious. There was a new Danish girl who couldn't speak a word — younger than me, and even more terrified as she was made up, her hair yanked by the roots and held high in the hairdresser's hand.

"The police, here?" I muttered to Jolie. Nausea clenched my belly: a dizzy, rootless dread. But that was exactly the point: fewer of them on the streets.

"The place is teeming. Even the chief is downstairs, relaxing in the countinghouse." The man in the portrait, down at the Préfecture. I'd seen him from time to time, being whisked through the halls by Madame Jouffroy. "Best to do it right under their noses," Jolie said. "The way they least expect."

. . . Flare of match light; moth flutter against my hand, a key turned in one lock, then the next; through the gate on its rusty hinges that wheezed a hideous, heart-slamming *au revoir*. I slipped back a screw of paper with a few coins into the boy's waiting shadow of fingers. He knew the movement exactly.

The fresh, cold air caused me to gasp. Immediately I began to shiver in my thin garments; damp crawling up from slippers to knees. For a moment, forgetting the existence of weather, I turned my face up to the black sky. A light rain was falling. A match was needed to grope behind the odorous rubbish pile — it sputtered, fizzled . . . finally, after an eternity, my fingers latched on to the hemp texture of a sack. I seized it and fled: down the rue Simon Le Franc, around the corner, where my useless footwear was dumped in favor of street shoes; past the corner of Pierre au Lard, the raucous laughter of a café following my steps; into the shadows of Saint-Merri. There, under the pitted and blackened eaves, with the scent of the *pissoir* at my back (even then the church wall was a watering ground for the unfaithful), I pressed my back against the wall and shed my tissue-weight clothes, using the damp chiffon to blot at my face and scrub off the rouge. Tore the terrible bangles off my wrists and struggled into more solid fabric: a dress dreadfully creased, smelling of a stranger's sweat, but a luxury of heavy woven stuff, substantial against the skin — and the fit was good; Jolie had chosen well and I thanked her for that. A cloak, sturdy against the rain; a shawl for good measure. (To whom had these things belonged — the Danish girl? Someone else? And under what circumstances had she given them up?) As promised, Jolie had knotted a few extra coins into a handkerchief.

But I had lingered too long. I took a quieter pace to calm my racing heart, slipped through an alleyway and down a set of blackened stairs on the tiny rue de Bon, past a knot of workers clinking bottles, across another street, under gaping window holes where linen flapped, ghostlike — and finally, beckoned by the magnificent lights of a cab stand on the rue de Rivoli, I flung open a door that I could not afford and, barely able to gasp, gave the driver the address of the only place in Paris I knew.

Chairs were legs-up on the tables, and Claude was wiping down the zinc. A single dark-coated figure sat hunched over the bar, a nearly empty carafe in front of him. Another late-nighter keeping Claude from his supper and bed. The drinker sat up straight when he felt the draft as I parted the drapes and stepped inside; unfolded himself like a knife. "*Salut,*" said Chasseloup. "Where the hell have you been keeping yourself?" He inclined his glass in my direction. "I am celebrating tonight. *An Unknown Girl* has been sold."

~ 10 ~

L'Absinthe

THE RAGGED-EDGED PARIS map was tacked onto the wall above Chasseloup's divan, exactly where it had always been: The rounded, fawn-color form of Paris was shaped like a breast; Notre Dame a brown marker at its center and the Seine a blue vein coursing through. It was crisscrossed with black lines, inked with curling italic labels, illustrated with tiny monuments, hospitals, gardens. A dark-notched perimeter surrounded the city, where fortresses orbited like guardian planets. FORT D'ISSY, BICÊTRE, FORT DE NOISY, ROMAINVILLE, MT. VALÉRIAN — names that would in the not-distant future become imbued with a universe of meanings but were then merely words, strangers one had not met. Fortifications, city walls, buildings of stone and brick and mortar and glass; skirts, crinolines, and at last — the corset, the tightest of all, formed concentric circles of girdling. Not for the first time I reflected on the term for Paris's perimeter, the *enceinte* — and its world of double meanings.

This window, at least, let in light: even at this hour of the morning, cast its delicate beam on the map, on the tumbled bed linen and Chasseloup's white thigh, with its delicate dark hairs, like tentative sketch marks on a tablet. He was stretched full length, his breath long and even. *Morning light: who would have thought it such a miracle?*

My old lover had been pleased to see me: a blurred supplication of lips and fingers. What was it about those cow eyes, that loping stance, and those bony knees that made me forgive the man? He'd given up absinthe because he had read Henri Balesta's tales of ruined *absintheurs*, he said; and taken the man's words to heart. "'Nothing vibrates anymore . . . everything is dead. Only remorse, that last record of his sinking, survives——'" Pierre had felt remorse himself, he said. For half-ruining himself with the green bottle.

Even before we'd climbed the stairs, my flesh had become another kind of wall, cold as clay or whatever lies on the Seine's riverbed. Chilled from my long dash across the city, a headlong flight to the corner where memory lay, I was cold but even more aware of the sensation on my skin. It was not just the heavy dress that lay like a hard shell of varnish. The emotional senses that had once met those of my body had vanished, as though blood, nerve, and flesh were severed from feeling. For a moment, when Chasseloup's hand caressed mine, I felt an abstraction of tears, a mood or remnant of a feeling, but when he reached for me with all the familiarity of a lover, my consciousness veered away; wandered to the Paris map and its ring of fortresses; to the wrought iron pattern of the balcony shadowed against the wall.

A regulated body divides itself from memory and desire.

Chasseloup did not seem to notice a difference, and I convicted him on a dozen counts for that.

Afterward I lay awake, bubbling with distress. My body was telling me that it was not time to sleep but to wash out (although I had no bowl or syringe) and it was unpleasant not to do so. My stomach pinged with hunger and sent up a complaint for midnight supper. But here was Chasseloup, immovable as a tree fallen across the path.

At first daylight, he was fresh and eager again, like an infant to the suck, and I drowsed insensible, a dry-teated nurse chafing in surprise. When finally he swung his legs to the floor, I turned over and dropped off . . . woke, much later, to sun harsh and dazzling;

illuminating the dust in all the corners of the room. From the open window, traffic sounds and midmorning merchants' cries.

I was alone. A marvelous rush of air, fresh and cool, billowed in, bringing the lavender scent from the bunches always carefully tied with twine by the old street vendor. Children's shouts. And then I knew just from the sound and the scent of the air, even the soot-laden Paris air of the Impasse de la Bouteille: it was May. And here was an edge of something, what lies between one world and the next; the place where the hem turns under, where the outside becomes the inside, and the reverse . . . a place on the verge of a change; and a quiet ecstasy tingled through me like the first greening of gray winter stalks.

I looked around; took inventory. It was an indigo-colored dress I had worn, of heavy linen gathered at the wrists and flat across the bodice; a thin shawl printed with a paisley design. Compared to my earlier borrowings (a lifetime ago), these items reflected a lower rung on the social ladder; a working girl might have worn them on a Sunday. I wondered again at its original owner and in what circumstances she now found herself—not unaware that in some measure, I owed my freedom to what she had left behind. The full, heavy skirt went over my head with an odor of sweat and vinegar . . . No underthings, and I hadn't even missed them. A gray cloak.

Within Chasseloup's cupboard lay signs of domestic improvement: bread and *confiture*. Butter. Mustard. The new, fashionable kind of coffeemaker; tins labeled FÉLIX POTIN: cocoa, honey, coffee, peas. Bottles from a water man—so Chasseloup no longer drank from the pump. Starved, I tore off the end of the loaf and smeared it with butter and fruit; shoveled old newspapers off the table . . . then seized one back.

The model for *An Unknown Girl* may once have been a denizen of the Mabille pleasure gardens, a suggestion stiffly denied by the artist and his representative. The painting's buyer, that estimable owner of the concern Maillard et Cie, professes no interest in the identity of the sitter, but so apparently besotted is he that he has initiated a bidding contest for her hand — the one made of canvas and color, at least. *An Unknown Girl* will sell for a fortune.

A shaft of sunlight pooled over the newsprint, my stained and wrinkled skirt, and a puddle of soiled linens on the divan. From the street rose a babble of children's voices. A small tide of orphans, perhaps a hundred in all, dressed in red smocks and caps — stood at the mouth of the Impasse. A black-winged cadre of nuns gathered them, moved onward, and the piping clamor faded and passed. Irritation swelled in me like a boil under the skin, a festering site of infection that inflamed and subsided, trapped and unable to surface . . . *a fortune?*

Chasseloup's boots clomped down the stair from the studio sometime after that. Paused before the door, then passed. Echoed down, down. Down to the courtyard, the street.

Of course, the man had money now — he could go out and dine.

"For God's sake. A man has to eat." Chasseloup sluiced water into the basin, more energetic than I remembered him to be, and washed his hands. He must be using watercolor. I folded my arms and stared at him, biting my tongue. Oh, a man does, but a woman? *She* eats her own hand, saves the other one for tomorrow!

"Your beard is dripping on the floorboards."

Chasseloup shook his head; droplets scattered. "And I have no damned towel." He bent to search in the mound of mildewed laundry. Finally he said, "You want to stay here, do you?"

"No."

"You have another place?"

"Not just now."

"Let me guess. You are hard up." Glancing at my dress.

"I was in a pinch and had to take every stitch to the Mont."

"The money from the painting comes in installments. Vollard took his cut from the first and booked a trip to Africa. I owe my father for loans — and everyone else, from the landlord to the water man. At least I'm not drinking cholera. Now, of course, Vollard says there must be a follow-up. Everyone does, except for Duport and I don't give a damn about him . . . Did you read the *Gazette?* He nearly had the best of me. But as they say, 'The artist who does not paint the woman of his era will not endure.' Do you want to sit for me again, Mademoiselle Rigault?" Chasseloup eyed my mess of a dress.

"You'll need to pay me, this time around."

The painter stretched his long arm, circled it round my waist, and drew me toward him, then somewhat away. "Phew, can you take these rags to the laundress?"

"*Your* linens are nothing to brag about, Chasseloup. I'll take them along." His glance softened and that phantom of emotion crept through the room like a fog. Chasseloup leaned his cheek against the top of my head, briefly. I tipped my chin up to him, felt the brush of his beard, which smelt faintly of linseed. Then shook myself free. On the stove, the zinc pail was steaming with the last of what the water seller had brought, bubbles rising from its silvery bottom. That old pail.

"Stay here if you'd like. Really."

Paris was in a forgiving mood: lilacs and chestnuts had burst into bloom, children played with hoops in the streets, shopkeepers opened their windows and doors to the breezes, and café tables came out on the boulevards. Chasseloup's atelier clattered with messengers bearing invitations; students come to look over his "technique," dealers to sell paints and canvas. Artists previously unknown to these quarters regularly stomped up and down the stairs; and visitors, well-wishers, and the curious climbed them, not to sit in front of a tripod in rented clothes, but to pay their regards to the new medalist. The entire studio, in fact, was all easels and props, sketches, studies, and armchairs facing the buttes; Chasseloup's own with a smoking jacket draped over the back. The clothing racks had been relegated to a corner, I noticed, on the day Pierre invited me up for a trial.

A velvet-covered box stood at the center of the room, upon a chair of tufted pink satin. I pulled the tacks out of the long wooden dress box; unwrapped a garment from its rustling bed of tissue. The dress was beautiful: deep green shot silk, like leaves seen through shafts of golden sunlight, with tiny embroidered buttons up the back to the neck. In a second box lay, collapsed, a crinoline, a drifting hollow cage. I fastened it at my waist, felt the curious air around my knees. The dress, Chasseloup explained, was a wedding gown based on an eighteenth-century design; and green was the most ambitious color in the painter's palette. And so the "unknown girl" must be dressed in it, dressed in green. An artistic challenge.

The fabric was stiff and carried the scent that only new fabric has, fresh from the bolt. Its gored panels were cut to flow smoothly over the crinoline; flatter the waist and pouffe out behind. My fingers fumbled at the button loops. I tried with damp palms to smooth the skirt, but where it was cut to flatten in front, reinforced by whale-bone, it bunched outward. This was only emphasized by the over-skirt, a piece of drapery made to part like a theater curtain over my middle.

"I will use an old technique, an underpainting—and layer the green over it. The painting will be about language, the voice of de-sire, emerging from centuries. Vollard thinks we should call it *An Unknown Girl at Nineteen*. Nineteen is a symbolic number."

"If she's *unknown*, how can you say she is nineteen? And her desire is probably to pay the grocer and her rent," I said, fuming, struggling with the buttons. "May we do without the overskirt?"

"The woman of the nineteenth century is beginning to voice that for which she yearns. The painting is about that initial moment, her departure from the mute and into what she longs to express—"

"Is that the latest topic at Vachette these days?" Pierre some-times brought me what was left from his dinners there with his new-minted set of fashionable friends. "From what I can tell, the 'woman of our era' is like the pot you boil water in. Useful until unneces-sary." I was snappish and tired, despite the weather.

"There's no reason for you to speak that way." Chasseloup had a peculiar look on his face. He was silent, and continued arranging his supplies. But a demon (or two) persisted in my guts, wanting to bring the whole matter to a boil.

"You've never asked once who she is, where she came from — your 'unknown girl.'"

Chasseloup was silent, then finally said, "What? You're angry. Because I had to go to Croisset to finish — or for having some success at last, some hope of a career?"

"You never gave a thought to what would happen when you left, that I'd be thrown out on the street — "

"I had arranged for you to stay!"

"It wasn't a legal tenancy, any fool knows that. And with the rent in arrears — "

"For goodness' sake, we had just met — I didn't know where you'd come from, where you might be going."

"And you didn't care enough to ask."

"And *you've* been in a fury ever since you've been back, avoiding me every night. Eugénie, I am grateful you've agreed to sit, and of course we are creating a kind of . . . story, but I've tried to help, really."

"Whatever happened to your other ideas? Badinguet's social accidents, *the rings of the wealthy pull down their carriage shades,* all of that?"

"A man can't eat political commentary, not these days."

"Can't dine out on it, you mean."

"Eugénie. It *is* a good painting . . . How is the dress fitting?"

I gave a last, weary tug at the fabric, but the tiny buttons would not meet their loops. I said, finally, "It's not going to . . . fit."

Chasseloup stepped behind the screen and kneeled down. "How have you put on weight, living on milk and *soupe?*"

"Oh, Chasseloup . . . I'm not nineteen. And I'm — " I took his hand, gently, and placed it on the green silk of my belly.

PERNOD, DUVAL, CUSENIER, JOANNE, read the silver stamping on the bottles, a shop window full of them. Liquid emerald to take you beyond the horizon. Slough of green silk, opalescent, viscous . . . *Remorse.* I can tell Monsieur Balesta — that remorse does vibrate; and with such terrible motion that you are sick on it, like being dropped from a height into churning, merciless waters. It's not only absinthe that is the cause, and no storyteller's description would help us tonight.

"I'm sorry, I'm so sorry," he said.

That painting, the first one, had been made from some truth passed between us across the studio — *my present cure* — that current, Chasseloup's sightline, my pulling taut; or like the bright streak of a meteor in the late summer sky, one we had seen at the same moment, calling out to each other. I hesitated, I did. The words were formed and on my lips.

It's not yours, Chasseloup. You've nothing to do with this.

I looked at him over the carafe, the two filigree spoons set over tall glasses. He was fiddling with the sugar. "Where is the painting, actually?"

"Crated up at the Palace of Industry. Waiting for its owner." Chasseloup poured; the liquid in the glasses turned milky, opaque.

"I'd like to see it. After all."

"Yes, well, without you — I don't know. My plate of trout would have had to win. As it was, the poor fish never got a second glance!" He laughed.

I laughed, stopped.

It's not yours.

"Oh, come. Even Vollard said — "

"Vollard? He thought *An Unknown Girl* was unfinished; I had to fight him to submit it. And he wasn't wrong; I was up on a ladder painting in the background on hanging day. But, one way or the other. Maybe only because Chasseloup is near the beginning of the alphabet, before the judges were tired. *Salut.*"

"So." My hand trembled on the glass.

"And thank *God* it has happened this year; I couldn't have held out."

I hesitated. My hands slid down, down to my belly, still wrapped in the fabric of the green dress. Chasseloup brushed my cheek with the back of his palm.

Whose life was worth saving, an artist's, a woman's, a child's? . . .

The green burned the back of my throat as it went down, trickling through my hollow, tenanted body. The first swallow tasted like poison, and my whole being reached for the second. Chasseloup stretched and yawned.

"Now I'm starved . . . Shall we go out? Find something that fits from the racks. Vollard's idea is that the unknown girl remains a secret until the next one's done." His voice sounded far away, a purring sound, *shh-shh*, a cat's tongue rasping against its belly. The absinthe green snake coiled around and around us; it felt like my belly glowed in the candlelight, the warmth of the stove. He pulled a pin out of my hair, which stayed in place. Silence filled the room like a sad, opalescent cloud.

Even then I wasn't certain. I wasn't a good liar.

"We both have snakes," I said, "sitting on our heads."

"I was just thinking of a snake, how did you know?"

He leaned down to my lips, our glasses tipped, and my hair came all the way down. We set aside our glasses and I reached for the soft brush of his hair. Hunger of my hunger, Chasseloup — present, firm-fleshed, warm — not a memory, not a dream; not a lump of clay, not broken-hearted, or broken. He was real — flesh, blood, and bone real; and I had been uprooted, plucked like a weed, fuzzy, jagged-edged, unwanted — to plant myself, try, again, to send pale shoots down into the cold clay of the earth . . . and he was dark-jawed, looking down on me from his towering height. What does the gardener feel for his weed?

"We die from lying long . . . With flowers, and with women." He was trembling all over, wormwood soft, swallowing the bitter with the sweet. "I'm sorry, you know . . . Let me take care of you. I can, I will."

. . . Did he say it? Such slight words, to kindle a thing. Ah, but it was such an old dream, returned to like a nest even after the forest has burned, the scarred road cleared for another passage. Even my compatriots at the *maison* had kept it locked in their hearts: a dream of care and order, gardens tended; fruits heavy on the vine. As impossible to abandon as to think of the earth leaving behind its sun, around whom it has revolved for lifetimes.

I reached for Chasseloup like a rope across an abyss. *Tie the knot, secure the cord. Quick — quick, before the wolves come.* We lay tousled together, in front of the stove, where the flame began to lick greenishly, and Chasseloup's hands stayed tangled in my hair.

Very late, we floated downstairs and took a flyaway to the Closerie des Lilas, to dine under a vaulted ceiling, panes of rainbow-colored glass reflecting a thousand lights. Tobacco smoke and wild violins; an expanse of white cloth, scattered candlelight flickering off wineglasses and flower petals. Melt of Brie on a grape leaf; Chasseloup's cow eyes and close-trimmed beard. Champagne bubbles in my nose; tongue tasting the sour of pickled vegetables. Around us shimmered dark suits and bare shoulders, jewels dangling from ears and wrists; a woman's voice speaking, the soft gust of her perfume. Men who were poets and men who were painters.

Later, in the small hours, on the divan under the map, in the spooning half-circle of warmth, in a wakeful, wormwood-dreaming state, I felt the infant already in my arms, her head, or his, lying against my breast. My belly was flat, and whole; and the whole awkward, girdled orb of Paris — in fact, the entire globe of earth — was again well.

11

RUE SERPENTE

ORMWOOD IS AN ANCIENT plant, known through the centuries for its bitterness as the bringer of calamity and life's extreme sorrow. But its history turns back on itself, contradicts. Wormwood's essence was also said to void the guts of worms, cure melancholia, free virgins from the scab; heal the right eye of a man and a woman's left; comfort spleen and liver; repel moths from linen chests. It prevented drunkenness by producing euphoria without inebriation . . . even cured the pox. In Roman times, winners of chariot races were required to drink it as a reminder that even within victory lies sorrow. Because of its bitterness, wet nurses wiped their nipples with its tincture to wean infants; and so it perhaps represents the first bitterness of time's passage. According to legend, it was wormwood that grew up in the path of the serpent as the prophetic creature departed from Paradise: and that was the faint sound of Paris's late spring: a rustle through the leaves; barely an exhale through dense foliage, then a slow and poisonous unfurling.

The following morning Chasseloup (an adept with his new spirit lamp and balancing siphon) made coffee and brought it to the divan.

I should rest, he said—but he wouldn't mind a chop and a salad of spring greens, later on?

His boots echoed on the stairs and I lay for some time under the breast of Paris, sipping at hot, dark liquid; gazing at the iridescent dress coiled like summer leaves in its coffin box. Eventually I got up to rattle the money tin; and found its contents replenished for once. As a result, the coal man filled the bin with black lumps, and the dewiest and most delicate lettuces at the vegetable stall went into my basket, along with red-and-white radishes, long, bright spring onions, and waxy potatoes the size of a baby's fist. Two good beef chops, fat-streaked and on display in the butcher's window, were tucked in as well, and the man in the blood-soaked apron instructed me on how to grill them. A small crock of goose fat was procured for the potatoes. And the wine-shop keeper stood on a ladder and reached for a bottle.

By evening, the table was set and a small, careful fire bubbling. Lettuces had been torn; the grilling pan (first scrubbed of rust) was oiled and heated; wine poured. My hands shook as I waited for the sound of boots on the stairs. Chasseloup finally came down; and without stopping to wash his color-smeared hands, cupped his palms around my waist.

. . . Paint fingerprints all over the newly laundered and fresh-scented indigo dress, which only made us laugh. It was midnight when we tore the end off the white loaf. But the chop was perfect. Tender and rare.

So, now the floor was swept; the sheets and linens clean. We had cabbage and carrots, beef bones and onions; bottles of red and occasionally a three-franc chicken in the larder. Our little ménage was a household, not just a box in which to keep ourselves. Hours regularized, which probably surprised a few at the Trap and Vachette.

I had not intended to name him as the father; it was against the Code, the law of the land; *recherche de la paternité* it was called, I knew that much. And I had not named him; we had slipped and slid into it; he had thought it himself, had as much as *offered*—and I—with accusations on my lips—had accepted. Pierre Chasseloup had a decent heart in this careless city, and he had turned me up-side down. All of this had the unpleasant consequence of making me more aware of my shame, and defiant about it.

Outside, people now seemed different. I was aware of distinctions: which girls were likely *inscrits;* who were the possible clandestines, *non-inscrit* or *insoumise* — girls not on the Register but "working" nonetheless, on the boulevards and in the arcades, sucking the clientele from the *filles en carte.* Such competitors were the subject of much conversation at Deux Soeurs; indeed, they drove many registered girls into the houses, where they could be assured a clientele. Thus the spying-and-telling was carried on — the denunciations and tips, true or false, that landed many a young woman at the Préfecture. There, if she could not give a credible report on her morals, the name of a "protector," or a solid job and family connection, she went on the Register and joined the ranks of the *inscrits.* With my new double vision, some movements on the boulevards and in the markets, previously opaque, became clear.

And it was impossible, now, to abide in the capital without sharp reminders of the way things could go, and perhaps bring my house of cards tumbling down. One afternoon at the *poissonnière,* a flurry of movement caught my eye; an abrupt, almost silent scuffle. A clerk cried out; a couple of matrons dropped their loaves. Two gendarmes in flaring gray overcoats stepped smartly through the crowd. Then suddenly a display table was overturned — a brief chaos ensued and then they had a girl by the arms. These were twisted behind her back and I was close enough to wince at the wrench, at the pale of her cheek; to see the flounce of her skirts.

"Carte!" demanded one of the officers. He was answered by a final, faint sob of protest, and the girl was borne off, a limp knot fluttering between two gray coats. My legs went weak and watery, as though her protest had passed to me like a baton, on a wave of humiliation and fury — hers, my own, or both.

Carte de brème, carte de brème! the girls at Deux Soeurs called the *carte* our street-level counterparts were required to carry, naming it after the flat white fish. "It's only after a few days that it begins to stink!" However, obtaining one (which is what the law required me to do) involved re-registering at the Préfecture. Since doing so would result in my immediate arrest as a debtor-runaway, the very thought made me sick with dread.

The fishmonger shifted his gaze; for a moment his eyes bored into mine. Then he looked away, back to the matrons shaking themselves like elegant dogs. The citizens of the capital carried on with their loaves and fishes and pastry boxes wrapped with string. Only the tourists gawked.

In practice, on the street, the Brigade des Moeurs didn't check information in the Register before apprehending a girl; rather, they judged her by her dress and behavior, and then stepped in if they pleased. She might be a registered girl who had committed some infraction, or a *non-inscrit*—a "clandestine" who really did have something to hide. Or she might be merely an innocent going about her business, who somehow aroused suspicion. It made us all vulnerable and helped explain why nearly all women disappeared at dusk; why they wore this or that—playing, as adeptly as they could, this guessing game. I took to avoiding everything I imagined an *inscrit* might tend to do, the places where she might go, and how she might attract the eye of the Brigade—easier said than done, because *inscrits* were forbidden to behave or dress in any way that could be described as tempting, a quite inclusive category. As a result, every unescorted female under thirty was behaving in approximately the same way—suspiciously, in the eyes of the police. She was presumed guilty unless married, rich . . . or a real *cocotte* decked out in finery and driving her carriage through the Bois. I did not yet understand this contradiction, how that other tier of women operated—as open and brazen as tulips in June, plying a trade in kings, princes, and the empire's wealthiest men.

Some of Chasseloup's grocery money went to a cheap gold-colored band to slip onto my finger whenever I left the Impasse—it went, I told myself, with my condition, and provided camouflage. I was rather proud of this innovation; marriage was a sacrament of the church, and most girls would not dare go so far. I shopped always in crowds, avoided the arcades and boulevards; took care to steer clear of single men, or girls who might view me as "competition." I walked without stopping or appearing to look up, while making a covert study of gray coats: where they traveled, at what times; where they ate and attended the *pissoir*. Whom they noticed or stopped; what they did, when they did it. It was a lonely business, shot with bouts of alarm.

As for what I was wearing, the indigo gown had stood me in good stead. It was proper looking, not too worn, and nondescript. I had let out its side seams a little, gusseted them with fabric from the hem. And soon it would be too small.

Chasseloup and I seemed to have crept around to some kind of understanding, but matters were hardly settled. His only interest in dresses concerned the one he wanted to paint — so I resorted to the only solution I could come up with — the secondhand market back on the rue du Temple. Near the Mont de Piété and only a stone's throw from Deux Soeurs, and for all I knew, another of Françoise's trawling grounds. But after another week, need had gotten the better of wisdom.

The fripperer's bins were a sea of secondhand flotsam: ancient handbags, fossils of shoes, shawls of every fabric. Crinolines hung like giant birdcages amid Turkish carpets, mantillas on strings, racks of whalebone stays, and tattered point lace. Hordes of shoppers behaved like pecking flocks, like the ruckus of a goose pen. My arm was one among many raking hastily through the bins, clutching at sleeves or a bit of hem, tossing and clawing for any decent scrap: nothing dyed too bright, cheap-looking, or gaudily trimmed. Bursts of argument flared when opposing hands grabbed at the same bit, and bargaining and bartering clamored all around. We all wanted the same rare item: a suitable dress in summer fabric; decent gloves, a bonnet, a pair of shoes not entirely worn through. A few of these dangled overhead on hooks, just out of reach. Their prices, written on fluttering yellow tags, were nearly as much as those in the shops.

A serviceable stretch of sepia-colored material fell under my hand, but no sooner did I tug it out from the pile than I felt an opposing pull. Tired and frustrated, I cried out just like my noisy neighbors and seized it harder, determined to win or tear the thing to shreds. We struggled for a moment, then the other side abruptly let go, nearly dropping me into the lap of the *patronne*. Astonished, I looked up. My opponent was tall, sloe-eyed; red-gold hair falling from its pins.

She grinned and dived, tossing a moth-eaten tippet in my direction. I gasped, dodging it. And she came slouching around the bin, irreparably herself, dressed in a man's smoking jacket over a dress that had seen better days. The *patronne* glanced up and jerked her chin. *Out of here, with you.*

"What are you doing, you little idiot?" Jolie growled. "Don't you know this place crawls with Brigade boys?" And the world rolled around again — turned up its nether side, and peculiarly, it looked and smelled and felt like relief.

We passed through high-walled, cobble-broken streets so narrow, we had to flatten ourselves against the walls when a vehicle passed. Workshops sat chock-a-block: an iron filer, a gem polisher, a window of watch chains. Walls painted with advertisements for VINS and BI-BERONS. Finally we turned into an alleyway even more cramped and ancient, the walls leaning in so they nearly touched at the top. *Rue des Vertus.* Haussmann's work carts had apparently passed it by.

"Virtue takes a narrow path," said Jolie. "This street's all ours." She parted a set of ragged door curtains, ducked inside. My eyes adjusted to the dimness of a room furnished with a few chipped marble tables barely bigger than plates. A kind of café, a no-name place without window or sign. Jolie dropped her bag, a cloth sack tied with a drawstring (like a thief's), disappeared, and came back with a *pichet* of thin-looking wine and two glasses.

"I used to live up on the corner," she said. "Six floors up. My window looked onto Gravilliers. Once I thought I'd live and die here. Still — it's the only café in Paris where we won't be bothered . . . You're growing past your clothes; is that why you were at the Tem-

ple? You shouldn't, you know. What's that on your finger——?" Jolie divided a cache of tobacco. It lay in fragrant, curly little piles; she
methodically separated and smoothed cigarette papers and deftly
rolled the first.

"You're out of there, then?"

"Bit of a tip-up with Françoise."

"Not on my account, I hope."

"Well, what if it was?"

"I'd be sorry to have put you to trouble!"

"You are nothing *but* trouble. But no. It was over Bette. Some
cigarettes, Françoise's private cache that she kept to sell to the *michés*——not cutting the house in on her markup, don't you know——but
I had tipped Bette to light-finger them. Françoise caught her in the
business, looking for them under a stack of chemises in the parlor——I'd told Bette where they were! But she doesn't have the hand
of a thief, alas——"

"Poor Bette!" I had to laugh, imagining the scene, the submistress red as a beet and buzzing mad.

"I've deviled her anyway, Françoise, for selling under the table.
But Bette can't afford to lose her job, she's got two little brothers
to support, and a father with the gout. Jouffroy and Trois weren't
too hard on me; they helped me make an arrangement. Didn't want
to lose their submistress over a pile of cigarettes! Well, it's summer
anyway——a good time for fresh air."

She got up and slouched over to the bar for a light. Women relaxed on mismatched chairs, smoked, poured wine from their *pi-
chets.* They didn't appear to be the right kind of woman, nor the
wrong; and a spectrum of wardrobes was represented: from shop-
ping-arcade gowns to maid's dresses to eccentric combinations like
Jolie's. All mixed together; these women just *were,* as though they'd
a right to be there. One sat alone reading *L'Opinion.*

"You see?" said Jolie, sliding back into her seat. "That's what I
want to do."

"What?"

"Read. Know without asking, for once. There's a school near

where I stay now, just around the corner in the rue Hautefeuille. A teacher there will see me for free. Now—what have *you* gotten yourself up to?"

She poured. And poured again; we passed her rolled cigarettes between us. I told her I was staying with Chasseloup, and she eyed the ring on my finger again. "So. Model marries painter, happy ending? I may not read much, but I've heard the fairy tales."

"It's a fake," I said, uncomfortably.

"Ah." And then she pushed back her chair. She had to go and meet Louise. Her teacher. When she said the name, her eyes sparked.

A few flights up the stairs on the Impasse de la Bouteille I stopped to rest, breathing heavily; a few provisions and my stash from the rue du Temple weighed me down. Madame-who-lived-on-the-fifth gave me her fisheye stare through her cracked-open door. Chasseloup was dining out, which was just as well. He and Jolie jangled in the mind like two animals that should not be placed side by side in cages at the menagerie at the Jardin des Plantes.

A sooty stain had accumulated on the wall over the stove because of my enthusiasm for cooking with a more inspiring range of ingredients. I lit the stove, though the coal was down again; tossed a few bones into the pot and cut up a carrot and an onion. Then took up the brown-flecked fabric from the fripperer's bin. A solid in a dull color, but rich enough to gather into graceful folds.

From the window, a pool of light from one lamp, then the next, as the lamplighter made his way. He lit the nearest lamp, then the one across from the hat maker's porte-cochère, and passed on to the rue Montorgueil. It had begun to rain; the street glistened. A lone girl, bareheaded, with her shawl pulled around her, appeared in silhouette under one lamp, then drifted to the next. For a moment her face turned up, as though to look at me, and I shivered with her chill, not my own. The sky was black and I closed the shutters.

I had planned to use the indigo dress as a pattern to make over the new one, and then use some additional fabric to expand its waistline, to create two serviceable garments. I separated the waistband from its skirt, ripping seams and pleats. Slowly; I was no seamstress. When I checked the soup again, the fire had gone out and a skin of whitish fat had congealed on top.

After I'd relit the fire and returned to my work, I noticed something had fallen out of the indigo dress's waistband. A pale square of pasteboard, about the size of my palm, which had been sewn inside. Inscribed with a name—a female name. I knew what it was.

Carte de brème—carte de brème—it's only after a few days that it begins to stink! The genuine article, dated and stamped. I had no such *carte*. But the original owner of the indigo dress did. I'd been carrying it all along.

Voices from the hall shook me from where I sat staring at it, pins and fabric scattered about. Chasseloup's voice and another man's and a third voice, lighter. Feet stamped; umbrellas were shaken. Flare of the gas lamp just inside the door. The flicker lit up a girl's blonde curls, her elbow-length black gloves, as she tugged at the fingertips with her teeth. Her other arm was linked through Chasseloup's. When she saw me, the girl's lips widened into a silent O.

"Sweetheart," she began, in a clotted voice.

"Eugénie! What are you—? Vollard needs a drink, so I invited him up—" Chasseloup's voice slurred like an idiot's; his posture was half-reeling. A cloud of liquor over both men, with the chill of the night; the third of the party angled into the tiny room.

"I just want a look at that canvas you claim is not blank." Vollard glanced in my direction and began to laugh. "Why, if it isn't is the 'unknown girl.' I'd heard you were back in the picture!"

You may remember that that year, tropical flowers were the fashion—orchids, hibiscus, and gingers grown through the winter in heated glasshouses. Melodrama was in vogue too; a commodity in itself—it was the kerosene that the empire burned. What was in me was also ready to ignite, although I could afford neither melodrama nor orchids; and a quickening voice might have told me so, had I cared to listen. But cold fury at seeing the girl hanging on Chasseloup's arm, and panic and humiliation at the sight of Vollard—whose shoulder I had all too recently dampened on a sofa at

Deux Soeurs—carried me, in three steps, across the wedge-shaped room, from the divan to the stove. I flung open the window; with one gesture seized the soup, cold as rain under its sheath of fat, and dashed it to the street, bones and onions and carrots—hurling the pot after it. I wanted to hear the clatter all the way down, six flights, to the street, smash iron against stone. Some buried, long-banked rage—at the whole nauseating faithful ignorant attempt at—*what?* I grabbed the fresh white *ficelle* from where it was resting and flung it after the pot.

Chasseloup had retreated to the cupboard alcove, his back turned. Vollard was pouring himself a drink. The girl had not made a move to leave—just the opposite; she settled herself on the divan. Her eyes were narrow and too close, and her white fingers were smooth. She looked stupid as lead, and determined to get her lousy coin for the evening. I took a look at her, and she at me, before I decided—well, it was hardly a decision, not a strategic move, but a furious, impetuous one, almost a bodily reflex, like vomiting.

"Wait!" called Chasseloup, but I was done with waiting.

Down the million stairs, flinging myself around each landing, dizzy at the bottom. Nausea, emptiness at the center, as I headed toward the river and Notre Dame. I walked to keep moving, to keep myself from thinking. *Inside me there was a ravenous something, tearing at my guts, keeping me from being still, from any clear thought.* Three flights down, I realized that I was wearing only a dressing gown of Chasseloup's. It was raining. And I had left the *carte* on the divan.

The next morning, Chasseloup paced back and forth, jacket smeared with paint, stub-bristled brushes clutched in his hand. Pieces of sailcloth, odd-shaped squares, tail ends of rolls, their corners peeling down, were tacked up over every surface, in various stages of *imprimatura;* some chalked with figures in green outline; still others, painted over to be started again. The green dress and its crinoline lay in their twin coffins.

"And where did you find *her*—the blonde girl with the rat's teeth?" I'd ended up sleeping in the studio upstairs; hungry and ruing the fate of the soup pot. "You tell me that you care for me — I make soup every night, wait for you to come home, go on sitting for you, not for a sou but for a promise — of what? For you to finish another — pack of lies on canvas for old men to sweat over — and then treat me as you please. Oh, God help me if I *ever* step up on this box again."

He stared at me in rigid fury.

"Pack of lies, indeed. God help me if I ask you to."

"Well, why not? It's worth it to you to finish. Rack up a second medal; Vollard will get you another fortune — "

"When you had your tantrum and threw the pot out the window — which, by the way, could have killed an innocent passerby — you left something behind."

My hands went cold, then my feet and legs, and the tip of my nose. My hands moved instinctively to my belly. The damned *carte* from the indigo dress. We both stared at the flimsy square. Chasseloup holding it between his fingers like something putrid.

"It's not mine."

He gave a sharp, short laugh. "A week ago Vollard told me a story I had the sheer vanity not to believe. He told me . . . because I told him of your condition. I wanted his advice. I had gone to my father, I was even thinking of — God help me — ! I believed I had painted an — innocent girl. I refused to believe the picture could be compromised in — this way. Or that you could have been."

This time, I was the one who crossed to the studio's windows and stared at the buttes. Stared a long time. Finally I said, "You left — for Croisset. Let me make your eggs and sew your buttons, and collect your brushes and carry your things to the train, and you waved goodbye without a word. You never paid me what you should have; never bothered to ask where I might stay, nor if I had the means. I was a little fool come in on a train from the provinces. It doesn't matter. It's not my name on that *carte* — "

"Do I even *know* your name?"

"I said it's not my name. I told you my name!"

"Yes, an empress and a rabble-rouser; maybe you got it from the papers."

"It's not my name on the *carte*." I stopped, and heard myself. "But it might as well be, Pierre."

"Gustav told me that when you came back — *got out* — he even went so far as to pay off what he called your 'debt.' What you owed to some Madame So-and-So — because he wanted me to paint you again."

"He did that?"

"He said that otherwise you'd be hauled in by the Morals Brigade and unable to sit. So you hardly have a complaint against *him*." Chasseloup's voice was hard again. "But I don't care for that arrangement. I reject it. Please leave. Go back to — wherever you came from. I don't wish to see you. And *if* it's true — that you didn't fall into this situation until after you sat for me — you could have done a thousand things before you went where you did."

I stood white and mute. Responses circled, washed through my mind like water sucked down a cesspool. "I was cold," I said finally. "I'd lost everything, and then I lost you."

"Eugénie." Chasseloup picked up some brushes, hands trembling; mopped his face with a paint-smeared rag. "Is this child mine?"

Some piece of me splintered, broke away.

"No, Pierre. No, it's not."

Chasseloup turned away. "Then — please — go. Let me paint in peace."

Color bled everywhere — on his flesh, on mine, on the green dress lying embalmed in its casket. On the floating white shawl I'd worn to the Closerie des Lilas; and on the pasteboard *carte*, in the dust where Chasseloup had dropped it. I picked up the thing before I went. It was the least I could do for her, whoever she was.

"You've really screwed the thing, haven't you?" Jolie rolled a cigarette and refilled our glasses, wide-mouthed jars from a shelf. The wine was slowing my racing thoughts. "Your Stephan was nothing but a *miché*, and this Chasseloup is a *bébé*."

"I don't know what else I could have done."

"I'm sure *that's* true . . . *Salut, chouette.* Oh, don't look like that. It's not so bad as you think." Jolie wore a faded velvet wrap over her shoulders; strands of hair were clinging to her skin. A sleek tanger-ine-and-cream cat dozed on the bed; she curled tighter when a draft rippled the ragged length of lace at the window.

"That's Clio, and the furniture is bought and paid for, from Al-bertine on the rue du Jardinet—"

"All of it's yours?"

"My friend Odette was stashing it for me. She's an old pal from when we both lived on Vertus—but she didn't live there long; she moved up in the world! The stove's in the hall, so there's no heat, and it's shared among nine of us. But it doesn't matter; this place is a palace."

It occurred to me that just a short time ago, I would have exulted in this paradise—a tiny silk-festooned matchbox under the slope of the roof, over a café, with Jolie. In one corner was a narrow bed covered with a strip of purple cloth. In the center of the room was a rose-colored chaise, pocked with cigarette burns. A small table was marked with bottle rings, more burns, and streaks of black; a stack of tattered old books—a primer, a book of fairy tales—and the possibility of a decent supper: bread and grapes, cheese, a bit of *saucisson*. A bag of fish heads for Clio, dripping onto the floor. The cutlery was all silverplate, and mismatched, some of it heavy. Salt cellars and napkin rings.

"You know what?"

"What, *chouette*?"

"I'm at least half-glad to be here."

Jolie had uncorked a bottle and looked at me, eyes half-closed. "All right. First things first. You still owe Jouffroy?"

"It's been paid."

"I wondered. Otherwise they'd have caught up with you by now." Jolie gathered the wrap around shoulders and stretched her long arms to the ceiling. She reached for the tobacco, rolled another cigarette. The cat stretched and yawned, jumped down and me-owed, brushing against my skirts. She had green eyes as well. "Clio, do you want your fish? Not really a hunter, are you, my cat? She lets the mice run right under her nose." Jolie hitched up her dress as she bent down to fill a saucer. Her legs were so long that her knees nearly came up to her shoulders. Her skin was like milk, her eyes like stones under water. "So—are you back in the game, going to register as an independent? You'd be good if you wanted to—the *muffes* know contraband when they see it."

I looked down at the ripening fruit of my belly. "I was sick on those men, before, at Deux Soeurs. And now—like this—"

"Well . . . what, then?" She drained her glass and bit the end off a sausage.

"I have a little modeling job, for a sculptor." She was a friend of Pierre's—Mademoiselle C—who was living off her inheritance and sculpting in a pocket courtyard studio on the Île Saint-Louis. She was intense, slate-eyed; her brow gathered like a storm; her hair a dark mess of ringlets pulled up in a chignon. She had a ferocious excitement; a vibrating tension that bounced off the old sand-colored walls. Mademoiselle C had no patience for conventional art. *You might as well visit the morgue as the sculpture rooms at the Palace of Industry during the Salons. White hands. White breasts. Drapery. Wings. White wings, on angels. Scrolls and busts. The same model, in the same pose; copy the academics, bloodless, bleached. They never work from life,* she'd said. Her gaze dipping and swimming over the curves and shadows of my swelling belly. "You fell from the heavens. How many *enceintes* could I get to model for me? I'll tell you, not one."

"She'll need me for a while longer. Could I stay with you for a bit?" I remembered Jolie's lecture, that two *inscrits* could not share lodgings, although I didn't understand why not. "I know we have to be careful."

"Mmmm. I'm glad you're here, anyway. It was lonely before."

Jolie did not lounge under street lamps, kohl-eyed and spotted with rouge, but made herself into an indescribable sort of person. Her dresses had theatrical touches but were still demure. Plum-red silk rustled over colored petticoats and jet-buttoned boots. Her hat, veilless, was trimmed in black velvet; her hair swept up and scented with men's cologne that she kept in small stoppered bottles. She carried a knife in a soft leather casing in her boot; never wore a shawl or a cloak in any weather or carried a handbag; yet she glittered like a soft, shimmering jewel. Before going out she poured two neat brandies into thin-stemmed glasses; drank one and then the other. If it was raining, she took a large black umbrella.

Down the stairs, Jolie greeted all the neighbors with a *Good afternoon, madame,* or *How are you today, monsieur?* She took soup to the old ones; sometimes brought in flowers or tobacco, laughing at her little bribes to old Madame Boudet, who, she said, would happily march down to the Préfecture herself, were it not for Jolie's bits of shopping. When she reached the street she tipped her nose up, as if to see how the wind blew, and when she came home, she hitched up her skirts and dumped out the contents of her pockets — dozens of them, sewn into her seams and a sash around her waist. She divided the money into piles: bills and coins in orderly stacks. Jolie had a circle of regulars, and the odd one out; she didn't seem to be partial to any one of them. On the rue Jacob, around the corner from Galopin Vins Fins et Ordinaires, was a room — I wasn't sure from whom it was rented. Jolie joked about the "poor Brigade boys," by which she meant the gray coats of whom I'd been so afraid, and I assumed someone had to be paying them off.

When she rattled the key in the lock, Clio made a graceful leap off the chaise and abandoned my lap for the door. Jolie looked flushed and sparkling, vivid with her hair and her colors. She'd had a reading lesson with Louise; she always looked happier on those nights.

"So, what have you been doing all evening?" she asked.

"Writing." My usual scatter of nibs and ink pots on the table.

"To that Chasseloup? He's your ticket, probably lonely and drinking himself to death. All along, he enjoys your services, makes a fortune off your face, and suddenly he's high and mighty? *And* you let him off the hook. Anyone would say he owes you."

"No, they wouldn't, Jolie. No one would say it."

Tears welled up and spilled over. The evenings were long, too long, with thoughts circling and jostling, contending like fighters in a ring. And also, my sittings with Mademoiselle C had taught me what I knew, but half-denied. My defiance, my careless-seeming courage was not, in fact, true acknowledgment of my situation, but partly an inability to accept it—and to plan for it. I had refused the ergot and the angel maker to defy Françoise; to cling to some vestige of the past. Now life was calling me from childishness to womanhood and I wanted to shirk, shrug it off. My divided Selves, somehow, had navigated my path thus far—and even now, I could not speak with a single unified voice.

Jolie came around the chaise and sat, lit a cigarette. Dumped Clio into my lap to stretch out her neck and start a rumbling purr, from deep in her creamy orange belly. A velvet sleeve brushed my cheek, a hint of men's cologne.

"Well, *I* say it."

"I wasn't writing to Chasseloup."

"What, then?"

"Just—a sort of diary. I feel like I've been—split down the middle, drawn and quartered and divided up until there's nothing left. Ever since I came here, really. And now—soon—this baby."

La Maternité was the place poor women went when their time came. Peak-roofed, high-gabled, overgrown with shrubbery; I had even seen a young woman cross its wide, dark threshold. I took some comfort from its looming presence, its very existence a testimony to my situation. To read the papers, one would think only women with christening-cup collections gave birth, but La Maternité put the lie to that.

"I've been thinking about it. Remember my friend Victorine? She was turned away there and at Hôtel Dieu, and ended up having hers on the Pont Neuf. To get into the hospital you need two character witnesses, a certificate of morals, proof of residency—and *then* they do their best to kill you. The place is so filthy, even Françoise has given up on it."

"Really?" I closed my eyes and Jolie rested her arm around my shoulders. My back ached, and I couldn't breathe. These days I could not sit, or stand, or lie down—could do nothing, it seemed, but wait to burst like a rotten melon—and I tasted salt again; it couldn't be helped.

"Come lie down, you are in a terrible state." Jolie scooped Clio under one arm and took my hand. I sank the bulk of my poor body into her mattress while she unbuttoned the back of my dress. "You should be sleeping here. I'll take the chaise. No—really." She put a drop of oil and cologne on her palms and began to rub my back, then the stretched, hot skin of my swollen belly, with her cool hands. The tears came like a flood, in great gulping sobs.

"When my brother, Henri, left to join the army, I felt as bad as you do. And not just any army—he was just a thief from the Paris slums but he wanted to join the Turcos and go to Africa, and he did. I never believed he'd go, but one morning he was gone, just as he'd said. He left, and then I had to learn to be strong. I thought I knew all the tricks, but I just had to learn them all again. Thought I'd die for sure. For a while I wanted to."

"What did you do, Jolie?"

She was silent for a moment, considering.

"Well, figured out who my friends were, to start. Real friends, not just those with their own interests at heart. I had to learn to tell the difference. Make the best of both." Jolie had a talent for it. At Deux Soeurs and outside—I could see that much through my haze of misery.

"All right, let Chasseloup go hang for now," she said finally. "I'm not going to forget what's due. But I'm not going to leave you sobbing by the side of the road, either." She sat up. "Now, where are my knitting needles? Clio, let go!" She laughed and tugged the ball of yarn from the cat's claws. Jolie had been knitting an infant's blanket in the small hours before she slept.

12

AN ARRIVAL

ALL SUMMER, THEN, we stocked up. Champagne and absinthe, mismatched bottles one at a time, and opium — soft granules wrapped in paper, nested in pocket bottoms. Jolie was crossing off the days and planning an impromptu party at the rue Jacob, as the hour neared; she put everyone she knew on notice. The plan was that after I'd returned to the rue Serpente with the midwife, the guests would stay and put bets. A send-off, with the money going for a layette.

"An *apprentice* midwife," the young woman offered, holding out her hand. "I work with La Cacheuse on the rue Monge." Mathilde twisted her blonde curls up into a knot, secured them with a comb, and opened her black bag to show the stack of clean white linen. La Cacheuse was an abortionist; angel making paid the rent at her mistress's outfit, Mathilde said, but she was happier delivering babies when she could.

"La Cacheuse helped out with Odette," Jolie said. "Did the job for her with ergot of rue and a porcupine quill."

"No, with mistletoe," said Mathilde. The tea had come from mistletoe that grew on an old oak in the center of the village where La Cacheuse had grown up, Mathilde explained. The villagers never allowed the road builders to cut it down, so the old oak had stayed and the road divided around it. The tinctures made from its mistle-toe now supported half the population, and it was shipped to Paris by the crate.

"Kiss under it at Noël, swallow it at Lent, is that it?" said Jolie.

"Something like that," agreed Mathilde, giggling. "Oh, it's so lovely here! What a nice room, but no stove at all?"

"We dine out," said Jolie.

It was just the three of us at the rue Jacob flat, one large room with broad floorboards, old wood beams, and mahogany wainscoting. The place was furnished with a wide bed and a yellow satin divan. Layers of drapery shielded the windows; thick brocade and tulle and lace. On a sideboard was a full set of glasses and decanters. The flat was funded by Jolie's "regulars," Jacques and Jean-Paul and a third whose name I didn't know. When she wasn't there, she rented it out by the hour, an entirely risky setup.

Mathilde rubbed my back while Jolie cooked the opium over a small brazier, stirring it with honey and pistachio nuts until it was a viscous-looking, sticky mass. "You'll need it," she said. "And so will we, once the creature starts wailing."

"Be careful of those coals, Jolie. Take that thing over by the window or you'll asphyxiate us." Perspiration beaded my forehead, trickled down my neck.

"I'm not opening a window," said Jolie. She was on edge because there had been raids the past few nights and a few of her pals had been arrested and gone down to Saint-Lazare.

Mathilde soaked a flannel rag in cold water and passed it to me; Jolie set out her cache of bottles on the sideboard. She dipped a spoon into the opium mixture, and I rolled the sticky mass onto my tongue. The paste's bitterness penetrated the sweetness of the honey and was barely masked by the crunch of green nuts.

"You know, m'amselle, when the baby is born I can take it to the hospice for you. That way the nuns will take care of it. Depending on the time of day, the guards might ask questions, but I've done it a few times for La Cacheuse so I know my way around." Her voice faltered. I stared at her. "Well, it *is* what's done."

"Certainly not," I said. "Never."

"Think it over, m'amselle. It's quite usual, you know."

"Don't bother, Mathilde," said Jolie, bending over us.

Champagne, more champagne, as the door opened and closed. Odette, Jacques, Jean-Paul, others I didn't recognize. Jolie had asked if I wanted to invite Mademoiselle C, but I couldn't imagine the sculptor mingling on the rue Jacob with abortionists, opium eaters, and Jolie's gentlemen, who had money, but in a shadowy way that brought pickpockets to mind, even if they wore good boots and starched linen.

. . . Babble of voices, laughter.

Jolie lit candles, small ones that dotted the room, and a big, flaring candelabra for the center. From my corner of pillows I watched them flicker as the perfumed smoke of opium — what hadn't been made into sweets — rose up in coils. The room was not large, but more and more people came, sat on cushions on the floor. Lips were pressed against my cheeks, fingers tousled my hair, hands rubbed my back, my neck; someone unfolded a fan, brushed me with a breeze. There were ribbons for luck, a silver filigree baby spoon, a tiny blanket edged with lace. I got up and then lay down; another glass was pressed into my hand.

"Put up your bets," Jolie called out. "Boy or girl, and the time of birth. *Boy or girl . . . winner takes half and the rest is for Eugénie and the baby — a girl, then, at midnight; a boy at 12:45 . . .*" Voices rose, a laughing babble, smoke and chaos. A colored scarf lay on the floor, amid more wrapped packages and ribbons, the *chink* of coins added to coins.

I was beginning to feel dizzily outside of my body. Pain eddied in and away; I could imagine it going on and on, never getting worse, or better. Someone put the cool ivory tip of a pipe between my lips; I sucked it and filled my chest with deep, sweet smoke.

"You'll like Odette," Jolie had said. We had something in common, she pointed out, as Odette had tried modeling for artists, or "taken a walk down the rue Bonaparte," as Jolie put it. From across the room I caught a silvery glimmer, a flask tipped to her lips. Odette was a generous woman, with beautiful round bare arms, tonight dressed in a salmon-colored gown that crossed over her breasts. And peacock-feather earrings brushed her shoulders. She looked a little like a painting—maybe one of the nine muses. The one who played the flute.

Odette settled down next to me, tipping absinthe into a glass from her flask, an embossed oval. She drank it neat, *la purée*, as stylish women did, omitting the water so they could keep their lacings tight. Odette leaned in and murmured, "You're a braver woman than I, Eugénie . . . I always knew she would have been a girl, Beatrice." She pronounced it French-Italian, *Beh-AH-tri-cheh*, her tongue caressing the syllables. "Beautiful, blessed. I talk to her now. Tell her everything." She paused. "She'd be eight years old . . . But I was young and could never have kept her." Odette gave a shudder and her feathers shimmered. "In France a woman can politely decline by way of mistletoe, and there's no shame in it. But you are a brave young thing, and I salute you."

A pain, huger now, tore through me and I gasped, but then it passed.

Odette, Jolie had said, was orphaned at thirteen, the only child of elderly parents. She had no other family and was taken in by an older man who had been an associate of her father's. He was married, a wealthy gambler who loved the races, and kept her. It was a pampered life, full and extravagant. Odette had enjoyed a private flat, all of the clothing and jewelry she could want; evenings out and as much admiration as a beautiful young girl could receive. She had books; time on her hands to read. But then her protector lost his fortune and died soon after, in a riding accident. He'd made no will. At eighteen, Odette was left on her own.

"Jolie and I met up when my situation wasn't so different from yours," Odette was saying now, helping herself to an opium pistachio that floated by on a tray. Then she held up an absinthe spoon from Jolie's collection. "One of Henri's finds, no doubt. He knew every dodge, that boy. False-bottomed boxes, coats with double pockets, packs of cards. *Faire la souris, faire la tire,* tricks with knives and cards, *le rendémi,* a trick done with a gold coin, *la morlingue,* a way to steal a purse . . . *coupe de fourchette,* a two-fingered pocket picking; or his *vol à l'Américaine,* which I believe involved a buckskin jacket. Henri could clear a restaurant of its cutlery in under a week. A magician. Of the lower sort, I mean. You should have seen them, and this one"—she waved the spoon at Jolie, across the room—"they called her 'the little nurse.'" Odette's voice eddied and retreated as a new pain, sharper, doubled me over.

"Mathilde . . ." I gasped, and wobbled to my feet.

"Oh, you have plenty of time," a woman's voice said. Not Mathilde's. Arms eased around me, settling me back among the pillows. Laughter.

The scarf on the floor was full of baubles and coins. The blanket Jolie had knitted held a place of honor on the bed. *Remember to breathe.* I could not breathe; and suddenly, sick and terrified, confused by the opium—another pain, this more quick coming on than the last.

"I *must* go," I said, pulling myself up again by the edge of a chair, my legs unsteady. "*Now.* Mathilde, it's time." I spotted her sunny curls across the room, head lolled to the side like a rag doll. A bolt went through me; my palms were damp. "*Mathilde,*" I cried out, and struggled to my feet.

Jacques's arm was twined around Jolie's neck, an empty glass dangling from two fingers. On her other side was Jean-Paul, who lived at the Bourse and was, I thought, in love with Jolie, though she couldn't care less. "Jacques and Jean-Paul have made very nice pledges," drawled Jolie. She pulled me down toward her, kissed me on the mouth. "We had seven girls and six boys," she said. She reached down into her boot. "Jean-Paul, tell Eugénie what you just told me."

"Mathilde is enjoying the party too much," I said. "Is someone here? At the door?"

BANG BANG BANG.

"I'm not expecting anyone," Jolie said blearily, "but you never know."

BANG BANG BANG.

My insides collapsed, then gave way like a child's water balloon.

Warm liquid gushed down my thighs as though I'd been holding it back with all my strength. Panic hissed and flittered through me, my knees buckled, and another pain moved through me, flash fire and flood, all at once, and I started to sob. "*Jolie,*" I said, "Mathilde — you've got to help me — "

"We're all going to be arrested," groaned Jacques, struggling to his feet. "*Merde.*"

"Oh no, we won't," said Jolie. She reached down to her boot and drew out her knife, folded it into my palm. "Take this," she said. She lunged to her feet, half-falling against Jacques. Pulled a bottle of absinthe out of the crate and pushed it into my arms. "And this!"

"Jolie, Mathilde is — "

"I see her. Jacques, you'll have to go with her — get her out of this room."

"Me?"

"*Yes,* you. I'll send Mathilde right after you — ! *I love you, chouette,* I love you — !"

BANG BANG BANG, went the door again, then the loud thump of a boot heel, outside.

"I love you!"

"Jolie, what are you doing, what should I — "

"The back stairs! *GO.*"

"*We love you!*" sang out a clutch of pistachio eaters from a corner, looking up from their spoons. Jolie lifted the guttering candelabra high into the air, streams of sooty smoke rising from each wick, and memory slithered back, back — to the shimmer of crystal-ensconced flames when I was in Stephan's arms at the chateau, his face before me now, clear and full of laughter. Boot heels crashed against the wood, crack of the door, pain doubled me over, and Jacques caught me before I fell.

Jolie brought the candelabra to the window and flung back the brocade. She held the flames to the gauzy tulle curtains, and fire licked them up faster than lightning; the curtains caught like they were meant to burn. Flames reached the ceiling, and spread.

"Jolie, don't," I said weakly, leaning on Jacques.

"FIRE!" she yelled, as gray smoke filled the room. Hands pulled me to my feet and pushed me to the door, open now; Jacques gripped my elbow.

"*Fire, fire, fire,*" echoed the chorus, as they coughed and waved through the smoke.

"Wake *her,* wake Mathilde," I said into the chaos, but no one heard, the door broke down. The gray coats burst in, grabbing people, choking in the smoke, but in the melee, Jacques pushed me through a second, hidden door, propelled me down the back stairs and onto the street.

"*Mon Dieu,* I am a lucky man tonight!" Jacques sang. Drunken father-to-be, warding off the police. It was dark and quiet, all of the shops shuttered tight, and his voice echoed off the walls. The big clock face read five past midnight. The night air was a humid, sticky breath, and I clutched Jacques's arm.

"I can't walk," I gasped. But there were no cabs.

He had to half-carry me up to Jolie's flat, up seven flights. "Don't leave me alone," I said, after Clio butted her head against my legs as I fumbled for a taper between searing bouts of pain.

"Are you all right now?" asked Jacques, hovering over me in the dark.

"Go get Mathilde; please go back and get Mathilde."

"You told me not to leave."

I started to cry. "Don't leave, but DO find Mathilde!"

"Sure, sure. I'll have her right back here." His boots clattered down the stairs, echoing like a bucket dropped down a dry well.

The windows were open; gusts of wind blew the ragged lace. The wind had come up suddenly, and it even felt cold, strangely cold, without a fire. I lit all the candles I could find. The pains were on me for real now, one after another in waves. I uncorked the absinthe and drank straight from the lip, and barely tasted it going down. My head lolled back against the chaise; the pains rolled me forward —

Stay conscious, stay awake, just hang on — I crouched on the chaise as well as I could, pulling the sheet over me, shivering. *Mathilde, where was she* — *?* Blackness like icy water closed over my head and I gave in, let it close over me before struggling back to the surface. My breath came in gasps. *Breathe,* the midwife had said.

It was more like drowning, though, gasping for the surface — and nausea, green-bottled, long-necked nausea clutched in one hand, Jolie's knife in the other. I eased myself down to the floor, braced my back against the chaise. Clio had retreated, her fur tangerine-orange against Jolie's purple shawl on the bed. She licked her white belly, licked and licked, her pink tongue bobbing; just a cat performing her ablutions. The minutes clicked past on the white-faced clock; the hands moved past the numerals.

"Jacques!" The moan did not seem to come from me. But Jacques became Jolie and Jolie Stephan, and Stephan Pierre, and Pierre . . . Mademoiselle C . . . and a girl with long fingers and rat's teeth. Ten, fifteen, twenty minutes; half an hour, an hour . . . I was cold, it was freezing in the room, and the pains came one on top of the next; finally, and finally, I knew no one would come, not Mathilde, or Stephan, or Pierre, or Jacques or Jolie; no one, no one at all would come to assist this birth. Even if I cried out Stephan's name, as women were said to do — that grave declaration in extremis that could be nothing but the truth — no one would hear it.

Then another, a new kind of pain, the most immense of them all, making the others measurelessly small in comparison — this cut through the opium, the absinthe, slashed through my abdomen like a jagged knife edge. This pain was a bolt forking down into the furrows, it ripped me from the earth, uprooted me, held me, strangling and naked, white, tender, earthbound roots, straggling legs hanging in the air — it was enormous, that pain, it was everything I'd ever feared, and hungered for.

The cry was a thin sound, but too far away . . . I started to sob when I saw, finally, the crown of the small head, the tiny heaving chest — eyes screwed shut, a mouth open in an O, to bellow . . . held the tiny, fragile, blood-and-mucus-charged pith of my bones. I struggled to pull myself up, to turn the small infant body toward mine. It — *she* — was a girl.

A girl. Poor wailing scrap of a thing, jinxed in the womb—my vision went black, and I breathed. I had made her, alone; nourished her with my body, had given birth to her, alone. *Alone. My daughter.* Pain echoed through my body like a bell tolling, tolling, and tolling. The storm had rolled by but in its wake, fires . . . the blackened spires at the forest edge; and women coming down the road with bundles bound to their backs with ropes, with cord.

Jolie's knife was still clenched in my fist, and the throbbing, blood-charged, still-live umbilicus bound this infant, this daughter to me. I found it, wrapped it around my hand. *When do I cut it—now? when?* It seemed she would die if I cut too soon, cut her off from me, from my body, from everything—the cord, quivering, wet, pulsing with my dark blood, cries of the infant—cries, *Oh please, be quiet.*

I shut my eyes tight and pressed forward with the blade. It did not want to cut through; the knife trembled, I was not strong enough . . . *Please, God, let this be all right, let me not kill her, let Mathilde come.* It slipped through, finally; severed us, the knife trembling—and for God's sake, what now?

Wrap her, clean her, she must be wrapped, swaddled—what to put around her, all the linens were with Mathilde—*Mathilde, damn her*—but my shawl, my shawl—it was somewhere here. The room began to turn; slowly I shook myself, I felt ill, was going to black out; she was crying, but wait, she had to be covered.

Was she dying?

The shawl, when I found it, was not the plain one I had pulled around myself at the rue Jacob; the shawl, as I wound it around my daughter, was different, much more beautiful; it was like a living thing, a whole garden, it was twined with roses in a delicate pattern, in red and gold and purple, with green, winding thorns.

"Isn't it lovely against the black?" Berthe's face turned toward me, pale in the candlelight, fiery in the mirror.

The infant stopped crying then, as though the ghost of her grandmother had come into the room and taken away her fierce little wails. *Is my mother dead, then? Has she forgiven me?* Standing on the stairs, face turned toward Auch, palette box under her arm; Charles's arms wrapped around his wet nurse, Virginie. Berthe's gloved hand resting on his head, and mine, bare, red with my daughter's blood. The infant was quiet at last as I slipped under the black waters, and all I could think was *I already love her too much.*

Sunlight glared through the high window, poured in onto the rose-colored upholstery of the chaise. Black flies buzzed in the heat. The clock's hands said three and all was very still. The heat had finally returned; it wasn't cold anymore. The *thwap, thwap* of a cat's paws on the floor; Clio meowed, slapped her tail against my face, and went to sit next to her bowl. The world was a remote, sunny, quiet place, and I had been gone for a very long time. If I moved, even a little, a point of pain throbbed on my forehead.

It pulsed. It grew, that pain. In my head, as it did after I'd come into the Porte Maillot, and everything went black—and then, lower down. I was lying on the chaise, under a cover. Felt down cautiously for a stiff, bloody gown, but no, what I encountered was soft. The sheets were damp. I pushed back the cover and looked down for the dried mess of blood—yet there was nothing but the folds of a fresh white nightgown, a garment I'd never seen. I moved and felt some bandaging, bulky between my legs. There was no blood anywhere; the chaise had been made up with clean sheets. The pain in my head gave an awful cold-edged stab, the room went bleary then, and everything was fogged. *It was quiet . . . too quiet . . . why?* I remembered, clearly enough, cutting the cord—what had happened after? Where was the baby; had I harmed her? Should she not have been nursed by now? Or had Mathilde emerged like a lost devil, to take her to the *tour d'abandon*—

"Jolie?" I called, my voice weak and hoarse with panic. *"Jolie!"*

Clio stared at me golden-eyed from across the room, her tail twitching . . . No Jolie, no baby, no blood.

"Madame Eugénie?"

I lifted my legs over the side of the chaise, pressed my feet tentatively against the floor. They were puffy, swollen, useless things. Braced my knees and rose a little, unsteady, until a ragged pain tore from below.

"Madame Eugénie—oh, thank goodness you're awake." Mathilde appeared, breathless and flushed.

"Mathilde, you didn't—I swear, if you took her to the *tour*—"

She stood in the door with a small bundle in her arms. "No, madame." (I was madame, now that I'd given birth.) "You told me no, so I took the baby so you could sleep. She is a lovely little thing; hold her! I'm sure you are right to keep her, but—well, La Cacheuse told me to do everything to change your mind; it is so difficult to have a baby all on your own with no husband—"

"Shush now, Mathilde." I held out my arms.

"Where is Jolie? What happened—?"

"What happened? What *didn't* happen! But there was a back door and I got out in the smoke!"

What Mathilde said, in essence, jumbled together with apologies and a few more attempts to convince me to follow her employer's advice, was that after Jolie had set the draperies on fire, and the police had stormed in, and everyone was coughing and confused as the police were trying to make arrests—Jolie had jumped out the window. "Gone out" was the way Mathilde put it. They all heard a sickening crack, and leaned out and saw her dress in flames on a glass roof one story below.

"Oh, God," I said. "And now she's at Saint-Lazare."

"I believe it, madame."

The red-faced scrap slept in my arms, eyes squeezed shut. Eyelashes finer than the hairs of Maman's tiniest brush. Pink-bow lips, the faintest dark smudge of an eyebrow, as if smoke had touched her brow. Tiny fists, fingernails.

"You've had an eventful entry," I murmured, and then asked Mathilde if the cord was all right.

"Oh, it's fine—I fixed it up a bit. And look what I brought." She reached into her apron pocket, an ample one, and pulled out the blanket Jolie had knitted and a few of the trinkets from the rue

Jacob, all wrapped in the colorful scarf that had lain on the floor, and a set of clothes for swaddling, a donation from her mistress. An envelope stuffed with the bet money. The scarf had a burned edge, and smelled of smoke. And I forgave Mathilde a little.

"What are you going to name her, madame?"

Berthe, I said to myself, softly. Closing my eyes, burying my head in her shoulder, I inhaled the sweet, worldless perfume of an infant.

13

THE GARDEN

S HE SLEPT IN A SMALL orange crate, lined with scarves and
scraps of fabric, like a gypsy child. When she woke, I nursed
her. Mathilde visited to pronounce that she was doing well,
to bring us a half-loaf and a bunch of red-and-white radishes, and
to tell me she had found an *abéqueuse*. Every mother in Paris had an
abéqueuse, even if she could not afford one. I told Mathilde that this
"madame" would not engage a wet nurse, and she looked troubled.
She removed the bandaging from between my thighs and my body
felt tentative, afraid of movement. Exhausted past all remembering,
until Berthe's cries roused it again.

I ate the entire bunch of radishes, even the leaves, with the salt
that was left.

Berthe wailed; I lifted her from the crate. She was hot, the little
one, and no wonder; it was sweltering under the eaves, it had not
rained in weeks. The Seine was not much more than a muddy rivulet, ebbing and sucking at its stone bed. The cries of water sellers
were heard more and more from the street. With her lips clamped
around my swollen nipple, her warm, silky head cradled in the
crook of my arm, I tucked my feet up on the chaise and dropped
into a kind of drowsy quiet, taking her rhythms, the tiny suckling

movements, deep into my body . . . saw that she had his eyes, his brow; his ears, nose, and lips.

He was written all over her. Stephan.

When she was quiet, all I wanted was to sit with the blinds down and a piece of cool wet cloth around my head, hands cupped around my still-swollen belly. My mind, usually so full of racket, emptied, stilled, and lit, again and again, on an image: pollen-heavy stamens; flitting insects. Some notion, some scent; roses, lilies nodding on their stems. Gardens. A mirrored pool. I suppose it was inevitable that my thoughts would finally circle back and rest there: the garden, with the roses, lavender and yellow and pink, the buzzing insects, the water splashing lightly in the fountain. The gardens, the roses. Berthe in her cradle. Stephan beside us. *Peace*. Peace, *rue de la Paix*. It was different now; everything had changed. Now we were closer. She was here.

My earthly possessions now consisted of the indigo dress and the sepia-brown curtain-muslin skirt, two chemises and a good skirt and top; a variety of underthings, a pair of calfskin boots, worn at the heels; two pairs of stockings, a hair ribbon, four petticoats; a set of stays and two combs. Berthe possessed Jolie's knitted blanket, one set of swaddling cloths, one silverplate baby rattle, one pewter baby spoon, two ribbons, a cloth, and two pink, flowery notes. The betting wins, amounting to about seventy francs. Aside from that, a few notes and coins, loose among the mismatched pewter and silver, remained from Jolie's hoard, the rest having gone for celebratory provisions.

In the drawers of Jolie's flat I discovered packs of cards and a fist-sized ball of dirty wax. Aside from a few books lent by Louise, Jolie's sometime-teacher from the rue Hautefeuille, there was only one item of value: the man's pocket watch that Jolie had looked at, the very first time I'd met her, the very first night, at Deux Soeurs.

Pinkish gold and buttery smooth, the winding knob made a soft *tick-tick-tick*. The lid was engraved with a design of twining curlicues and ribbons, and folded open on a thick hinge to reveal a moon-round face with gold filigree hands and black numbers. It was a rich thing, heavy and old and fine. How might she have come to have it, I wondered. Could it have been a sentimental gift, a payment of some kind—or was it something Henri had filched?

In the orange crate, Berthe slept; Clio kept watch from the chaise, flicking her tail at slow-buzzing flies, casting green-eyed cat gazes down at Berthe, of whose small life she seemed to have appointed herself guardian. I closed my eyes.

My feelings for Jolie had thickened over these months together. I had, more than I'd admitted, waited for her while she was gone; watched her dress and brush out her hair; was jealous of the time she spent with Louise (and suspected their meetings were about more than learning to read). But she was slippery as an eel. I thought that she cared for me; but if she moved toward me (and at moments, she did), she would soon retreat; slide away into the world of her friends and lovers. I would never fit there, no matter how much I might wish to, how hard I might try. Jolie could keep others off balance if she wanted to; play one off the other, leave confusion and yearning in her wake; it was how she had learned to live. A heart thief; a thief. But—was that fair? She also had a fierce sense of justice, was loyal to a fault. The two braided together and you never knew which side would turn up.

It was sickening to think of her at Saint-Lazare.

Clio looked up at me and meowed; she knew it was about time for the mackerel woman to send up her call from the street. The knife slid easily into the fish's belly. Jolie's knife could cut an apple, an umbilicus, or a throat. A knife of Balzac, and the boulevard stories in *Paris Illustré*. Later, after Berthe had nursed, and Clio and I had shared a mackerel, I sat down again by the window; counted again the money from the drawers, what was left from the bets at the rue Jacob. The gold watch ticked; I briefly considered pawning it but decided against that. Who knew what the watch meant to Jolie, and when I could redeem it? Eventually, between the hypnotic rounds of feeding and drowsing, I decided upon a plan.

With the first jolting lurch of the train out of Saint-Lazare Station, it was an uncoiling, an unwinding, a returning to rights. My body let go from my ankles to my neck into the cupped palm of the train seat. The rocking motion suited Berthe, and my own spirit lightened as soon as we passed through the *enceinte*. It was the exact reverse of the trip we'd made together when she was — oh, had I but known it, would I have made the journey at all? By Versailles she was sound asleep.

One had become two, two would soon be three. Mother, daughter, father. Somewhat out of the usual order, but so be it. The garish images and smells, the ghosts and cries of the city retreated behind us with every ticking turn of the wheels.

We disembarked at the tiny station west of Le Mans. *"Last stop,"* the coachman was saying. "Last stop!" He swung the door open and extended a hairy arm to hand me down. No porters here. No horses or mules. Just dusty grass, unhitched carriages, and stable boys leading the horses to feed in a tumbledown barn. *A thousand leagues from Paris and all the better for it.* Tufts of soft grass grew between the rugged ties of the railroad tracks; the station itself was built on a human scale, with a small single platform, a waiting area, benches of drowsing old men in place of the vaulted ceilings and turbulent crowds. As the passengers alighted, loved ones embraced them; carriages were waiting. The coachman hoisted my bag down from the top. Berthe was crying in her basket. Only we two remained, and all was still. It was near dusk.

"Where you heading for, madame? You and the little one — "

"For La Vrillette. The big chateau?"

"La — what? Near here?" His expression was blank. Not a local, then.

I took the road that forked to the right; my feet recalled the turning. The sun had begun its descent and the sky over the vineyards was purple now, at its height; rose and lavender where it met the tips of the cigar-shaped trees. The very air seemed to vibrate, holding the shapes in its substance, sky and land, and the heat of the earth had softened. Tall purple flowers by the roadside; a warm, sun-baked scent, my feet picking among the ruts as if they knew the pattern . . . ruts, those deep ones in the Gers, in my sabots.

No sabots now, but dusty leather-soled boots made for walking on cobbles. And we were alone on a precarious road. *Our* road. I saw the wizened old farmer from whom Stephan and I had gotten our milk. He stared—his eyes falling, briefly, to the infant in my arms—as though we were two ghosts. The sky had gone from purple to gray, and the moon was a pale, full circle against the horizon. And then, the gates of La Vrillette, the drive; the crunch of gravel underfoot. There it was, just as I had dreamed and remembered.

In the half-twilight, the long rectangle of the mirror pool was overgrown with a carpet of lily pads, their long stems invisibly trailing under water like tangled hair. Black-winged insects darted and skated over the waxy tops; dragonflies and wasps circled. The front gardens had gone to seed. The grasses looked as though they had not been cut back for a year; the drive was choked. La Vrillette looked as if it had not been inhabited since the day I left.

Winter, spring, summer, and nearly another fall; rain had beat down, the sun had shone, and the turrets still stood out in the soft dusk, lavender on slate. But the house had closed its eyes; its shutters were fastened; the front entrance padlocked with a chain. I lifted it and let it drop, with a heavy clank. Berthe was quiet; I shifted her to my other hip.

In the back gardens, the roses were still in bloom; a frowsy, gnawed-petal bloom. Only one bush appeared untouched: a miniature rosebush with partially opened flowers and tiny pink buds, clenched tight like Berthe's little fists. As I moved closer, I could see that some of the petals were brown-edged, perhaps from the heat—but no. Each tiny rose, perfect from a distance, had a black, writhing center. Burrowed deeply in each flower was a black, shiny-winged, red-spotted beetle, a living toothed thing, head buried in the center of the flower, legs pushing inward, sucking at that rose-sweetness, working at every wilting bloom, destroying it from the heart.

The stone benches that framed the pool were covered with stiff lichen; rough to the touch, pale green against gray stone. I remembered wondering how this scabrous covering, like a disease of the stone, appeared so lifeless, yet was living still. Taking its nourishment, somehow, from sun and wind and stone. Berthe's tiny hand reached up for me. Her tiny bow lips found their site, and sucked.

My thoughts drifted; the sun fell.

. . . Stirring our soup on the little coal stove in the hall on the rue Serpente, next to the stairs, with the stink of the latrine close by. Staring at the soot-blackened walls, waiting my turn to cook, while our neighbors, Madame Boudet, or the old monsieur to whom Jolie brought tobacco — boiled their cabbage or fried their onions in oil. And then, further back — that other part of my life, the part I held back — that stain, that beetle-gnawed blight on my soul.

. . . Ebony cane, silk waistcoat. The one who said *"Relieve me of myself, mademoiselle,"* before plunging. The ones who laughed, pulled me close, reached around my shoulders for a glass of champagne. And: playing to their moods; laughing at what I did not find amusing; keeping things moving until coin rang on marble, and the rubber bulb swooshed, everything trickling back down my thigh.

It was the same with him, a voice said. Her taunting contempt.

No — !

Where is your Stephan, then? Not in this bolted, abandoned place in which you find yourself, and a baby, and no one else?

Darkness fell, and Berthe's mouth slipped. How she could give herself up to oblivion in my arms. I dipped a cloth in the pool, wrung it, and in the soft light, wiped her face, the muddy smudges of travel clinging to her. Her legs had filled out; her chest, when it moved, was a shade less fragile; her skin, touched with moonlight, was whiter, more opaque; the blue veins, which had been faint as though painted by a tiny brush, had receded behind milk-fed flesh. The umbilicus had begun, already, to heal. So small and perfect she was. Baptized now by the waters of La Vrillette and caught in a web of the past; her small life charged, already, with her mother's burden. If she were a rose, the dark beetle already hummed and circled; it lit and waited, pulsing, hungry, for her center to open. I walked again through the detritus, through the tangled gardens. Berthe in my arms, as the moon rose high and bright.

. . . Better, then, if they were going to live so briefly, to weave their images into a shawl, paint them on canvas, carve their shapes into crystal. Inanimate, impregnable, frozen. Safe. *Sain et sauf.* Let's have a picture and prefer not what breathes and dies. I slipped from the bench, made a blanket with my cloak, and took Berthe from her basket. And we slept that night under moonlight, my body cupped around hers. Peltless animals. Naked and shivering.

I dreamed I was on a sea journey. The waves were black and choppy; clouds massed in the sky. I stood at the side of the ship, my hands clenched around the iron rail. A woman, one of the passengers, had fallen ill. She had slipped past consciousness and had to be taken off the ship. Two seamen eased a small wooden rescue boat from the deck, on thick ropes; dropped it, dangling, toward the rocking waves, down to the water. I and another were to take her. We descended by a rope, into the boat, and the sleeping woman was lowered last.

The little boat's planking was old, honey-colored wood. Deep grooves, tobacco-brown, worn between the boards. The sick woman lay in the center of the boat, stretched along its spine, her face to the sky. My companion was in the prow, oars dipping, down and up again. My own oars were light in my hands — too light, as if pushing back the waters with a feather. I didn't want them to cut the ropes to the big ship — but they must, they must cut them; the ropes were already frayed.

"I am not strong enough!" I called up to the sailors.

"Let go!" the other rower shouted, her voice nearly lost on the wind. Gold-red hair blowing over her shoulders.

"Let go! Let go!" They were all shouting now, coiling the ropes back up onto the deck.

The wind whipped through my hair, blew my shawl, which was nothing against the cold — I pulled, pulled with all my strength, and the little boat moved into the waves.

I woke to the sun, with Berthe's blanket wet with dew.

The morning light shone on two things. A stone garden statue of a woman: sinuous, rounded, nestled in a patch of weeds, riding a feline beast, like nothing to be seen in Paris. And it had not been there before, when Stephan and I had stayed at the chateau. The second was the face of a pale, obedient girl: the one who had laid our fires, brought our provisions. Léonie carried a basket over her arm and looked astonished.

"Mademoiselle—madame?" Berthe stirred in my arms, then screwed up her face to wail. Our former serving girl, arms folded, looked from me to my daughter.

"What is this statue?" I asked, as though Léonie had just brought the eggs, laid the fire.

"It was a present for the birth of his nephew. For the child of Madame Sophie, from Monsieur Stephan. My father put it in the roses."

"This garden is crawling with beetles."

"Yes, they came thickly this year. Is she—is she yours, madame? She is beautiful, just like a rose."

"Where is Monsieur Stephan, Léonie, do you know?"

She looked up from under her lashes, her eyes flicked over me, frankly assessing. She backed away. "Why have you come here, madame?"

The third thing I saw that morning was a memory of green eyes and tangled red-gold hair; a pair of efficient hands, tying coins into a knotted handkerchief; spiriting the indigo dress out of a creaking armoire; defeating Françoise. Hands that had soothed my aching flesh; fingers that had knitted in anticipation of an infant, lips that had not betrayed their word. Jolie had held me when I cried, found a midwife, thrown a party, paid off the Brigade (I suspected) so I could stay with her on the rue Serpente, and jumped out of a window so Berthe could be born outside the walls of Saint-Lazare.

The road home was not easy. But it was our road. Mine, and Berthe's.

∽ 14 ∾

Tour d'Abandon

Back in Paris, the rue Hautefeuille was a bustle of evening, of women carrying loaves and packages, men with newspapers rolled under their arms. Hooves clopped on the cobbles, and the screeches of the oysterman mingled with cries of newsboys. A close damp saturated the air, a portent of evening rain. At the florist's, tall stalks of red and purple flowers stood in buckets next to long-stemmed roses—red, pink, yellow—and small pots of tender-leafed ivy. Next door in the butcher's window, plump, white chickens for roasting and stewing, nestled on beds of green. My reflection before them was swaybacked and pale, a wavering liquid in the glass; the bodice of my dress dark-stained from too many hours away from Berthe. My blood was weak and needed meat; I dug to the bottom of my purse and left the shop quickly with the bloody, soft parcel—cuttings of tripe and brains, the cheapest of the lot. Leaned against a street lamp. *Nausea.*

The first of the raindrops pelted against my packages, and pinkish liquid seeped through the parcel, mingling with the milk stains on my dress. Carriages passed; their wheels dipped into the ruts between the cobbles, spewing up muddy water. The kiosk on the corner of the rue Serpente had pulled its shutters but still allowed purchase of a copy of *Le Boulevard* for small change. Mathilde's flutey voice carried all the way to the first landing, Berthe wailing in her arms. Mathilde was waving a sheet of paper, the birth certificate from the *mairie*. Our household was full up with fresh certifications; I'd gotten my own when I re-registered at the Préfecture. It wasn't hard, once I located the right line and followed the girl in front of me, asking no questions. I was paid up, thanks to Vollard; and the Dab on duty at the Préfecture confirmed that I had recently given birth (so my lapse in adhering to the schedule for the *visite sanitaire* was accounted for). They required only a birth certificate for Berthe, for which Mathilde, as the midwife in attendance, could file. I was now, after a few weeks, within the law and in possession of the *carte*, which was how I was able to keep my key in the latch and tripe on the table at Jolie's flat. It was remarkable what I could do—for Berthe.

"Mathilde, let me get up these stairs and I'll take her—"

"The young woman may be *père inconnu*, but she's legal tender; that's a cause for celebration," called a second voice from within. Odette sat on the divan, draped in a paisley cashmere shawl and pouring absinthe from a flask, her lovely oval face cool and smooth as alabaster. She took her drink almost neat, adding only enough water to make the green stuff drinkable. Odette's luck, as Jolie said, always turned like a sunflower, and she'd escaped unscathed from the incident at the rue Jacob.

"You needn't stay laced for us," I said. "Relax and enjoy your poison." But she was used to it now, she said. Liked her wormwood bitter.

"She's not *père inconnu*," said Mathilde.

I had taken the certificate and folded it, not without a glance at the facts and dates. "Mathilde!" I said. My hands shook as I took Berthe from her arms. I'd always have a vinegar bath, after my working evenings, but tonight it would have to wait. Damn these gossiping midwives.

"Nothing suits her today. Usually she's such a quiet one, isn't she?" said Mathilde.

Odette handed me a glass and was staring at me with something like concern. A weak, murky fatigue shadowed me, and the nausea. So much so that I had even wondered if I was sick or (worse) pregnant again, and douched out with Jeannel's. On better days the fear ebbed back; on bad ones it seemed to represent something else, deeper, formless, shadowy, as though I was standing behind my own body, pushing it into the abyss.

"What's this about the father's name?" said Odette.

"It's right on the line, on the birth certificate—de—*what?*"

. . . Pursued by my relentless roiling guts, keeping the roof over our heads, cosseting the neighbors, and appeasing the Brigade boys who patrolled the block. Mathilde came in the evening to look after Berthe, until I returned at the Regulation-dictated eleven o'clock. It was true, the night before in a mood of defiant rage, I seized a sputtering pen, filled its unreliable gutta-percha reservoir with ink—really, I needed to go back to the dip pen and inkwell, or just a goose quill, which had been good enough in the Gers. I had inscribed my own name, *Eugénie Louise Rigault.* And wrote his name on the line for the father: *Stephan de Chaveignes.* Bold as you please, managing to stave off a blot, and thrust it toward Mathilde to file.

"Well, a toast to your daughter, a citizen of Paris," said Odette smoothly. We clinked glasses. I didn't like to drink much before I nursed, but the bitter trickle of emerald offered a dose of respite. The little flat was a fortress of domesticity—mended furniture tied together with silk scarves, mismatched cutlery, and jars as wineglasses. Clio an orange coil on the divan.

I glanced down at the bloody package. "If I'd known you were coming, I'd have gotten something better."

"We can order in from that little brasserie around the corner. What's it called? Chevet's. Mathilde, will you go and fetch it? And join us as well; you look like you could use something. Roast chicken and salad and a bit of cheese. And coconut meringue. We can't do without that. Here, give me a pen, I'll write it down."

When Mathilde was out the door, Odette said, "What are you doing to yourself, child? Planning an early grave?"

I tipped back my glass. "I'm all right. It was nice of you to come."

"Well, that night I saw how things were."

"Yes." I remembered our conversation.

"Eugénie, did you really—name the father? You wrote it on the birth certificate?"

"I did."

"The Code Civil prohibits it; it's *recherche de la paternité.*"

"It's the truth. What can they do about it?" I muttered.

"Whatever they please, I suppose. But you should be more careful. Your situation is precarious enough." Odette sighed and kicked off her shoes, resettled herself on the divan.

I changed the subject. "We were interrupted, weren't we? The other night when you'd started to tell me about how you met Jolie."

"Yes, on the rue des Vertus—I first saw her at a little café, the only decent place down there. Holding court."

"Yes, she took me to that place."

"You know, I'd had my old man, who took care of me after my parents died. For six years—from when I'd just turned thirteen—life was perfect. Oh, he's not the beast that you think, that people think—he didn't touch me until I was sixteen, and I loved him by then . . . No one ever knew why that filly reared up and threw him. He was a cautious rider." Odette took a tiny sip and continued.

"I was very young, and took up with a friend of his, much younger—handsome—a beautiful man, a wonderful lover. Four months of bliss, then catastrophe. He was the one who broke my heart. The father of Beatrice—if she'd lived."

"Ah."

"One day he just—disappeared. Didn't come when we were supposed to meet, never turned up again."

"Just like that? But why—" Futile question, my own question. All the same, it was my constant companion and slipped into the room like a restless child. *Why, why, why?*

Odette sighed. "Oh, they get in over their head. Think they can afford to keep a mistress like the rich ones do, or their fathers did. He'd known my old man, gone to the races with him—he was there on the day of the accident and I ran into his arms, a sobbing girl. He promised to take care of me, but he couldn't afford where I was living then and put me up in a rat hole on Vertus. I didn't care; I was grateful and fell in love with him immediately. Not like my old man — but in that mad, jealous way, always worried he would go off with someone else. He did care for me, I think — but he outpaced himself. He'd inherited some money and didn't prefer to spend his time making more of it . . . But then, when he left — I was hard up. I saw how the women were living, but I wasn't like them. I'd loved these men — I wasn't selling my body, wouldn't dream of it. But in the eyes of society it was the same. I was ruined goods. Of course."

Odette tipped back her glass, rearranged her skirts. In my arms Berthe had quieted enough to let me listen, and I unlaced my stays to try her at my breast.

"So, what did you do?"

"You mean, after I visited La Cacheuse and sent Beatrice back to the angels? I looked up my lover's friends, met up with them if they'd speak to me. Most of them didn't. When I could, I went to the old places — Vachette, Café Anglais — but Paris was a fishbowl. I kept seeing people who'd known my old man or my lover, and Vertus was a terrible place, filthy, and I couldn't bear it, except for Jolie. She came and went, but she always circled back to see how I was doing. Her brother, Henri, was still around then, and he took care of some things for us even though he was barely more than a boy himself. He and his band kept us out of the hands of the worst of the brutes lurking around there — I'll always be grateful to him for that. Then one night on the rue de la Grande Truanderie — I was eating *tripes à la mode de Caen* with probably the last upright citizen in Paris who'd be seen with me. He'd known my old man and I suppose he thought I needed comforting. After dinner he introduced me to the captain of a sailing ship, *The Pharamond* — named after the first king of France, and his favorite dining spot when he was in town. I liked him well enough; he seemed kind and knew the ways of the world. We kept drinking Calvados and it was the best night I'd had in a while. He told stories and I saw that nothing could shake him; he made his own rules for how to live. He asked me to sail with him, and my old man's friend as much as told me to go, get out of Paris, and have an adventure. The first place we sailed to was Barbados, on a sugar run. That opened my eyes, I can tell you.

"But enough storytelling. I just stopped by to see how you were. And now I do see." I shifted Berthe on my arm — she was already heavier, growing, moving in new ways. Tonight she was not sucking well, though. Her tiny lips fell off my breast as though she couldn't remember what it was, as she had done when she was first born.

"Listen, Eugénie — you're no good at this end of the game. You need someone to take care of you." Odette shook her head. "You're naming *de-whatever,* but going out fast and cheap; doing this blind and dressed like a servant — it's a death sentence. You're either above or below yourself, I can't tell which."

I had no answer to this, because she was right.

"And you must stop walking around as though you deserve to be whipped, like you've done something wrong."

"If I hadn't, surely things would not have turned out this way!"

Odette tossed her head. "You didn't organize the world or the Préfecture of Paris. Why, I'm sure if it had been up to you, you'd have done things quite differently, and so would I."

Mathilde came back up the stairs with the bag from Chevet's. On squares of brown paper we served roast chicken, steaming and delicious, with crackling, fragrant skin. Odette cut the wedge of Camembert and said, "Mathilde, how do we find Eugénie an *abéqueuse?* An honest one, I mean — not up to the usual tricks."

Mathilde said she could find some names, but when she announced what it would cost, even Odette looked startled.

"So many of them nurse for the rich women," said Mathilde. "Or the hospice." She glanced at me. A brief silence fell.

Then I said that I couldn't imagine entrusting Berthe to a wet nurse . . . My milk was all I had; I needed to give her that much.

But the next day Berthe wailed inconsolably, making a wild sound that would challenge anyone's reason, and she hardly took any nourishment. Her little head was hot and seemed only to get hotter, even with cool cloths applied to it. When she at last cried herself to sleep, I slipped out to the baker's; but by that time no day-old bread was left. He took a few sous off today's loaf, but with a tired look that told me not to ask again soon.

———•••———

So, it was a typical evening; neither a dull nor a busy night on the streets. Or perhaps not so typical. I'd been feverish and thin-skinned by noon; a bit of chicken liver turned my stomach; wine tasted bitter, water too thick. Mathilde was late. By the time I went out my breasts ached; Berthe had slept through another feeding time and now I was afraid she was sleeping too much. Mathilde had put her hand on my daughter's tiny furrowed brow and pursed her lips.

The man who stopped was large, not tall but solidly built, with a heavy beard. A suit neither good nor bad; he was self-contained, the kind who paid his way. Soon after I saw him I felt the pressure of his hand, his big fingers, with knobbed, swollen knuckles. Twitched my hands away; I didn't like to touch, to see too much.

Hôtel Picot, I told him. "La Ratière," Jolie called the place; a *hôtel de passe* that let by the hour. The lobby was a pretense of respectable decoration, with a tatty carpet, skeleton chandeliers, chipped-paint filigrees; beyond it was a stair with a grim, sarcophagic smell; the odor of pickled, rotting things. The rooms were passably clean. No one asked questions.

An iron band pressed around my head, that familiar need to ward off—when he reached for me again, I pulled back as though my hand had entered a hive of bees. He stood, looming and uncertain, but I was no help to him. Through his trousers I sensed a quick swelling, heard the hard intake of breath.

I said, "Get me a *paff* if you don't mind. If you go down, the barman will get it." When he left I met my own eyes in the glass, steadied myself against my own gaze. That much I'd learned to do.

His thumb hooked around two glasses and the neck of a bottle, and he knew his purpose well enough. I drank down the brandy, but it just churned in my guts. I lay down with my head turned and my skirt pulled up—this is why I did it on the cheap, so as not to be involved—my bodice buttoned to the neck. But this one grunted and jerked his thumb up to demand that I undo it—as he wanted the top of me as well as the bottom. When I hesitated, he moved quickly despite his bulk, swung me round and nimbly fingered my buttons, my front-lacing stays. I barely had time to gasp before he was on his knees, burying his face. My breasts were pendulous and aching with milk, their areolas a dark, mottled red, and wet with the thin fluid that escaped. A soft low growl rose from somewhere within him as he sucked them, then ground his face into the softness of my belly. I fought down bile, fury, wild despair. *Berthe, they belong to Berthe* . . . Then I glanced down at the top of his head, his pale scalp where the hair parted.

I'd sensed the thing even before I saw it: a hard chancre, coin-shaped, swollen and angrily red on his scalp. I reached for my bag and pulled out a sheath, one of those tough, abhorred little membranes that the tobacconists stocked and the men hated.

"It's too late for that," he said, breathing hard.

"I am a mother, monsieur — please."

He felt my resistance, flared to it like a match to a gas jet. Without answering he pushed me back and turned me over, pulled up my hips; I pressed my fists against my eyes and braced myself to take the heat.

A sharp crack. What?

I am a mother . . . What?

And then, I was *not there* — not on the bed, not anywhere. The mattress eddied out from under me, and I had a brief sense of vertigo, of falling.

Sometime later, I don't know how long, I was watching the scene as if from a corner of the room or the top of a long flight of stairs. Like the slow, round eye of the photographer's camera, I took in the tangle of sheets, a glass still standing, half-filled with amber, another tipped over. Crumpled dress in a pool on the floor; the corset's dangling strings; trousers in a heap. The last imprint on the air was our voices, shimmering, palpable . . . *It's too late for that . . . No!* And then a liquid quiet, like a plunge below the water's surface.

The woman, then, face-down. Dark hair scattered on the pillow, a limp hand, fingers curled. Flailing over it, his shirttails, blue-white in the dimness. The consciousness that was myself, but not that body, saw it: detached, curious . . . When had it last been my own, that poor, numb knob of flesh? It moved a little, with the man's frantic jerks, a rag doll hunched under his bulk; or the ribs of a carcass hustled to and fro, the hunter's fist clamped to the back of its neck. A black shape, boot to the ribs—bloom of red blood against the white—

"Don't worry so, my dear." My own voice comforted the body. Or was it another voice, comforting me? "But I am a mother!" I wailed. And to be that was to be a thing of blood and matter and gravity; congealed, stuck to the earth—as though I had flown to the moon and come down, down and down again . . . A silvery cascade shivered through me; images, poetry, strange words as in a dream.

It may have lasted just seconds, a minute. A cry—a piercing child's wail—Berthe's, or my own? Flash of pain, silvery, an ethereal cord to the body below, pulled me back down, back and back and down. Fingernails bit into the flesh of clenched fists, stiff linen scraped my cheek; knees pressed into the ticking. I cried out from within my own throat; the man grunted and stopped. In that moment I moved enough to twist and reach for the bell pull, the bell that would bring the concierge or someone else—because even at La Ratière we had a bell pull. But help did not come quickly, not at Picot's.

. . . Catch of a buckle; snap of suspenders. Chink of coin on marble. A shadow standing over, briefly, hesitating maybe, because her body had stopped moving again, didn't come to, and he didn't really know what to do about it, did he? Finally, the door pulled to; his boots echoed down the hall. I rolled to my side without breathing and tried to slide my feet back on the floor. Sharp pain stabbed under my ribs; I coughed and felt a terrible pain somewhere beneath my armpits, and the taste of metal. I spat blood onto the coverlet and, shaking, lay back down. Blood from my tongue, where I'd bitten it, not from my throat. That was good. Sometime later the knock came.

"Problem?" said the concierge.

"Just help me stand." Knees shaking. Salt of tears. Tang of iron on the tongue. Love congealed to matter, brought life from the heavens to earth; love, here, was abandoned and betrayed. Berthe was too little, love was merely nourishment, is that all it ever was?

My thoughts were confused and the concierge was waiting, and not for me to stand on my own. I shoved my chin toward the coins. He collected his tariff. I made my way down. Numbness set in, to help.

On the street, the wind had picked up. The damp, rain-scented breeze turned chilly, reaching from my heart to my knees to the marrow center, to the last part of me that held any warmth. Something rose, licked at my guts. *The way his eyes went to my milk-heavy breasts. The filth of him, the disease, the ooze inside me still, and the shadows of all the rest of them. The filth of him — of all of them — sick on everything inside me.* Only a narrow rectangle's width in front of me, a small square, blackness pulling at every edge. I walked that narrow width, black-bordered, like mourning.

It was late when I reached the rue Serpente, took Berthe, and put off Mathilde's questions; she gave me a reproachful look and hurried off. Berthe's brow wrinkled in a wail; her cries pierced the air and undid what was left of me. I did my best to cool her head; bathe her hot little body, the anesthetic of urgency deadening me enough to get her wrapped in her blanket. I stumbled against the table, still strewn with the detritus of last night's feast. Newspapers. Bills in dirty envelopes, no sooner emptied than re-sent again. Underneath, a letter to Stephan — begun, not finished; the pen had leaked and ink dripped blackly down the page. My breath came shallow and fast and the pain pulsed fiercely. Scrabbling through the pile I found a blessed thing — Odette's flask; silver and oval shaped — and half-full of the green stuff. I longed to be like Odette, with her lovers and adventures. I tipped it back, its taste raw and bitter and unsugared, but I nearly retched. *Your situation is precarious enough!*

From the hall came the rattle of the stove, probably the movements of our neighbor, old Madame Boudet. I managed to open the door a crack, to let in some warmth from her fire. Looked over at Berthe in her crate and my numb heart flooded. I could hardly bend to rest my hand on her eggshell-thin skull. Its soft spot on top, barely covered with membrane, the blue veins pulsing, beating with the blood I'd given her. She stirred and made sucking movements with her tiny rosebud lips; flailed her little hand in the direction of my breasts. Her cheeks flared, rosy. She didn't understand how she felt, the little scrap of a thing.

"You'll feel better tomorrow," I whispered, then eased back on my heels. I felt feverish myself, weak, nearly out of my body still, with shuddering flashes of the man at La Ratière. I felt my own forehead, damp with sweat. If I had been infected—by this one, by some other—I would poison the very air my daughter breathed, the milk she sucked. Pass disease to her as surely as I gave her the blood of my veins, the milk of my breasts. And if I had a broken rib, it would be impossible to lift her.

I let my heavy head fall onto the table, roll over on one arm. *Le Boulevard* on another page showed pen-and-ink figures of a man and woman standing before a dark, square opening in the wall. Her hair bound in a scarf, like a working girl's; he looked sorrowfully on. The cutaway showed the arch of a cloister and the peaked cap of a nun receiving their bundled infant through the turnstile; and a row of cribs. Hospice des Enfants Trouvés.

Berthe woke. I took her from the crate and fastened her lips to my breast, but she fell away. Her lips slipped off the nipple and her back arced; she began to wail in earnest; her whole body stiff with heaving sobs, as if she knew what had been there earlier, where I had been; and something in her feverish body resisted . . . the infant's flesh was nearly translucent, white, milky pale as a candle. As I stared down at her, I saw through the skin to the bones behind it; the eye sockets, the nose, the eggshell skull; Berthe's little head; and the green stuff spoke for me . . . *You think your eggs are on the fire when only the shells are left!*

From the hall, Madame Boudet's stale cabbage lingered.

For a bare moment, the ink-blotted letter paper lay across the fire as though capable of resisting flame. But slowly, at its leisure—the coral edges of nearly spent coal sucked at its corners. Line by line, blackened and devoured. The question *Why did you not love me?*—sparkles and fades. Then the paper turns silky, like petticoat layers, like tulle; crumbles like an old dry rose. Disintegrates into fine flakes of pure white ash. One wants to burn more and more, just for sheer satisfaction. One wants to burn—*everything*. From within the anesthetic of absinthe my thoughts began to line up, cold-cut like stones.

Of the two of us, my case did not warrant assistance, but hers did. Berthe had the right to be nursed by those mandated by church and state; clothed; cared for. Once I was rested, better, back from the dead—when Jolie was out—perhaps then. Between the two of us we might find a way. If Jolie didn't go back to Deux Soeurs. I filled the pen again.

This child, I began, on a fresh sheet; then struck it out.

My daughter's name is Berthe Sophia Louise. She is feverish, and she will not take my milk; as I cannot care—I am afraid that I cannot care for her and that she will die. I will come back for her as soon as I am able. She is my only star in a dark sky.

I folded the note in four, made a small parcel: cap, blanket, spoon, bonnet; slipped a small bracelet from my wrist, bone beads and coral, and put that with her too. I unfolded the certificate from the *mairie* and stared at it. *Berthe Sophia Louise Rigault* was listed as having been born on August 28, 1861, Paris, third arrondissement, under the care of Mathilde Sainte-Anne, midwife. My name was on it; and Stephan's. *The truth*. The illegal, Code-defying truth of the matter.

Berthe was wailing again, her small chest heaving with sobs. A sharp pain, stronger than absinthe and delusion, tore at my ribs. Should I strike Stephan's name, blot it out? Let it stand? Keep the certificate, not leave it with Berthe? But that did not seem safe for her, to be without an identity, lost among other lost infants in this vast city. And without the certificate to identify her, how would I ever reclaim her? So I folded the certificate as it was; tucked it into the bundle.

I'd not be able to make it on foot, not as I was. I would have to take a cab.

"*A direct train for Charenton,*" Jolie's voice echoed, somewhere behind my ear. She always said that absinthe took you straight to the asylum for lunatics and brain-rotted drinkers. On the street a gas lamp's watery light shone on a colored image affixed to the side of

the building on the corner of the rue Serpente, a huge playing card,
the ten of hearts. GRAND ESTAMINET 4 BILLIARDS read the advertisement, but now the red hearts seemed to be jumping off the card,
as though on springs; leaping down to the street. Heart after heart,
one leapt and the next came after, as though when one tumbled, the
next naturally followed; they had no independent will, these hearts.
They filled my arms like red flowers, a sheaf of tulips. My dress was
an apron, and I caught them as they fell. Berthe was a sobbing sheaf
of tulips in my arms.

The red flowers had become hearts again, shrunken, wrinkled
little hearts, and now they covered her face like blotches. Not hearts
but chancres like the one on the man at La Ratière, covering her
cheeks, her little hands. Her chest rose and fell too fast, with shallow, heaving heat that rose through the shawl, and I clutched her.
The driver raised his whip; brought it down like the hammer of an
auctioneer. Going. *Gone* . . . Absinthe could do funny things; now it
was doing them to me.

The latched wooden door covered a small opening set into the seam
of the wall; inside was a wooden basin like the kind in which bread
dough rises. No blanket to make it soft, not even straw. I wrapped
Berthe and squeezed her small warm body, nuzzled the soft fold of
her neck where the blanket gaped. She had been crying all day and
all night; now she was quiet. Was it her way of telling me that she
was ready, that others could take better care of her? She stared the
way animals stared — quiet, waiting for a feed bucket. Empty or
full? *They* didn't know. Only the bearer knew what she could, or
could not, provide. I closed my eyes. A final clutch at pity; an In-
tervention, the Divine Hand. But not a tingle, not a whisper; not a
brush from the fingertip of fate. No voice at all, not even a mocking
one; nor a reproach.

It began to rain. Lightly at first, then a steady chilling downpour.
I had spent my last sous; nothing was left for a fare home. Berthe's
blanket dampened; fat drops splashed her hot brow, soaked the brim
of her bonnet. The wormwood wore thin and my chest and ribs began a stabbing beat of pain. I wouldn't be able to carry her far.

Colder in the night air, I pressed against the stone wall. The rain came harder, Berthe stayed quiet, waiting. I began to cry . . . After all, I could come back and get her; I could come back—even Mathilde had said something like that; at least I thought she had.

Berthe just fit inside the small opening, with her blanket and her bonnet, but the rain started to fall in, so I closed the hatch to keep her dry.

In this way I blamed the rain.

Water, water. The night my waters had broken for her . . . and she emerged, drenched and stunning us both; now she was passing through a womb of stone to what waited on the other side. *Dry linens; the arms of nuns.* One of us, tonight, could be dry and warm . . . I grasped the handle, smooth under my fingers. Its mechanism moved easily, worn by many such turns. Then I waited, ear pressed to the small wooden door. Nothing from within, no cry. No creak, nor wheeze of hinges from the opposite side. Alarmed, I turned again, now in the opposite direction. Would she suffocate? And I had forgotten to kiss her goodbye—how had I neglected that? I needed to cover her head with kisses! But the device did not turn that way. I rattled the wooden door, then pounded. Oh, on how many doors had I slammed my fists, before and since, but none like that one. Then I realized with horror that Berthe's crumpled birth certificate from the *mairie* of the arrondissement, the one signed by Mathilde, and with Stephan's name on it, in violation of the law—remained in my hand. A sick feeling gripped my guts. *Please. I have made a mistake!* I pounded again, and sobbed.

The rain fell, as rain does. My arms were empty, the new weightlessness as unbearable as their burden had been. The night guard had been off taking a smoke. He returned. I shoved the paper in his hand. And then I walked.

. . . Zigzagged alongside the spikes of the padlocked Luxembourg, past Saint-Sulpice and over the rue Bonaparte where the models waited; past the École des Beaux-Arts where Pierre had studied; all the way to the quai Malaquais overlooking the Seine, where the stone parapet was cold and damp. The Seine was too low to drown in just there; the current not swift enough, people said. If you wanted to do it, better travel upstream. But they also said you could drown in a teacup, if you wanted to.

How easy it would be to lift my body over, slip down the other side! The water would break with a quiet splash; and it would be cold, the current swift and strong . . . God help me, I had died a hundred nights; I was used to dying; now I just wanted to make it stick.

When I awakened—if you can call it awakening—I was back in the garret, face-down on the floor in a glare of sunlight. My head a rain of a thousand hammers; hands so swollen my fingers would not bend. They laid pale against the stained planking, nails broken and ragged as if they'd scraped on stone. My body throbbed and the damp fabric of my dress was clammy. Something stirred. Clio?

"Mathilde?"

"Are you back among the living?"

I rose as if a string pulled me up, but my chest and ribs wrenched sharply, and I caught my breath fast. The light hurt, as though I was staring into the sun. Jolie was on the chaise, filing her nails. Crutches on the floor. Her eyes shadowed underneath and her long, red-gold hair was scalp stubble, shorn like a fallow field.

"You are wrecked, *chouette*. And where is the young lady of the house? I thought I'd hear her wailing by now."

I laid my head back down.

"Come here, *chouette*. What's this?"

"I was at Picot's—La Ratière. The guy took it out on me. Oh, Jolie. How did you get here?"

"They dropped two charges. Procuring and missing my *visite sanitaire*. I'm left with 'willful destruction of property' and a couple of broken legs, but Nathalie Jouffroy guaranteed to cover the damages to the rue Jacob place. So I'm sprung. House arrest. With a whole doctor's bag of tricks from the Deux Soeurs' Dab too."

"She did that?"

"Seems Nathalie didn't want to let me rot in there. A few m'sieurs have been asking. Or maybe it's too dull for Françoise without me! But I won't go back before I'm mended. So we'll fix you up. Fix us both up." She paused. Empty silence; a void. "Maybe it's for the

best, where you took her? I saw the newspaper picture. And old
Boudet said you'd gone out with her, late."

My fingers curled up then, into fists, hammers pounding. The
hammer's friend was a chisel that struck a crack in my heart, deeper
than any other; splintered it; made it a shattered, split thing.

I must have slept awhile, because it was dark when I came to the
surface again, and the hammer blows had stopped. An infant's thin
cry — but no, it was Clio, meowing from across the room, holding
a vigil next to Berthe's crate. The cat did not come as she usually
did to lick my hand with her rasp tongue, butt her soft ears into
me, climb onto my chest to knead herself a place, each paw sinking
before she settled. Her meow was reproachful, as if she knew everything. A pillow was under my head now, and some cloth bound my
ribs. A bottle of drops of some kind.

"Are you awake, *chouette?* Here, *soupe* from the café. We both
need it." I slithered and slid until I reached the divan and could lean
against it, and Jolie's thin arm, and could feel the hard splint under
her skirt. Her fingertips were light, spidery against my cheek.

Oh, questions — so many, about what would be, how it would be.
My milk-swelled breasts had only just begun to ache, and that was
the very beginning. Soon I could not sleep, only sob for the pain,
until at last we sent the café boy for Mathilde, after he'd brought us
our *soupe,* so she could show me what needed to be done.

BOOK III

GALLANTRY

Gallantry is like war; to win one must employ tactics.

— MOGADOR, *Memoirs*

~ 15 ~

A Dinner Party

JOLIE'S LEGS RESTED on a hassock, her cigarette burning in a saucer. Her head, with its stubble of hair growing back in like summer corn silk, was bent over a maquette in dim light. The slant-legged table was cluttered with paints and brushes, water jars that had been last night's wineglasses, and cartons of labels and sachet packets stenciled in outline, to be filled in with color — their product due on the shelves by Saint Martin's Day. Clio had settled atop an open box like a hen on her nest, ginger fur fluffed out over the edges. Jolie slid the labels out from under the cat and dipped her brush. Someone or other had a brother in Grasse, where they were inventing perfumes for the Paris stores; one of Jolie's friends had set her up as a piecework painter. Our provisions were to be paid down by finished labels at a few sous apiece for a man named Guimper, a task stretching to infinity, or at least until Jolie was on her feet.

"I was a lucky fool, wasn't I? Thought the roof would hold and I'd go down the drainpipe. The next thing I knew I was at Saint-Lazare with a lousy straw bed and a bowl of horse broth. I stared at it till I cried, and they locked me in and wouldn't give me anything better until I'd stopped. Horse soup, the cure for hysteria." Jolie tapped water from her brush so abruptly that she spattered

Clio, who flicked her ears and, stiff-tailed, abandoned her carton for a bathing session at the other end of the flat. I laughed in spite of myself.

Jolie continued. "I was just thinking about that fat Jean-Paul at Jacob, who had just been saying to me — before the door was banged down — that if he ran out of money he just went out and made more, like the soup pot that fills up again. There he was, swilling champagne that I paid for with both legs. Now for all his love notes I don't see *him* darkening the door . . . Idiot. Make me a cigarette?"

Within reach of Jolie's long arm were *Les Malheurs de Sophie* and Perrault's fairy tales, gold stamping faded on its battered spine; but she had put those aside for the newspapers and a book called *La Case de l'Oncle Tom,* a pirated translation of a story about the American slaves, contributed by the schoolteacher Louise. It was the American Civil War that had really taught Jolie to read, squint-eyed, over accounts of the Battle of Bull Run, with Louise. Even I had to admit that Louise was formidable, sashaying around town with a man's certainty. I'd never met a woman like her — unafraid and no one's supplicant, even though she was neither rich nor married. She taught evening classes at a school for working people — not *les inscrits,* of course — but she didn't have qualms about taking Jolie on the side. While they discussed the Army of the Shenandoah, I smoothed the pages of spine-flayed books, visited the water pump and the cesspit, and traded Jolie's finished labels for cash.

"Guimper will reject those heliotropes. That color isn't on the maquette," I said, examining the latest batch. Strung across the flat from the door to the back wall were strings that dangled the delicate advertisements, a line for bergamot, one for lavender, rose, and so forth.

"This is not exactly one of your art salons, *chouette.* No one cares as long as I stay inside the lines."

"Guimper checks them under the magnifier and subtracts for every one that's not right."

"Why don't you take this last batch and tell him we need cash

toward next week. And slip in a question about those *académies*."
In the coloring-in business, the most lucrative work, if you could
find it, was hand-tinting the rosy tones on pictures of female nudes
engaged in various contortions. So far they had eluded us.

"The police are all over those; business has dried up."

"Just in Paris. For the export market they turn a blind eye."

"You've been reading the papers?"

"We need more than perfume to pay for your shopping trips, my
sweet."

I went to the window and stared. Our small household was precariously afloat on cigarettes and brandy; sugary treats and panicky
self-denial; liberal doses of the Dab's laudanum. Ever since my terrible encounter at La Ratière and the fateful moment at the *tour*,
the slightest tremor shook me, and Berthe's absence gnawed at my
insides like insects hollowing out an old log. I felt her presence the
way a soldier misses a lost limb, and blamed myself for severing it.

On the rose divan I delved for sleep; awoke with aching teeth
and fingernails biting into my palms; thoughts racing. Some yearning, still-childish fragment in me sobbed and cried out for — *what?*
Those who knew, who should have known, might have helped,
could have, *should* have. *Should have what?*

Still, Gascon bones knit well, and thanks to Mathilde my milk
had dried and gone. My besieged body was my own again. Jolie's
injuries were slower than mine to heal; the Dab said it would be
dead winter before she went down the stairs, which probably meant
spring. Still, she displayed the same steely will and bleak good humor she always had. Even with two broken legs she was still holding
up the roof . . . But how long could it last, getting by on rags and
bones and packet labels?

On my last trip to Guimper I had stopped and stared in the windows at Hédiard, Paris's gourmet emporium near the Madeleine.
The "colonial display" featured a pyramid of hairy, wrinkled, head-
shaped, and finger-shaped fruits. An advance on two weeks of sachet packets and labels was hot in my pocket and a wicked urge to
cheer up Jolie carried me, trying not to look like a vagabond, inside

the magnificent portals. I whisked past the chocolates, cheeses, cascades of sweets and savories, and all twenty-nine types of French mustard, and I negotiated the purchase of a "banana," which the clerk ceremoniously wrapped in tissue and boxed like a gift. Jolie declared it delicious and, after she had devoured the fruit, sampled its bright yellow skin, which, after all, was too dear to waste. A few hours later she was sick as a dog and declared war on all colonial fruits thereafter.

"If you don't paint according to the maquette, I am coming back with a pineapple."

"Don't be late or you'll miss Odette's chicken."

"Roast fowl and a fresh round of advice?"

"She just wants to be a friend, *chouette*."

"Hédiard has a new chocolate tart," I said, changing the subject.

"Maybe not, I've invited Louise."

"She doesn't approve of tarts?"

"She calls them 'pacifiers for the middle class.' She doesn't mind us."

Doesn't mind *you*, I nearly said, but bit my tongue.

An hour later I came to be watching, rather diffidently, a white-aproned boy too young for chin hair demonstrate to mutton-chopped old gentleman how to delicately remove the pines from a pineapple; golden juice dripping from his knife. To one side, a cartful of bright lettuces, cascades of sticky-fresh *haricots verts*, radishes glowing like damp jewels . . . all this glut, this plenty. Down another aisle, displayed like the empress's tiara, was the *tarte du jour*. Creamy dark chocolate, the bitter kind, topped with halves of fresh walnuts, ripe from the Périgord. Dear as the bottom of a pocket; a tourniquet between misery and my pumping heart. (Around the corner a replica could be had for half the price; but its chocolate would be grainy, its pastry stiff, and the walnuts would be last season's.) My ribs began to twinge, along with my head; the dank sniff of Picot — La Ratière — was a shadow amid the heavenly perfume of coffee and chocolate and washed cheese rinds . . . Holy mother of God, I dreaded being back on the streets. I was dragging my feet, had already missed a health check.

"I'll take one of those, please," I said to the clerk, and watched while he took it from the pastry case and placed it in a fine red-and-white box, tied it up with gold string. It cost all I had, of course; and my heart pounded giddily until I was once again outside, slapped by the cold. So what, Jolie wouldn't care the money'd been spent; she'd grin like a cat.

Back at the rue Serpente, candles flickered and the labels and paints were pushed aside. Roasted beets and onions steamed on the hall stove and the aroma of brasserie chicken heralded the luxury ahead. Clio, from her roost on the label box, eyed Odette's peacock-feather earrings. Odette had acquired a government protector and a gigantic new flat near Notre Dame de Lorette. Louise had turned up with a stack of books and nothing for the table. With her sharp features, plain skirt, and pulled-back hair, she made a marked contrast to Odette, tight-laced, lovely, and perfumed as usual. Jolie reclined, looking with wry amusement from one to the other. Odette was deep in conversation with the schoolteacher, whose bank of knowledge apparently did not include the finer points of how an iron latticework of rules meant to deprive us of our last free breath.

" . . . And, in the recent announcement by the chief of the first division of the Morals Brigade, Paris Préfecture de Police: 'when a woman is virtuous, she does not live in furnished rooms.'"

"Why in the world is that?" asked Louise. "What's wrong with renting a girl a few tables and chairs and a bed to sleep in?"

"According to the Préfecture, the only honest way of obtaining a chair is to marry it. Rented furnishings prove that she is wayward and has abandoned domesticity."

"What I don't understand is why we aren't allowed to share a flat," I said, joining the conversation. "Even if the furniture is bought." Living under the same roof, Jolie and I were at anyone's mercy. If Madame Boudet, on a bad cabbage night, decided we were an immoral influence, she could complain about us.

"Because they think you're setting up in business for yourselves. The boys have to take their cut—the doctors and the police and the tax-revenue people, and so on. Of course, it's not how they put it.

But take it from me, I've heard them talk. In private, they don't even pretend it's not the reason."

Louise mused, "For centuries the whole question has been up for debate, of course—but as I understand it, the teeth of the present system come from the work of Parent-Duchâtelet in the 1830s."

"Yes, a doctor who made a study of sewers and drains and then moved on to describing women along similar lines." Odette shook her head, peacock feathers shimmering. "But I'd rather approach the entire matter as a businessman would. Just look around at the money circulating these days—the ordinary man doesn't know what to do with it. In Paris even the worst of enterprises turns a profit. Not just silver and gold, but tin and lead as well, if you know what I mean. If a woman saves and invests—who, really, should mind if she takes a lover or two? It's an invasion of privacy, if you ask me. When I'm too old I shall retire to the countryside and plant a vegetable patch. I already have my eye on a slice of land just outside the *enceinte*. Darling cottage there already. Or I'll build." She reached for the bottle that Jolie had uncorked and poured wine into four jars.

"It sounds simple enough," said Louise. "There's got to be a catch."

"Sure, there's bound to be a Morals Brigade officer prowling around whom she hasn't paid off," I said. "And a rat on every corner to tip him off." I reached for a thick-lipped glass, sipped blessed relief.

"You'll see. Lucre makes legal—the laws will have to catch up. These fellows up at the Hôtel de Ville cling to the tolerated houses, their silly rules, uniformed officers arresting women to a fare-thee-well. Meanwhile, 'respectable' fashion follows the *cocotte*, because you have men of every class throwing cash at women to whom they are not married," said Odette. "Count the carriages in the Bois, of an afternoon. Love, sex, and money all going around like a carousel, and like as not the women are driving, married or not. Already the gray coats can't keep up with how the styles change—we've got them on the run. It's only a matter of time."

"Odette got lucky early on," remarked Jolie. "She found a ship's captain and sank him."

"Sank himself, just helped me in the meantime," Odette retorted.

Louise said, "Louis Napoleon has bloated Paris with debt and floated it on profits from the *tolérances*. The proceeds from the regulated houses drive up rents past any price a normal market would bear — that's how the speculators are getting rich, on inflated property values, and they are gunning them until they crash."

Irritated, I said, "Meanwhile, until one learns to manipulate rather than to love — the Brigade, the doctors, and the madames make a ransom off our backs?"

"Oh, *love*," said Jolie. "Eugénie, are you still puzzling over that?"

"I'm not puzzled, no."

"If she is, she's not alone," said Odette.

Louise said, "And what about you, Jolie, did you get 'lucky'?"

"*I* am out of service at least until March. And this one here" — Jolie's hand floated in my direction — "never did learn how to ply her *carte* without cracking a rib; now she has a broken heart from the loss of two *amours* — well, I think it is two — and a baby."

"A baby?" said Louise, looking at me. I closed my eyes.

"And where is the 'author of the child,' as the law calls him?"

"Well, where do you think, Louise?" said Jolie.

"Have you considered bringing a case? Of course you cannot claim paternity directly, but you might be able to get a judgment for damages to your person, reputation, your ability to earn an honest living."

"Really?" said Jolie, incredulous.

"The Code Civil was framed to protect legitimate children and family bloodlines. Seduction and abandonment of young women en masse was not the desired result."

"I think it serves their purposes nicely," said Odette. "Plenty of bastards for the army, cheap labor for the factories, girls who are dumb and willing — "

"There have been precedents in law for support," said Louise firmly.

"Even if you're on the Register?" said Jolie. "What judge would believe one of us pointing the finger?"

"What better argument than that a woman's other prospects have been ruined?"

Jolie snorted.

"Certainly, a lawyer would have to prepare a clear case," said Louise.

"Lawyers have to be paid, or so I hear," said Odette drily.

Jolie said, "Shall we dine? Odette, this bird smells like heaven!"

"So, now that you've jumped out a window, are you finally ready to move up in the world, *minouche*?" asked Odette as we drew our chairs around the table to a meal that, at least for Jolie and me, was Balthazar's Feast.

Jolie laughed. "Is that possible?" To Louise, she said, "I'm the only guttersnipe here, picking out my alphabet. These two have gone to school; they can carry on with whom they please. You'll have to take us as we are, Louise."

"You knew enough to get yourself out of Saint-Lazare," said Louise, and I wondered, not for the first time, why she was here and what she wanted from Jolie. What everyone else did, or something else?

"What those nuns taught I could write on a thumbnail," said Odette, pouring again. "I learned everything I know from my old man's library."

Jolie helped herself to salad and a leg. "A band of thieves raised me—I was the little one who took care of them. Iced their lumps and black eyes with what I scraped up from the fishmonger. My first trip inside, I'd been picked up for stealing ice. At the *poissonnière*."

"It's a favorite spot with the gray coats," I said. "Even Odette prefers chicken."

"You should have seen the two of them, Jolie and her brother, Henri. Pierrot and Pierrette of the bandits," said Odette.

"But oh, the girls at Saint-Lazare back then! The packages they got, the flowers—from their madames and lovers. And they acted like being inside was nothing. While I, flea-bitten and half-starved—and I thought myself tough—cried like a baby. And I'd put up with a lot by then. But when I saw *them* cry, it seemed like an adventure—maybe they were crying over a *lover*. Where does a kid get those ideas? I never even bothered to look at the old women, of course. Dead sticks in the corner."

"And what happened?" asked Louise.

"I made friends with a girl who was a bit older. She told me that when I got out, she could get me better work than thieving, and I'd walk on a carpet and wear a pretty dress. I'd never seen one."

"A dress?" said Odette, munching on a thigh.

"A *carpet*."

"When I met Jolie we were both living on Vertus, and she did wear trousers from time to time. To think she signed away her life for a rug!"

"A cheap copy from a Paris factory, in the first dump I worked. And not much in the way of a dress." Jolie chuckled. "But *this* time—this last time at Saint-Lazare, Nathalie Jouffroy found out I was there and sent a box to me—so I was the one passing out sweets. But do you want to know something—out of the corner of my eye, I could see only the older women now. As if I'd opened the closet door and found them, like Bluebeard's wives. But still breathing; that's the curse. When you're young, you can't see where things lead, and why is that?"

"No education is complete without 'Bluebeard,'" remarked Louise wryly.

"What drags us down, in the end," Odette mused, "is taking care of everyone else when we can't scrape up enough for ourselves. How is it that we think we can *be* and *do* and *care* for everyone else without being able to take care of ourselves first? Not in this world." She looked across the table, nodded at me. "You may have loved that baby, Eugénie, but soon you'd have been afraid to keep her near you. The daughters just become what the mothers have been."

A silence fell over the half-picked carcass, the empty jars, which Odette refilled . . . How could I ever have envied Odette? The woman was made of marble.

"And do you think that pretending you are a capitalist changes that?" Louise said finally to Odette, just short of acidic.

"I'm no better than my neighbors, Louise . . . Peel me a beet, *minouche*?"

Jolie wiped chicken grease from her mouth with the back of her hand. Speared a beet, stripped its charred skin off, made ruby slices. She dropped one on the white cloth, staining it. I looked down, felt tears well. *How long could I go on asking her to be strong for us both?*

"Your heart is leaking and if you don't stop it up, you're going to bleed to death, *chouette*. All over the floor," said my friend abruptly.

Louise sawed off the last chunks of meat and offered the plate around.

"Jolie and I have been studying the case of American slavery. I'd be interested to know how much each inscribed girl is worth to the city of Paris."

"I saw sugar slaves in Barbados," said Odette. "Are they worth very much?"

"For the price of a healthy young man you could probably build a chateau on your little plot of land. *That* is what the Confederacy is defending. Its wealth in slaves," said Louise. "I don't believe that Paris will easily give up Regulation. Not until there is something else to put in its place. Or — the women refuse."

"I don't see many refusing," said Jolie. "I've never seen so much competition on the street."

"Set them free and educate them," said Louise. "*Then* you'll see."

"I don't know what army would fight to free us," I said.

"An army of the just," said Louise. A brief silence fell over the onion skins. "Meanwhile, I wonder if you could organize a trade union. Negotiate for some basic rights."

Odette yawned. She stared at the schoolteacher, a flicker in her pale eyes; the same twitch of the lips Berthe used when my father spoke. His Limoges notions, she called them; as if Limoges was as distant as China. Papa would give her a gentle, helpless glance. Jolie looked doubtful. I swallowed; closed my eyes. Metal, the taste of metal always now in my throat.

"Louise always gets to the point," said Jolie, finally. "That's why I asked her to come. Is it time for chocolate?"

With the taste of *poulet rôti* and wine and now the bittersweet chocolate melting in our mouths (even Louise had liked the tart), the mood around the table mellowed. I said, under the rosy tinge of wine, "When I was young I wanted to mean something, to be important to someone, or to do something larger than myself. Once I thought *the point* was to be of use. And to care for those you love."

"*Use* in the sense that you mean it is an eighteenth-century idea. Now the meaning has been corrupted, and it means the strong using the weak for their own gain; it has led to instrumentalism." Louise nodded to Odette. "From your notion follows self-mechanization and the death of the soul. And yours"—she turned to me—"your conception of it foundered on the rocks of a new meaning. Living in the past has put you at the mercy of others."

"That's what we've been trying to tell her," said Jolie.

"I think she just falls in love with the wrong men," said Odette.

"Oh, they're all wrong, Odette."

I persisted. "So, what *is* the answer, Louise?"

"It is a weak society that depends on wars abroad and selling women's bodies at home. A sign of internal rot, like marrow disease." She paused, gestured to Odette. "But I don't mean to moralize. Until society grows stronger and women can earn a decent living, the money you make should be yours. You should be able to have your furnishings and live in your flats any way you'd like." Despite her brave words, Louise looked as though she was still mulling it over.

"Hear, hear," said Jolie.

"Well—getting back to the point of the evening—first we need to figure how to keep any roof at all over these two pretty heads, and Clio in mackerel," Odette said.

I'd drunk a lot of wine. A vinegary feeling coursed in my blood, a stubborn, full-stomach-and-gunpowder sensation. I leaned forward. "No, I want Louise to tell me the point of what she is say-

ing. The point of — of *living*. For *us*. As we are *now*. If it is not just
that we are wretched, meant to be endlessly punished to remedy
a sin — to be held up as an example. If we are just being used for
the profit of others, which is not what they say, that — that is — " I
stopped, confused. "What are our lives *for?*"

"It's not such a mystery," said the teacher, slowly. "Life's purpose is to learn and to grow. To be able to sit at the banquet the
world offers, to eat and drink your fill, you as well as anyone else.
You, Eugénie, and that other one, that so-called empress whose
name you share — are not so different . . . You too have the right to
a defense. Believing it is the first step."

Odette sighed and pulled out a tiny lacquered snuffbox. Jolie's
eyes were shadowed. I stared — perhaps unfairly, because no one
had been more generous than Odette — at her plump caressing
hands as she delicately mounded a pinch of aromatic tobacco between her left thumb and forefinger. She took a long sniff and said,
"Louise, this revolution of yours — because that's what you're talking about? The rights of man, guns in the street, et cetera — I think
that is the 'eighteenth-century idea.' Finally a woman with her wits
about her can live more or less unencumbered, and I mean to do
it. Your ideas led to the guillotine." Odette sniffed again and sat
back. Her peacock earrings dangled, catching Clio's attention as she
sprawled against the faded Perrault. The cat pricked up her ears.
Jolie lit a cigarette. Looking over at her, I felt my heart give a stab.

"I would not actually call living by the *carte* unencumbered," I
muttered.

"The *carte* is an egregious insult. I've said so before . . . Care for
a pinch?"

Louise shook her head. "For the moment, I was talking about
trade unions. And litigation on behalf of fairness." Looking at me,
she said, "Be more generous with yourself. If you are not — who on
this earth will be, for you?"

"What do you mean?" I asked, low-voiced as Louise. The table
was covered with bones and cups and crumbs. "How?"

Odette cast me a sad glance. As though I was naive and rustic; as,
in fact, I was.

Louise said, "That gold you must find for yourself." She rose and plucked a label from the line. Turned it over and scribbled on the back. "Come and talk it over with others who are also asking the same questions, if you'd like. Jolie knows where the school is." She left it, got up for her shawl. "Now, my friends — I am due at a meeting. So it is good night, for now."

We listened to her boots echo down the stairs.

"School indeed," said Odette, raising her glass. "To the Bastille, more like."

"You're going to be short a bergamot," I said, turning over the paper on which Louise had written.

"My legs hurt," said Jolie. "The bones aren't setting right, I can feel it." She closed her eyes; she had gone pale and a sheen of sweat lay over her brow. I went to the window and opened it; the air felt like lead, again. Louise had rattled our chains but left the padlocks without their keys. I found what was left of the laudanum, helped Jolie to the divan. She'd been running through the stuff like wine. "*Chouette*, you're a darling."

Silence settled as the glint of candlelight flickered over empty plates and jars.

"So, to business?" said Odette. She found a pen and tested its nib against her fingertip.

"What do you think about what Louise said," I began, slowly. "About — suing for child support?"

Odette said, "Do you want to know what I think?"

"Do we have a choice?" said Jolie, easing back on the pillows.

"That the ground has been torn out from under you, Eugénie. And you have to build it back up again, stone by stone."

"Like Haussmann and the rue de Rivoli," Jolie said languidly. Her eyes were a little glassy; the laudanum was sinking in.

"The best lawyer in the world isn't going to get you what you don't feel you deserve. You need to face them. All of them, before you ask any lawyer to do the job for you. This painter —"

"I told Odette about those newspaper articles and *An Unknown Girl*. I thought she might know how to get these *michés* to pay up," Jolie said.

"Yes, Mademoiselle Cat's-Got-My-Tongue—why was it Jolie who had to tell me?"

I sighed. "Believe me, they don't think they owe me a thing. *You* know, Odette."

"I want to see those clippings."

I went and rummaged for them, my gray and fraying little stack of newsprint. The past spring's Salon columns from various papers. Odette became absorbed in them, and when she surfaced, said, "So—fill me in. Who was it that paid off what you owed to those villains at Deux Soeurs?"

"Vollard. He's a sort of—he organizes business for Chasseloup. He sold the painting."

"For a fortune," interjected Jolie.

"Hm. So—how did he come to pay your debt to that place?"

"I saw him there. After I left he wanted me to sit for Pierre again, to paint another *Unknown Girl.*"

"Presumably, the second time around she'd be *Known.*"

"That's what I said. But they thought I could still be *Unknown* because—I wasn't in the press, at the parties—"

"So?"

"Pierre got angry and refused. When he found out where I'd been."

"After Vollard had paid up? . . . He had qualms, but Vollard did not?"

"This Chasseloup is a bit of a prig," Jolie said.

"So, Monsieur Vollard is out his sum. There's one point."

"Whatever it is, I'm missing it," said Jolie. Her heavy lids were half-closed and she was stroking Clio's tawny belly.

Odette sat back and tapped her fingers together. "I think that the subject of *An Unknown Girl* has to be launched into society. We can throw a big party. The press will eat it up. Vollard—he might just jump at the chance to get Chasseloup's name in the papers again. What do you think, Jolie?"

"With what kind of lettuce? Who'd stake us?" Jolie, still pale, had rallied but she winced when she moved.

"I have an idea," said Odette. "Nathalie Jouffroy . . . Well, why not? She could front us the money and invite her friends. We'll have to have them lining up like German princes at a caviar bar, anyway, to get you two through the winter with your chocolate tarts."

"Well, she'd know how to work this thing, if anyone would. I've never understood this art business," said Jolie.

"It's a fairy tale people want to believe."

"Leading to cash being thrown in Eugénie's direction?"

"More at a figment of their imagination, but the money is real enough. I've seen stranger things happen in this city. So if you want my opinion, it's worth a try."

"I suppose it's odd that people spend a fortune on a picture at all," said Jolie. "Paint. What is it, really?"

"Chasseloup will never go along with this," I said.

"Oh, you might as well go for the game and try, *chouette*."

"I'll tell you about this Chasseloup," said Odette. "I heard of him, back when I tried modeling. He's been around forever. By the time you came along, not a model in Paris would sit for him; he'd run through them all. He was slow and never paid, never turned up when he was supposed to. Everyone but this Vollard had given up on him. Without you, he'd have been left painting a plate of turnips and then having them for dinner. Now he's got his little corner on fame and fortune, but I've known an artist or two in my time. They all need to chase the press like it's their last hope."

"And if we have this — party, then what?"

"You *do* make me sing for my dinner as well as bring it along, don't you," said Odette, yawning. "You are set up for society. You have gone public; you are *launched*."

"Will I be able to get Berthe back?" I asked, my voice flat.

"Stop making yourself sick on regret, *chouette*. Let me squeeze that bottle," Jolie said, reaching for the laudanum.

Odette said, "I'll tell you one thing. You need to come out of your child's world of '*If I do this, may I do that?*' Wait to be told and I'll tell you what you'll get."

"Or the police will — there's one sure bet," Jolie said, with mock cheer. "Things can always get worse."

Odette said, "What do you think, Jolie? About Jouffroy."

Jolie looked thoughtful. Even now, I didn't know her whole history with Nathalie, how well she knew the woman, and on what terms. "She does love a party, when there's enough in it."

"Is she interested in art?" Odette riffled the stack of clippings.

"Sure, why not?"

"Eugénie will have to propose it," said Odette firmly.

"You mean to her? Jouffroy?" I shuddered, remembering my last encounter, sobbing into a handkerchief with the woman towering over me, an iron fist dressed in flamboyant colors, spinning her yarns about wealthy courtesans and ignorant girls. *She*—so confident and certain, bent on culling and selecting—deciding who would live and who die, for that's what it was—she had never seen Lucette's ashen face in the mirror when she put on her kohl and rouge, or heard Claudine weep after a rough night, or listened to Banage's black jokes. Nathalie Jouffroy was never around to hear the silence that fell when Delphine's name came up. And the morning the Dab took Lucette—she hadn't even been allowed back upstairs. I knew because before I left in my own haste, I found her few belongings stuffed under the pallet—among them, a bent and stained *carte de visite* of an older couple wearing photographer's rentals. An empty envelope addressed to Germinie, which must have been her real name. A ribbon; a rhinestone hairpin. No, Nathalie Jouffroy never went far afield of that bank-vault parlor of hers, the countinghouse where she reigned with Émilie Trois and the chief of police. Jolie railed about the Morals Brigade but I didn't find our own keepers any better. If anything, they were worse. Closed their eyes to what was happening under their noses.

"I won't, I *won't* go back there," I said violently.

Jolie drawled, "Well, she's right—if they meet, it shouldn't be there."

"And you'll have to be dressed," said Odette firmly, turning to me. "I don't mean in what you're wearing."

"We can knock something together," said Jolie. "Go look now, if you'd like."

"No, not your bits and pieces, Jolie. I mean Eugénie must be *dressed*."

Clio made a leap to the tabletop. Reached up her paw and batted Odette's bright feather earring. Odette laughed and gathered Clio onto her lap. "You want to bag a peacock, do you?" She passed me a fresh sheet of paper and a bottle of ink.

"Yes, put the ink pot to good use, for a change," said Jolie, helpfully.

Odette said, "If you play your cards right, you'll be better off than you are now."

"All right," I said slowly, testing the nib. "All right."

Jolie clapped her hands, once. Clio jumped down and stretched, since it was time for the mice to start scratching in the walls.

"But I need a new nib. No scratches or blots." I knew what letters should look like; I'd checked my mother's, often enough. I had a good writing hand. Even the nuns at school said so, though I doubted they would say it now.

16

THE MARCHANDE

Fᴏʀ ᴀ sᴘʀᴇᴀᴅ ᴏꜰ days, then, in the dying November light, while students settled down to their books, artists to their ateliers; as my nearest of kin, leagues distant, hurried to prepare foie gras for market, and Jolie painted perfume labels and read Rousseau, *The Social Contract* propped up on boxes of envelopes, I was remade before the cracked mirror on the rue Serpente.

Odette enrolled the *marchande d'habits,* a kind of traveling wardrobe bank. Madame Récit looked you over with a practiced eye and then lent, at a stiff tariff, what had been culled from Europe's bankruptcies and its best boudoirs, once she ascertained what a girl could pay off, given the requisite ambition and the right clientele. Once she set your price, no shot silk or Indian cashmere would be too expensive; no gilded button, soft kid, ribboned linen, or faked-up Valenciennes lace. From her boxes came giddy clutches of rhinestones, knots of tiny beads; hats ticklish with marabou and ostrich; silks in magenta, sunlight, and silver; crinolines of a fashionable cut and breadth. She had embroidered dance slippers and silk stockings wittily striped or delicately worked, lacy and gossamer-fine. Lorgnettes and opera glasses. Umbrellas with carved handles; tiny confections of evening bags. Everything gone first to the frippery tailor or *rebouiseur,* who brushed up a dulled nap with thistles, pasted over tears, stitched new linings, and ran an inked quill over faded seams. Récit knew the sleight of hand and how her troves could effect marvels of fortune turning. She was a sort of *rebouiseur* herself: making over her clients, women of the better classes whose reputation had undergone wear and tear, those who had entirely fallen off the social ladder and lived now by their appointment books. The balance was made up of those like myself. Aspirants.

Jolie watched and smoked and painted and the rue Serpente garret became a bazaar. Clio dove and hid among the valises and folds of fabric as whalebone tightened around my ribcage. "Enough, enough," I gasped, fearing for my fragile, newly reknit bones; but Madame said that a cracked rib would be the better for it, and her pearl-gray silk floated and settled over the cage of an undergarment like redemption. Next was a ball dress of chiffon and lemon-colored satin; then a high-cut creation in aniline violet that hitched up to show a bit of boot and a good deal of six layered petticoats. As I rotated in front of the mirror, the feeling of silk and other fine stuff felt like blood returning to my veins. Jolie turned a page and licked her brush. "'*Man is born free, but everywhere he is in chains.*'"

"Poor bastard," said Odette. "Got rid of five children at the *tour*, never laced a corset in his life, and he still died a madman . . . The boots need some color; use the embroidered ones. Gloves too pale, black is better with the ivory umbrella. No lace, take it off the collar, and the Comtesse Dash herself could scarcely make any improvements. No jewelry. And the handbag is atrocious. Find another."

"If you have to go to the trouble to carry a handbag, you'd better be sure it's stuffed to the gills. I'd rather a skirt with a dozen pockets, myself," said Jolie.

"Aren't we just talking about one evening?" I ventured, as Madame Récit's fingers twitched and fussed.

"I am growing ambitious; what do you think, madame?" said Odette.

"She's a glory, demure with a touch of the wild, rustic but decorous."

"Or decorated," said Jolie.

"Perfect as a picture!" said Madame, clasping her hands, although I failed to see how violet silk was demure. But the view in the mirror was felicitous, we all had to admit.

"Now, these half-corsets precede the full. You won't ever want to appear unlaced, even in your own boudoir."

"Clio won't mind," said Jolie.

Odette intoned sonorously, as if reading from a *cocotte*'s instruction manual: "To cultivate a clientele, you'll have to start reading the society papers and the financial news. If the money is in rail, go to Legrand. If it's in textiles, to the rue Saint-Marc at midday, to Lyonnais. When it's in art, the rue Drouot. When the Bourse goes up, the *courtes* go up. And when the Comte de Whomever is marrying Mademoiselle de Something-Else, you'll find out where he buys jewelry and luggage. In which case the odds are better than roulette."

"Not by so much," said Jolie.

"You're just lazy, *minouche*."

"No, I don't want the trouble of some old *muffe* falling in love with me."

"Love is your trump in the commerce department, my dear," said Madame Récit. "Now, with you, I could perform miracles." She dove once again into her bags. "Might I tempt you?"

"No, but thank you anyway," said Jolie, as though declining teacakes from a gracious hostess. I suppressed a laugh.

Madame Récit fostered the notion, soft as a whisper, that whatever the difficulty, she alone provided the remedy: the armor against the world's troubles and the ill-deserved feminine plight. Murmurs about Mademoiselle So-and-So's bad luck, or the Baroness-of-That, all over the society columns but no baroness at all and poorer than she looked. She barbed and placated; scolded and persuaded; soothed and remonstrated; dripped like laudanum. Plucked and tacked as though fine dress was a privilege she alone could grant. Only at the very end, after I had signed the promissory note, did she fall into a plaintive tone, that of the old woman past her talent days, and wouldn't we know it ourselves, in time! . . . Ah, well: the very seam of grief, the stitches that held in place the injuries of the past; it was the thread leading to the future, was it not?

When the *marchande* had gone, Jolie said, "If you're not careful, between that old ragpicker and what you let the *michés* walk off with, you'll be the one whose pockets get picked."

"But maybe not pickled," said Odette.

"That's what *you* think."

"Oh, you," said Odette. "Even you wanted off the rue des Vertus when I met you, and what song are you singing now?"

"I'll take my own chances. I have since I was twelve."

"It's easier when you're twelve, *minouche*. After that you have to work."

I groped behind me for a chair. "Can I be unlaced now? I feel dizzy."

"It's just the vertigo of a sharp rise," said Odette.

Later, we were alone and Jolie stared at the pile Récit had left, a taunt of luxury against the pitted floorboards, atop the slant-legged table — a jumble of pilfered mismatches. Jolie, lovely as always in plain French calico, was languid and ominously quiet. Knitting again, with wool from an old shawl I'd found at the Temple market, unraveled and smoothed. I fingered the fabrics, lined up pairs of shoes; exhaled into the stony silence.

"*Now* you think this is a mistake," I said. "There are so many silly girls out there; can I possibly do worse?"

"Silly girls have dumb luck, something *you* haven't stumbled on, if I have to point it out, *chouette*."

"You can't afford to jump out any more windows for me, Jolie."

"Oh, it was nothing, *chouette*." She'd taken a turn for the better over the past two weeks and was almost her jaunty old self again.

I sighed. Picked up the promissory note with my name on it, whose terms and amounts seemed direr than they had earlier. "Odette does well enough for herself," I said.

"Sure. She wants to see the world, she finds a ship to take her there. Or for a certain flat, she locates some *miché* who owns the building. But you don't know what it is you want — do you? And now you're in hock up to your eyebrows." Jolie looked up sharply over her knitting needles.

"What is it?"

"Are you—still waiting for that other one—the child's father?"

Did it matter to her, then? This girl that Louise wanted to teach, and Madame Récit yearned to dress—a girl who had made love to me and made my heart ache and broken her legs on my account, even though she shrugged it off. Jolie's guess was alarming; it rattled me. Stephan had left me high and dry in Paris, and now I felt the rustle of silk (another flag of the country to which he belonged) lying, soft and sinuous, against my skin—was this just another steep and costly betrayal I was engineering for myself?

"No," I said. "I'm not."

"Who is he, anyway, *The Unknown Man*? . . . *Père Inconnu*? Paint me a picture, *chouette*."

But I could not, not for her. I did not know which Stephan to paint—the man I had loved, or the one I hated . . . And besides, I loved her too.

It was nearly eight, and dark with lowering clouds as the cab rattled to the quai des Grands Augustins. The wind picked up toward the Seine and chilly gusts whipped at my skirts—the pearl-gray—as I stepped down, full of dread. I shuttered my qualms—I owed them nothing now, I reminded myself—took shallow breaths into my narrowed lungs as I stared into the black river lapping quietly at its banks. Madame Récit's knotted-silk reticule dangled on its chain from my wrist. Ridiculous. Jolie was right about that.

The *maître d'hôtel* threaded through a honeycomb of corridors, stopping before a panel, which opened with a tiny key.

It was warm and close. Suffocating even, inside the velvet-covered walls of a private dining room. A white-clothed table was set for two; banquettes flanked the walls and a palm frond arced above the furnishings, brushing my cheek as I seated myself. A giant bouquet of thick-petaled flowers exhaled a dense perfume. For all its grandness, yet another lock-and-key room in which to wait for this woman. From the corridor, a murmur of voices, a quick burst of laughter; the rustle of a crinoline. Then Nathalie Jouffroy entered, a blaze of white-blonde hair combed back into a chignon; her cold eyes gray or blue, gray or violet. Her skin was powdered to opalescence; emeralds sparkled on her fingers and at her throat. Naples silk the color of old, soft gold. If you were to sculpt her, it would be in heavy metal. Bronze.

"*Remember you have help from every newspaper in Paris,*" Odette had said. I felt for the little reticule, my pouchful of clippings. My future in my hands, if only I could spin straw into gold. I was far from confident.

Bowls of steamy bouillon appeared, clear and golden, and the panel clicked shut. We stared at each other briefly, in silence.

"Have you been well, madame?" I said finally, in a low voice.

"The Bourse is up. International trade is fine, rail brings in the tourists, which quiets my investors. Marriages seem to be more unsatisfactory than ever and the example for gallantry comes from the highest seat in Paris. As for us, you'd think there was not another tolerated house in the city. We hardly complain."

The bouillon was removed and silver domed plates put in its place; a small fortress covering pungent flesh with a sweet glaze. Under Madame Jouffroy's dome rested pale curves of shrimp; commas against a creamy, saffron-colored sauce.

I swallowed a bit of pheasant that under other circumstances might have been delicious, although it was not as tender as it might have been. Nathalie Jouffroy's speech was slow and imperious; a sharp reminder of the business at hand and by what means it would be conducted. I remembered her tone, its certainty; the shadow of resistance that I felt in response. I wanted to dislike her, but feared her more—we all had at Deux Soeurs, feared and played up to the madames. Except maybe Jolie.

Madame continued. "I appreciate your taking care of our Jolie until she can come back to us. So many of our guests value her." Light glanced off her like moonlight over a lake; its loveliness shielding the eye, the mind, from the ravaged shore behind, and I knew, suddenly, that I was already in her debt; it was more than likely that we owed her for more than laudanum and the doctor.

"Jolie never lacks for admirers," I murmured.

"And you, have you done well for yourself? You do look lovely, the gray becomes you."

A waiter changed the dishes again; now a wrinkled fruit lay in a pool of caramelized sauce. I stared at the plate.

"Thank you, madame. I wrote to you," I began.

She smiled drily. Her face was parchment, finely lined under the powder.

"Because our first meeting was such an . . . unqualified success? . . . Perhaps since then you have gained some control over events?"

"I was quite ignorant, madame." *And you used your advantage over me.*

"Ah. So you fault us for your situation," she said, reading my thoughts.

"No. Only myself."

"Still, you do not appear to be awash in self-pity."

I cut into the fruit; it was a prune stuffed with *foie d'oie*, specialty of my own province, where, far away, a goose's throat had been tickled by a goose-girl or an old woman. I tasted it and swallowed and it seemed to stay as a lump in my throat, like undissolved tears. The past — my own past of fruits untasted, just ferried to market and sold. Now I was tasting them.

"*I* think you are angry," she continued. "It's reasonable that you are looking for a scapegoat. It gives you a bit of color but enmity will not serve you well, my dear. It is a relinquishing of self-control. So you have lost the first round of your battle with life; you must find satisfaction in the rematch. Your *revanche* must be in the marketplace . . . Capital is the great equalizer, and we women can be glad, at least, for that, yes?" Nathalie Jouffroy smiled slightly and fitted a thin cigarette into an ivory holder. A silver pot was set on the table, with teacups, and cakes on a salver. A waiter appeared; lit Nathalie's cigarette and went away. The very walls were a sweating greasy velvet nap. I knew that she had agreed to this meeting for her own entertainment, like Clio's sport with a mouse. Yet her eyes, her smoke, held me captive.

Wordlessly, I opened my tiny reticule, passed my clippings across the table. The letter Odette dictated had outlined the proposal; now I had brought the evidence.

"Ah yes, Monsieur Vollard," she murmured, briefly absorbed. "So the notion is to trade on your — infamous status — one that we shall have to recall to the mind of the press? But if it was so easy, all the little fishes in the sea would swim in champagne."

"Water will do for me, madame."

"As hard as he tries, Monsieur Haussmann cannot seem to bring good water to Paris. So it is champagne or the gutter for us . . . The senior Chasseloup is well known in our circles. I don't know the son."

I leaned in; for a moment, taken by a grudging curiosity about this woman who had bargained with the devil, caught him by the tail; and now, for her, doors opened. Swung shut, when she desired them to — the doors of her parlor countinghouse, behind which she disappeared while the world ferried to her exactly what she wanted. A look passed between us: hers implacable, mine curious, despite myself. I hesitated.

Jouffroy reached up and pulled the bell rope; a waiter appeared so quickly, he must have been stationed outside; and left and returned, with pen and ink pot, a stiff-spined ledger, and a tray of chocolates. The flowers breathed out perfume.

"So you are looking for a backer, and why should I object, after all? I have had a good year; I can afford a few experiments. And you have done me a favor by taking care of my girl. If you succeed it is good for us all. If you do not, I am sure we can find other ways of making use of you."

The panel swung open; I glimpsed a domino-clad woman; a man in a dark, fine-cut suit with snowy linen and a silk cravat, waiting there. Nathalie stood and extended a gloved hand; clasped mine, briefly. Then she turned and passed through the narrow opening; a check fluttered on the salver in her wake.

Of course, I could not imagine all the ways in which this new debt would have to be repaid. But I would learn.

17

CONTRABAND

"**"A**ND WHAT A CURIOUS collection of souls it was, last night at La Palette in the auction-house district, assembled from a mysterious social register to toast Pierre Chasseloup's *An Unknown Girl* and meet her flesh-and-blood counterpart. The young woman in question, Mademoiselle Eugénie R—, lately of the province of d'Artagnan, was forced, due to circumstances, to abjure the glare of publicity during this year's Salon. Gossip would have it that Artist and Model became estranged over the course of creation; the painter finally secreting himself at Croisset to put finishing touches to his canvas. Last night the young belle, dressed in a gown apparently made of spun honey and silver cloth, accepted a bouquet from her painter.'

"There," said Odette. "Sweet, isn't it? Chasseloup would rather have eaten those camellias than hand them over, but Vollard was on hand, with sharp toes on his boots." She reached for the coffeepot from the divan, where she was stretched out in a velvet morning coat. Jolie was curled up asleep on Odette's brass-inlaid sleigh bed.

"Here's another, from the generous and kind-hearted Duport: 'A Pandora's box of infamy opened last night just north of the rue Drouot (appropriately positioned between the art district and the municipal slaughterhouse), an evening of pandering celebration of a medal-winning Salon artist and the much-touted "reunion" of painter and subject. Ill-considered appearances by Paris intelligentsia set against the whirligig antics of imperial hangers-on . . . the sight of the chief of police adjacent to Madame Nathalie Jouffroy of Strasbourg and Biarritz was one much to be regretted. Not present was the painting's actual purchaser — Maillard, of Maillard et Cie, nor, of course, the painting itself. As for the demoiselle's Paris itinerary, it lists such notable stations as the Préfecture de Police, a *tolérance* in the rue du Temple, the maternity hospital for indigents — altogether a history more to be pitied than celebrated (which may explain the absence of the estimable Maillard). Prince Victor's attendance was this morning denied by an aide who insisted that he had been asleep by nine.'

"Now, there's some investigative reporting for you. Do you think Duport put his back into it, or did Chasseloup tell him your story?"

"Not Pierre. He'd rather throw himself under an omnibus."

"Vollard, then? . . . So the scoundrel has written about you; what more do you want?"

"I never set foot in La Maternité," I said shortly. I was dizzy with a champagne headache; last night was a blur of chandelier light, straining violins, faces from opposite worlds shuddering against one another. Jabbering voices amid noisy chaos; my ribs gripped by ferocious baleine as the room whirled. Pierre drunk and not speaking to me; Vollard following us with his eyes. Later, Chasseloup across the room, drinking more and laughing with his smirking coterie. Any notion of rekindling Pierre's affection (it had occurred to me, cravenly) dried up like a puddle in the baking sun; and soon I was only dancing with men I did not know; one with small pinkish eyes, a white piqué vest; another with skin like a baby, who spoke French but said he was an American Indian. Nathalie Jouffroy's parting growl, her approving grimace stretched over her powdered parchment skin as she drew on her gloves.

"Enjoy the champagne, my dear!"

Another man taking me up and away, again. Later, half-delirious, looking for Chasseloup, needing badly to speak to him — why? I couldn't remember now. But he was nowhere and the journalists were settling in for serious pleasures at the zinc. By the end of the evening, Vollard bending seamily over my hand as though flies and dirt clung to my honey gown. Odette had declared the evening a success.

"What now?" I asked. Odette yawned and stretched like a big cat. Jolie appeared, scowling and rubbing her eyes.

"Yes, what now? That champagne was cheap, by the way," she said.

"We wait. Like spiders on a new web."

In fact, Odette won the bet. By evening, a gold-wrapped box arrived via the concierge to Jolie's flat on the rue Serpente. It lay squat and elegant on the burn-scarred table littered with the remnants of paints, crumbs, the morning's papers, and flecks of tobacco. Jolie was painting and didn't lift her head as she said, her voice full of doom, "Did you see the concierge head-to-head with old Madame Boudet, after dropping *that* on us?" She eyed it as though it was a stinking carcass. Since last night, her mood had suddenly reversed. Clio stared out the window, twitching her tail at sparrows.

I slipped my fingers under the folds of foil-backed paper. The box bore a label from a fancy confectioner's shop on the rue de la Paix. *Marrons glacés,* honey-soaked chestnuts. A note, penned in black ink:

My thanks for providing a rare evening in which the Known improved greatly upon the Unknown.

Jolie said, "I suppose we'll eat sweets for supper? Because we don't have a single sou around here."

I picked up a sweet from the box. "Look," I said. "Cash."

The candied chestnuts were individually wrapped, but not in ordinary paper: bank notes had been folded around each of the sticky nuggets. Jolie put down her brush and stared. The notes clung together, and to my fingers as I tried to peel them off.

"Give them to me." Jolie took over, dabbing at each with her painting cloths, then clipped the bills up on the line. *How* much? We counted again. My friend raised her eyes to the notes now fluttering gently, then said softly, "Look at Clio; she's flicking her tail."

"She doesn't like me these days, even when I smell like fish."

"Where did all this loot come from?"

The envelope showed an address on the avenue d'Antin.

"That's where the Confederates are waiting out the war. What is his name?"

"Beausoleil." I stared at the slanting signature.

"Maybe he is a slaveholder!" Jolie stared straight at me for the first time since before Récit had come around, her eyelids heavy. "Eugénie. I think something awful is going to happen."

"Something awful has already happened," I said.

"You can't — this man could be — "

"What? An art lover who likes candied chestnuts and just — "

"Wraps them in hundred-franc notes like a madman? Oh, Eugénie, I just — want to go back to the way it was." I stared at her; Jolie was not herself. I tried to joke her back into her customary insouciance.

"The way it was when? Name one time we should go back to."

"I spoke to Chasseloup last night, you know."

"Don't keep me in suspense."

"Well, I wouldn't say he is remorseful. But he is not without regrets."

"He only came at all because Vollard forced him to — and you think I can crawl on my knees to him now?"

"I don't think you should take this money. Send it back. Then — "

"What?"

"We'll figure something out." I looked at my friend, bony and wide-eyed, her hair in tufts. Last night she'd worn a great plumed hat all evening; the rouge had stood out on her cheeks, her eyes were laudanum-bright, and I knew she'd been worn down, she'd lost ground with this injury.

"I'll tell you what I'm figuring out," I said. "I'm starving, and I'm going out to bring us something hot, and then I am going to sit down and see what we owe to those screeching violinists and Ma-

dame Récit and—God knows who else. Old Boudet and the concierge, for not telling on us all of this time."

"I told you, I *don't want it. Any* of it." Jolie made a funny choking
sound and I realized I'd never seen her cry before, not once, and I
went to where she was sitting and kneeled down. I wanted to put my
arms around her but didn't dare; she'd shake me off.

"Jolie. Is it so bad, Odette's stunt, having this money, what?"

"You don't see that it—it changes everything. It will change.
Everything."

"You're the one who said I was living in a dream world," I said,
more gently.

"Well, now I think it was me. I've been living in it . . . Eugénie?"

"What is it?"

"Nathalie Jouffroy spoke to me last night too. She says she needs
me back."

"Oh. Oh, no." My throat constricted; I swallowed dust.

"I can't believe it, I look like a scarecrow. And I—I don't want
to go. I want to—be here, and paint, and see Louise and read
more—and you, *chouette.*"

Then I did put my arms around her, as if two girls like us could
hold the world together. Just like that.

Jolie was asleep when I returned, later, with hot potatoes and trout
and a bottle. Hanging on a new line next to the dry bank notes were
a whole string of labels that should have been heliotrope but were
painted entirely red.

------•••------

"*Embracevirtue Avertyourcourse from the Abyss Renounce sinful ways
Turn to God?*" the young woman said in a tremulous rush, as though
asking an implausible question. She was about my age, pretty; eyes
fastened somewhere on my breastbone. My knees pressed uncomfortably into the wooden edge of a prie-dieu.

The wide doors to the Hospice des Enfants Assistés had brushed
open silently on oiled hinges. Soot-shadowed floors, vitriol-drip-
ping walls; the smell of soured milk and the air dense with the au-

thority of the church, like a fist closed around the throat. This was
a day—of all days, the first Monday following the revelation of
the unknown girl—on which I was permitted to file a request to
discover Berthe's situation. A wide-eyed, sober-cloaked girl handed
out tracts; a collared chaplain rushed down the corridor, whispering
to a black-coated surgeon. Sisters of Mercy milled in dark skirts,
crucifixes glittering. At the end of that hall, a corridor branched off
into yawning halls like those of an elaborate tomb. The clatter of
sabots echoed; then a line of small children appeared, marching in
file. Two by two, silent and unsmiling; first boys and the girls behind them; the younger holding the hands of the older. They were
a wan bunch dressed in identical blue *cottes,* medallions dangling.
At the end of the line, several paces behind the last pair, trailed a
single little girl, smaller than the rest—too small even for the tiniest
worker's smock, in a gray pinafore. She clomped along on sturdy
little legs, a scowl on her face. A long, exhausted sentence punctu-
ated by one small, fierce dot.

A dozen of us—reclaimants, petitioners, defiants who considered
ourselves worthy of news—perched on the benches at the end of a
polished corridor. One or two visibly pregnant, others with heaps
of piecework sewing; our shawls and cloaks damply shoved under
us. One unabashed girl was reading *The Charterhouse of Parma.* Another did nothing but cry and wipe her eyes on her sleeve, but not
for being moved by literature. From time to time a lay sister, hair
skimmed back under a veil, came forward to call a name, and we all
looked up.

Imagine, I wished I could say, now, to this girl who sat rigid before me under the cross's weight, *a village in the hills, where finches
dart and poppies grow by the side of the road, and the wind blows up in
gusts, and hailstones are the size of moons. The land is as beautiful as
you are; Paris is a distant and charming place!*

I raised my head, refusing to budge until the mutterings were
finished and at the end I was given a flimsy fold of paper:

THE STORY OF JUSTINE.

Justine, innocent and good of heart, falls and is abandoned.

Justine gives herself body and soul to Redemption.

Justine corrects her state, retreating from Paris, returning to her province.

She marries; returns her husband (a profligate) to the Faith.

Justine is duly rewarded with legitimate children.

At the end of this day, with our crumpled Justine tracts in our hands, we filed past the sisters who, black-skirted, hush-footed, never looked up. *Monsieur le directeur* had had a demanding schedule, was too busy to take on the Mothers; and the tears of the Invisibles were left to be mopped by the Virtuous.

"Is this always the way it is?" I asked the girl who'd been reading Stendhal. She shrugged.

"We are done with Justine, at least. The tract handlers will be at La Maternité tomorrow."

"Do they really expect us to leave Paris without knowing about our children?"

"It doesn't apply to me; I was born a block away. But they have to let us sit here; it's the law." She tucked her book under her arm. Cries of infants echoed down the halls as doors to the wards opened and fell shut as we passed. Sisters on hurrying feet. The hospice doors brushed shut behind us.

What I'd learned was no surprise, really. To retrieve a child the hospice required full reimbursement for care; a marriage certificate; assertions of paternity or filiation. I had none of these, but not to appear would have been to relinquish my claim to Berthe; and so I had gone — just to say that I existed. It was a beginning. And I allowed myself some meager congratulation for that.

Voices drifted down to the fifth landing as I made my way up the stairs of the flat on the rue Serpente. I stopped by the hall stove. The door stood ajar, which was not usual. And a small crowd seemed to fill the tiny rooms. Jolie, disheveled and in a kimono, was on her hands and knees next to the bed. Two men in gray coats.

"Clio, come here, sweetheart!"

And another woman, the least welcome face in the world. Pointed chin, slippery dark hair, and lithe, boyish. Heart pounding, I stepped back. *Here it is, again. Police. Françoise* — the submistress from Deux Soeurs, to do Nathalie Jouffroy's dirty work.

"Françoise — help me get Clio, I won't leave her!"

"She'll be fine." The submistress's voice a glissando whine.

"Do a thorough search of the place. Smells foul enough," said one of the officers.

Creak of wood, clatter of an umbrella to the floor, and a tumble of hatboxes.

"Enough contraband here to stock a store."

"These yours, or does another one stay here?"

"Just storing things for a friend," said Jolie.

Guttural laugh. "Stolen goods; it's police property now."

"*Clio!*"

A hubbub from within, a crash and a yelp, maybe from one of the men. I took a step back, felt for the banister. A tiny mouse was a gray streak out the door, Clio an orange blur racing after it, both of them darting into the privy. Mind frozen, my body moved of its own accord, but leaden, as if in a dream. Or as if you are dead and the spirit stamps its foot in frustration — *the body cannot budge, I cannot move it anymore . . . !* But the body did move, through the viscous air. Oh, cowardly body — yes, I ran away, hating myself at every step I took farther from Jolie and the flat . . . Down and down, and down again, away through the courtyard. Past the pasty, rancid face of the concierge as she lolled on her seat.

Much later, when I came slinking back, I couldn't find Clio anywhere; she didn't come when I called. Jolie's pots were knocked askew; water ran in painty rivulets across the slanting floor. The latest wad of packets, painted, dry, neat, and ready for their wrappers. IMPERIAL BATH SACHETS. A few labels still clung to the line; a final box of blanks stood forlorn in the corner. Bottle of laudanum, empty. Armoire pegs bare. My rental clothes gone. *Crinoline, lace camisole. Worked stockings. Beaded purse. Gray shot silk. Lemon chif-*

fon. Brocade gloves . . . Marrons on the floor, coated with grit and
dust.

Uselessly I picked up Jolie's paint pots, her color boxes and
brushes. Stared at them as if I had time to think about it. But the
gray coats would be back; they already suspected what was up. And
Jolie was on her way back to Saint-Lazare, or Deux Soeurs—or
both.

And like the hands of a clock, the finger of blame came back
around. I knew I could not have saved her. And yet, and yet. With
my knees pressed on the prie-dieu at the hospice, under the gaze of
that wood carving of a girl muttering pieties in the bowels of the
place that had swallowed up my daughter—I had wished to forgive and be forgiven; to be washed clean. What was on offer was a
faked-up absolution applied under impossible conditions; a travesty
of what any God would offer, wielded by blunt and grasping hands.
But my desire, my trapped and impotent longing—that, at least,
had been genuine. I would have cried; but I was dry-eyed with urgency now, and had no more time to wait. Left Clio a paint pot of
milk.

. . . Stark light from the gas lamps staring in through the slats in
the shutters of a nowhere-*garni* room on the outskirts of the city,
where the poorest factory girls slept; the kind of place you go to
just to be invisible; that I'd never been able to bear before, not while
Jolie would take me in. Selfish, self-serving wretch that I was . . .
And the dark suffering hole of a dream. The same one, just past the
eyelid of consciousness. They came when most needed; the warp
and weft of what was beloved; as it had been loved. Sometimes,
physical selves tumbled together as they once had; supple and lusty
and strong. I had dreamed of Stephan; of Chasseloup; tonight—of
Jolie. The dreams did not discriminate, or trade in guilt or moraliz-
ing; but were epics of breath and bone; spark and softness imprinted
in a place that could not be erased. Sometimes great baroque plots
occupied my nights: letters, secrets, intrigue; sensuous deceptions,
messengers, and stolen moments. A proscribed love; a great, chival-
rous love; a medieval love. We traveled on canals (Venice?) or ran

away to some battered, ramshackle place. Sometimes there was a rival between us . . . woman or man. Dreams of quarrels; of making up; arguing and parting. Of country banquets, of poetry unfurling.

The dreams were not hope nor expectation; not even desire. Just a part of me, a current, a draft, an infiltration—gust before the storm; then the storm itself. I needed them; they were some comfort, but my dreaming nights dismantled and unfit me for life. Dreams abandoned me to scraps of daylight, left me raw and empty, less fit for the kind of survival that others lived for, or seemed to.

That night I woke past midnight, at an hour when night looms for desperate hours. On a terrible *garni* pallet, shouts behind the thin walls, ferment from the privy in the hall to which I was afraid to venture; and Beausoleil's money crinkling underneath me in the stays I still wore, in bed—I saw a small girl carrying a slop pail, patiently, waiting, walking. *Carrying it forever.*

And that night, I discarded a burden I myself had carried for a very long time—lifetimes, perhaps. *That voice—hers. My mother's, accusing; full of reproach.*

Petite salope!

Tossed it over the parapet, watched it gush and eddy away.

And I said, aloud to Jolie, *I know you are strong. You are strong enough.*

When morning finally broke, it was a cold dawn. I made a list—not the first of my life, nor the last. *Move rooms.* That was item number one.

18

WATERS OF PARIS

Among Americans, apparently, there are those sufficiently impressed that one has managed to climb out of the gutter and onto the curb that it does not matter by what means, or if one's undergarments are splattered in the process. History, although it haunts the empty purse, is forgotten in the glare of daylight on new currency, and the blessing of blindness pursues any gain — though it should not be such a mystery that every flowing tide also has its ebb. Still, natural laws were irrelevant as a bolt of drapery fabric shimmered and was taken down from a shelf on the rue de Rivoli; textures and weight tested with a finger. Carolina's finest — a combed medium staple from the Sea Islands, soon to be among the last in Paris; the rest of it rotting in bales on docks, the result of a blockade of the Confederate ports, said Beausoleil. Zachary-Gabriel Beausoleil.

His father was French, a new-world aristocrat; his mother's line Acadian and Souriquois, exiled from Quebec — as I recalled him saying as I matched my feet to his exquisite steps, dancing at La Palette. He had grown up on a sugar plantation near the Mississippi River, and "in town," in New Orleans. A man of wit and lassitude, of disguises, who inspired confidence, perhaps because he was anx-

ious about nothing—not money, nor love, not even war—though
war was the reason he was here, in Paris.

Our first meeting was at a Rivoli tearoom, looking each other
over a little warily on our silk-striped chairs. I was still at the *garni*
with nothing but the clothes on my back and his money in my stays,
glancing over my shoulder for gray coats and wondering what a
slave owner could want of a girl in a painting; why he would send
her candies wrapped in cash. Beausoleil was a striking man of about
thirty, I guessed: blond; robust but delicate; with rosy skin and a
tawny bearded chin and quizzical blue eyes; a nose that looked like
it had once been broken. It had, he said. When he was a boy. In soft,
Creole-accented French, he explained that he preferred silk to cotton; the rue Royale in New Orleans to the plantation; and if there
must be wars, financing rather than fighting them. He spoke of his
dedication to the Confederacy; to his preference for life over art.
And in bed, men before women. I choked on my tea.

He set down his cup with a measured hand. What, he asked, was
my relation with Chasseloup? Because he guessed that nothing was
as it seemed, that night at La Palette.

I was a poor storyteller and a worse liar, and his frankness inspired my own. I told him that, indeed, the entire evening had been
a reckless stunt; had left me high and dry and ashamed; lost me my
dearest friend and the roof over my head and made a fool of a man
who had once helped me. If not for the sticky bank notes, I told him,
I might be dead now, or worse.

The man listened. It had been a good performance anyway, he
said—a beautiful night. The flowers perfect; the dress divine. My
charade with the camellias gracefully done; even more so as the last
stand of a desperate soul.

"You and I," he said, "are romantics . . . confederates, if you
will." He laughed. Said he thought we might get along. What did I
know about Creole life in Louisiana?

Nothing at all.

"*Perfect,*" he said, linking his arm with mine as we left our teacups behind.

So we fell into step, Beausoleil and I. Arrived at an agreement and it all happened very quickly, like the sudden rise of a gas-filled balloon.

I liked him. Appreciated the directness of our transactions and that his soft lips never sought mine, for I was not in the mood for a lover. Our entire enterprise together was to enact a fiction, not unlike the night at La Palette itself. Beausoleil told me about growing up in the *garçonnière,* the separate quarters built for young men, apart from the main plantation house and looking over the cane fields and slave cabins. How his brothers and cousins, but not he, went out to those cabins at night for the coffee-colored girls; Zachary-Gabriel preferred staying in the *garçonnnière.* Later, he learned his own pleasures and suffered a broken nose as a result. But on the back streets of the French Quarter, with dusky young men, freed black men; and others who didn't live by the stiff etiquette of plantation circles, he knew who he was. Paris was another story. His country was at war; he had serious business to do and preferred discretion among his fellow expatriates. And so my evenings were his, but my bed was my own. I understood how to make his life easier—and he, mine. "Our Louisiana brothers" indeed, as the Confederates were sometimes called in Paris. *Nos frères de Louisiane.* The man was richer than Zeus.

On the rue du Mail, across the Seine and a universe away from the rue Serpente, stood a wagon piled high with mattresses—some plain, others with striped ticking, a few with straw falling out, and the occasional goose down. Bedding was heaved down from the balconies of apartment buildings and bundled out of doors to the upholsterer's men; feathers and straw filled the air. It was spring, the time of year for coming and going, and renewing of beds, and the women who slept in them—lovers, mistresses, and the enterprising. Everything changed for the season up and down this particular block. I arrived with a fresh cache of rented dresses—lighter, summery fabrics now—a stack of creditor's notes, and the retrieved

Clio meowing in a box. Installed as though making camp on the edge of a precipice.

My new abode was a busy hive of lacquer-box flats off a curving, polished stone stairwell in a building of identical suites next to the Hôtel de Bruxelles Meublé at the intersection of the rue Montmartre. Across the street was a café and (for possible convenience) a branch of the Mont de Piété. Clearly it would not do to become attached to possessions, but that was not my present worry; today's weather was springlike again, the air full of arrival.

The stairwell itself greeted the visitor with a wall mural of beaming putti, their festoons of ribbon trailing over a garden of rosette-nippled, plump-thighed nymphs. From the treetops, a bright sun showered light.

My rooms consisted of a *petit salon* for receiving company; a bedchamber overlooking a courtyard; a cupboard alcove and miniature tiled stove to the back, near the servants' stairs, and the privy (shared). The foyer doubled as a dining room. All unfurnished, but the main *salon* was bright with balcony windows overlooking the rue du Mail. The building's upper stories had been fashionably renovated as a roof veranda; its windows caught the sun and offered a home to a humid stand of palms and a struggling persimmon. This, I learned, was the place for the building's tenants (all of whom had certain attributes in common) to gather in the afternoons. This building was a sort of live-in *maison de rendezvous* although this was neither admitted nor discussed by Amélie, Lili, Francisque, or the others who had cultivated the stock market's rise and the ensuing exchange of favors. They all (except Sylvie, who sang in the opera, at least during opera season) traded in monthly allowances; migrations and peregrinations — the races, the carriageways, opera, theater, and balls; spas and watering places. My new neighbors would not for a moment think they had anything in common with *les inscrits* — poor castaways kicked about by life, working the *tolérances* or the streets, or girls who had had the bad luck to fall in love with a turned back. The constraints of Regulation were not for them. If one had enough credit to float on and a string of wealthy protectors, one needn't duck around corners like a thief. It was as simple as that; in other words—not simple at all. Personal histories were held as closely as playing cards up in the glass palace.

The back stairs, once meant for servants but now reserved for private assignations, were carpeted in a plush and silencing crimson. Maids' quarters had been put down in the basement, English-style, and were regulated by a concierge known as La Tigre, who reigned over the tenuous boundary between the streets and privacy and, apparently, more than that. She held or delivered the mail as she pleased and could be prevailed upon (or not) for numerous small helps. Madame Récit was acquainted with La Tigre, and it was she, the *marchande,* who had connected me to this place. Beausoleil paid my way in.

And so. If rain fell, it now spattered against windowpanes secured with a catch while a light fog rolled in over Montmartre. If Hédiard chose to introduce the whole coconut (you could never guess from a meringue that its principal ingredient resembled a human head complete with hair), it could be delivered to the door, although possibly to the distress of one's maid. I hired one almost immediately. Her name was Séverine, and soon I could not imagine how I had ever lived without her.

I wrote to Jolie at Deux Soeurs to let her know that Clio was safe. I did not hear back.

By autumn, my little escritoire (Beausoleil had found it at Tahan, *fournisseur de l'empereur*) was piled with messengers' envelopes, ivory, white, blue; invitations, solicitations—receipts engraved with the names of florists, *parfumeries,* Galopin's Vins Fins et Ordinaires (our old wine shop still had my loyalty); Potin's provisions. Thanks to Beausoleil's generosity and his excellent taste, I now regularly visited shops that I had once passed with my head ducked—those that sold preserved quail eggs, rose water, and long pods of vanilla. *"Don't forget these lovely things,"* sang the clerks, pointing out silk irises, carved ivory perfume boxes filled with ambergris or sandalwood. Gifts at Noël and for New Year's, 1863, included a striped umbrella with an ivory handle, a brass-clasped wallet in Moroccan leather, lace gloves in cream, and a cherry-colored cashmere shawl. The little bells tinkled as we stepped out onto the street, winter's chill brisk on our cheeks as we passed into our carriage.

In six months, Madame Récit was paid (the principal, if not the interest, which was pushed off). Beausoleil insisted that I make the acquaintance of one Mademoiselle Colette (trained at the atelier of the English couturier Worth)—she of round hips, heels tapping across polished parquet, with her cashmeres and silks, buttons and lace. Beausoleil's world, his taste; the people he saw and the warm press of his hand on my elbow—it all offered every possibility to forget. Maybe that is why we loved it so much. Sometimes it shocked me. More often, I simply gave way.

It was a heady, fairy-tale version of Paris. The brilliance of the capital cried out, beckoning as it had for so long—and did still, as the day traffic slowed to the flicker of gaslight, then picked up to the evening pace. It was so cold and glittering, so whirling and bright. The commerce of fine things eased our passage, each of us hurtling forward into the unknown. One would do anything at all to keep it going. And we did—oh, we did.

Beausoleil. We became a fixture among Paris's expatriate society, a situation that Gabriel invented, stage-set, and dressed; it suited him exactly. There was a great flurry of socializing; and musicales—soubrettes at pianos draped with the Confederate flag, theatricals with great, ghoulish puppets of Lincoln, the American president whom the Southerners thought the very source and center of evil. Outside those circles, there were drives and races, theater, the opera, and dinners served à la russe until rings of wine and the remains of parsley sauce, rinds of cheese, and sucked bones littered upholstered-and-tasseled salons, where we stayed until dawn. Dizzy with drink and smoke; lightheaded with the blur of gaslight; senses taut and buzzing. The American Southerners had a way about them that enhanced reputation and fortune in Paris; they were passionate but not eager, refined but sufficient unto themselves; biding time until they could return home to their fields and gardens, their brave soldiers, the slaves they said they loved like family. A number of these dark faces attended the Confederates in Paris, and in France they were, technically, free—at least as free as servants could be. These black-skinned Americans ran Paris errands, wore Paris clothes, and strolled the boulevards as men and women in full possession of their rights as citizens. Certainly, I had slipped into such habits myself, with Beausoleil as my amused teacher. It was easy to acclimate. So terrifying to consider falling back.

In my off hours, card games and gossip with my compatriots on the rue du Mail, up on the veranda with the potted palms. In this way, summer-autumn-winter and spring, again.

Odette settled herself across from me in the open carriage, looking like a tea rose in her rustling taffeta. Her equipage was painted with a rose motif as well. A landau to the side of ours, top folded down for a champagne party, was emblazoned with the garlanded words FORGET ME NOT, the lover's plea. And the mother's.

On that particular morning I had made my trip to the hospice, the sole and significant concession I made to my own past—never missing a visit on the permitted date as though vigilance alone was deserving. What it was possible to learn was whether a child continued to live and receive the state's assistance, or if she did not. Now, having spent time in those corridors, I understood how poor the chances were for her survival—and I dreaded going. However, not knowing was worse. Odette thought me lugubrious.

She tapped her fan and and the carriage started with a jolt.

"So," she said. "The sun rises and falls with Beausoleil, does it? You have tucked yourself into a narrow bed, Eugénie. Rumor has it that you are marrying him." Even Odette did not know the exact nature of the arrangement.

"No, when the war ends Gabriel is to marry his cousin, so the estate is not split."

"I suppose it's just as well; those charming Southern ladies cannot be so open-minded at home as they pretend to be here. But then you need to diversify, my dear. Has anything caught your eye?" I hesitated. My eye did not want to be caught.

"All day now he receives the battle reports from the brigadier generals about how badly the war goes. The least I can do is not scheme behind his back. "

"But you have to think of the future, Eugénie," said Odette, sighing.

"I am thinking of it. I have filed a petition to reclaim Berthe . . . You have to do it within two years."

"You *are* stubborn, aren't you?"

"Lili Duval is studying dental science. She says Berthe should have all her milk teeth now. Four front, her central incisors; four lateral incisors on each side, four first molars, four canines. Four second molars, lowers first." Odette occasionally joined our card table at the rue du Mail, so she knew my neighbor, Lili.

"Charming. Last I heard, she was doing spirit readings at the Psychologic Society for a bunch of monocles. Has she given up the planchette?"

"She has learned that in Mexico City, men don't allow dental surgeons to touch the mouths of their wives, and the women are all in terrible pain with rotting teeth. With a Paris degree all she needs is to put a notice in the papers before she sails." We under the palms and the persimmon had come up with the wording for advertisements: *The Painless Paris Extraction; Gold Fillings for Less than a Wedding Ring; Evening Session for Ladies in Molar Distress.*

"We are still at war in Mexico, you might want to mention to her. And I know for a fact that Lili cannot discuss molar distress in Spanish." The French-supported Hapsburg, Archduke Maximilian, had been crowned Maximilian I of Mexico. Even though neither the Mexicans nor the Americans recognized him as emperor, Lili had already booked her passage.

"She says by this time next year Haussmann will have paved the Mexican Champs-Élysées."

"And an American one in Louisiana? I hope you have been keeping an eye on the papers because your Beausoleil is likely to sink himself, along with his cotton frigates."

"I do read the papers."

"*L'Opinion* and *La Presse,* or *Le Patrie?*" She tapped me on the wrist with her fan. "Do you want a tip? Take your money out of the 'American Bastille,' if you have invested any. France will not go with the Confederacy in the end. Lincoln's Proclamation turned the tide."

"The emperor is still sympathetic. At least, Gabriel believes he is . . . I don't have anything invested, Odette." I sighed.

"Louis Napoleon can't have everything he wants these days. He's in trouble — just look at the results of the parliamentary elections — Orléanist nobles, independent liberals, republicans — he is surrounded by opposition. Even the empress distances herself from this Southern project. No matter how lacking the Yankee Northerners are, no one but the emperor is comfortable with this question of slaves, and goodness only knows why he is."

Beausoleil himself was frankly contemptuous of this question. To hear him speak, the Negroes lived in the midst of their families — were family themselves. Gabriel spoke fondly of the nurse who raised him; the cook, all of the house servants he had grown up with. His letters home included greetings to them all, including the midwife who had pulled him from his mother's womb. He pointed out that the European poor were stuffed into factories and starved off their land; even to open the paper in Paris was to hear of the scourges of the underclasses, the filthy slums, the cholera-infected water. As for the infants abandoned at the hospice — that seemed to him the profoundest insult of all. Not even slave babies suffered that; they were suckled by their mothers, he said. He was sympathetic to my plight with Berthe; he'd even pulled some strings with his influential friends.

Odette raised her small whip; we jolted forward at last. "Reclaiming the child is one thing, raising her is another."

"Gabriel thinks I should take the case to court."

"Fine for him, since he's not planning to marry you."

I ignored the comment. "I need a witness who will testify that I and — Berthe's father — lived together at the time of conception. I have located the house girl who took care of the place where we stayed."

We crawled amid the colorful carriage traffic, past manicured flowerbeds and smooth-pelted, artificially sylvan lawns. The fountains, usually sparkling, were dry. All of the capital's fountains were dry that whole summer long; all of Paris impatient for Haussmann's long-promised waters to flow over the aqueducts and into the taps and fountains.

Odette leaned out and waved as we circled, to say a word to Madame "de V —," cinched in oyster velvet and ostrich, looking too warm for the weather and every bit like the fat-purse cut-purse she was. A water seller moved among the stagnant crowd with his greenish bottles; Odette again snapped out her fan.

"*That* water is right out of the Seine taps." Behind Madame de V was another recognizable vehicle, Giulia Barucci's open-air Italian carriage. Giulia gestured toward the water man and then waved at me. We had met at one of the American parties; she was known for extravagant stunts, such as dropping her dress without warning before European potentates, and was rumored to have been the mistress of the prince of Wales. Giulia was dreamily beautiful, with masses of dark hair. She had a daughter, Giulietta, who lived at a convent in Rome, out of harm's way — at least most of the time.

"So you are going to see her, this maid?"

"I have arranged to meet her."

Odette snorted. "You'd best be careful. In order to claim that your reputation has been damaged, there has to be proof, and that proof has to be that there is a baby and that the man is the father. And that sounds like *recherche de la paternité* to me. And where *is* the man? . . . Eugénie, are you listening?"

"I don't know where he is."

"But this house girl might? Is the family wealthy?"

I put up my hand. "I've already said too much."

"You can put me down as dying of curiosity, then."

I looked off into the distance, at the colorful array of carriages.

"Any news of Jolie?" I said. Even saying her name made my heart ache, caught me in a sticky tangle of emotion.

"Just that she left Deux Soeurs and went to Chevillat."

"Oh! She has left Nathalie, then? I've written to her a few times—but not a word. I've missed her terribly. I wish—"

That it had all gone differently; that I was not possessed by an inchoate guilt—

"Try Chevillat. How is Clio?"

"La Tigre's favorite; she dines on mackerel and herring every night."

"Everyone has moved up in the world, then! You must introduce me to the infamous Giulia. *La Barucci.* Perhaps she will emerge from her dress."

When we finally reached the cascade, we were surprised to see sparkling water pouring over the gray rocks, a verdant mist and a happy crowd milling in the moss-scented air. Every droplet available to the empire must have gone to create this artificial tumble.

19

RECHERCHE DE LA PATERNITÉ

THREE MONTHS LATER, I stood on the Turkish carpet of the office of *monsieur le directeur* of L'Assistance Publique, my ivory-handled umbrella dripping from the rain. First I had been summoned to the hospice director's office, then redirected to L'Assistance Publique, and then the rain had arrived all at once. A set of small bronze-plated shoes stood on the desk, and enshrined on the wall was a portrait of Madame holding an infant in her arms, which, I suppose, elevated her to sainthood. Berthe's second birthday had passed, and in the weeks since, I had been nervous as a cat. If we were reunited soon, she might not remember that we had ever been parted; but this illusion could not be sustained much longer. My appointment had been put off for a week, then another—the reasons, as usual, unexplained, while I waited in the hospice corridor. Then, without warning, I received the summons.

My documents were ready; triplicate copies. Beausoleil's friends and my persistence had nagged my petition from the nether end of a bottomless pile; the *directeur* himself had been blizzarded with supplications: from friends of the comtesse (the hospice's patron and the author of the Justine tract), American doctors, Baptists of good standing, even a famous *chanteuse* for whom—as we learned—*monsieur le directeur* had a particular fondness. I had run a gauntlet to get here, a flurry of favors traded, outright bribes, and had been run ragged between administrative offices. Exceptions could be made—harlots all over Paris had repossessed their children; the convents of France and Europe were full of them. The trick was to become one of that lucky group, and on that road I had traveled far.

My petition, as it now stood, attached a statement of income and attested that I was prepared to reimburse the hospice and the state for Berthe's care. I would guarantee her welfare and fees at an appropriate school if it was deemed "most proper" for her to live in a convent rather than at home with me. My profession was listed as companion, employed by a well-placed New Orleans socialite who had very little idea what she was signing, late one evening, on the piano draped with Confederate colors. At any rate, I *was* a companion. Chaste as a nun, for that matter. Some language had been included about matters of status currently under consideration by the Paris Council, asserting that I had "reformed" and was not practicing my assigned trade. Even that my enrollment on the Register would soon be expunged—a prospect supported by no evidence, though Beausoleil's lawyer had promised to try to pull it off.

The second part of my plan, however, had stalled. I had traveled by rail to Tours, accompanied by Séverine, and found Léonie blinking in the dusty sunlight at the excavation site of the rediscovered tomb of Saint Martin, a meeting we had planned through an exchange of letters. Beausoleil's lawyer had located the girl. (It was marvelous what lawyers could accomplish. My present situation afforded many such revelations of their ease in dealing with life's various affairs; and my surprise was always a source of amusement for Beausoleil.)

I had chosen the site for luck. Stephan and I had met around Saint Martin's Day. But Léonie—now blossomed into a young woman of sixteen—shifted her feet and evaded questions, casting pleading looks from under her lashes. She appeared diffident and furtive, anxious to get back to her post—a different creature from the quiet but self-assured girl she had been at La Vrillette, when she so devotedly laid our fires and set our table. She was presently employed in the home of a railway official in Tours, she said, but declined to disclose anything else. I asked her to walk with me, explained what I needed. Tugged at her memories of La Vrillette — did she remember us there? Did she know where Monsieur Stephan resided at present? On that question, she demurred ... His family? Her gesture seemed to indicate that her former employers were not entirely unknown to her (and I wondered, then, about the existence of the railway official). Finally I pressed a letter upon her and paid her a lordly sum to deliver it. She pocketed the money and promised.

She in her plain dress and apron, averting her eyes — while I reassured her from the height of Mademoiselle Colette's latest copy, in my fine linen skirts and pale gloves. We stood in the shadow of Saint Martin, the saint who had cut his cloak in half and shared it with a beggar. Léonie took the letter and I saw that her small hand was chapped, the nails ragged. Had her hands been so hard-used before? I could not recall. And then I had to hurry for a cab to return to Tours station.

Now, at the august offices of L'Assistance Publique near the Hôtel de Ville, the *directeur* shifted his feet under the desk, folded and unfolded his spectacles. He rustled a folder of papers on the desk. He was not smiling.

"You have received the itemization of costs incurred in your daughter's care?" he said.

"Yes, sir."

"So you can see that a good deal of time has been spent on your case."

I bowed my head. "Yes, I am grateful."

"Despite your nearly impossible status," he continued, "your friends' influence caused us to spend an undue amount of time persuading the Mothers' Aid Society to look kindly upon your petition — no small matter; and one in which our offices endeavored for discretion. The Christian Mothers surely would have followed. And as you know, the functioning of the hospice, the welfare of our many children, depends on these patrons, our volunteers — and they do not necessarily—look kindly on a case like yours." He cupped his furrowed brow and tired eyes briefly with the palms of his hands, and sighed. Did it indicate a softening of demeanor; or merely a breath between one problem of his afternoon and the irksome next? He was not a terrible man.

"Surely you understand the law," he said. *Surely, surely.*

"Yes, of course."

"And you have worked very hard to make yourself an exception—so—forgive me, Mademoiselle Rigault; your actions make no sense." My heart lurched.

" . . . Monsieur?"

" The birth certificate . . . was not in the proper case file. But it has now been found." He slid it across the polished surface of the desk to me now, the document I had thrust into the hand of the night guard, the certificate that had not accompanied Berthe into the *tour*. Of course, I knew what it said. Or what it *had* said, because the name on the line identifying the father was now effaced by a black rectangle of ink.

"After all that you had accomplished—to conduct a research into paternity, put forward a claim involving one of the foremost families of Paris, to deliberately violate article 340 of the Code Civil? What—*what* was your intention?"

"I don't—sir, what do you mean? I have not—" But indeed I had; I had inscribed Stephan's name on the certificate; had put a letter into Léonie's hand.

"The birth certificate has been corrected, but you have made it untenable for me to proceed. I believe that you are in possession of further detail on this matter from the family's legal counsel. If not—certainly it will be forthcoming. Case number 3568 has been closed to further inquiry."

He rang for a Sister, and one appeared to see me out.

Furiously, horribly, back to the rue du Mail in a pounding squall. In the summer's heat the downpour would have been welcome; now the streets had become running torrents, clogged with cabs and omnibuses. Finally home to sift through the foul matter of receipts and visiting cards; scrawled notes for debts at cards; Lili's draft of the dental advertisement; opera programs. Menu and seating plan for a private dinner for twelve, including Gabriel and his newest *ami-coeur,* a dashing young man never seen without a very fine leather riding crop. A note from Mademoiselle Colette about boots in mauve calfskin, *very unusual.* Bill for eight baskets of violets, third notice (for what occasion?) . . . Galopin's statement for the last order, a dozen bottles of champagne, as many of red and white; seven of port; one absinthe; and a Tennessee bourbon, special-ordered . . . Had some letter been buried? What did he think, this *directeur,* that I could attend to everything? I had no bevy of sisters all neat and tidy in their caps, just Sévérine . . . although I now remembered that La Tigre had slid an envelope on top of my stack and murmured something I could not now remember.

Finally, it was discovered between Mademoiselle Colette's most recent note and a perfumer's bill. And a note from Beausoleil — probably about tonight's engagement — what was it, dinner, or the theater and dinner late?

On behalf of the aggrieved party and on pain of prosecution . . . Illegal breach of article 340 of the Code Napoleon forbidding *recherche de la paternité* . . . Cessation of correspondence with the referenced aggrieved and his immediate family . . . The registered prostitute Eugénie Rigault to be placed under authority according to the provisions of the municipal council.

Signed, stamped, and sealed within an inch of its life and embossed with the insignia of a Paris law firm.

I sank down into a Louis XV bergère chair, covered in striped silk and chosen by Gabriel. Stared out the balcony window, down to the rue Montmartre. The hotel, the café, the Mont de Piété. All of the evening comings and goings. *Recherche de la paternité* . . . All that I asked — that my dreaming, impractical Self had asked — was that

Stephan acknowledge the past. I had written to the Stephan I had known, the loved man. And also because Beausoleil's lawyer had told me that I needed material proof of our liaison.

I saw, now, in a sudden, cold light that the sort of truth my letter requested was out of the question. It could not possibly have been understood as I had intended; not in the shadow of legal proceedings. So why had I clung with such a grip, maintained an allegiance to what was long over; courting destruction, throwing myself down an abyss? I should have known better. I *did* know better, but had refused what I knew . . .

The rain cleared, casting a waning sunlight over the geraniums. The warrant stared up at me from the escritoire; its graceful curved legs holding up a pile of indulgences.

Stephan. In a certain way, the warrant was the first solid piece of evidence that Berthe's father was anything but a dream. Was that—in the midst of the eddying whirl of what had become my life—what I had needed to prove?

I wondered when the police would pound at the door.

At last, I brought myself back and opened Beausoleil's note. But it did not concern this evening, or any other evening. It consisted of several paragraphs, not the usual brief lines about our rendezvous. What he wrote now was that the French ministry had reversed its position on the matter of the empire's support of the Confederacy. The government ministers denied ever having approved such support, which had been the subject of Beausoleil's careful negotiations (involving the building of French ships at Bordeaux and Nantes to come to the aid of the Confederate ports) . . . Now, instead, a pact of neutrality was to be affirmed. France would favor neither side, North nor South. "*We have lost a good deal in the matter,*" wrote Beausoleil, in the same hand that had once penned "*the Known improved greatly upon the Unknown.*"

Beausoleil, for all his love of theater, play, and illusion—knew what was real and what was not. I might be interested to know, he wrote, that the marquis de Chasseloup, Pierre's father, Napoleon III's former naval minister, had been the one to issue this official reversal of France's position. *"And now I am called back to New Or-leans. Matters do not proceed well at home after Vicksburg, and now losses in Tennessee and north Georgia. If you can see me off tomorrow I am your most grateful servant, &c. When I am gone, I hope you will remember me for sending you a sweet—and brief—reprieve from your own battle while we fought ours. I wish you every good luck in your af-fairs, and await news . . ."*

My throat was parched. I sat for a long time, until the sun had set and the geraniums disappeared into the dark. From below, evening traffic clattered; iron wheels rumbled over the cobbles. Lamplight-ers now in their silent progress down the street. Reflections of the lights shimmering in the puddles left by the storm. Sévérine came in on cat's feet and lit the gas; cautiously inquired . . . It was unusual, of course, that mademoiselle was not dining out? There was *soupe*, she said. Just a *bouilli ordinaire.*

Clio stalked in behind her and vaulted onto my lap. "Hello, faith-less friend, where have you been?" She began to purr. "And why do you love me only when I have a bad day?" I buried my face in her rumpled ginger fur.

20

AN INK-STAINED HAND

Does the story, in the way it is told, open a window into the soul's fortress or place yet another stone to block the view? These events have been related as they unfolded; as accompanied by my feelings at the time or as I remember them to have been. But every life takes on its wrinkles, like lines on the face of an old madame—and who could have foretold her particular destiny in the tracings on a girl's palm?

For a while, when not writing wasted love letters and petitions, I squeezed my own suffering down to an inky fingertip. This effort did not come continuously but in fits and fragments; stained and laden with debris and ill-cut from the start. Slipping like the awl that leaves an inarticulate scratch. Like Madame Récit's finery mender, I brushed, concealed, restitched, and revised; eventually it seemed that even as my life occurred, I had hardly lived it, referring always to an unseen past or future. Forever at an impasse, shot through with doubt; assigning both agency and blame to others and yet my own words formed another kind of betrayal. Writing was intended to burn and to exorcise but its effect was the reverse. For in writing down there is no forgetting; in editing, contouring, shaping a thing, what has been omitted looms in the mind. Recorded with pen and ink, blotted and stacked in unruly sheets, the events, both those presented and left unrecounted, were ever with me, as in a dream in which one never runs hard enough to escape some threat. As ink stains water, billowing out and suffusing it, one substance entirely occupies the other until matrix and infusion are one. Thus is suffering formed and transmuted. But meaning accrues slowly, not in a cataclysm, and always unexpectedly.

For a period on the rue du Mail, while I enjoyed Beausoleil's protection, food in the cupboard, and a maid to walk to the laundress, my days turned into a fury of revision at the little walnut escritoire (a surface too narrow for the task); a feverish search for the logic in a flustered tale of lost loves, ateliers, coal bins, and stone walls; butcher shops and dank corridors. Here was a word from Bovary, a whiff of Balzac; the cesspools of Zola and Huysmans's vinegary indigestion. Madame Sand's trousers and cigar hardly appeared; but very often the tinsel villainesses and heroines of the Seine bookstalls, and all the urgency of uncertainty. Giulia—a different woman in private than in public, came to the rue du Mail to read Veronica Franco aloud, translating from the Italian as she went. Little Giulietta accompanied her beautiful and celebrated mother, played quietly with her doll on the carpet while Giulia read: *"To eat with another's mouth, sleep with another's eyes, to move according to another's will, rushing toward the shipwreck of one's mind and body . . ."* We both sat on the rug in front of my little balcony and wept. At the disappointments not only of our own lives—but centuries of lives. Franco taught us that.

But finally, my efforts added up to the story of one for whom all stories had failed. Perhaps if any of us live long enough, the skin and bones of life accrue to prove every word false. Every novel and painting; every lover; every war. Storytelling does not stand up to facts. Maybe that is why we do it, to compel the facts away.

What I have written here is mostly true, insofar as anything is.

The trip back to La Vrillette and to the rose garden was a fiction to assuage the heroine's honor; the girl I wished I was. In reality there was neither the faith nor will for such a journey, nor could I afford a train ticket, and my better self foundered on life's more with-

ering details. Léonie did not find me there; although if she had seen
Berthe in my arms in a garden of roses, perhaps her heart would
have been in a different place, at Tours. Perhaps mine would have
been.

This Eugénie, in her pages, did for good reason loathe the life
thrust upon her, and did not see any part of it as resulting from
her own choice. She did (at the *tour*) stand miserably in the rain,
with the child for whom she was not prepared. The letters to her
old lover—those were burned up in a stove. The one pressed into
Léonie's hand at Tours—another story she wove around herself, or tried to. Life rejected them; slapped her with the threat of
arrest.

She was angrier than she acknowledged. All around her, arguments bubbled about how a woman's life should be conducted.
But the general view, even if it luffed and flapped perilously and
shifted with the winds, invariably fastened itself where it had always
been. To the female body as container and vessel for all that was denied, despised, left unsaid. And since there was a good deal of that,
whether in the gutter or the champagne bucket, it was in that role
that our sex was most necessary. Shadow figures, negatives; blank
pages, dreams.

Soon after Beausoleil departed—I don't remember how long, exactly—a column appeared in one of the papers. An *inscrit* (it was
always an *inscrit*, never a girl or a woman), age twenty, *quartier des
Martyrs*. Doors of a coal stove ajar; a haze of soot on the walls (and
in that terrible heat). Mattress stuffing wedged under the door. Her
suicide note was printed. It read, *"I am called Banage. My brother is
an actor at the Gaîté."*

Banage: from Deux Soeurs. Bones like a bird, turning over those
brass tags, as many as could be fit into the hour. Until that brother
got the part he deserved, the starring role, the one that would prove
the poor boy was the world's exception.

After that I began to notice them again. Girls with a netherworld
pallor beneath their bonnets; with packs of white cards in their

hands . . . MAISON DE SOCIÉTÉ, MAISON DE PLAISIR. The capital's madames had prevailed upon the Préfecture to allow the doors
to open and their indebted captives to leave behind, for an hour, the
saturated odors of sweat and perfume and drink. The grimy chandeliers on frayed ropes, ill-concealed by a crumpled, dusty sleeve.
Rope, cord, umbilicus, garotte, noose. Tourists stood and gaped at the
bits of cardboard; know-it-alls nodded and smirked; businessmen
pulled their collars up smartly, fooling no one, not even themselves.
Their tight, conspiratorial moods, these girls; lofty, vagabond,
defiant.

. . . One of them. Installed on a bench near a dry plot of ground;
cards stashed behind a bush; her face mushroom-pale. She shifted to
catch the sun, lifted her bonnet so light would warm her face. How
low were her reserves? Had her guts weakened; did she hover on
the verge of fever, malaise, the brink of collapse? With each passing night did she feel the coil tighten, awaken to find her own hands
scrabbling at her throat, pulling at what was unseen, what choked
off her very breath, what wanted to hang her from the garret beams?
Ghost of an emotion, welling up . . . *bitter memory, too-green apricot,
skin-split. A dry August, no rain. Sabots in the ruts.* I swallowed hard.
Forget me not. *Forget me now.*

Haussmann's water not yet in Paris and yet — from nowhere — a
trickling, dripping sound, behind and above — *where?* A drip like
agony. Hypnotic, that drip; if you didn't look around, it could even
be the sound of light rain on leaves. A rivulet dripping down a wall,
cutting a darker groove into the mottled stone. Or a long slow leaking through the body, fluids, vinegar water pumped up from a rubber bulb, running, trickling, cold then warm, down a thigh; a shift
hitched up above the waist. Ablutions, afterward; back turned to the
bed with its tumbled linens.

Excellent linens now on my own bed; a thousand threads under a
thumbprint.

The girl on the bench twitched her skirts as an old man swept up
dirt and leaves with his twig broom. Pigeons pecked at the ground.
Little boys drove their hoops; soon it would be twilight and they

would all go inside and this girl would retrace the steps she came by, because she was hungry; or perhaps — if she was just hungry enough — she would not.

I thought of defecting to America. Lili and I plotted and planned because Mexico was somewhere nearby, so we could visit. She booked her passage, but I dragged my feet. In the end I could not resolve to leave the soil on which Berthe — somewhere — lived. Beset by a stifling fury — yearning for all that had been denied — I was contemptuous too of my own vain, self-justifying tales.

. . . Dark moods, then. Without Beausoleil's protection, his comradeship, and his social whirl, I was once again at the mercy of forces stronger than myself. Besides, I had acquired tastes beyond my ability to pay. Gabriel's parting gift kept my bed linens out of the Mont de Piété, but it wouldn't last forever. For the practical reader, it may seem that more prudent investments could have been made — that it would have been wise to pay off old Madame Récit's interest as well as principal. Ah, but Mademoiselle Colette's new dresses were so immediate and urgent. The wine merchant's wares too; and the florist, and the tobacconist. While Nathalie Jouffroy, over in her countinghouse on the rue du Temple, bided her time, like a spider on a glittering, treacherous web.

It will already be clear that I was never a Bellanger with a garden of pleasure in a smile; a clownish, fun-loving Cora Pearl. Not a bewitching Giulia Barucci — nor the heroine of *La Dame aux Camélias*. Oh, I heard the stories of how it used to be, when there was more to it than commerce. Great claims were made for the old Paris: its wit and festivity, its narrow and winding streets, the charming personages winking down on us now, shaking their ghost heads and tugging their ghost beards and wishing we were having a better time of it during the reign of commerce. I found myself less and less able to contour my talents to any mold, though, and as time passed, became ever more the unknown girl; unknown to myself most of all. No one had told me that a Self is built up slowly over a life, and that all of its splits and fissures, gaps and weaknesses — its strengths and structure — come in time to be understood. Our small world, in fact, told us the opposite: that we were born in perfection, and either preserved ourselves morally and physically, or fell and decayed. Thus time became our enemy. At least I saw it as mine.

The last recourse, then, was surrender. To cease excusing myself with reasons that fell apart like old silk; attempting to defy the forces outflanking my army of one. Perhaps, as I learned to slip the *passe* so long ago to a slight girl called Banage on a velvet sofa, my course was already carved out. Finding the world's disgraced and abandoned in a sunbeam on a bench, mending and shaping them like a *rebouiseur* to the dispossessed. (Anyone would shudder at that girl's story, a common one, but I will not tell it here.) Some might even say I saved her, and the others like her, if you want to stretch the truth. Truth has its stretchers. But my own truth-sized truth died with the warrant from Stephan's lawyers and the threat of arrest. I was not like Jolie; I knew I could not survive Saint-Lazare prison. The goose-girl, finally, had the last word. Procurer of *foie d'oie* and other delicacies and desirables—with that dogged Gascon heart, bound to finish what she so rashly had begun—oh yes, she knew how to bring a fatted duck to market. How to save the day by the skin of her teeth.

Of some matters, one does not write accounts. One prefers not to, especially at times when life's business proceeds apace, leaving little time for inky reflection. Instead, at my escritoire—bills piled high, a heart leached of passion, and eyes that could see only impasses, I wrote to Nathalie Jouffroy. She, of course, was one of my creditors—the only one who never pressed. I'd been in her debt since La Palette; and after that, she had loaned me money to pay my legal bills. Her response came quickly. The dessert course of our long-ago dinner.

It should be clear, by now, that the business of Regulation was a very busy one indeed; and I became one of its pillars. At first I merely wrote Nathalie's letters, as there were always matters at hand between Deux Soeurs, the Préfecture registry, and the Paris Council. Also, correspondence with the "women's bourse" at Brussels, where the regulated were bought, sold, and traded. (Later I traveled there myself, in first class. It was not the kind of place you might think: for example, my trips there involved dining with the same jewelers who catered to clients on the rue de la Paix. But jewelry rentals were a secondary business at the *maisons de tolérance;* a beautiful young girl dressed in emeralds and nothing else might raise her price considerably.) My duties broadened once it was understood how useful, in fact, I could be; how faithful to the causes of Regulation; the issue of public health; the Code Civil, the Préfecture . . . aiding the proper course of the new *inscrit;* drafting letters about proposed variations in the articles — suggesting appropriate delays in the licensing of new houses, for example. *In the name of administration and the public good.*

As far as matters with Stephan's family went, arrangements were made to stave off prosecution and ensure that nothing occurred. This was my last shred of justice; the final, defiant fragment upon which I built a precarious structure of stones and bones, of the tears of girls on benches, and the cold hearts of their lovers. Lesson learned: those hearts could always be counted on for the bank account. *Why* it should be so is a question for the poets and philosophers — although they don't seem to have much to say about it.

In the spring of 1865 we had the news out of Appomattox, and there was much jubilation in Paris on behalf of the freed American slaves. Beausoleil wrote to tell me that he had married, left the property to his wife to manage, and settled in New Orleans. I must come and visit, he wrote.

In 1867 came the final disaster for Maximilan and Louis Napoleon's Mexican adventure: the proposed "emperor of Mexico" was shot by firing squad; all of the European ladies sailed home. Lili, who had finally saved enough for her passage, turned around mid-Atlantic with her case of dental instruments. She returned with a heavy heart for the Mexican wives, for whom there was to be no relief.

Odette was more often between lovers now — and more often at the card table at the rue du Mail. Jolie surfaced once she had risen through the ranks at Maison Chevillat, settled in as one of the "seniors" of the establishment—reassuring clients that all was right with the world, keeping younger recruits in line. She was eligible for paid holidays now, and wrote that she wanted to go to Trouville because she had never seen the sea. Would we like to come to Trouville, Odette and I? Her bold scrawl on paper imprinted with the name Chevillat. A pilfered supply.

Three times a year, as before, I made my trip to the hospice. Demoted again to the corridor, subjected to encores of the pious ruminations of the Good Ladies. The benches outside the director's office were weighed down by a fresh crop of tear-stained faces, the newest novels and knitting patterns. I was the senior stalwart, intransigent—but the state continued its allotted payments; and this was some indication that Berthe lived. So I watched the sisters come and go, listened to the *nourrices* gossip, struck up the occasional conversation. I collected many stories in that corridor; but mostly just waited, as the law allowed, with neither strategy nor hope. When he passed, the director did not look my way. But he knew I was there, a needle in his side.

Thanks to Haussmann's new aqueducts and reservoirs, my rooms at the rue du Mail were eventually fitted with water at the sink. Clear, clean waters of the Dhuis River flowed from the taps; and soon after, at least a portion of the Paris citizenry could not remember when the drinking water and the cesspool were contained in the same courtyard. The old builder, indeed. And the new.

And slowly, slowly, in those waning days the clocks ticked, and I knew myself to be growing away, at last, from childish things.

. . . How does a woman learn to doubt herself? When does it happen, and why?

But the answers take us to insalubrious realms, and finally it may be better to go to dine; finish the evening with a brandy and a good cigar, if we possibly can. Let blessed silence fall and these sorts of questions fade like a puff of smoke.

BOOK IV

DEBACLE

Since everyone must dine, even those who want to wage war,
around six o'clock the streets were passable.

— MOGADOR, *Memoirs*

21

DECLARATION

W E WERE NOT—any of us—paying attention when it began, the beginning of what we all now know as the *end,* during a sultry stretch of July 1870, in the nineteenth year of the empire. The mood was languorous, up in the glassed-in veranda at the rue du Mail. Odette and I made fans out of *L'Opinion Nationale* because there was nothing much to read in it. The playing cards had slick, hot surfaces as we dealt tarot or played *manille* (silent *manille,* talking *manille, manille de misère;* a *manille* for every mood, but always the same game). There was some imperial bluster about a Hohenzollern candidate for the vacant Spanish throne and the typically inconsiderate behavior of Prussians. Visitors to the apartments on the rue du Mail included rather more of those in uniform, colorful and stiff with gold and silver braid; but this wasn't so unusual. Francisque and Amélie often expected such decorative persons to take them to dinner. Lili occasionally mentioned how ruinously expensive small things had become, combs or a pair of gloves. Francisque, porcelain-lovely, was impeccable as always; she minded her popularity assiduously but seemed to live at some distance from herself—more so with the passage of a few years. Amélie was warmer, sympathetic, and better read; to hear her speak, one would never believe she was a *cocotte*. Amé came from an old Dijon family (she was on familiar terms with the varieties of mustard) but had wanted to go on stage as a girl, and no good advice could stop her. A string of suitors from generals to opera tenors occupied her, keeping La Tigre lively, lest they mix up their evenings. Lili, dimpled and adorable, cultivated paying jobs beyond a string of protectors, though it did send her bounding in several directions at once. They lived by their wits, their lovers, the prevailing winds of fashion — the discretion and management provided by La Tigre, our "concierge" — and the stock market. The Bourse's current lurches up and down caused Francisque palpitations, and Lili to comment that she hadn't felt so seasick since Mexico Bay.

I dealt tarot; gave my opinion that things would pick up. Everything depended on how you wanted to look at it, and one might, indeed, choose. Shuffle and strategize your bets, avoid the struggling runner, and allocate to the stronger, as we did on the grassy downs at Longchamp. Diversify, put it off your own shoulders, never take things too seriously. Keep a cushion in the savings bank. This had been Beausoleil's attitude, and I had worked to make it mine.

The empire had its share of grumblers and a fresh helping of critics, to be sure. Louis Napoleon was not as young as he once was and suffered from gallstones. But his signature style continued unabated: balls and masquerades and all manner of extravagance and *volupté* at the palaces, at the Tuileries and Compiègne. Imperial mistresses and dalliances came and went, and the demimonde, the world of fashion that was the empire's assiduous imitator, was on parade and as spendthrift as ever. France had survived the Mexican disaster and made a shining tableau of wealth, beauty, and social progress in a giant glass dome on the Champ de Mars two years past. The Great Exhibition showcased Paris as Europe's glittering jewel, and the whole world, it seemed, arrived to view the macadam-paved streets under sparkling gaslight, the parks and boulevards planted with trees; even the new sewer system was available for tours. Louis Napoleon had reviewed thirty thousand splendidly outfitted troops,

cannon, and artillery; he was saluted by the Russian tsar and the
king of Prussia and, with great and solemn ceremony, accepted a
prize for his model workers' dwellings proposed for the slum districts of Belleville and Ménilmontant. Working people in their blue
cottes and dull-colored dresses came to this exhibit to shift on their
feet and stare, dumbfounded, at the display.

Still, the past year's elections, after all of the strikes and disturbances, had resulted in some liberalizations — freedom of the press,
for one. We at the rue du Mail now fanned ourselves with *La Lanterne* and its brick-red cover, as well as the other papers. A new crop
of journalists faulted the empire's tyranny; its tarnished-silverplate
arrogance, ominous indebtedness, tinsel parades and spectacu-
lars — but in our hothouse quarters these rumblings remained on
the periphery. Closer to our own affairs, a few socially intended
novels produced a flurry of anti-Regulation opinion and clothing
drives for the "victims of Saint-Lazare," though I was never sure
what cause would be served by dressing up these unfortunates and
putting them back on the streets — certainly not an overturning of
the social order as we knew it.

My career had progressed. It consisted of servicing and adminis-
tering the empire's appetites; feeding the dragon's maw and avoiding the flames myself within a system ill-founded and corrupt to
its heights. Voluptuousness, beauty, and certain other qualities were
desired in great variety — a thousand versions of the game were
played, but in fact there was only one — inking the uninscribed.
Fishing up young migrants; siphoning off from the thirty thousand—
odd Parisian "freelancers" some number to augment the Préfecture's bulging Register, clearing the streets for tourists, and assist-
ing the tax office. After the Préfecture had stamped cards and doctors had examined eyes, mouths, fingernails, and hair, and prodded
at nether regions, I picked and chose for Deux Soeurs and its competitors; took what was raw, naive, unformed, and ignorant — contoured and shaped that rough material, that feminine clay, for use,
for admiration, for profit. I did not pretend that these efforts served
the "public good." For any girl, inscription meant erasure from the
world of possibility, her head pushed beneath the dark waves, and

I was Charon at the riverside, plying the ferry into oblivion—one of many boats for those who seemed as determined to throw themselves into hell as hell was to have them. Sometimes, temples throbbing, stomach queasy, I wanted to say *"Run, run"* to the girls I met. But most had run already, and this, here, was the place they had reached.

For each who found a place in the pantheon of poisoned goddesses, though, hundreds were swept aside: back to empty *garni* rooms; into service, or to relatives who did not want them; they were banished to the provinces, to the nunnery; to the bridges and to the madhouse. Back to make their way as best they could; back to nothing and worse. And I didn't know to whom I was doing the greater favor or the lesser. I had carved out my niche; even surpassed the likes of Françoise, who had never made it past submistress before she left to marry herself off to a second cousin.

Dimly, perhaps, I was aware of having lost the thread of the real, but what was real—and if one decided, what was to be done about it?

A (pseudonymous) gossip columnist once described a few of my first-class passengers thus: *"Mlle. Julie, a brunette with sparking eyes and a Spanish foot. Mlle. Dina, an intrepid rider of the Bois de Boulogne, possessed of a rosy mouth, embellished with pearls. Annette M—, an English milliner, fair complexioned, with rosy ringlets and black eyes. Gabrielle La B—, a Creole retrieved from a host of angels, fallen to earth. We must applaud a certain 'unknown hand' for bringing a sparkle to the foothills of Montmartre and to the better of the tolérances . . ."*

"Well done, my dear; I can see your stamp on this," Nathalie Jouffroy would say of a season's lineup of the willing and warm-fleshed. She appreciated my seriousness about the "refurbished" although she preferred to spend fortunes on "starts" at Brussels—acquisitions that often ended in a mountain of debt and urgent trades down the line. But that is what kept her in the footlights of the half-world; in the adored swirl of intrigue. Émilie Trois was always there to pick up the pieces. Trois would assess the line and say, "But now

you must find us some merchandise as well. After all, we're not entertaining Olympus here. The human animal just wants to be fed."
And so I went down to the previous night's trawls at the Préfecture, negotiated the raw materials, then brushed up and refitted them for the Deux Soeurs salons. As for spying on my own kind — that popular empire occupation of tipping off the Préfecture that Mademoiselle So-and-So was down on protection and ripe for the Register . . . information was conveyed, but never out of revenge, and my friends knew they could trust me.

On the writing desk Beausoleil had bought me, an overflow of correspondence; pens and blotters; ink and seals.

> To Monsieur le Préfet: Mademoiselle D— wishes to convey that cruel reversals of fortune have driven her close to the final act of despair. If she had not been kept back by religious feeling she would have succumbed . . . Her circumspect conduct, the care that she has bestowed on her parents, and that which she lavishes on her children have been deserving of the esteem and consideration of all worthy people; not being able to work, she begs for authorization to receive into her house six women of quality . . .

> To Madame Jouffroy of the Maison des Deux Soeurs: I take the liberty of writing to you to ask if you are willing to enter into business relations, and to know if you want any English girls of the age of seventeen. —Albert, hairdresser, Leicester Square, London

And a hundred more like them. I had learned to exhaust my energies at such work. When it was finished, for a day, a week, or a season — such fearsome effort at my little walnut-inlaid writing desk, or rattling around Paris at night — I harbored a further ambition, a secret, poisonous dream: that my service to the Préfecture would, at last, have amassed enough chits and credits that I might request my own erasure from the Register. After all, I had not practiced my "trade" for years, even while I was young enough to have a future. That summer, with business proceeding briskly (even though tourists had drained from the boulevards as though a plug had been pulled) and with the empire's functionaries cemented into their secure and lucrative positions — my intention was to get myself erased from the Register before the year was out.

Under the potted palms around the card table at the rue du Mail, Francisque fanned out the hand she'd been dealt with a lacquered fingertip.

"Odette has not been with us for three weeks! Is she in love?"

"Or in trouble?" Amélie shook out her chestnut curls, sending hairpins scattering.

Francisque gave her a dark look. "Lili, what do you think of holding another dental clinic for molar distress?"

"I've got my eye on an excellent instrument case at the Mont." Lili was thumbing through a used textbook on horse anatomy. Her latest passion was veterinary science, a field she swore was expanding too quickly for men to keep up.

"No, really," said Amé. "What if she is?" She raised her bid and played the Fool, which won wry comments all around; then caught my eye.

"I'll see what I can learn," I murmured.

It was true that something had taken hold of Odette, the strategist prepared for every new hand. Neither too loyal nor too fickle, she never lost her heart nor gave it away. Every one of her lovers felt lucky to have her, and their protection usually outlasted the duration of the affair, which is how she stayed afloat — that, and market tips. Such a career required endless diplomacy and vigilance and Odette seemed immune to fatigue. But her last affair had ended badly; I suspected she had allowed herself expectations. Or loved him a little more. It was an odd point for her to stumble upon — so obvious, like a stairstep one has gone up and down a thousand times before.

Again the next week she failed to appear at the green baize table. The air was charged and torpid; pent up. The kind of evening when the storm threatens but never breaks, and even Séverine, usually so placid, walked around like a thundercloud, spilling a drink without a murmur of apology.

"No word at all?" said Amé. "Eugénie, have you heard anything?"

"Yes, I believe she was . . . detained." Jérome Noël, the original agent of my inscription and still Nathalie Jouffroy's close connection at the Préfecture, was out with a summer grippe. I'd made delicate inquiries via his deputy, Coué—a real stiffneck who was always haunting the arcades or hauling in trembling milliners and ladies out shopping *sans chaperone*.

"Monsieur Hibiscus, I'm afraid." Francisque turned white.

"Catastrophe," gasped Amélie. "He denounced her!"

"Coué didn't say as much, but he wouldn't."

"Monsieur Hibiscus" was an importer of exotics and dwarf palms who had been courting Odette for months, showing up at her door with giant bouquets, a parakeet in a gilded cage, and once even an iguana. Her dance of innuendo and resistance had occupied much of the spring; he did not meet her standards, and besides, he lived nearby and therefore was a risk. When we'd last seen Odette, she was determined to confront him directly.

"She's retained a lawyer," I said.

"You've got to be joking," said Francisque. "She wants to bring a case against this *frotteur*?"

"Against the police, actually. For violation of privacy," I said drily. "I gather she gave them a list of protectors as long as her arm. Under duress."

"I would have liked to hear the names on that list," said Francisque. Odette was not one to identify her lovers.

"Is it *possible* to sue the Préfecture?" asked Lili.

"Even *La Lanterne* doesn't go that far," said Amélie.

"What lawyer in his right mind would take the case?

"I hate to think what it will cost her," I said.

"Goodness, it's hot," said Amé. "Where is Séverine with the drinks?"

We had not even begun the diversions of *manille* when one of

Francisque's officers arrived, a *chasseur* in the Imperial Guard — de Ligneville, I think it was; his picture was popular on *cartes de visite* and that evening he looked as though he had just sat for his photograph, tightly buttoned, sashed, and braided into his uniform; boots polished and saber at his side. He declined to sit; we suspended our conversation; turned our sunflower heads toward his bright armor.

"Let me be the first to tell you," he said. "The government of France has declared war."

"War?" said Francisque, and her milky skin paled perceptibly.

"The breach is caused by the Prussians' absurd idea that a Hohenzollern could ascend to the Spanish throne."

Lili looked startled and put down her textbook. "But Prince Leopold was withdrawn!"

"Bismarck brushed off France's demand for an absolute guarantee that he would stay out of Spain. So it is an excellent opportunity at last to drive the message home. Put the German question to rest once and for all."

"So much for the finer points of diplomacy," said Amélie. "Whatever happened to *Il ne faut rien brusquer?*"

"I thought that the whole issue of the Hohenzollern candidacy in Spain was nothing but a tactic," I said. "A — kind of Prussian taunt, to see if France would take the bait?"

Amélie said, "Any trifle can be made serious when men want to go to war." She looked pensive. She too had been prickly of late, and I wondered why.

"There, you're wrong," said Lili. "It is the empress who wants this."

The officer laughed. "Yes, she says, 'I shall go to bed French and wake up German if this is allowed to continue!' You will see," he said smartly. "It will be brisk, victorious, and very good for us all." Francisque pulled on her gloves. We picked up the cards and dealt, three-handed.

The next day, as it may be remembered, if anyone cares to recall — the imperial curtain rose on its last spectacular show. The declaration was complete with costumes, wigs, and makeup. Carica-

tures of Germans with drooping mustaches and long pipes appeared
in the papers; French soldiers, decked out with flags and plumes,
paraded with trumpets; parrots were trained overnight to squawk
"To Berlin!" The major papers were bellicose and frantic over the
notion of a France encircled; gassily inflated it to the level of an
international incident, one to be quickly avenged. It sounded more
like a duel than a war, with the French army eager to prove its met-
tle, and I remember my initial surge of irritation, a helpless sense of
the absurd nature of the thing — even as the boulevards filled with
marching troops in brilliant colors and excited little boys jumped
from foot to foot. Tempers were touchy; the weather too hot. Some
critics ventured to suggest that despite outward appearances, our
army was not prepared for a conflict with the Prussians, but these
voices of reason were rapidly denounced as traitors, as was anyone
else who opposed the war. The Bourse soared. Francisque relaxed
and dined out every night, generally at the Jockey Club. Lili procured her dentistry kit; Amélie, between engagements, took to reading all the leftist papers. I felt uneasy, unable to concentrate on the
great volume of paperwork on my desk. Still no word from Odette,
but I had a few scrawled words from Jolie, proposing dinner. Since
Trouville, we'd gotten together only a handful of times, which Jolie
attributed to her employer's demands.

In late July, Louis Napoleon and his son, the prince imperial, age fifteen, embarked from Saint-Cloud to the front lines. Soon the papers
and broadsheets were shouting about the "invasion of Germany"
and proclaimed that the prince had retrieved a bullet from the victory battlefield in his hand. Badinguet knew what kept the *quibuses*
in their seats.

Should one blame the long-throttled journalists? Their censored
pens spewed only the flimsiest tittle-tattle, copied out messages
from the imperial press office, and blared them at a loud, incessant
pitch. Even the best among us were distressed, distracted. To live
under the empire was to be blinded by the flare of gaslight, diverted
by a thousand glittering inventions and the clatter of trains. Preoccupied by the movements of the Bourse, the building up of the bank

account. The full-bellied and fur-lined looked over their shoulder, feared the rising tide of the dispossessed, and soaked their hearts in champagne. The poor were ill and dreaded the landlord's boot and the Brigade; they were happy for military conscription, the higher wages of war, and the ability to direct their misery at an enemy at last. It was what we knew: to be childish, credulous concerning our leaders, zealous, and unprepared; to rely on compromises, however shabby and inadequate. The abyss between poverty and plenty was decorated, façaded, landscaped, and policed, but still it loomed ever larger; the brisk whirl of commerce — dizzying, maddening, unnatural — was our chosen distraction. But the number of Parisians who could with certainty find Saarbrücken on a map in July was roughly equal to the quantity of fresh eggs inside the city walls six months later.

Jolie leaned back, balancing her glass on her long fingertips, tossing back her hair, which was falling from its pins, and I felt a pang for her spark; her small, bright explosions.

"What do you think about Odette?" I asked. "That Coué is a devil; he thinks every female over the age of twelve should be registered. I'd make a bet he was involved."

"He may have met his match. Suing the Préfecture, indeed." Jolie laughed. "Our excellent friend. I've missed her."

The weather may have suggested oysters on ice, but we were eating from a pot on a charcoal brazier, and the meal was calf's stomachs simmered with a steer's foot. It was Jolie's favorite dish, served at a hole-in-the-wall near Les Halles; a late birthday celebration, and she *would* take it out on us with tripe. We had eaten a lot of it together, once. When my big belly was shoved against the tabletop in our little match-to-a-haystack flat. And it was as hot as it was then; another long-ago July.

My friend's features had hardened just perceptibly; eyes a little deeper under the lids; her tall, languid body a shade more gaunt. She — who had never favored the ascetic, even if she had to tear apart, fumigate, and sew her attire back together (sometimes in a way that did not exist before) — now wore a mossy-gray elbow-patched dress that blended in with the smoke, her hair a flame above it. An umbrella, a battered green one, leaned against the table. As always she was strangely alluring, the scent about her, and my own toilette felt fussy and dilute by comparison. For her birthday I had given her a pair of gloves in peacock silk and a bottle of gentleman's cologne. Removed from their boxes and stripped of their tissue, these lay on the table between us, incongruous amid the tripe pots.

"You look more like a Blanquiste than a *grande horizontale,*" I said, spooning up a gelatinous serving. Jolie reached for the carafe, and her hand trembled enough to allow the neck to slip and the wine to spill.

"*Merde.*" She leaned across the table. "I'll bet you don't lick your fingers like that at the rue du Mail."

"That's why I'd rather eat more often with you."

January was when I'd last seen her. Louise in a man's trousers and Jolie in a long cloak, both with hair pinned up under caps. They had been following a funeral cortege through the frigid streets in a steady rain, shouting, part of a crowd led by the old revolutionary Blanqui. (I had been on my way to the florist, making preparations for a dinner party we were to hold that night at the rue du Mail.) The funeral was for Victor Noir, one of the increasingly noticeable brash-voiced men who wrote against the empire. The boulevards were in a furor because the emperor's cousin, Prince Pierre, had shot the journalist over a disagreement about the terms of a duel, a dispute concerning criticism of the empire in the press.

Louise and Jolie were a pair of jubilant insurgents — sooty, drenched, exhilarated; Louise brandishing a French navy pistol. She showed us how the smooth curve of its grip fit her palm, demonstrating its mechanism as easily as a cook breaks an egg. "And whom are you planning to shoot — Prince Pierre?" I'd asked. Louise still had her schoolmistress's demeanor, but it had a new edge. When she spoke — about barricades going up and the guns echoing those of 'forty-eight and 'ninety-three — the air crackled and you could almost smell the powder, although she didn't answer my question. Jolie had interrupted her, plucking her sleeve and calling her former teacher "Clémence" with a familiar joking affection. My heart had snagged, then. As it did now, remembering. I didn't want to lose Jolie entirely; but what did that mean? It was impossible to see much of her; she sent a note when she pleased; half a year might pass before the next. One could more easily capture smoke in a fist. Harder to admit were the alterations in my own life that had created distance between us—my new-money companions, my comings and goings with the Préfecture and Nathalie Jouffroy. Those we did not discuss.

A shot went off now in the street, very close. I jumped, nearly upsetting the brazier.

"You'd better get used to it," said Jolie, who did not pause as she moved the spoon from the *tripière* to her bowl.

Earlier that day, more troops had stretched across the city, still celebrating the successful attack at Saarbrücken. Lines and lines of soldiers, all the regiments and battalions brilliant and colorful, a coxcomb display in their various uniforms—tight Zouave breeches, bright blue ballooning Turco trousers, ten thousand kepi-covered heads. Drums and horns and flags, colors flashing in the sun, and flotillas of cannon on the Seine, all tying up traffic for hours. Now with the festivities over, the participants caroused through the streets, with shouts and the breaking of bottles, gunshots and singing, heading off to rout the German bakers from their beds.

"I've missed you," I said. "Where have you been?"

She looked up. "I'll tell you something. I've got news; I'm off the books."

"What? Have you left Chevillat? How in the world did you manage that?"

"Infirmary Saint-Lazare for a month of mercury. And then another stint, compliments of Chevillat's Dab, at Hôpital de Lourcine—where, on the whole, the food was better."

The wine tasted vinegary, suddenly unpalatable; shreds of stomach lining and carrot congealed on my plate.

"Why didn't you tell me?"

"Well, it was sudden, you know. They just whisk you away. The mercury makes you sicker at first, so I had to recover. They don't let you send letters from Saint-Lazare; and no visits to speak of because they don't want the *souteneurs* coming round. Then Chevillat offered me a second round of mercury and a submistress's job. Or to pay me out. So then I had to think things over, and I have. I've decided to leave . . . You don't have to look like that; I'm not going to fall over tomorrow. Syphilis has three stages; I'm only in the first. My whole life is ahead of me." She gave a black laugh.

"It's the tripe," I said quickly. "You know I only eat it for you."

She scraped up the last of the sticky remains.

"So." She paused. "There's no reason for me to stay around here. I'm going back to where I came from. To Belleville."

"You can't do that."

"Why not? People live there, you know."

My guts clenched. I knew Jolie had grown up in the slums on the eastern outskirts of Paris; even more overcrowded now, since Haussmann's demolition had pushed thousands there from the inner rings of the city. Seething warrens of illness and poverty — Belleville was a place to leave if you could, not to go back to. "The air is bad, the water. The — I don't have to tell you." Cholera, typhoid, putrid vapors. I looked at the gifts of gloves and cologne, ludicrous. "You'll be dead in six months."

"You should see the place we've found. It's in a huge block of apartment buildings. From the street they look like slum palaces, but inside the walls have been removed between the separate buildings, and our hall is just like one long boulevard, way up high. Everything goes on there, it's like a village, with street vendors and workshops and cafés, even a *bar à vin*. Everyone knows everyone else. You don't understand it, you don't *know*. It's not *lonely*, it is *living*. Mothers and babies and old people and young ones. We'll all help one another. Share and share alike."

I gave her a look.

"Well, rob each other, then. But not the way they do down here. It's not easy to get a place up there, but we did it."

"We . . . who?" *Louise?*

"Henri."

"Your brother?"

"He's been a prisoner, but he's released. He's out past Prussian lines, but he'll get in." She leaned across, fierce and tender, her mouth turned up like Clio's used to when she settled down to her fish heads. "It isn't the cage that feeds the bird, as they say. So I'm going to fly now. In whatever time I have left." And she laughed. Her old laugh; and it made me gasp with loneliness for the rusty velvet sofa and Clio's soft belly fur. But how, on the rue du Mail, with money to burn up on peacock gloves, with Sévérine to brew the coffee and go to the laundress, could I miss those terrible times? Jolie, her voice clear as a bell, calling down as I clomped up the stairs from the rue Serpente, the strings of some unaffordable package tangled around my fist, stopping on the landing below to catch my breath. Shouting up for her to guess what I'd brought. But I was the one who hadn't been able to give them up, those indulgences, those comforts.

"Will you ever wear them?" I fingered the silk gloves. "This is your old cologne!"

"They are pretty things. But maybe I won't wear them to the barricades, *chouette*."

"It won't come to that. This war will end very soon. Everyone says so. It's not as though the Prussians can invade Paris —" I stopped. Jolie looked pensive, as though she was about to speak, but another shot sounded close by — so near we both flinched; the shouts of drunken off-duty soldiers rang in our ears.

"They think they can shoot all the Germans," said Jolie. "But they don't realize that then they won't have their bread or morning *Kaffee*. Not to mention, the streets won't be cleaned. Did you know that most of the street cleaners in Paris are Germans?"

"No . . . You can't go back there, Jolie."

"Eugénie."

"*What?*"

"You're up to your old tricks, living in the past. Everything is different now. Shall we have a coffee?"

After we parted, I hiked my skirts over the debris left from the army carnival, the spent bullets in the gutters. They say that when Paris first let out its laces, expanded its girth, and under the empire and Haussmann breathed beyond its ancient perimeter, the old cart horses stopped where the city gates had once been, stood stock still, and would not move, despite the fact that no toll taker, no wall stood before them. Even the drivers' whips did not make them budge. Perhaps it was my old friend who was galloping ahead, out into the new, unknown city.

Francisque, Lili, and I shopped the sales for wool petticoats and crinolettes (the newest improved shape in dresses) in department stores hot as ovens and crowded to bursting. Markdown signs had sprung up out of season and suddenly; the aisles of the big stores showed riots of violently colored fabrics, winter boots appearing from nowhere alongside polka-dot neckties and pink gloves and parasols; a chaos of paisley shawls and vests, all hastily cut from the same bolt. Customers fingered ready-made clothing in a frenzied delirium while pickpockets, dress destroyers, hair snippers, and *frotteurs*—all the disturbed minds of the capital—were out in force.

"I don't see why everyone is worried, with thirty thousand Prussian prisoners and victories at Forbach . . . or is it Froeschwiller?" said Francisque, struggling with a stretch of red flannel that didn't seem to know what kind of garment it was. Other conversations flurried around the racks.

"No, Saarbrücken was the victory, Forbach a retreat," said Lili.

"What do you think of this? Laces from the inside, so you can change the shape of the loops in back."

"No, Woerth was a victory as well. The dispatch was posted," said a young woman with a variety of crinolettes in her arms.

"Where?"

"Bourse."

"I didn't see it, but I heard the same," said a second woman.

"I've heard that the Prussians have surrounded Strasbourg," said a third.

"Never! *Who* says?"

"Lili, you are going to have to take out the planchette to tell us what's what," said Francisque.

"All we need is a decent news source," snapped Lili. Since the war had been on, it had been impossible to get any papers other than French ones, which reported only victories and, perhaps, empire-favorable lies.

"Why *did* the crinoline have to become so wide, and what will we use the old cages for now—protecting plants this winter?" someone behind us complained.

"The empress set the fashion wide so the emperor couldn't reach her—"

"All the doors in Paris had to be widened so the empress could fend off her husband? The old toad."

"I have to say, these new ones are worse. All these tapes and laces and bands to flatten the front and flare out in back; we are going to look like huge beetles with wings extended."

"Whom does the empress love, then?"

"War, and chocolate, and her American dentist," said Lili, tossing a stack of shawls over her arm. "You've no idea how hard I have tried to meet him!"

On the way back, we passed cafés filled to overflowing; the streets stank of alcohol. Men and women alike reeled along the boulevards and around mountainous refuse. Most were celebrating the victory at Woerth, but one rowdy group nearer Montmartre was singing about the imperial prince: *"So* Monsieur fils *picked up the enemy's bullets, which someone laid down in front of him!"* The heat had gone on so long we were ill with it, and not a breath of air on the horizon.

"The whole city is drunk," huffed Francisque, her usual perfect façade ruffled and overheated by the time we finally reached the harp-playing stairwell cherubs at the rue du Mail. We had settled ourselves with cool drinks provided by La Tigre; ferried up by Séverine. "I hope the boxes will be here soon." In the crush, we had all assigned our purchases for delivery. We looked at one another over fizz and lemon.

"Aha!" I said, flipping through the day's mail. La Tigre had sorted it and left it on a tray as usual, which was just one of the means by which she knew all our business. (To be fair, it was practically a job requirement.) "From Sylvie; she must leave Vienna." She had been touring there with the opera. "And Odette, finally . . . posted from London."

"Open it!"

A handful of news clippings fluttered out from between the pages of a letter. The first was from *Illustrated London News* dated August 6. Lili snatched it and smoothed it out on the tea tray.

Lili said, "Oooh. Look at this." And we did, while our drinks sweated in the heat. The picture was very different from our own artists' renderings, printed in the French papers. It showed peasants with flat spades, in a pelting rain, burying bodies on a battlefield. *Burying the French dead at Woerth,* said the caption — even I could read that much in English.

"Could this be?"

"Here is the *Pall Mall Gazette,* with no pictures. Dictionary?"

We picked out the words, one by one. "You don't have to be a medium to see what is going on," said Lili pensively.

"All of the battles — Forbach, Froeschwiller, Woerth, Spicheren — were French defeats?" asked Francisque, puzzled. "Do you think the English papers are telling the truth? Spicheren is near Saarbrücken, I think, but the army won there. Didn't they?"

"Well, the prince imperial . . . as we know . . ."

"Yes, yes! Who could forget?" said Lili. "I think that — this is why they won't let this news into France."

We sat silent, and Séverine removed the tray, casting a questioning glance at us as we sat still as statues, with a few pieces of newsprint where the cards usually were.

"What does Odette say?" asked Francisque finally. "What is she doing in London?"

I scanned the page and read aloud, summarizing. "The Préfecture's violation was . . . classified as a crime rather than an offense, so the matter was referred to the *ministère public.* We applied to him, and he put the complaint in his wastebasket in the name of the 'Principle of Authority.' According to this good principle, the police cannot be tried for a crime. And we cannot prosecute that *frotteur* for reporting what he believed was a crime."

"So you *can't* sue the Préfecture," said Lili.

I continued. "'My lawyer then sent a letter asking that my name be expunged from the Register —"

"*What?*" exclaimed Francisque.

"He denounced her for rejecting him, so she was put on the Register, of course," said Amé.

I kept on reading. "But meanwhile, the police had the right to arrest me whenever they liked. As a result, at my lawyer's suggestion I have removed myself to London. In fact, he has accompanied me. I am seeing the sights and sitting out the war. And we are investigating the work of some English women who are suing against the Act of Contagious Diseases. Please tell Lili that I have seen an excellent dental surgeon . . .'"

Later that evening, to distract ourselves, we went to see that famously bawdy queen of the *cafés chantants,* Mademoiselle Thérèse, who was doing a special performance at the Gaïté. We were accompanied by a group of officers: de Ligneville, de Montarby, Savaresse, others. The chorus was satirically costumed as revolutionaries of the past century: soldiers with ancient rattling swords, peasants, bourgeoisie, and so forth. The scenery was fragmented, falling apart. Thérèse herself wore a red skirt with blue stockings and a white sash; with her sleeves rolled up washerwoman-style and her bodice very low, she sang "La Marseillaise" with great and winking fervor. We all laughed along with the rest. "How we love to mock ourselves," said Francisque. "Odette will miss that, with the English."

So Odette left before the Paris walls closed, and that alone was worth the price of her lawyer.

22

CRISE

STRASBOURG, NOW: EVERYONE spoke of Strasbourg, first in low tones, then at an escalating pitch. "How is the defense going, what is happening?" "Strasbourg holds out!" "That city cannot be defended; it is riddled with spies." "London reports that the Prussians have opened fire." "Strasbourg is a proving ground; Paris is next. Look at the structure of the Strasbourg walls." "The Prussians would not dare. We are five times the size of Strasbourg!" "Do you think we are next?" Eager chroniclers, boulevardiers of the conflict, were available for consultation. One could clock the moments of change, when something became something else. Certainty became doubt; Strasbourg went from being distant to very close. The new fashion in panniers turned into the "bulletproof" silk bodice. Carelessly extravagant dinner parties became canned goods from Potin's, scurrilously hidden.

We went from solid ignorance to greater familiarity with maps, and eastern railway lines, and where they could be disrupted; the status of the fortifications girdling Paris. Fleeting rumors were heard about uniforms, sugar supplies, absent battle gear, and phantom victories. The papers continued to present bloodless marches and brave scenes. On any given day, flags flew from windows and victory lamps were lit; the next, the flags were snatched from sight and the lamps extinguished. The nonstop "La Marseillaise" ceased its drone and an eerie silence fell; a single pair of boots echoing on the cobbles the only sound. At the rue du Mail, nerves ran high; Séverine was forever running up and down stairs with cold rags, smelling salts, and pots of tea for someone's *crise* and looking as though she could use some relief herself.

By the end of August, the heat was intolerable; travel on foot beyond bearing. Waste clotted the gutters; mountains of rubble and garbage had grown up like barricades; the Seine ran turbid with waste. We lifted our skirts and held handkerchiefs to our faces to walk to the corner. The *fouille merdes,* the cesspool workers, the sewer-and-rubbish men, had all been German and they had either left or been shot, just as Jolie predicted. No one had considered the consequences of this robust defense of the capital. In every corner black flies clustered, and with them arrived the flux of watery diarrhea, cholera's first sign.

Jérome Noël's hair had thinned, his jowls thickened under his Louis Napoleon beard. It was nearly a decade since I had first stood before him, a pale, trembling girl, as he presided over the Register of the *inscrits*. Now, as lieutenant, he made his lair in an interior office with a green-shaded lamp, with his silver-framed photographs of Madame Noël and the children dressed in their Sunday best, along with a framed *carte de visite* of the imperial family. Noël carried upon his shoulders a burden of licensing, regulating, and policing upper-echelon *tolérances,* but he was a clean-desk man and actually disliked corruption. He made a great effort to conduct proper research into families, to keep underage girls and foreign traffic out of the *tolérances* and clean bills of health inside. In many ways he was an admirable officer and these past few years I'd seen a good deal of him. However, a summons to the Préfecture was a bit out of the usual; generally I reported directly to Nathalie.

And so, turning down his corridor and tipping my nose to the fevered activity there, the rushing of uniforms to and fro that late August—I wondered, what next?

···

"You have been helpful to the Préfecture, Mademoiselle Rigault, your contribution to the public health. But a matter of greater importance has arisen."

Noël seemed nervous; his well-nourished paunch pressed against the edge of his desk. Noël had inked me; Noël held the power of erasure, and it occurred to me that I should seize the opportunity before it was too late. With this precariously ill-planned war, a capital seething with anxiety, train stations filled with our former clientele — any remaining visitors and the fleeing well-to-do — how important was arresting girls under street lamps? Noël's pale mustache hairs twitched.

"Madame Jouffroy is a native of Strasbourg. You have traveled with her, from time to time?"

"Yes. But not to Strasbourg."

"A beautiful city that will never fall."

"Surely not. If there are setbacks, they will be turned around." These were the patriotic utterances of the day, and I faithfully recited my part.

"Persons of Prussian or German extraction were turned away from the Maison des Deux Soeurs from what date forward, if you please?"

"Why — I don't know. Certainly the clients have always been international. Perhaps Madame Trois — "

"You are aware of Nathalie Jouffroy's aliases?"

"No." *But who doesn't have other names, on our end of things?*

"You defend her, Mademoiselle Rigault?"

Defend her, Nathalie Jouffroy? My employer, the woman to whom I owed my relative freedom — who was I to defend her or not? However, Noël's words set a dozen scenes playing through my mind: Nathalie on the arm of various uniformed officers; Nathalie speaking German, in which she was fluent (but also in Spanish); Nathalie before her mirror, dictating letters while at her toilette. Nathalie on her way to Baden-Baden this past July. Vain, self-absorbed, preoccupied with anything that offered a diversion or turned a profit — and who had half of Paris at her beck and call. Never mind which half; the woman had her admirers, some very high placed . . .

So Noël was turning his back on Nathalie, who has lined his pockets and has done him a dozen favors a week for fifteen years.

I was the tiniest of cogs—not even the speck of oil on the smallest gear of this vast administrative machine now being dismantled and put to another use; from peacetime surveillance of the *non-inscrits* to turning up Prussian spies under every rug. Oh, I'd gone down the road with them—find this girl, that Brigade officer, these theater tickets, or that racing box. Around every bend, a new helter-skelter set of urgencies. Now it was spies, supposed spies, possible spies, someone's idea of who a spy might be, a neighbor one didn't much like, an old score settled. Was it a sign that Noël was out in the cold at the Préfecture if he was sniffing round Nathalie, betraying his line commander in yesterday's war? Did he need a promotion from poor girls to Prussian informants; was I the day's best prospect?

"She has always been Nathalie Jouffroy to me," I said quietly.

"No information at all, then, Mademoiselle Rigault?"

"I know you understand, sir, that my desire is to offer my best efforts to the Préfecture."

"Mademoiselle Rigault, I am aware of your service and your circumstances. I recall you standing before me as a young girl . . . perhaps unjustly. However, you have had opportunities that others have not, to learn and improve yourself. If you can be helpful to us in the matter, when the war is over you could find your situation much changed. Now. Let me share with you a few facts about the woman you know as Nathalie Jouffroy."

The promised papers arrived at the rue du Mail for my signature the next day. A stew of accusations—purported dates of travel, meetings, engagements—Noël had run down a list of names I had never heard. I sat with the papers at my desk, crossing out words and clauses; deleting facts to which I could not attest. Sick-headed, queasy, and sleepless . . . Oh, I wanted to save myself once and again, a final time, for good! Should I trust Noël, denounce Nathalie, risk my livelihood on a chance? Would any of it matter; would it just go with a fistful of others into the dossier? I didn't know what was true; wanted to have it both ways, get off the Register and stay in Nathalie's good graces; have it all matter as little as possible and go back to *manille*.

Oh, but you've forgotten, it is war and everything has changed. Around the baize table, with our English-French dictionary and the *Pall Mall Gazette*, we learned that the emperor was so ill, he wore rouge on his cheeks into battle, and the empress now slept in her clothes. But I was too distracted to play cards, and that evening it was my headache that Séverine ministered to with cold cloths and salts.

Again at my desk, head in hands, pressing a damp cloth to my temples. I could no longer focus my thoughts . . . Once this Prussian mess was over and done, Noël needed to marry off his Josephine properly and send little Louis to officer's school; he was looking for his best chance. Of Jouffroy I could believe anything. What was black or white; what would save my roof or salvage my soul? I felt corruption breaking over my head like a stormy wave at Trouville bringing in a filthy tide . . . and if one decides not to drown — *what?* That had been the question since my painted life with Stephan at La Vrillette cracked and turned brown. And at Trouville . . . what had I learned? That at life's ebb and flow, I was an apprentice.

While Jolie and I stood on the beach on our brief holiday, watching a storm roll in and the white spray scurrying up the flat sands, catching women in their bathing dresses, making them run — she told me that she loved Louise; that Louise was, perhaps, her first real, first unrequited passion. I learned that she had loved her from the beginning; through the fairy tales and the Civil War and for all of the months after that, whenever she could see her, wherever she was. That it was hopeless every time, for Louise loved nothing, and no one, but her revolution. "She really *does* want the *inscrits* to organize into trade unions," said Jolie miserably. "That's why she came around at all. She thought I could help the cause."

I stared at the gray sea, hearing but not hearing; not wanting to hear. The roar of the wind and waves provided some cover for my stricken heart; for I had my answer at last. Finally I said (rather traitorously), "It's not the worst idea in the world. Think of Banage. And Lucette, and Olga—whatever happened to Olga?"

"Saint-Lazare infirmary happened to Olga, what do you think?"

My friend stared out to sea, frozen in her unhappiness. Written all over her face, the familiar strain of love that, at least for a time—sees only itself. The waves roiled in and out; taking away what had been on the beach, throwing up something new. And now, and now—Jolie was ill and I had to run and catch up to a war.

I stared down at the papers. The war would end somehow; all wars did. I could end my own—wipe the slate clean. I filled the pen's reservoir with ink, wiped its nib . . . I had not heard from Nathalie for weeks; my employer had stretched her summer holidays, been absent since she left for Baden-Baden in July. To gamble and take the waters at the Rhine bathing palace whose grandeur rivaled that of Versailles. I thought about Olga, smuggling pastries up from the kitchen at Deux Soeurs so we could share something sweet . . . Saint-Lazare for Olga. Baden-Baden for Nathalie.

It seemed likely that she was a spy. What Noël said had made perfect sense, although I was no witness to any of it. Lacking the heart to consider it further I riffled through the pages of the document to find the line for the signature.

"A moment please, Madame Eugénie?"

"Yes, what is it?" I had not slept well and was late in rising; had not called for Séverine. Now my maid sat stiffly in her going-out dress and gloves so neatly mended, the stitches were invisible, and my heart sank. Her sudden good humor over the past few days now seemed too brittle; and I had overheard quick, fiery bursts of conversations with La Tigre. I wondered, not for the first time, if the girl begrudged us her service; but she was an excellent maid—more than a maid. She was essential to all of the business in which I was involved. I tried to recall where her family was. Normandy. But she was not close to them.

"I'm sorry to give you my notice, Madame Eugénie. But the Prussians have gunners around nearly every fort; they mean to starve us out just like at Strasbourg, over the winter. I have taken service with another lady. She says there are many more Prussians than — than — is thought — and Paris is full of spies. Anyone with any sense is leaving and I have to go and pack her tonight."

I threw the pen at the wall and spattered it with ink, hardly missing her nose. Sévérine ducked.

"Sévérine! When?"

"Tonight, madame."

"You can't — *tonight?* That's not any sort of notice — where are you going?" I had no time to interview replacements. "Are you ill? Take the day off. Sévérine — what I mean to say is — it is a very bad time." I had Noël's document to deal with, and everything required haste, as though it had to be done before the city burned down; but what would it matter then?

"It is worse than you think, madame, if I may say so. I will leave my things; the lady is to give me a new set of dresses to wear, she is very —"

"A lady — what lady? Are you going across the Channel? To Brussels?"

Sévérine closed her lips. I knew that expression of hers; indeed, I had relied on it. Her discretion.

"Yes, yes. All right, then. I hope you are not leaving it to me to tell La Tigre; she relies on you too much — and Lili —" (Since Beausoleil had departed and Lili had come back, she and I shared the services of Sévérine.)

"I packed Mademoiselle Lili last night." Sévérine's freckles stood out on her pale nose; and her curls were escaping from under her bonnet. Now I started in shock.

"*Lili* is going?"

"Sailing tomorrow, madame. On *Napoleon III* from Le Havre to New York. I believe she means to try again for Mexico."

"Well, at least one further errand is needed. To the Préfecture."

"I'm so sorry, Madame Eugénie."

So I did not have her services to convey the document on that day. By the time I carried it there myself, the man at the desk was Coué,

and he told me that Noël had been reassigned to a post on the battlefield at Sedan, a fortified town at the edge of the Ardennes forest
and near the French-Belgian border, reporting under General the
Marquis de Gallifet. Gallifet's wife, the marquise, was famous for
having made a dazzling appearance not very long ago at an imperial
costume ball, dressed as a white swan. All the papers had written
about her costume. So Noël had his promotion after all.

I returned to my escritoire with the denunciation of Nathalie
Jouffroy still in hand. I broke the seal and removed the sheets, took
stock once more of the document, my amendments to it, my bold
scrawl at its foot. I had not wanted to give it to Coué; didn't trust
the man. Then, on an impulse and without knowing why — not for
loyalty to Nathalie, and nothing to do with Noël, Coué, or any of
them — I tore the paper to shreds.

Perhaps I knew in some way that it was growing late for spies . . .
growing late for the Préfecture, had any of us known it.

Sometime in the middle of the night, or toward morning, the roaring began. A dull torrent from the direction of the Bourse, filtering
in and out of dreaming night. I threw open the shutters, opened the
window to the watery sky, and leaned out, as the roar resolved itself
into a clear syllables.

DÉ-CHÉ-ANCE!
ABDICATION.

And so. As the world now knows, on a crisp day in early September 1870, not even two months after his declaration of war, Emperor Louis Napoleon III surrendered to King Wilhelm of Prussia
and Chancellor Count von Bismarck on the battlefield at Sedan. His
troops, 104,000 men who had staged a gallant burst of fighting worthy of the last battle of Troy, were taken prisoner. His regent, Empress Eugénie, fled the palace with her American dentist, abandon-
ing her breakfast egg, hot and freshly cracked with a silver spoon.

And the roaring of Paris started a day that was to become glori-
ously sunny, perfect September weather. The citizens were muster-

ing for the empire's end. And the streets, even at that hour, were filled. A solid river of people marched toward the center, to the Hôtel de Ville. By evening, the Third French Republic was declared.

The war, Louis Napoleon's war. It had been lost; but for a moment or two defeat receded. Who had wanted to fight it? Not the tarot-and-*manille* players, the gossips of the rue du Mail. Yes, yes. We were to learn who wanted it, and why. But for an intake of breath at the dawn of the new republic, we had peace without an empire, and the Age of Reason made a brief reappearance. Reason, that old-fashioned, past-century notion? We breathed it for whole moments at once, saw things as they could be. Honored the republic soberly that bright September, with the corpses of Sedan not yet surging back through the gates. And with passion, tearing down the emblems of empire. The words PROPERTY OF THE PEOPLE were chalked in front of the Tuileries. Busts of Napoleon III thrown into the Seine.

Jérome Noël returned from the Sedan battlefield as one of the dead. The man who had inspected my hands for signs of softness, had labored over my inscription and thousands of others; who had transcribed my intelligence in the name of the public health, collected what information I had to offer—but never erased me from the Register. This man shot in the line of duty, carrying a message for Gallifet. Inspector Coué, persecutor of milliners and lately, of Odette, was set to replace him at the Préfecture.

And then suddenly—as it seemed, though in fact it was not so sudden—a lull took the place of the clatter and chaos, the flags and "La Marseillaise"; everything became businesslike. New proclamations were unfurled on the walls, replacing the winding, deceptive discursions of the previous regime. The current message was brief.

The enemy is on the move toward Paris.
The defense of the capital is assured.

～ 23 ～

DEBAUCH

BUT THE WEATHER WAS brilliant, and the gutters and fountains again dry as an endless stream of people and product surged through the Paris gates like a misguided herd. Not only was the enemy "on the move," but so was everyone else; and the population of the capital was changing. The well-off tumbled out of the city with their locked trunks, tapestry bags, horsehair luggage, and servants; those on the outskirts moved into the center. No one wanted to be trapped between the Prussian army and the Paris walls; Paris, at least, was sure to be defended. Wagons lined up one behind the next, piled with household goods, as goats and chickens straggled behind. Families trudged with their bundles; children pushed loaded carts down the tree-lined streets, trampling the city's sprucely trimmed shrubs. Young men came to enlist with the National Guard. Any streets not filled with marching and drilling soldiers were overrun with girls in clogs and caps, with women carrying infants; farm boys driving pigs and sheep to any open space, including parks, courtyards, and buildings whose ground floor had been vacated. The formerly clean-swept boulevards were littered with household detritus: coal and vegetable peelings and lost laundry; the squares were filled with animals; clotheslines were strung between tree branches. Provisions rolled in too: piles of cauliflower,

leeks, and turnips; apples and plums and pears—sides of beef and
pork—great wheels of cheese and tall tin containers of milk. All
the countryside's harvest was hauled, hand over fist, in through the
perimeter walls as though a great and torrid feast was in the offing.
Apples fell off a cart, but there were so many that the urchins didn't
even scramble for them.

The girl was barely more than an urchin herself: sharp-angled
knees poking out from her thin skirt, and thin elbows jutting from
the sleeves of her dress, not much more than a rag against the cold.
Deep-set eyes and loitering on the corner of the rue Montmartre,
but she looked scared and out of luck. The lead medallion of the
abandonnée around her neck.

"Finette *is* my name," she said, her chin forward. She insisted
that she had been promised employment at the Black Cat, but they
had turned her away for being too young.

"Finette is a famous dancer, and you are certainly too young to be
she."

"I'm sixteen," she muttered.

"Let me see your medallion." My chest tightened as I touched the
small flattened bullet of lead, the hammered disc heavy as a heart,
dangling on a filthy cord. *How old? Too old.*

The string was made up of sections, one knotted to the next, to
enlarge the circle around her neck. The bit closest to the metal disc
was black and frayed. She'd tried to scratch off the number—as
though everyone wore medallions and it was only her number that
gave her away. I hated to see them on the street so young. The year
she was put under state care was still visible under the scratches:
1857. An unmothered little gypsy, an air creature brought up on
noxious fumes. The soles of her feet were black. Callused and bare.

"Who promised you the job on the hill?"

"If I didn't he said I'd be sent to the coffee grinder!"

"He was lying then. They send boys only to Cayenne. Not girls
of your age; you are thirteen if you are a day."

"They *will* send me to the coffee mill, he told me so."

"From where?"

"Saint-Denis."

Tiny sparkling chips in her grimy earlobes.

"And he gave you earrings, so you will do whatever he says?"

"I *don't*. Not whatever."

"Well, you're in luck today. I need a maid." I dangled the medallion. "Or you can go back to where you belong. The hospice doesn't like to lose track of its own."

She looked afraid.

"If you come with me I'll show you where to take a bath and where you'll sleep, and give you supper, if you ask nicely. And a pair of shoes."

"A bath . . . in a bathing tub?" she said doubtfully. "Will it be warm?"

"Quite hot," I said, looking her over again. "And a lice comb."

"I don't like to wear shoes," said Finette.

The name stuck.

La Tigre would give me the sharp side of her tongue for hiring a maid off the street; Francisque and Amélie would never share her. But her big gray eyes, and the way she said *I don't*, suggested she might be honest and bright, under the grime. I would send a note to the Préfecture about illegal procuring out of Saint-Denis. For all the good it would do.

Soon Finette, with freshly scrubbed fingers, was ripping stitches in a pool of gaslight, tearing out the seams of Séverine's castoff, which could make three gowns for her. La Tigre folded her arms and gave me a *look*.

"Might you do me the favor of lacing me up for tonight, madame? I'll teach her tomorrow how it's done."

Lights from a hundred apartments glimmered like underwater diamonds from my carriage window, and the earlier hubbub of the streets had subsided. Swimming through a silky liquid, the night spread loose; the moon was three nights past half, waxing, high and bright; clouds scudded by, obscuring then releasing it. Tonight's supper was in honor of my friend Giulia, our celebrated *Italienne*,

who like everyone else was leaving Paris. I dressed as though it was
the last celebration in the world, in midnight blue silk and black lace.
The wind came up as the driver slammed closed the carriage door;
I pulled my cloak tighter. It had a swan's-down ruff that tickled my
neck and ears. An autumn moon; chill in the air — the first real cold,
the shivering kind; the first night on which fire must be lit — the real
change, the one that doesn't relent back into summer's arms.

Flickering tapers in the chandeliers and the flash of waiters' dark
sleeves; a rising din of conversation and popping corks. A hubbub;
a whirl, the pouring of wine; a clamor as some Russians arrived.
(Did Russians remain in Paris? Apparently some few.) The white of
Giulia's famous shoulders and neck, where her creamy skin met the
curve of bodice. Giulia, with white camellias in her hair, kissed me
on each cheek and on the lips and placed Giulietta's hand in mine.

"Be a darling and watch out for her, Eugénie. She so wanted to
come, I couldn't say no, and I had to promise my life to the nuns to
let her out." Giulietta was now eight, a lovely small princess with
wide, dark eyes and tendrils of hair escaping from her too-adult
coiffure; the dress she was wearing was a miniature, though more
demure, copy of her mother's. I had watched her grow, playing on
the carpets in my rooms at the rue du Mail when Giulia came to talk,
to cry, to read poetry on my little balcony. I would have loved to see
more of Giulia, but she must play "La Barrucci" and tour the capi-
tals of Europe. She was a captive of her fame; I did not envy her, as
did most women — certainly Francisque and the others. The Russians settled themselves, tipping back small, cold glasses of vodka; a
draft blew through a crack at the tall windows. I squeezed Giulietta's
hand as conversation swirled, and her big eyes smiled at me.

. . . Haussmann's dismissal, how it had proceeded. The new opera house, which would have more than two thousand keys to un-
lock its every compartment, door, and secret (over the consommé, a
brief argument over the exact number of keys). And then to the war.
Dawn's rosy tinge had been shaken off the republican transition,
reassuring us all of the quick hustle back to business. Order must be
put to the appalling situation that Louis Napoleon had left behind,

and the man assigned for the job was the Breton general Trochu, a career military man known for his dull and lengthy proclamations and his criticism of the army. Unpopular with the imperial rulers, he had since been installed as governor of Paris and charged with the capital's defense. Trochu's "Plan" was the talk of the boulevards and the papers . . . We talked of the sugar shortage. Money and how to make it, under the circumstances.

Heads swiveled as a startling, dark-skinned boy entered the room. He had almond eyes and a beardless chin, was dressed in a coat of sapphire silk and a close-wrapped head covering. He preceded a gentleman in a beautifully cut suit; Indian silk, in a European style. Giulia's mellifluous voice rang out from the other end of the table.

"Enough of this! *Monsieur le comte* is just in time. He will divert us with stories of India." The boy, with the eerie air of a dream, pulled out a chair; he stared straight ahead as though none of us existed. A waiter circled with a dish of caviar on ice, offering servings from an ivory spoon as the man crossed to kiss Giulia's hand; nodding to others here, bending there. He caused a ripple in the room. Eyes like soot stains, full of sulky irony.

Hadn't I known all along? Whether the thousandth, or the ten-thousandth night; it was just a matter of time, of place, of one coincidence too many. Still, the shock shuddered up through the floorboards, flooded up my spine with a spinning chill.

" . . . Near Chandannagar," he was saying now. "An indigo concern." Uproar of Russian laughter. "There is a reason it is called 'the blue devil of Bengal.' Most of my Indian stories, I fear, you would find the opposite of diverting."

Giulia called out, "Have you met the fakirs? Do they sit in the center of fires or bury themselves in sand up to the neck?"

"At Mozufferpore there *was* a fakir who stood on one leg for seven years," said Stephan. The turbaned boy was holding his master's chair as though he had been standing for a decade himself.

"But *why?*" whined a woman in a saffron bodice.

"To show that the body's decay has no meaning."

"How can that be?"

Speed the body's deterioration, release the pure spirit from its mortal envelope — perform miracles so the people will believe. But perhaps it is only a trick they do for alms ... Laughter. "In fact it is no easier to find magic in India than in France, madame."

He turned momentarily toward us, toward Giulietta and me; then murmured to the woman on his left, sharing a laugh. I did not move an eyelash, cry out, or faint. Just put my arm around Giulietta's shoulders, too bare for a child of her age; she was shivering with excitement. The girl picked at a plate of tiny silvery fish, stealing glances down the table at her mother, at everything: wide-eyed, taking in every word and color and sound, including the visage of the dark-skinned boy who must have been near her age, but who was so still, insensible almost, even as he listened — and he must have heard, even though he seemed to be attuned to distant music.

Monsieur le comte was seated across the table, a few chairs away. His glance traveled past me to Giulietta, and returned, a flicker of recognition, a question, a hesitation; he faltered. Lost his syllable and fumbled with his fork, set it down.

Two waiters stepped to his side, and one to mine.

"Champagne, Madame Eugénie?"

"Water, if you would."

The banquet room heated; became suffocating and stuffy. The long, silk-festooned windowpanes were fogged from the heat of food salvers, conversation, and the candle sconces and chandeliers. Finally, someone opened a window and a gust of cold air swept down the table, flickering the candles, which started to gutter and drip. Giulietta was shivering. I turned my eyes away; removed my shawl and wrapped it around the girl. The Indian boy was watching too. His eyes seemed to absorb light.

"Close the window," someone called out. The party had divided — the raucous side toward the hostess's end, and the quieter toward where Giulietta and I were seated. Stephan made the fulcrum. One of the Russians, rather than draw it shut, flung it more widely open. A drunken "La Marseillaise" filtered up from the street. Shots went off.

"La Dame aux Camélias requests her pleasure!"

"What, Giulia wants the window open?" someone asked.

"But she is a Roman; she loathes the cold."

"Mama," Giulietta cried, her full attention now fixed on her mother. "You have a grippe!"

"What is going on?" asked a woman across from me. Giulia had pulled her seat in front of the tall window.

Stephan said, "It seems that the Russians are placing bets on how cold Giulia can get before she decides to close the window. She has taken them on and declares she will sit through the night."

Giulia loved a bet and I felt sorry for anyone who wagered against her. She *would* sit there all night; she would strip naked and bathe in an ice bucket if she needed to.

" . . . To perform a miracle, or for the alms?" someone joked.

"It is a game you know, monsieur?" I said, across the table.

"I was simply translating from the Russian," said Stephan.

"Mama—don't sit by the window," cried Giulietta, this time in Italian.

"Sidonie, take her home," called Giulia down the table to her maid. "This is no place for a child." A Russian was dropping ice where La Grande Puttana's last string of pearls stopped. Waiters swirled in black and white, tapers guttered, and the wind fluttered camellia petals like snow.

"What do you say? Thirty minutes, an hour, until dessert? Or can La Benini, La Grande Puttana, sit here until morning? I will bet with her that she cannot die; the blood of her heart is ice already, her lungs are the lungs of a Siberian sturgeon."

"Place your wagers, gentlemen." The laughter went on; a woman snapped her fan and rose . . . Courses came and went in quick succession. Wine was poured, and poured, and poured again.

. . . And why this night of all nights, why now? With the provinces invading Paris; sheep grazing in the Tuileries; Normandy apples and Cantal cheeses thundering through the gates, and carcasses swinging from hooks on uncurtained wagons, the entire line of food supply stripped naked, revealed to all? When the empire was now a stage set torn down, its costumes shivered off? Or because I had finally learned that in Paris, night was day, daylight was darkness;

mortal flesh was money, and to love was to kill yourself. When I had achieved my own footing, on that rotted ground.

Strands of Giulia's hair had fallen down over her shoulders. One of the Russians had seized a bottle of seltzer and used it to drench the hostess. This encouraged further sport and an entire pitcher of ice water was dumped over her head. Giulia's beautiful gown was by now almost transparent, clinging to her skin like drapery carved into marble. Water ran in rivulets over her neck and shoulders, soaked the notes and bills scattered around her, the camellia petals and gold coins on the floor around her chair. Her face was icy, then ashen; expressionless, she was as a white statue, cold, perfect, uncracked. It was vile, but I'd seen worse at these affairs.

Guests put down their knives and forks even though the courses were still coming, and a few departed, leaving a gap where conversation had been. Across the table, my one-time lover allowed a waiter to refold his napkin. He looked uncomfortable.

"You are perhaps unfamiliar with this sort of performance, monsieur," I said.

"It is not my preferred form of entertainment."

"Then you have not been in Paris very long, for it is hardly rare here."

Next to me, Giulietta started to cry, silent tears running down her reddened cheeks, and she needed a handkerchief. "Mama has the grippe," she gulped. "But she told me not to move from my chair, whatever I did."

I looked around for Sidonie. "Don't worry," I said. "Your mama is just playing a game. It's not a good game, but it will end soon." I spotted the maid, and beckoned to her. "Sidonie! Aren't you taking her home?"

"She coughs up *blood*," sobbed Giulietta.

Stephan said, "In the Indian scriptures it is said that he who forgets the suffering of women shall be born in the body of an owl for three separate lifetimes. A room full of owls, then, in a hundred years, don't you think?"

"Why, *your* old place was hooting with them, wasn't it, monsieur?"

Stephan stood up halfway, pushing aside some lemon-colored dessert. His face turned bone-white; his gaze went again, immediately, to the girl. The boy in blue silk turned and stepped ahead. I hugged Giulietta, handing her off to Sidonie.

"She is Giulia's daughter," I said calmly. "Lovely, isn't she?"

"I am sorry for her," he said abruptly, and turned away.

Behind me, coffee was being served and some of the party had lost interest in the betting; they had gone off to smoke. Giulia sat alone with a small hubbub around her; she looked less like marble now; colder and more wretched. I went to her and closed the window, kneeled at her side.

"Giulietta has gone with Sidonie," I said. "But I promised her that the game would be over soon, Giulia. If you get up now, cross the room, and leave by the side door, I will embarrass these Russian *faiblards* into paying up. My driver is outside. Use him; I will get a cab." Giulia did not keep a driver in Paris. My friend did not answer; she was in some sort of trance. I had never seen anyone so still.

Finally Giulia's chest heaved in a trembling sigh and she tried to stand. I took her arm and steadied her. But I wanted her to leave that room on her own, splendidly dripping ice, past the Russians and out. I kept my hand on her back until she could. Then drew the Russians' ringleader aside. Stephan was gone. *Damn them all.*

Later, hurtling over the broken cobbles in a cab, the driver spurred the horses. Narrow streets, high walls. Broken panes stuffed with rags. VINS. RESTAURANT. BOULANGERIE. CHAMBRES À LOUER, rooms to rent. Rooms, rooms. Always rooms and nothing there. My head rolled back against the seat of the cab, against the cracked black leather, and I steadied myself against the sharp jolts and turns. The carriage pulled up; the door swung again. There, just in front of where I stood on the corner of the rue Montmartre, was a flock of ghostly geese pecking the dust. Escapees from a farmer's cart, newly pulled in through the Paris gates. And there, for all the world like another ghost, was a ragged, wraithlike goose-girl, her arms wrapped around an enormous bird like she was holding its wings for dear life.

24

SURROUNDED

THE QUIET WAS LEADEN and the room cold; no fire had been lit. A heaviness like an invisible cat weighed down the Marseille quilt bunched up around my neck. A dream stuck like fog; that Lili was examining my teeth and giving me saffron-colored flower petals to chew, saying that the stains they left would show where my teeth were weak. My head was pounding from the after effects of vodka and champagne. *Giulia, Russians. Stephan.* I huddled under the quilt and shivered. It was cold enough now for the gray goose-feather duvets to be brought out. Finette must learn how to clean out a hearth without spreading ashes on the carpet; to place saucers under coffee cups. The cold brew left on my bedside table was bitter.

Finally I threw back the bedclothes and went to my desk, tugged at the blue ormolu bell pull. In the compartments were scrolls of outdated correspondence, Noël's overflow (such is the fate of the functionary; it doesn't matter that one is dead).

Do not, M. le Préfet, deny me the consolation that an afflicted mother so much needs . . . My son, dead in honorable service to France on the battlefield at Sedan, now I beg of you not to refuse me an honest means of living, a license to open a tolerated house . . .

What to reply? *Not only is your son dead, but also monsieur to whom you write, along with a good number of your prospective customers . . .* Request for a loan of funds. Letter of introduction needed. The usual, from Deux Soeurs, an urgent request for three new girls. (How did I become their avenue of first resort?) Two more required at another house, "European languages preferred." (How to interpret that—fluency in German, in preparation for an occupation?) One candidate "of excellent quality" required at the discreet and expensive meat rack tucked behind the Louvre . . . Stacks of letters.

Nathalie Jouffroy had surfaced—in the form of a sheet of stationery from the Hôtel Royal Champagne at Rheims, where she presided amid green-topped gaming tables and black-and-white roulette, doubtless consorting with the Prussian generals. And suddenly I understood, in a slow-headed haze, where my maid had gone—no one but Nathalie could have made Sévérine jump so quickly! Nathalie must have made a flying trip back into Paris to pack her things and corral the most reliable hand to be found, Sévérine. How many errands had I sent the girl on to Deux Soeurs, back and forth. Nathalie had had ample time to assess my maid—I was surprised, now, that she had stayed with me so long. In fact Sévérine had been loyal to a fault, given what Nathalie would pay her.

Of course, at Rheims Jouffroy needed a capable hand to assist and cater to "the Blackamoor," as Noël had liked to call her—the Spanish African beauty, Nathalie's precious investment—a registered girl raised from the obscurity of Salon Trois, up through the ranks, to become one of the most highly desired courtesans in Europe; and her billets-doux and appointment book and sheaves of roses must be expertly managed. Nathalie would fly to the moon for "Camille," as she was known. And Jouffroy's own newspapers, her financial pages, must be managed just as she liked; her café au lait served tepid, so she could sip it slowly, without any change in its temperature. She had abandoned Paris with her jewel just as Giulia was preparing to do, and the city would close like a trap.

Somewhere in the depths of my desk was what I was actually looking for: the sheaf of correspondence from the lawyers, a summary

of where my case stood with the de Chaveignes. My lawyer recom-
mended that I agree to drop any claim of paternity in exchange for
my liberty. But I had developed a sharper taste for justice and had
requested another solution: damages, reparations. In short, a payoff.

In reply, my representative had stated that because of my status
on the Register, not a judge in Paris would rule in my favor. Pursuing it, I would spend more and gain less. He then suggested I publish
a memoir full of salacious details.

At the bottom of this detritus was another sheaf of loose papers:
stained and blotted notebooks. Diaries and letters begun long ago,
on hesitant afternoons and empty evenings. I had examined these
in light of his suggestion — but the tone was naive, angry, lacking
insight. I was unable to step away from the events of my life and
refashion them; instead, my old ink-stained wounds thrust me into a
labyrinth of doubt.

I had put down my stricken pages with the haste of a convict
tripping over herself to please her jailer, pursuing chits for favors
with the Préfecture, securing myself against arrest, and nursing the
vain, tenuous hope of the *inscrit* — that once off the Register, with
all record of my existence there expunged, and with a perfect record
of hospice visits, at least I could reclaim Berthe and my own good
name. Even this, I saw, had been a fictional bargain with a nonexis-
tent judge and jury. However, with Noël dead at Sedan, Coué pol-
ishing his desk ornaments — Nathalie at Rheims and the Prussians
on the doorstep — it had all, perhaps, come to a fitting end. Thus
the world taught its lessons.

Ah, and here — in with some hairpins and a pile of dust — was
my *carte*. It bore no recent record of medical inspections, no stamps
of renewal; was never requested by the police. A relic except for the
bare fact of its existence, the lingering, poisonous fact of it, and the
chain of consequence to which it had led.

"Madame?" A soft knock. Finette, looking surprisingly demure
with her hair pulled back, wearing a hand-me-down of Séverine's,
and precariously carrying a fresh pot of hot coffee and some warm
milk. I sighed.

"Yes. Good morning. What is it?"

"You rang the bell and La Tigre told me to come up."

"Can you ask her to show you, please, about the bed linens and the hearth. And I will have a letter shortly."

"Yes, madame. But she sent me to tell you also that you must get out for provisions soon, before everything is gone. The others, Madame Francisque and Mademoiselle Amélie and she have gone out, hours ago. I went with them to carry parcels. So—now may I finish the hearth? I have brought some spent tea leaves; otherwise the ashes scatter." I blinked. La Tigre had created a miracle, or else the girl had finally realized her good luck.

The others had gone for provisions. That explained why everything was so quiet.

Across the street, lines for the Mont de Piété snaked down the block; a steady stream of birdcages and kettles, mattresses carried on backs; bedsteads dragged behind cartloads of chairs and tables. Every last citizen of Paris, in addition to the hordes of bewildered newcomers, was exchanging whatever he or she could lay hold of to trade for ready cash, to make purchases on the black market. The flying rumors did not concern battles lost or won any longer, but food. What was where? Who had it, and at what cost? How much was stored for absolute emergency? A peace agreement was expected, but days passed, then weeks. Every morning we rushed out to examine the pronouncements plastered to the walls, hoping for an armistice, and each succeeding day offered no news—only the new government's lukewarm assurance that provisions for a city of two million souls could last for an indeterminate period of time. But at Strasbourg, the people were starving to death. And the march of the Prussians toward Paris had already reached Versailles.

At an under-the-counter up Montparnasse was a long, shifting line of the well- and better-dressed. We all watched one another, darting our eyes at whoever stepped past with parcels and packages, as though the quantity of goods carted away by anyone in particular was an indication of what was to come. Certainly it was as good a measure as any: the papers argued and said nothing.

"Her husband was an empire man, and she's got only one salted ham—maybe old Badinguet still has something up his sleeve," a man behind me whispered.

"Oh, it's all just a precaution. We'll be handing out hams on the street at Noël."

"Or shooting horses by then."

"Trochu has a plan, you can count on it." *(A plan, a plan. The man has a plan! PLAN, PLAN, PLAN! Mon DIEU, what a fine Pla-a-n! Thanks to him, nothing is lost.* That's what they sang in the streets, with mocking, eerie prescience.)

"If Châtillon is lost we will be girdled tighter than Mademoiselle Thérèse after dinner." The present worry was that if the Prussian army established itself on the Châtillon plateau to the south of the city, three of the forts protecting the capital would be vulnerable. And from Châtillon, shells launched by the Krupp cannon, which had been admired so recently at the Great Exhibition, could reach the heart of Paris.

"Trochu will defend Châtillon to the last gun. He's not mad, just a Breton."

"Yes, and a Catholic, and a soldier, as he is fond of saying—and a pessimist and a procrastinator! My money is on Gambetta, now there's some fire!" Léon Gambetta had proclaimed the republic from the windows of the Hôtel de Ville; some thought he was the only Frenchman capable of raising a defense of Paris. His handsome profile made Amélie swoon, although Francisque declared him common. General Trochu, head of the new Government of National Defense, was monklike and forbidding as a toad, and favored by none of the women—though we certainly hoped he could save us, just like the old *muffes* we couldn't afford to hate.

"It is Belleville Trochu is afraid of. He'd rather answer to a German than to the mob."

"Madame P, have you taken all the fish heads, as well as the fish?"

Boxed English biscuits, strings of dried fish, sardines, salted beef, and confit; Liebig's meat extract, "Extractum carnis Liebig"; parcels of Chollet's desiccated vegetables. Rounds of waxed Dutch cheese. Tea. Coffee. Sugar (very expensive, as was salt—they had run out of salt at Strasbourg, it was rumored, and could not make a decent sauce to cover the rats). Flour and rice. Casks of wine and one of Armagnac. I opted for a generous supply, took a few parcels, and ordered the rest for delivery.

On the way back, boulevard traffic was slow, and several of us from the queue shared a cab. Then the carriages were diverted and re-routed — another parade approaching? But the republic was less taken with parades than the empire had been, and this one advanced without fanfare. The gentleman beside me, supplies captive on his lap, drew out a small spyglass. Many carried these devices now, either to look at their neighbors or to go up to the heights and study the fortifications.

"I think these marchers have come from Châtillon." After looking, he passed it along, and we took turns watching the columns of soldiers — lines and lines of infantry marching toward us. Some ramrod straight, with placards on their chests — others barely shuffling, like sleepwalkers, or with an attitude of sulky defiance rather than the customary bravado. Their soldier's caps were reversed, and coats and trousers turned inside-out — even those of the proud Zouaves — and if they were armed, we could not see it.

"They must be deserters." The first of the ranks were now passing quite near. I craned my neck to see that one soldier had broken from the line and was moving from carriage to carriage, shouting. When he reached ours he stared at each of us in turn.

"*NOUS SOMMES TRAHIS!*" he said, and then again, hoarse and urgent — as if I had not heard, or as though he expected an answer, he repeated the words. *We are betrayed.*

"Why is he saying that?" asked Madame P, with her stock of dried fish heads, which she said were for her cat. "What does it mean?"

"Trochu betray the French army? Never! These deserters all love to claim they are betrayed," said the spyglass.

To look into their eyes, though, was to feel the creep of something familiar. Of deals made far above one's head, out of one's view; destiny on the chopping block.

———

Rumors were whispered, although not among the likes of those in the black-market line. Some said that in the wake of the failure to produce an armistice, Trochu's "Plan" was not to fight but to capitulate to Bismarck; but that he could not do it too soon, for fear of a popular uprising. Even now, some murmured that the police were not safe on the streets in the working districts of Belleville and Ménilmontant, where men (and women as well) were all for taking up arms against the Prussians themselves. So the French army was being trickled out in its insufficient numbers, with few supplies and no defensive strategy; an army of show to appease the population and keep them busy in the *ambulances*, the makeshift hospitals that had sprung up all over the city to take in the wounded (which were few) while the government dithered and debated. But looking at their faces, it was difficult to believe these soldiers were deserters. I wasn't sure what it meant; no one was.

"So what is going to happen *now*," asked Mademoiselle Fish Heads, whose simpering was beginning to steam the windows.

"I would prepare to walk, if I were you, mademoiselle," said the gentleman with the spyglass, gathering up his parcels to disembark. "It will get you into condition for the time, God forbid, when we have eaten all of the cab horses in the capital."

Something terrible had certainly happened. At the rue du Mail, my neighbors were up in the atelier with telescopes — palm glued over one eye, as children will do. The roof gave a view all the way out to the Fort de l'Est. On the horizon appeared bursts of white smoke, each vanishing in a puff. We watched until dusk; the lights from the fortifications flickered like gas jets; and cannon fire sounded hollow and dull — just, as one diarist would later describe it, like the *clunk* made by an oar as it struck the side of a boat. We waited; watched. In the streets, people gathered uneasily at the kiosks for any news, even opposing reports. But now there was nothing. No word. During that brief, uneasy interlude between *now* and *forever*, the flicker of doubt replaced the lick of gaslight. Now the thunder that we heard signified no storm; it was the sound of many keys turning in many locks, the distant tumult as bridges exploded over the Seine, and the rattling closures of the gates. The capital was being cut off from the rest of France. Châtillon had been abandoned; it was now held by the Prussian crown prince.

In the following days, usual activities were suspended. Theaters remained dark, orchestras silent. Mail and news from outside ceased and the usual chatterers seemed to be stunned mute. The landlords had fled like rats off a ship, so no one was collecting rent, which changed the tenor of certain things. At the Préfecture, most of the Morals Brigade had been conscripted for the army—even Coué was hurriedly recommissioned. Without the police, no distinction existed between *inscrit* and *non-inscrit;* everyone stood where they pleased in all of the old off-limits places: the Champs-Élysées, the Tuileries. Girls smoked, drank beer, undid their bodices, and headed out to the ramparts at midday because the National Guards made one and a half francs per day and were virtually idle, although no one understood exactly why. The Prussians did not advance; our army did not engage them. Opinions flew: that the Prussians did not dare attack Paris, the "beating heart of Europe, the city of cities; the city of men," as Victor Hugo had gustily written earlier that September. Or Trochu was negotiating to capitulate; or the Prussians had suspended their advance because they were so stunned that the French had not mounted a sturdier defense of Châtillon. Or we were all waiting for Gambetta to take charge and change tactics. With hardly any news to print, the papers turned to accusing the girls. In fact, from the very beginning of the conflict, the helpings of blame were generous: it was courtesans from the top, boulevard girls from the bottom, who had rotted the empire and debilitated the fighting forces of France.

With nothing else to do, Amélie and Francisque and I sorted through our gowns. Conclusion: none appropriate. Cherry satin, violet moiré shot with orange, sea and emerald velvets were bundled into the armoires, and only my drab cloaks, suitable for incognito trips to the Préfecture, were kept in use. Amélie volunteered for the women's battalion, the "Amazons of the Seine," but was turned away at the rue de Turbigo for lack of an escort to attest to her character. (Trochu later trounced the idea of a battalion funded by rich women's jewelry, disappointing fifteen hundred applicants.) Undaunted, Amélie set out to sew silk into balloons at a factory in the Impasse du Cadran. Our hopes now were set on the hot-air balloons launched from the buttes, sending military intelligence, mail, and messengers out of the capital. Léon Gambetta himself was to be ballooned out to raise an army in the provinces. These airborne vehicles were a bold and unlikely idea — but the only one proposed. And so we waited. As the last days of September crept by, Strasbourg capitulated.

In early October, the ration card was introduced. It was only a precaution, said the pronouncements on the walls; but the line leading to the *mairie* of the second arrondissement snaked down the block, and you would be surprised at who was standing there, waiting to get a card. It was stiff and blue, marked off by the days, and could be used in exchange for a single ration at the municipal butcher or two portions at a city canteen. It also specified the composition of one's household, and one's profession. (Francisque asked, "Do you think that they will have cross-referenced the Register with the ration cards?" — which made me pause, because who would think Francisque worried about the Register?)

"In this turmoil? The government that lost Sedan?" snorted Amé. "Besides, what do you have to worry about?"

"I think they are better at waging war against those poor girls than against the Prussians," snapped Francisque. She was having a morning of nerves.

"Not without Coué," I said. "Amé is safely a milliner."

"And I am a zebra at the Jardin Zoologique," said Francisque. "I dare them to challenge it."

"Household?" asked the official, now, at the ration desk.

"Myself, and one maid."

"Profession?"

"Private secretary," I replied.

"Too long for the line!"

"Scribe, then?"

"Better scribe than inscribed," I joked darkly, later, to Amélie.

In late October an aurora borealis illuminated Paris with a claret-colored sky. It was a beautiful sight; the heavens avid with movement and splendor; a rush of lights and afterward the most brilliant stars. Everyone stood in the streets and watched.

"It is some devilry of the Prussians, you can count on it."

"The heavens are cracking open to give Paris hope!"

"No, it means we'll have the coldest winter in living history."

Eugénie,

I sit here in my apartments—in the American colony of the 16th Arr. with the remains of the displaced Confederates, business exiles, divorcées, et cetera, all poring over the *American Register,* with a herd of goats in the courtyard guarded by a boy of twelve with a pistol. I cannot, of course, book passage back to Calcutta. Friends and Relations have fled down to the last Hair—and I have found myself unable to conduct any business whatsoever. Would you care to dine? Brébant vows to serve dinner every night of the siege . . . Yours humbly . . . S de C

"Wartime lover, oldest trick in the book," said Jolie, over one of my shoulders.

"You must find satisfaction in the rematch!" said Nathalie, over the other. *"Water or champagne, my dear?"*

And so, Brébant, week three of the siege. The menu and the mood a simulacrum of what it had once been; with white clothes, mirrors reflecting a thousand lights; flicker of gas lamps on the wineglasses, the dark windowpanes. Waiters' feet feathered across the black-and-white floor; men's suits set off the ivory shoulders of their companions. Wines—from vineyards now occupied by Prussian guns—were uncorked; silver came and went, and glasses, napkins refolded in the fleur-de-lis. All smooth as clockwork, no clumsiness, no ragged motions here. All around, the murmur of a hundred civilized voices: the optimists, the morbid, the war diarists and siege *flâneurs,* the stenographers of suffering; elites who had not managed to escape. Meat graced our plates because the grass in the parks stopped growing when the weather turned; there was not enough feed hay within the walls to keep the animals that were to be preserved for producing milk and butter. They were slaughtered for meat and sold to the highest bidders. We were aware of these particulars, now. Where the fillet came from.

"Have you noticed?" Stephan said calmly, knife poised. "All of the women are eating instead of pushing food around the plate . . . Eating, breathing, what will be next? Walking in the street?"

"Prussians eating at these tables next week?"

"Bah! Never! Not while I am standing. But it is ludicrous. Ten years in the jungles of India, every muscle yearning for civilization, and this is what I come home to? To be a prisoner in Paris."

"What brought you back?"

"Business on behalf of Bengal's blue devil."

"Indigo."

"Yes, and it is late in the day for saving French fortunes by a dark blue stain." Stephan cut into his fillet. "And I came to face down my own devil."

I cut into my own fillet. Tasted it cautiously. Bit into a mélange of carrot and *haricots verts,* as crisp and buttery as if they were real. "Where do you think they are getting these?"

"Jeweler on rue de la Paix has turned vegetable dealer, I believe."

"So here we are. Dining well."

Stephan looked up from his fillet. "I understand, Mademoiselle Rigault, that you are worth a minor fortune."

"I've had some advice, good and bad."

"They say that no one knows who your 'protectors' are, you have friends in the highest offices in the city, travel the world under aliases, modeled for a famous painting—and that after this mess is over, you plan to publish your memoirs."

"Absolutely not. You have my word."

"My family's intention was to prosecute this—our case— through our lawyers. However, our men are, at present, sitting in an English country house, eating some partridge or a pheasant and waiting it out."

"Is that why you have suddenly come to the table? When the case is reopened, which I will see that it is, I will countersue and the circumstances will be considered in a republican court, not an imperial one, where they may take a more appropriate view of 'research of paternity.'"

"Any government will need to protect family and property. Why, it will take years to sort it out, even if they do want to institute changes in the Code Civil."

"When the armistice is signed, we'll see where we are."

"The courts will be clogged with cases."

"In Tillac they used to say, 'When a man cannot cross by the bridge, he will cross through the water.' But they never said what to do when there is no bridge and no water either. A woman must invent a crossing that defies physical means. Have you come with a proposal?"

He slouched back against the banquette cushions; the space between us widened, cooled. "The prosecution was initiated by my family, you know—I had enough on my plate in India."

"That is a weak argument, monsieur."

"Very well. They—rather, we—do not want any illegitimate claim troubling the estate, which is in enough difficulty as it is."

"The claim is not illegitimate in any just terms. And it is not an incursion into your family's fortunes that is my interest."

"The Code does not see it that way."

"The Code, the Code! Even that Bonaparte invention was never intended to foster profligacy, which is all that it has accomplished. The hospice is overwhelmed. Women line up and cry in the corridors like ewes whose lambs are gone to the slaughter. If you had ever seen it—why, even you might cry. It is expensive to administer, this tenet of the Code, and the courts may well want to take a stand against it. With any luck it will be torn down completely."

"But until they do, if they do, nothing else governs the matter. The law is on the side of the estate and I am not going to war with my mother and my sisters. God knows I have spent the past decade making amends. A penance under sweltering Bengal skies so my family would not suffer."

"So your sister Sophia's feet would never have to touch the cobbles in Paris!"

"Now, I will not see them ruined while you swill away the hours with self-loathing Italian whores."

"Giulia is my friend; you could not know less about her."

"And this sanctimonious cant of motherhood—I cannot stomach it."

A waiter appeared to clear our plates; we stared each other down over the crumbs. *Who was this man?* Amends for what, and to whom?

"I have recently hired a new maid. She fell off a vegetable cart from Saint-Denis before the gates closed. Illiterate, filthy, doesn't know a fork from a fish knife. An *abandonné*, a runaway. Terrified of being sent to 'the coffee mill,' as she puts it; and nearly sold into traffic at the age of twelve. *That's* the sort of daughter you gave to the empire that restored your title, *monsieur le comte*."

Stephan gave a dark laugh. "You dress like a *cocotte* and talk like a Jacobin. I'm sorry for the state of your household, but if your daughter is anything like her mother she will figure out a fork from a fish knife well enough . . . Do you want to know of misery and blighted lives? I'll tell you, it is not in France." He leaned away sharply and stared out the dark pane, where the silk turban of his boy sat like blurred midnight, outside. "My mistake—all right—my hedonism and conceit and your benighted innocence—yes, I took advantage; I was young and human and graceless. I wanted my pleasure, and took it as offered—became drunk on it, I even believed I could not do without you, had every right to you. You were willing—as I recall."

"I had none of the sophistications of your world, monsieur. As you were well aware."

"But while we were dallying under the mistletoe in my uncle's house, he was collapsed over a roulette table at Nice—"

"Mistletoe! I should have boiled it up and used it as a midwife told me to. Men will never understand a woman's follies, no matter how often we repeat them before your eyes. All you can do is accuse, and rewrite the story to please yourself."

Stephan leaned forward. "And you think the courts—even if there are new courts—will take your part? Listen. I am attempting to convey to you the facts of the situation as they occurred, ones that you do not know."

"Oh, I can listen."

Indeed, it had become my stock in trade. I sat back and folded my hands.

"After we parted, I boarded a ship to Calcutta. I was to meet my uncle. Arrived at Howrah Station, went as planned to the Great Eastern Hotel. We were to tour his investments, go tiger hunting—then return to Paris. I waited a week, two, then three before a telegraph finally reached me. He had never left Nice. Died there, at the gaming table, leaving me his fine, empire-plated title and properties stripped down to the wainscoting and so heavily mortgaged that I couldn't bail them out in a hundred lifetimes. Some time thereafter, a letter from my mother pleading with me to put his affairs to rights; to take my place as head of the family, with all that entails . . . Discharge the debts. Provide a fitting level of support for her and my sister—that was understood. And I'd had enough of dancing with heiresses at Paris balls, if you want to know the truth.

"News travels fast in India—and not by telegraph. We don't know how it does. But I could not even leave the hotel; suddenly about a thousand Hindoos had assembled in the lobby and outside, waiting for me, waving papers in the air. These were people who had been ruined by my uncle's dealings, or so they claimed. I had to explain that he was not coming; I was terrified of being engulfed; however, the news appeared to delight them. Suddenly I was not being threatened but offered help of every kind. Loans, credit, help, arrangements, servants. I was virtually a captive; and one of them had a letter that had given the name of the indigo concern in which my uncle had sunk the last of his capital. This man became my *dobachy*—of course, he had only a random claim on the letter; who knows how he got hold of it! These documents are used as currency; they are traded like scrip. He turned out to be only an underservant of an underservant of the real *dobachy*. A moneylender. From this man I learned that my household was already assembled. Cooks, lackeys, hookah bearers, punkah pullers, clippers of nose hair—*saheb le comte* certainly needed a large staff—he even assured me I would have a language teacher whom I would find much to my liking. I tried to refuse and found that I had less sway over the situation than a Bengali boy of fourteen. I was herded on a train as far as Mozufferpore and went the rest of the way by *dak*—a relay of bullock wagons, bamboo carts, and ponies. Surrounded by a horde—their train fare already charged to my 'account'—into the mountains. I had no idea where I was, who I was with. The *dobachy* negotiated everything; it was entirely in his hands. We arrived at a series of fields, and a group of huts . . . Indigo." Stephan paused. "I hardly knew what it was.

"The plantation's manager was an Englishman. He recognized a desperate fool when he saw one; I had no idea what I was doing. Why, my idea of life was that of a Paris gentleman who lives between his tailor, the club, his mistresses, and the theater, with the occasional adventure abroad. I had intended to follow in my uncle's footsteps, indeed—had made a good beginning.

"Instead I was hired as a factory assistant; the last one had just succumbed to some kind of galloping fever. I was lucky in one way—the position of factory assistant was viewed with such contempt that most of my "staff"—all except for a few, about a dozen of the roughest and strangest of the lot, just disappeared. I had not a rupee to pay the ones left, and no idea why they stayed. But they knew. And the Englishman knew.

"I was installed in a bungalow near a vast field of waving plants that I would not know from a sheaf of wheat, speaking not a word of the languages, and left on my own—if you can call being surrounded by fourteen Bengalis, each strong as an ox, *on one's own*. My first order of business was to take another three days' journey by *dak* to an area the planter was preparing to cultivate, and to oversee the destruction of a village's vegetable gardens. The plowing under of their rice fields. And then, the *tumnee* . . . Of course, I did not know, either, what that was." Stephan fell silent, then resumed.

"It is the digging that precedes the re-sowing of these areas with indigo. That was my initiation, that first *tumnee*. Everything about indigo depends on a properly executed digging. It is all done with bamboo staves by men in a line, watched over by 'stick men' with even larger ones. If it is not done well, the plants fail, rot in the ground, succumb to blight, never mature. Much can go wrong with indigo. Sometimes you don't even know about the problem until fermentation, when dye cannot be extracted from the plants. Of course I did not know how to do it, but the men did and the stick man knew.

"I had the grace to be ashamed. But here was a group of strong-men calling me *saheb le comte*. They were ready to work, their families were depending on them, and if I did not pay them when their salaries came due, they would carry me out to the jungle. My *dobachy* told me this. Very politely.

"And so I stood by the edge of a field—a rotten, pillaged swamp of a field—and I watched them. At the *tumnee*'s finish, the English-man gave their salaries to me and in turn, I paid the men. Afterward I went back to the main fields and learned indigo. How it was made, what made it profitable, and how, in great detail, my uncle's proper-ties had come to ruin. What was owed in interest alone. How the Englishman—Charlton—had taken over, and with bad fortune. Too much land depleted, *tumnees* scamped over by *badmashee* coo-lies. Fields gone to opium—we can't compete with it. Too much security required to plant and harvest. Fifty years ago the system worked, but now it has decayed . . . So. Village by village, field by field—I worked with Charlton for a ruined decade. Oh, and it got more complicated—everything does. I can tell you the details sometime, if you are interested. Once you hear them, I defy you to try to outrank me in suffering."

Silence fell between us. Icy pins of rain had begun to strike the windows. I said finally, "Your boy—he will be cold outside. He must not be used to weather like this?"

"Mitra likes the Paris scene. He enjoys watching."

"But—what's happening?"

Heads had turned toward the window as though wind gusted over a field.

A clatter through the drapes, billow of cold air, then noses poked through the curtains, knees edged in, a knobby shoulder. Blackened faces and dirty hands. Stock still, chests heaving, eight pairs of blinking bruised eyes. A hush fell on the dining-room babble and everything stopped, as though we were waiting for something to happen—a hand to reach down from the heavens and pick up the vagabonds by the scruff of the neck! Forks and glasses halted in midair; fans snapped and gentlemen half-rose in their seats. *Would someone please fire upon these children?*

A man—short, squat, dressed in tails—shouldered between the tables and made his way back toward the kitchen. He reappeared with a basket of bread and apples, steady as the ox pulls the cart, looking neither left nor right as he passed the tables of silent diners. The drape billowed again behind him, as he stepped outside into the rain.

"Auguste Maillard won't settle the mob by throwing them crumbs," muttered a man at the next table. I felt cold, and my stomach turned over. Maillard: the man who had bought Chasseloup's painting.

"Feed them tonight; tomorrow there will be a dozen more, then all of Belleville, on our doorstep. Your table extenders cannot reach that far, Auguste!" Laughter, mean and nervous. Auguste Maillard's first successful patent had been for a dining-table extender; a generous and pragmatic invention, I had always thought, reading about him in the papers.

"I've never seen anything like it in my life," exclaimed a woman, folding her fan. "What do you think made them so bold?"

"A change in the weather," said Maillard. He turned full, then, and looked—or perhaps I only imagined it—in my direction; made a slight movement with his hand. I was trembling.

"It is Maillard," I said, uselessly. "He is still in Paris."

"I know who he is," said Stephan. "He was an investor in indigo, in the whole French colony. But he did not like the *ryot* uprisings; security became too expensive. Men like him sit in Paris, never tramp down a field, or sit down to hookah with the *zemindars*. They say Maillard is going toward the mob, but the mob will never have

him—not with his Saint-Simonian notions, unifying Europe for
the economic good and the rest of it."

"I heard that he—Maillard—shot his own horse to feed his
workers because they threatened to strike. A beautiful mare."

"One lives as one must, I suppose. Do you care for dessert? Figs
in wine sauce. Figs are dry; wine, at least—plentiful. As long as I
can dine, I intend to look at this siege as a strange but well-deserved
holiday. Unless of course—well, it is unthinkable that Trochu will
so botch the thing that—it will continue to deteriorate. How do
you know Maillard?"

"He bought the painting. The one you mentioned earlier, for
which I was the model."

"Ah. There is a painting, then."

"It was done just after I came to Paris, yes."

"And Maillard has it?"

"He owns it, so I suppose he does have it."

Stephan looked curiously at me. "Why, I must see it. You have no
idea how I—how I thought of you, then."

I had finally seen the painting myself; had read in the paper that
Maillard had lent it to be shown, and I went and saw it. The girl
in the painting was half-turned, looking over her shoulder, a white
shawl, like a cloud, drifting over her shoulder and down her arm.
The hair, dark; her skin, pale. A three-quarters profile. A hand.
Resting on the other arm. I could not look at it for very long.

I picked up my fork to stab a fig; placed it back down. Watched
shapes in the half-light; candlelight licking goblets full of wine, reflecting a hundred ruby flames. Stephan's account had made me feel
feverish in an ugly way. Toyed with; pulled to and fro; not unmoved
by the sad truths of the unseen world. The waiter came. He apologized, to Stephan, for what he called "the disturbance."

"It is all right," I replied. "It is the world we are living in now."
The waiter's head swiveled toward me; his lip curled, in a breach
of Brébant protocol; neither of us knowing where the other stood.
That was the true siege; the not-knowing, the curtain coming down
on all of the old tales we told ourselves.

Stephan helped me into my cloak, the one lined with rabbit. The street was empty now, quiet. No lamps lit . . . Indeed, it was getting colder.

We drove, silently, a hired cab. Careened through streets, barely missing pedestrians and farm animals; soup kettles, random fires flaring alongside the boulevards. The silhouettes of makeshift canteens, dark and empty now; little shacks made of a curtain and some old boards that served *soupe* in exchange for ration tickets. We stopped at a café for brandy; it was lit with candles as gas was under ration too (although it had burned brightly enough at Brébant). Drove again through the ruined landscape, its façade once so spruce and manicured. That now seemed like a bit of scenery for a musical, stacked to the side to be carted away. The Bois de Boulogne had been denuded; the trees felled for fuel and also so the enemy could not hide among them. The artificial lakes stood empty; the cascade did not fall. We hit a gash in the roadway and my head fell against Stephan's shoulder just as it had once before — a decade ago.

I loved him when he was an arrogant boy, rescuing me from my father's lingering ghost; I would love him again, a man caught in a snarl of my destiny. I loved him as women love: *despite everything.* Love needed; demanded and hoarded; hurled back, burned, and claimed again. Ash. *Dark hair; pale skin. A full mouth. Dark eyes. We invent each other* . . . I cannot tell the truth of it, for I will never know that; nor how, nor why the heart plays its tricks.

This carriage became that other one; the rustle of absent trees in the Bois became the leaves of La Vrillette; its empty lakes the dark rectangular pool before the house, and I closed my eyes and fell, and fell. The void-of-myself, minus the elegant trappings, plain as an empty belly, those first Paris days. It was as before, it was no different, I was no different. *I was not wiser.*

Our crush of lips was a thing guttural and inarticulate; no benevolent third between us. I had once thought it was an angel, a generous, lighthearted spirit, or a sprite of the fountains that had brought me to him; to ferry me out of disaster. Maybe Berthe, determined to be born.

In my own bed at the rue du Mail with the snowy coverlets I

turned toward him, took him against me. Felt the weight of his boots as they dropped to the floor. Unfastened his collar, the small, pearled buttons of his shirt. The place longed for again and again; coming back to what had been lost. My young, uncorrupted self. To breathe again as I once did, when my knees did not ache; the blue veins did not show in my hands.

Shivering, we undressed each other and his hips found mine in the dark; we were hungry, both of us urgent for that nourishment so long withheld, and I tumbled back ten years, a hundred. To a time unmarked, clean. My soul, light and strong, as it once was; my body firm and free; a young untutored heart. Heart beating; warm, live flesh — oh yes, the same scents, the same hands, the same body — the same kisses, brushing my lips; the heat of his breath, his mouth; the way of fingers, then lips — *how the body does not forget the smallest detail.* Sheets tangled around us; pillows, covers falling to the floor. At La Vrillette we had been like birds calling to each other. In the morning, at sunset; never tired. We flew farther; the distance grew, but still he called, and I answered; our voices overlapping, touching under heaven's arc. Then I called, and heard nothing — *ah!* Where has the other one gone? I called until my throat was hoarse; my ears strained for listening to the silence. And now he had returned. Our green wood had once burned, popped and smoked and smoldered; now it burst into flame with a fast, bright heat. And in the morning he was smoking by the window, the same.

. . . From there, a giddy plunge into a desolate world. With Paris besieged, friends departed, rations short — we were two vagabonds who could care less, and why not? . . . A joke between the two of us, penned in his slanted, graceful hand. Our rendezvous named, a place whispered among the knowing. *Invited guests only.* Illumined by guttering candlelight, guarded by waiters with guns, wineglasses were filled, plates adorned with peas and butter; with white bread; with beef and cheese from God-knows-where. I ate for the Eugénie who had starved, once. Who shrank at the *poissonnière;* skulked through the aisles at Hédiard; cried into her butcher's offal.

Stephan was, as I learned, an expert in diverting us from disaster; a master of the arch edge, the Parisian ambiguity, the elegant reappearance. Arriving unannounced at the rue du Mail with something as unlikely as a prune tart, a pat of butter up his cuff, a can of sardines or even a bunch of carrots. Once a set of teacups from the Mont, borne upstairs looped on his fingertips; and we had *soupe au vin* in them, that staple of the siege: wine boiled over the fire and poured on dried bread. His visits to the rue du Mail delighted Finette, especially after he brought her a pair of bangles.

"My silver and gold," she said, fluttering her arm in the air.

"More like tin and brass," I said.

We walked in Père Lachaise cemetery, quarreled in front of the tomb of Abélard and Héloïse, a filigreed fantastical structure, the house they had never shared in life.

"I wrote letters — so many."

"Apparently that is why my family is suing you."

"I only *sent* one. What would you have done if you had not been held hostage in an indigo field?"

"How can I say?"

"You can speak for your intentions!"

"I *intended* to come back for you."

"Is that true?"

"As true as a — callow young man knows. But Eugénie — sooner or later I would have felt the weight of my obligations. They kept me in India and would have dogged me here."

"India was an added convenience, then."

"Yes." He wrapped his long arms around me; fierce, tight. *Just to remember those arms. To teach myself what it would have been.*

Outside our world of diversions, the municipal beef was gone and goat's meat worth its weight in gold. Horses were scarcer; omnibuses infrequent; gaslight finally failed entirely. The government's ration was cut, and cut again. Troubled questions hung in the air — why did Trochu not call for a *levée en masse*? Why was he not fighting the enemy with every arm in the capital? For it was apparent that negotiations had failed; that there was not to be an armistice; the "Plan," whatever it was, had fallen apart. (Or worse — voices fell to a hush — *this was the Plan.*) From Tours, where his balloon had landed, the gallant Léon Gambetta had waged a successful battle with an army that had surged in from the provinces to support him — and that victory had given us hope, was celebrated in the streets and at the rue du Mail; we opened a carefully hoarded bottle of champagne. But Gambetta's achievement initiated a split between Trochu's command and his. Our defending forces were mired in disagreement.

Street barricades had been erected all the way up to Montmartre because the balloons went up from there, and the pigeons flew back with messages from Gambetta's flank. Red placards on the walls asserted the right of the National Guard to defy the government's stance of "negotiation," proclaimed the urgency of the Great Sortie — an overwhelming rush toward the Prussian lines with everything, and every fighting man, Paris had. With each success of Gambetta's, Parisian morale rallied even more toward him and against the stoic Trochu. Everywhere, in all the parks and empty spaces, the National Guard, citizen-soldiers called up from every quarter of Paris, from the wealthiest to the most humble, drilled and marched with orders — or without. They were a motley collection, variously uniformed, erratically disciplined — serving from their separate and distinct neighborhoods. They had one thing in common, though: they were all armed.

On the rue de la Paix where the luxury shops had been, a window displayed fresh-slaughtered rabbit surrounded by larks on green sticks; a necklace made of quail eggs and minnows. People stared and gaped as if these items were diamonds. At the grocers' there was only soap and candles; pieces of ship's biscuit laid out on paper. At the municipal butcher's, a final distribution of fresh meat. The ration now stood at one ounce, and for that, lines started before dawn and stretched under armed guard, all the housewives of Paris wrapped in blankets, with their *chauffe-pieds* at their feet. The black-market butchers displayed exotic horns — any recognizable meat cost half a year's rent. Rumors told of wheels of rotting cheese beneath the streets, sacks of potatoes moldering in the catacombs—the pillage of war profiteers. Now and then a pile of dewy green cabbages appeared to taunt us, a cartload of leeks or a display of "true rabbit" (meaning not a cat) sold at a ransom. *Pain de Ferry,* named for the mayor, was the municipal bread ration. It was a dark, unleavened mass made of rice, oats, straw, and components unknown. It could hardly be chewed, much less digested. Nothing tasted as it should. Vegetables smelled of old laundry; meat, an alleyway abattoir. To eat was to cause the tongue to protest at all available textures: chalky, stringy, moldy, soft.

I could only hope that outside Paris, wherever Berthe was, she had better fare than this; but because of her—and since the fall of Strasbourg, and then of Metz, where so many infants had starved—I had been quietly reserving small packets of food and delivering them to the hospice. The *nourrices* watched for us and sent an emissary, unbeknownst to the director. It was against the rules to accept such packages, but the Paris *nourrices* were starving; and of course, there was no transport between Paris and the countryside.

At the stations, those great iron-and-glass structures erected by the empire, the trains were stopped in their tracks. Ghostly waiting rooms, piled with cushions; a fine black dust covered everything. On the walls, peeling posters of vaunted holiday trips to the Vosges, to Alsace, to Nancy. To Trouville: to the beach, where papas had once forgotten workday propriety and hoisted their children in the air, indulging their freer, kinder selves. Trouville . . . where I had lost Jolie. Antique journeys now; every one of them.

Stephan joined an elite National Guard battalion, looking very fine in his uniform, and made himself popular with Finette and La Tigre by bringing them cans of potted horseflesh, army provisions. And finally the proclamations went up on the walls, the announcement for which we had all been waiting, the only solution—for Paris to gather as one and with a great shuddering effort of collective will, throw the enemy off our backs.

Dream: I was a woman, living well beyond my own station in life, in a great house with gardens like those at La Vrillette. The sky was dark, as though a storm was coming, and I paced among the roses, anxious for my lover to return. We had argued, Stephan and I. He told me that he had loved another woman, loved her even now. Her name, he said, was Aurore: Dawn. I was alone; yet still waiting; waiting, though betrayed, and I cried; long, wrenching sobs. For love wasted, badly spent; for passion reaping pain that could not be undone. It was not so much an argument as an evil thread laced from my belly to my lover's and back. I wanted to tear at the thing that I could not reach, the cord of misery between us.

I woke up delirious with fever, Finette standing over me.

"Has the sortie begun?"

"Yes, madame! And we are winning!"

"Has monsieur sent any word?"

"Nothing I have heard, madame."

"And you, Finette, you look well—"

"I have eaten your rations while you were ill."

"Good. No horseflesh for me. Just water."

When I could finally lift my head, my neighbors came in and told the truth in low tones. The Great Sortie had been a colossal and tragic disaster; Francisque and Amélie were working as nurses. They said that a hundred times we had believed ourselves saved—had again been told of victory—only to realize later that we were lost. They described how the dead and wounded were carried in on carts and borne by *bateaux-mouches* to the Seine docks. The undersupplied *ambulances* could not handle them; the losses were unstinting; unspeakable. Gambetta's progress too had been halted. And the government had no solution; could not capitulate for fear that all guns, purchased by local subscription and kept by the people, would be turned against their leaders. Affairs proceeded in a disjointed, arbitrary fashion; and we remained as we had been: surrounded.

"Monsieur de Chaveignes?"

"Oh yes, he is back, and all in one piece. Has asked for you every day since his battalion was sent back. He has been bringing provisions. I don't know how he gets hold of things, that man."

"Mine is a palm of narrow escapes!" I heard Stephan's voice again, from long ago.

"He's been doing it for a very long time," I replied.

25

FÊTE DE NOËL

MENU FOR DAY 98 OF THE SIEGE

Cheval à l'indienne (gray mare, "best possible flavor," curried)
Pigeon egg omelette with lark's tongues and field mushrooms
Petits pois (Potin's, black market)
Chou-fleur de Fort Courbevoie (from a farmer's mattress near there)
Rice pudding with rum and currants
Surprise dessert for true patriots
Wine, rum, green tea
Arsenic

NIGHT FULL OF HOLES; the air so cold it could crack. My guests arrived at the rue du Mail with tallow and candles, green wood and coal, sticks of old furniture and fingers of tree bark to burn; they had collected morsels of food and drops of drink, along with tales of gastronomic daring. Wood, food, drink, and weapons—ivory-handled dueling pistols, kitchen knives, a *tabatière* or two—a bottle of vitriol and one of petrol, just in case one required protection. Jolie—in from Belleville, which she now called home—collected all the armaments and locked them in an armoire downstairs. La Tigre had decamped to her sister.

Clio (who had been reunited with Jolie when she moved) jumped out of her basket and prowled her old haunts, whiskers alert, directing her pink nose to every corner, as if she knew that the menu was finally secure and the dog-and-cat cart long gone. Jolie crowed: "She has been almost invisible—absolutely circumspect, especially around small boys, and never sits inside boxes or bowls, to play *poulet* anymore . . . thus far she has evaded the butcher's cart. Have you noticed that even the mice have left?" It was one of the siege's mysteries; people said they'd gone over to the Germans.

The party was a masquerade. La Morte arrived wearing black velvet, with a red sash bearing the date 1871, and carrying a papier-mâché scythe; her friend La Résistance was draped in white, with a *tricolore* sash, and bared a pink-tipped breast. The Red Virgin was not, in fact, Jolie's increasingly infamous Louise—for which I was grateful. The Louise impostor wore a wide red belt and a rifle slung over her shoulder (she insisted it was part of her costume). La Liberté was a girl with tumbling black hair, draped in white; her escort a *sans-culotte* of the last revolution, carrying a mustachioed puppet head of Louis Napoleon. Jolie was dressed as Saint Joan in a short tunic and blue sash, her long legs in high boots.

"La Liberté is a bookseller on Rambuteau. La Morte I met at a meeting at Jean-Baptiste—they never say *Saint* Jean-Baptiste anymore and the confessionals are used as *pissoirs*."

"And Louise?" I said. "I mean, the real one?"

"She has been arrested again," said Jolie. "The first time was for organizing a resistance for Strasbourg. Now—I'm not sure, but—the police don't like her. They can't predict what she'll say, or who will listen." Jolie propped her feet up on a pillow and began telescoping the buttes for Christmas balloons. She was thin, her skin almost transparent, as though lit from within.

"Are you worried about her?"

"*Louise?* Never."

Amélie, just then, made her appearance as Madame Roland. (Francisque was at the Jockey Club, dining with her remaining gallants.) Stephan arrived from across town, wearing a black mask and a working man's *cotte*, slipped his arms around me for a distracted kiss. He had not been himself since the Great Sortie, I thought. Mitra, on the other hand, seemed more and more at home in Paris.

"What do you think Odette is having tonight?" I asked, settling next to Jolie. "Jellied wing of peacock, Devon clotted cream?"

"Where did you get lark's tongues, of all things?"

"Abatem — the deaf-mute boy from Deux Soeurs."

"Now there's an enterprising soul. Old Madame B's henchman."

"He has turned scavenger; he goes out to the scorched earth between the fortifications and the Prussian lines."

"Guess what surprise I have tonight? You are destined to meet my brother at last."

"Henri? Is he in Paris?"

La Liberté had taken to the floor with her violin and was performing a musical inventory of the empress's furs, recently "liberated" from the Tuileries. *"Twelve yards of otter,"* she began, with everyone clapping and stamping feet. *"Eleven silver fox — ten Spanish lamb, nine sable tails, eight yards chinchilla, seven marabou — "* Finette had taken off her serving apron and begun to dance, lively and fluid, her movements practiced and correct. She really was a dancer. Mitra sat nearby watching her; the two had, during the time I was ill and Stephan was at the front, become friends.

"There is the bell," Jolie cried, dropping her telescope and running to the balcony to hang over the rail. A gust of frigid air — then a man in a gunner's coat called up from below. "It's Henri!"

He and Jolie were twinned in height, Henri lean and muscled and not as thin as the rest of us. The planes of his face so defined they made the others look soft as brioche. Callused fingers. Fine boned, powder blackened.

"It's from the *tabatière*. Target practice." He wore no mustache or beard, unusual for a man. Clean, and hard. Clear, like cold, rushing water. Henri's eyes were Jolie's: green, like pebbles in a stream, but his hair was coal black. Under the coat, he wore a National Guard uniform and slung over his shoulder was an enormous sack.

"Where did you get — all of *that*, Père Noël?" From it he pulled items not seen in the capital for a month, not even at the blackest market: a cache of potted, smoked, and salted meats; Italian and Dutch cheeses, a macaroni-and-ham pie with wheat crust. Jellied pigs' trotters, apples and plums. Sugar-dusted butter pastry for dessert. *Sugar.*

"Do you have any idea what's rotting beneath the streets in this city?"

"Henri knows the catacombs like the back of his hand; he learned them when he was a boy. Everything the war speculators bought and hang onto while people starve," said Jolie.

"It's called 'revolutionary requisitioning,'" said Henri, breaking into a grin. "Is there any coffee?"

"We haven't seen it in weeks," I said. "Brandy?"

"I don't take spirits."

"Wine? No shortage there, the National Defense has allotted a hundred liters per citizen . . . No? Green tea, then. Excellent for the health."

"I heard you were a prisoner," La Liberté said. You could see she was a bookseller; they were all flirts.

"Yes. Near Strasbourg."

"How on earth did you get through the lines?"

"Friends."

"Ha!" said La Morte. "Prussian friends?"

Hours later La Liberté and a *sans-culotte* were on a sofa with a bottle of rum; La Morte was at the telescope. The Red Virgin had disappeared, hoping to buy cigarettes off a guardsman. Clio had come out of hiding and scouted for crumbs, which were few, under the banquet table. Rag ends of the party remained; all of Henri's contributions consumed as well as ours; not a morsel of piecrust or rice pudding remained, although the mousse of osseine stood untouched.

Henri stretched his legs. Long, and lean. High, polished black boots. "What is this surprise dessert? It tastes like chocolate-flavored dirt."

"Osseine au chocolat." Osseine was a government-distributed food substance made from slaughterhouse bones. It was supposed to contain four times the nutrition of fresh meat.

"They ate bone-bread during the siege of Paris of 1590, and died of it. Who can promise that a government recommending arsenic for health is not making osseine of human bones?"

"I've never seen a boot like that on a French soldier. You'll be arrested for a spy," said La Morte, prowling over with her scythe.

Henri looked bemused. "Do you know how they sleep, in a Prussian camp? They dig out a flat, broad cone-shape in the earth, and a bonfire is built in the middle. Each man sleeps with his boots toward the fire, head pointed outward, his gun above his head. Thus he is warm all night. And the French soldier? Sleeps like a hunted dog, each one for himself on the frozen ground, or huddled together for warmth . . . No tent. No fire. As often as not, no ration. Everything the Prussian does is managed this way and Trochu knows it very well . . . Which army do you think will win this war?"

"Let me guess. The Reds," said Stephan, lighting a cigarette, offering one to Henri.

"What *is* this Commune anyway?" pouted La Liberté, back into the mix of things and trying very hard to fasten her costume. "Now it's like the new religion."

Stephan said, "It's a collection of mercenaries, nobodies, wild-eyed Blanquistes, refurbished Saint-Simonians, Americans who need a new war—and women. In trousers."

"All rather outnumbered by the National Guard in Paris itself, our own brave citizens . . . Have I had the pleasure, monsieur?" said Henri, turning to him.

I murmured introductions.

"He looks like a sheep in that carpenter's garb, but he isn't one," said La Morte, charmingly. "He's an aristocrat. Show us, monsieur, what you are wearing underneath."

Henri leaned back. "You think that the Commune is so easily dismissed, that you can safely ally yourself with those currently in power—the general with a 'Plan' to betray his army?"

"You are calling Trochu a traitor?"

"No, I am calling him a man caught in the web of his own negative intelligence; who cannot help but see the faults in his own people; an individual without hope and too much control over the destinies of others. He represents the worst in us. Thus he is starving us out."

Henri turned to La Liberté. "There are those, you see, who would have us take charge of our own destiny rather than be bombarded into submission. That is the Commune, and it sounds like religion because it is about faith in ourselves."

"And that old prisoner at the helm," said Stephan.

"Blanqui predicted the problems with rationing in Paris back in September. Among other things," said Henri mildly.

"An aged revolutionary has to believe his life in prison will have been worth something, and his friends can't bear the idea that he wasted himself, either," said Stephan. "You nostalgics are always turning back the clock. But what's more interesting is the connection with the Internationale and Monsieur Marx. What do you have to say about that?"

Henri made an impatient gesture. "The issue at hand is this city and the Prussian army. Do we want reconstituted Bonapartists capitulating, as they did at Sedan, or do we want Paris to stand?" The two of them drifted to the side and soon were deep in argument.

"War makes strange friends," I murmured to Jolie.

"Ah, let them have their fun," she said, her eye plugged again to the telescope. We needed a balloon that would save us all. Some said that the Prussians would bombard us directly after the New Year.

I remembered her with Louise, marching behind Blanqui at the funeral of Victor Noir. At the time, I thought Louise was a Blanquiste, and Jolie was a Louise-iste; now I saw that between Louise and her brother, she was surrounded. I didn't know where I stood, myself. Somewhere between the two, on scorched earth, looking for edible roots.

"Your brother speaks well. I see why you adore him, Jolie."

"Blanqui has been back and forth to Paris and Henri has been one of his guards. But I shouldn't say a thing to you. Are you still thick with the Préfecture?"

"No, I was never promoted to Prussians. Or Communards. How did your brother meet that man? In prison?"

"Oh, Henri won't say a word . . . So what are you doing these days, *chouette*?"

I shrugged, glanced over at Stephan and Henri, head to head.

"Oh, that's a good use of your time. So, do you love him again?"

"It's war, who knows anything? Even my lawyer said that the only way is to negotiate with him directly."

"So, have you?"

"Not while we all may be dead anyway."

"I don't think you should waste yourself on him, *chouette*. But at least don't lie to yourself about it."

"You are very frank tonight." I stared out at the starry blackness. "I'm not lying to myself. I'm trying to learn the nature of the man who is the father of my daughter."

"I would have thought it was clear enough. There are two kinds of defeat. You fight to the death and have a chance of winning. Or—you capitulate."

"Oh, Jolie. I am not capable of seeing it in black or white . . . But what I want to know is how *you* are?"

"Well enough. I have my days."

"Jolie. There is something I want to ask. Why did you leave Nathalie and Deux Soeurs? She must have been furious."

"What does it matter?"

"I wondered. I heard she was a spy. For the Prussians."

Jolie laughed. "I wouldn't be surprised. She knew people . . . She wouldn't help me though. I mean, she wouldn't help Henri."

"Ah . . . Were you sick before you left? I mean—did you get infected there?"

Jolie lowered the telescope. "I suppose it's possible. But I think it was—after that. And sometimes, you know? Maybe I let it happen, so I could finally get out. Off the books, out of the game. Smacked right out of there, back where I belong. Don't get me wrong; I had a good job at Chevillat. It was decent. But I was never a lifer. And—"

"What?"

"I like this little tunic. It's quite comfortable without a long skirt." She crossed and uncrossed her legs with brazen abandon, demonstrating.

"Don't joke! Nathalie took you back like a cat who deserves her cream, and it was a death sentence. We should have done something—"

She gave a short laugh. "What? I was under arrest, beholden, in debt—what do you think you could have done? Or I? You've always lived in a dream world, *chouette*. You, Eugénie—are young, and *well*. But you can't run after the past. Your lover is right about that. The clocks in Paris will start ticking again, one day or another. And what then? He is not sentimental; anyone can see that."

"Maybe not."

"If you can't, you're half blind. Who is that boy, anyway?"

I glanced over at Mitra, who was giggling in a corner, now, with Finette.

"Mitra? He's taught me to make a bread from ground rice and dried peas, much better than *pain de Ferry*. We should send him over to the Academy of Sciences. And he tells the most amazing stories. So—what about you, Jolie? Are you a Communard or subscribing for Henri's sake? Or Louise's? *She's* not happy unless she's fighting someone and dragging half of Paris along behind her."

"Louise's is the name they'll remember long after we're gone. What the Commune stands for may be the best that comes out of all of this. Someone has got to remind the world that we are human. I'd rather go down shooting than have my nose fall off with the pox. And if the Commune prevails—well! That will be a whole new day. All of us just—walking around Paris like we live here. Can you imagine?"

Jolie had one ear cocked to the other conversation and now interrupted it, nursing her jelly jar of rum. "Henri, are you going on again about the Americans? Eugénie is known to be fond of the occasional American." I looked over. Henri's chiseled profile was not shadowed by the unmistakable siege pallor. Even Stephan had it now.

"Nothing new is to be learned from the Americans. They have not solved the fundamental problem, which is orderly use and distribution of resources. They are gobbling as fast as they can, hand over fist, and once they run out over there, they'll be in the same pickle as the rest of us."

"I've brought the tarot deck; let's tell our fortunes," said Jolie. "Find out what pickle we'll each be in for the New Year."

"'Fortune is on the side of the big guns,'" said Stephan, wandering over.

"Thank you, Napoleon . . . Watch out for the monk with the stiletto, then," said Jolie. She gave him a look of certain, keen loathing.

"Pardon me?" said Stephan.

"I mean that destiny is an individual matter, monsieur. Even on the battlefield. Eugénie, shuffle the cards and we'll have a prediction for the year of our Lord 1871."

"That's playing with fire," said Amélie. She liked card games in any form.

"I'm not afraid," I said, shuffling the deck and dividing it into three stacks. I turned over the Two of Discs, the Ten of Wands, and the woman closing the lion's mouth with her hands. Jolie looked over my shoulder and said, "You have been juggling opposing forces and in danger of losing your balance. Now you are coming to the end of an endeavor that has been a great burden. The outcome may either be successful or bring further blindness. The card is reversed. For the future: strength."

"How about you, *monsieur le comte?* . . . Le Pendu, the Hanged Man. The Six of Discs reversed indicates that you have a debt to repay, or that the way you are paying is no longer good, or that there is a gap between wanting and having—"

"Who is *monsieur le comte?*" said Henri, pouring himself a glass of water.

"Mademoiselle Rigault's lover in the proletarian costume; you have been speaking to him all night." said Jolie. Henri snorted, uncrossed his legs. "And Mitra's father, if I had to guess." She glared at Stephan. "What kind of man has a ten-year-old slave?"

Stephan leaned back and blew smoke from both his nostrils. Poured another drink and looked the slightest bit ruffled. I glanced over to find Mitra but he wasn't there. Nor was Finette.

"What is your argument with me, mademoiselle? Aside from the fact that you don't understand India?" said Stephan. Then to Henri he said, "Now, *that* is the place for a real revolution."

"A man divided, in a time of absolutes. A doubter where there is no room for doubt. The future depends on how you pay your debt, monsieur."

"You are enigmatic, mademoiselle, and your reward is that I do not understand a word."

"Which is it to be? Once you have recognized what needs to be done, there are — oh — so many ways to do it."

Stephan stretched and put down his glass, glanced over at me. I looked away. Mitra — could he be Stephan's blood son?

"Ah. Well. I'll be off to the Jockey Club, then." He was being ironic, but the assembled guests didn't quite grasp it. Stephan hated the Jockey Club. Although he remained a member.

"I heard they are serving that little brown bear from the zoo — that used to go up and down his pole, do you remember?" said La Morte.

"Do you think it'll be possible to get a rickshaw? Mitra!"

"He's right at home, isn't he?" growled Henri.

"Eugénie?" Stephan turned toward me. I sighed.

"I'm not feeling like bear, really. You go on."

It was more than a headache from La Liberté's singing, or Henri's long, blackened fingers wrapped around the water glass balanced on his thigh. He had not stopped staring at me since asking, *Who is monsieur le comte?* Jolie took my hand in her cooler one, then pressed the back of hers, still holding mine, against my brow. "Eugénie, you are pale, and burning up. Did you eat the osseine?"

"Eugénie, the *sans-culotte* wants his pistol," said La Morte.

"All of the guns are locked in the first-floor armoire," said Jolie.

"I've just been ill. I believe I'll lie down."

"Take her downstairs."

"I'm going, anyway," said Henri. "Allow me."

The dark hall; a draft, cold, from below. Frigid; the very air could crack. Nymph ghosts of the mural, golden toes and dimpled knees, painted chains of ivy. Scuffling from the street, three floors down, shouts. Gunshots. Shuffling feet of the National Guard. I was hot, dizzy, even though the stairwell was cold. It was fever again; I felt it now, watery blood, hollow bones. Henri and I stood together in front of the armoire by tallow light.

"You have the key; open it," he said.

"I won't help you steal from my guests."

"A bunch of natterers and idiots. But if there is a decent pistol, I'll take it."

Henri struck a match, kneeled. A cigarette, unlit, dangling from his lips. He took out a thin metal rod, *quick as a draft through a keyhole.* Before I could draw a breath, he had rifled the armoire's contents.

"Oh, I remember. You were a thief." His lips hot, rough, broken. One of his hands, twisting my arm behind.

"*Monsieur le comte* can't kiss you like this — can he?"

. . . *No. Not like this.* I wrenched myself away. The man made me nervous.

"You deserve better. And I thank you for taking care of my sister." My eyes filled with tears. In the end, I had done so little.

"Go," I said. "Go, now."

"I'll be back," he said, lower than a growl.

Back in my own rooms, I double-locked the door. No one, that night. Not anyone. Not Henri. *Not Stephan.*

From the balcony I watched the snow begin to fall; soft and light; the sky pale and moonlit as the fine starry dust filtered down through bare-branched trees. Around midnight it thickened, laying a soft blanket over the scarred walls and piles of refuse and upturned carts . . . All of it bandaged, forgiven; blessedly white. A solemn, sovereign whiteness. When the sky quieted, a high, still moon rose, and beyond it glimmered the Milky Way; I remembered the aurora borealis. For the first time in days, the cannonade had ceased, and down the rue Montmartre from the rue du Mail, unlit by lamps, the snow seemed to emit its own incandescence. And I was light-limbed — unburdened of flesh by fever and famine. It seemed, for a moment, that the rest of the troubles should evanesce as well, dissipate into the cold sky. That we could — simply — forgive one another and begin again.

Horridas nostrae mentis purga tenebras.
Cleanse us of the horrible darknesses of our minds.

26

BOMBARDMENT

WE HAD BECOME USED to the cannonade, the low rumble of fire and dull *thunk* of Prussian shells beyond the fortifications as we drifted into a disturbed sleep. It was the occasional, sudden stretches of quiet that were truly terrifying: during these lulls, mattresses were hauled down into cellars, pails filled with water, and sandbags propped next to doors, if one had the luxury of sandbags. News rations were as short as those of meat, by then. We survived on speculation, tidbits ballooned in by compatriots outside, pigeon-intelligence word-of-mouthed. Bismarck was said to be suffering from varicose veins as he had been eating and drinking to excess; gorging on food stocks ransacked from villages, guzzling champagne and wine with German sausages and French charcuterie — the list of Bismarck's pillaged meals could go on at length. We heard that he was bewildered that Paris held out; that his soldiers munched ham in the streets of Versailles and exercised their horses on the palace lawns. That Europe was appalled at such arrogance; and not unaffected by Paris's suffering. A pigeon-letter signed by a roster of supporters hailed besieged Parisians as heroes — but Europe did not reprovision its former playground nor come to its aid; and that was a bitter truth.

Beyond Prussian-occupied Versailles, our remaining armies were frostbitten and foundering on the mismanagement between Paris and Tours. We well believed that the Germans were debating as to whether to starve us out, attack us with infantry, or use their Krupps to bombard us to death. That they could not decide; and the Prussian crown prince had qualms about bombarding Paris. He did not wish to murder children, they murmured. Wrongly, as it turned out.

Hunger narrows vision, but finally the barriers of appetite fall. The body learns to fast, conserve, consume itself, and return with harrowing vigor. Once the New Year had passed, Parisians collectively understood that our days of food hoarding, the hovering shadows of suspicion of one another, would soon be done. Any day now, we would be under direct fire. The weeks of anticipation were more fatiguing than the moment itself; once on the brink, we straitened to the task. On every street, we took measurements between known gun positions determined by telescope or spyglass, and our front doors, as though we could predict the damage. Sandbags and pails were arranged and rearranged. Doors left unlocked, in case a passerby needed to take sudden shelter. A new camaraderie arose among us and it was something of a relief.

I had not seen Stephan since Noël. However, a cold and silent day early in January took me to his apartments across town, in the sixteenth arrondissement. In anticipation of the bombardment, the city-installed *ambulance* on the first floor of my own building was well-stocked with bandages, alcohol, and *charpie*—shredded linen infused with alcohol and carbolic acid. We had had for some time plenty of supplies but few wounded; in fact—Francisque was always looking for a stray colonel with some embedded shrapnel. I found Mitra alone; Stephan gone out to collect useless newspapers.

Mitra was stacking sandbags at the head and foot of Stephan's bed. He worked with care; each of the bags nearly as heavy as he was—but he placed them in such a way that they could not topple. Apparently he did not wish his master to be shelled in his sleep, a catastrophe that Stephan was convinced would befall him. Such a

THE UNRULY PASSIONS OF EUGÉNIE R.

still, silent boy; always watching. But Mitra could speak and read French; once I had found him cross-legged, turban unwound and hair ruffled around his small ears, in front of my bookshelf, with *The Hunchback of Notre Dame.*

"Mitra."

He came and stood, as he always did.

"You are so young to be away from home for such a long time, in a strange place with a war going on. Your mother and father must worry."

Mitra did not touch meat at all and so did not miss it. Rice was now the capital's only available staple, and we French hesitated before it; however, the boy — among other startling accomplishments — cooked it over the fire with spices, roots, and dried leaves he had brought with him. From Mitra I learned that wheat was not essential, nor was meat; and milk and cheese could be done without. Once we invented a dish of rice, rum, cocoa, and cardamom that could have passed in better times. While the dried peas held on, Mitra made curried soups and griddle bread. Between the three of us, the siege had broken down certain barriers. Over the course of these strange evenings, lit by the dull flare of the cannonade, an affinity developed between the boy and myself.

Now he dropped to his haunches. He looked up, and there was a hint of confirmation in the clear planes of his face, despite his café au lait skin. *His eyes.* I slipped off the chair and dropped to the floor beside him. The boy looked at me steadily, and I took a deep breath. "You must miss your parents, though?"

Mitra's eyes darted involuntarily to the door; he dipped his chin and shook his head. "I do not miss him," he said softly. He ducked his head again, this time more deeply.

"Your mother? Tell me about your mother, Mitra?"

The boy hesitated. *"Le dictionnaire?"*

"But you speak French perfectly well." The angles of his face rearranged.

"She teaches the Bengali language to English and French men

who come," Mitra said gently, and suddenly seemed older than his years. "In Chandannagar she is called 'dictionary of the bed.' She does not know that I know that name."

"Ah."

"My mother says my blood runs from two different rivers, the Hooghly and the Seine, and that I will live the first half of my life as Bengali, the second half as French."

I paused. "Maybe life was not meant to be lived by halves."

"But I do not want to be French, ever," said Mitra.

I would have asked why not, but perhaps we French were not at our best, just then. Maybe his words made sense.

"What do you want to be, then?"

"A writer of the Bengali language," the boy said, without hesitation. "Like the name my mother gave me, after Dinabandhu Mitra. The great writer of *Nil Darpan*."

"What is *Nil Darpan*?"

"A drama that shows others the unfairness of indigo."

"I would like to read it, then. Is it available in France?"

"I will be the one to make it become available down at the book-selling place by the Seine. After I go to school." Mitra looked at me steadily; I looked away.

"I should like to hear more about your mother someday. She gave you an interesting name."

"Dinabandhu Mitra said, 'A poor man's words bear fruit only after a lapse of years.' Please do not say anything about my plans."

I pressed a finger to my lips.

"I have bandages and brandy and ship's biscuit for you. And then I shall be on my way and we will say nothing of this again."

"You are going to the hospice?"

"Yes."

My twice-weekly deliveries to the hospice had carried on in the face of all; now, those of us on this particular mission waited at the garden gate of an adjacent mansion, amid the shrubbery — and we were called (by anyone in on the secret) the "friends of the widow Chateaubriand" because the house had been his and was now oc-

cupied by his ancient widow. The *nourrices* who cared for the infants
stayed on the hospice's first floor — the older children were above,
and they watched for us. We could see their pale faces in the windows.

"Thank you, madame." Mitra took a small allotment of what I
had brought. "Give the rest to the children."

"It is silent from the forts today, Mitra. The cannonade is quite
intermittent."·

"Yes. I must finish the sandbags, madame."

That night, Paris was soft and moonlit and starry, solemn and quiet,
eerily so, lit by snow and stars. The only sound was shuffling footsteps, usually unheard beneath the city's clamor. The next day,
January 5, the bombardment of Paris began. The first shells hit the
rue Lalande and the rue d'Enfer, near the hospice and the widow's
garden, where I had just delivered my package to the grateful hand
of a starving nurse. Thus far, this emissary told me, not a child had
been lost.

It went on for three weeks. Hundreds of shells every night, starting
at about ten o'clock. The cannon were fired at such an angle from
the Châtillon heights that the charges penetrated the heart of the
capital, pounding the hospitals and churches, the Panthéon, les In-
valides. The Odéon; orchids under glass at the Jardin des Plantes. In
shop windows stood dusty *tricolores* and the merchandise of another
era, but nothing but a tangle of iron and glass where the ceiling over
them had been. What was once a glass-enclosed arcade was now
open sky, clouds scudding, swept by careless January winds. Explosions everywhere. Fires.

A fiery mass of metal drops five paces away, and you run, forward
or back, realizing foggily that the direction to safety is unknown,
and nowhere. Vision narrows; streams with images. A well-dressed
man stands motionless as stone in the Galerie de l'Horloge — pale
as a root, jerked from the earth with glass shattered around him,
covering his shoulders and lapels. Gasping through the smoke and

grabbing my skirts up to save them from fires, ignoring all but the narrowest square doorframe into which to take the next step—an open door, a nod, a sip of water.

Amid all of it, during the days when the shelling was quiet I made my way to and from the hospice, situated in the target zone. On the Right Bank, we were still sheltered.

We citizens of Paris, whose world once appeared whole, saw it splintered to fragments while Wilhelm I of Prussia was crowned Kaiser of the Germans at Versailles. We gathered in cellars, filled more pails, stacked more sandbags, bound wounds with whatever fabric was to hand—the next action raggedly begun before the last was completed, a chaos of urgencies. At the rue du Mail we left the bath half-filled in case of fire, and between nursing shifts, Finette and I made a constant circuit up and down the stairs to watch from the roof.

Now, to our *ambulance* came a steady stream of the wounded, soldiers and civilians alike. Our cots and stretchers, provided by the city, were nearly filled. An English doctor had come through and taught us how to distinguish wounds from chassepot rifles from those made by shell fragments; how to wash an injury with dilute alcohol, to close its flaps and even to stitch them and dress the area in good-quality wadding called *charpie*. For a surface wound, we used a bandage with *charpie;* compressed it and applied linseed. We learned to distinguish between pyemia, septicemia, gangrene, necrosis, and frostbite. How to recognize the triage cases, which had to be sent to the larger tent hospitals run by the Americans, the Italians, the French, or the English. The doctor informed us that the amputees at all of these places were dying, and that the orderlies were drinking themselves to death.

My hands were red with the blood of a soldier of the National Guard usually stationed at the Fort d'Aubervilliers, but who had not made it to work that day. Finette attending, I bound a gash in his leg with a piece of an old nightdress while he clenched his teeth around a strip of corset baleine. We were now short of bandages; but it was only a flesh wound and I could help him with that. I had learned my limits, and those of our tools. This one was within my capacities. He would survive. He was even joking with me through clenched teeth when I heard footsteps close behind me, and looked up.

"You don't have to start like I am a German shell come through the door."

The man's trousers hung as though roped to his hips; he was hollow-eyed with siege pallor. He was passing by the rue du Mail and ducked inside. Pierre Chasseloup.

"Help me, then. This man needs to be lifted — over there, by the stairs." Our ministrations proceeded, absurdly, under the feet of cherubs, the curling tree roots where bacchantes resided in an unchanging frieze of pleasure — but we were now accustomed to such juxtapositions. I washed my hands in a bowl of bloody water. The iron smell no longer made me gag. My guardsman seemed to be resting, and I said I would get him whatever could be managed — horse broth and brandy.

Chasseloup said, "Do you have any more of it? Last night I — I can't even say it. What I had to eat."

"Come up, then. Take off your boots, they are full of *merde*."

"There is no *merde*. Nothing is left to produce *merde*."

Then I saw how weak he was, that I had to lead him by the arm to climb the stairs, to sit him down at the table by the window, on the silk-tufted chair. My provision shelf offered salted herring, pâté, dried apples, a rind of English Stilton. A few of Mitra's flatbreads, and cold green tea — a stewed bitter — from the morning pot.

"My God, it's Balthazar here. You are eating foie gras?"

"It is what you can get."

"From where? For how *much?*"

"It was a gift. It's all they ate at Strasbourg."

"It is not what most of us are eating. Coffee?"

"Yes, for the *ambulance,* but you can't drink coffee, not in the shape you're in. It will destroy your stomach. You can have my ration; I can't hold down horseflesh. Where is your blessed father?"

"Furious that I took a job with the Artist's Federation instead of the so-called Government of National Defense. Left me to rot. I've been sandbagging the Louvre."

I set out some apple slices, cold tea. "Eat slowly. If you can keep it down, you can have something more. Now wait, while I see to my guardsman."

Chasseloup was stretched out on the divan, asleep, when I returned, and when he woke, I fed him again and told him he could stay the night. By then I was tired too, and in no mood to go out and watch the bombardment, or even climb up to the roof. The past few nights it had become a gruesome entertainment; even a relief after the siege ennui, but now, one just desperately wanted it to end. *Perhaps it will never end. Perhaps—*

Chasseloup said, "I wrote to Maillard with my plan to take *An Unknown Girl* out by balloon. I can get it done; I know how. But he has declined, said that the painting is perfectly safe and he must spend his time seeing to the security of living Parisians." Chasseloup paused, almost out of breath. "The man is a cretin, he knows nothing about art . . . What is this I'm eating?"

"An Indian flatbread, with spices to purify the blood. Anyway, at Neuilly, *An Unknown Girl* is practically under the protection of Prussian guns." I knew where it was because Stephan had arranged to see it, just before the Great Sortie and before I had been ill. I did not know what he thought; when I saw him shortly afterward, he did not raise the topic, and I did not ask. Jolie had said that Stephan was not sentimental, but he had been sufficiently so to seek out Maillard and the picture. I didn't know what to make of it, really.

"You know where it is?"

"Don't get mad ideas, Chasseloup. I can't help you with Maillard. I've never met the man. And his carpets are probably worn out with the number of people marching to him for one favor or another."

"He cares about his factories and his men, but I am a madman for trying to protect my own work—my legacy?"

A shell whined; it seemed unusually near and the explosion rattled our teacups in their saucers. Pierre and I both jumped and peered out of the window, where we could see nothing. It was peculiarly maddening to hear and know and even smell the smoke, but not be able to see what was happening; even though that meant that the damage was still a distance away. Disaster was highly localized and omnipresent all at once. Pierre raked his fingers across his scalp. His hair was noticeably thin, and gray.

"Every time one of those goes off, I have some kind of nervous attack. My brains are rattling loose, my hands are always shaking. I can't hold a brush. That last shell probably hit the Sorbonne but it felt as though it was on top of us! I have been reading at the Sorbonne library when it is open. The damned Prussians aim for churches and hospitals and asylums — Christ, they may have to haul me off to one if they don't bomb it first."

"Have some more tea. It is much better for you than black."

"I may be dead by tomorrow morning. The painting is *my* legacy, and — "

"Chasseloup. Do you remember the story you once told me? About the artist, what was his name? With his sculpture of Mercury that he believed was his masterpiece — but he was on the street in the dead of winter and put his cloak around it so the clay would not crack, and it did survive — but he froze to death? What an idiot he was, you said! He could have lived to make another."

"Ha! I will never paint another. Old Badinguet once said that his purpose was to 'encourage the arts but discourage the artists.' That's how he wanted it, and it worked. Good God, before I met you I was cleaning rooms for half a loaf of bread and a slice of meat. Too humiliated to go to my father. I didn't want to paint you, you know. I already knew that I was beaten and Badinguet had won."

"But you did paint it!"

Chasseloup sat back. He said slowly, "Do you want to know how it happened? At Croisset, I could not do any of the scenes I had planned. I was preoccupied and out of focus. My training had been to study a scene, memorize it — a flower, a tree, a scene from nature, even a face — and paint it exactly, from memory. I hadn't done that for a long time, but that is what took over. At first I thought it was a hallucination, or the effects of absinthe. I was possessed by recalling every detail, like a dream where I was living it again, your skin against mine, the curve of your lips, the way your hands fell when they took a natural position — the way you stood when you were tired on the box and trying so hard to be still, because I had some insane idea that if you just stayed absolutely still I could capture you. The way you opened the door so quietly when you brought up the soup bones for us — I sobbed my way through the painting because my stupid rules did not matter at all. It did not matter if you were still. It did not matter that you were not there. It mattered that you had cared for me, we had cared for each other, and I did not eat or drink or sleep until I had poured everything into the canvas and it wasn't even done by the time I had to bring it back to Paris to hang it. Even on the train I was seized with new details; I was delirious by then. But I knew that I had done something good at last." He poured some more tea into his cup; his hand trembled. "Now, look at my hands. I will never lose this shake."

"It is just the bombardment, Pierre. We are all sick with it."

"That *Mercury* is at the Louvre. I crated it up."

"Whenever they end this — the shells will stop falling and your hands will be steady again, you'll see. And time — it's another trick of the mind, holding on to the past. I've had to learn that. I am always learning it."

"You'll see, the way they will end this war. Our so-called government will capitulate. They are already negotiating with the Prussians against Paris, which they can only see as the mob. That's why this has dragged on for so long. The National Defense will have the Prussian army occupy the city, and the working man won't stand for it. Belleville will rise up, the *levée en masse* at last — and we will have civil war. But the National Defense will have the Prussians to back them. They are all waiting us out. It's a travesty but it is the truth."

"What do you think about the Commune?"

"I don't know. I don't support the standing government, but I don't trust these Communards either. They are — a jumble of ideas, a shifting sand, they are grandiose; hotheads — idealists — they pin their hopes on Blanqui like he is Christ himself. I've heard enough of all of this from Courbet, dearly though I love the man, and he saved my life. At least, so far."

"So you want to escape in a balloon with your painting."

"Do you ever offer a man a drink in this place?"

"Wine and nothing stronger for you." I went to the sideboard and opened a bottle. Cahors red. Good for the blood.

"This—what is it, a sort of cake?—beats *pain de Ferry* by leagues. What did you say it is made of?"

I poured twice. Pierre wrapped his long fingers around the glass. Legs incongruously long in rough trousers amid my little rosewood furnishings. He smelled like a sick man, but I was used to that.

"It's a little piece of heaven here," he said. "Eugénie, I am just looking at you now. If I still could, I would paint you at this very moment. You have become dimensional."

"Stay as long as you like. Here, I will make a little fire. My scavenger just brought me a good quantity of tree bark and a few branches. I'll be back after I see to things downstairs . . . You know, it will start again soon, Chasseloup."

When I got back he was sitting in front of the hearth, sketchpad in his hand, a piece of charcoal in the other. God knows where he found it.

"Are you feeling better? It's good to see you drawing," I said gently.

Chasseloup dug into his pockets and extracted several folded and crushed bits of paper, furiously written over, with notes and crossings out.

"Do you know, I think that our creations are not much ours at all. That is, they are not really acts of genius and will by a single individual in the way we pretend they are. Imagine," he said, turning his glass and staring at the ruby liquid. "A kind of rag shop of heaven, and angels like old *triqueurs* sorting through the rags and bones and burned flesh we have left behind. These rag-picking angels are busy harvesting the soul stuff, separating it from the dross, the gross material. There isn't enough to go around, because we are careless down here. We fling it around and dissipate it; we don't know what it is that we are made of. And I want to find it, I want to make it. And then—paint with it. Do I sound mad?" He trembled violently. I picked up his hand again. Knuckles red and raw, trembling, his long painter's fingers.

"Chasseloup, I think you've found it. Your painting was all—

made of that." And there it was, for the world to see. For me to see, if I opened my eyes. I turned to him and rested my head, just briefly, against his shoulder and did not get the sick odor; just the heart beneath it. But my eyes were blinded with tears, and I blinked in the cold, bright winter light. This siege made for strange thoughts, impossible conversations; the bombardment was a hallucination; it made us mad.

"You allowed the world to see it; the judges saw it; Maillard saw it. I saw the painting too, Pierre. I stood before it and was furious, at it, at you, at Maillard for owning it—and caring so little for me. But when I remember it now I feel differently. It's hard to describe—" She was half-turned, looking over her shoulder, her cloudy shawl. The hair, dark; her skin, pale. A hand. At rest. A hand. A loved hand. And the face, mirrored back to me . . . *We were green.* I reached out, took Chasseloup's hand in mine. He accepted it. He was no longer trembling.

Another searing whine, another explosion—this one, closer. Shatter of glass, somewhere near. Pierre said, "You know, what worries me is not that the bombs will come all the way here, but—"

Silence . . . *I heard it; I must still be breathing.*

Pierre? Did you hear it? That one was close, wasn't it? Oh, your arm—don't worry—just a bit of glass, from the reverberation. I should have taped these windows; the glass is too brittle. I can bind it up. Just wait. Wait while I go down to the ambulance . . .

How does the page on which one writes become neither the accuser, the accused, nor a justification, but a vessel—the place where all can be held; can putrify, distill, and fall apart? It is not by listing events as they are said, or even as they seem to have occurred. I do not understand how events die away, turn on themselves, one leading to the next—and when written, seem insufficient to tell the tale. I am afraid that mine is a hungry, careless pen, scraping across the page. And when I look back at what I have written, it is a fever dream, a half-gesture, the glance over the shoulder; a catalogue of surfaces.

The siege, the war. Its story is a thin gruel, like ersatz milk made of oil and albumen, invented by the Academy of Sciences when there was no natural milk in Paris. Not nourishing, not life giving. Just going on forever in lonely pieces. One could write oneself into a starvation of fragments. I do not know how to hold such suffering on a page. There was a siege; some lived through it and others did not. They say that shells did not reach past the Pont Notre Dame, but there was broken glass that night on the rue du Mail, a singing lance pirouetting off Chasseloup's arm, severing an artery, the profunda brachii, according to the surgeon, once I had located a surgeon. Once I realized that my own bindings of Pierre's wound were insufficient.

Chasseloup died in my arms that night. But at least—at least we spoke, after such long silence. Forgave each other, and just in time. What drew him to my door that day? There were small miracles, as always. Life-and-death miracles, even.

And one day when they ask for stories of the siege, they will ask only, "*Mon Dieu,* did you eat the rats?" Oh, we ate them. We all ate them.

BOOK V

DEGREES OF JUSTICE

Time passed, and the unknown protector was not coming.

— MOGADOR, *Memoirs*

27

SURRENDER

THE SIEGE HAD LASTED three months; the bombardment three weeks. When the Paris gates opened at last and fresh winds blew in, we were surprised at the effects of our own stink—the wagoners and provisioners held handkerchiefs over their noses, coughed, and spat out the saturated odors of rum, horseflesh, and charred garbage; of a city's population living without laundry soap or hot water. Food carts barreled through the gates and we fell to our knees to look on such things as fresh-cut kindling, green cabbages, golden potatoes, rosy onions, and sacks of milled wheat. Fresh horse droppings on the cobbles were a source of wonder.

We had forgotten how to eat. Hungry, but unable to digest the goodness of food, we took bismuth with quince syrup to soothe our protesting, shrunken bellies. It sounded suspiciously like Bismarck but we took it anyway.

And we had lost this ill-conceived, badly fought, bellicose belch of a war; no quantity of leeks and carrots and flour could make up for that. Paris had suffered so thoroughly that we could hardly believe there would be no reprieve. On the walls was a war of proclamations and retorts.

*HAS THE GOVERNMENT OF NATIONAL DEFENSE
FULFILLED ITS MISSION?*

*FUTILE SORTIES, MURDEROUS AND INCONCLUSIVE BATTLES,
REPEATED FAILURES.*

THOSE WHO GOVERN HAVE LED US TO THE BRINK OF THE ABYSS.

YIELD TO THE PEOPLE! YIELD TO THE COMMUNE!

THE GOVERNMENT OF PARIS WILL NOT CAPITULATE

Adolphe Thiers, a wizened old goat born in the era of the first Bonaparte, replaced Trochu at the head of the government, and Léon Gambetta, Amélie's hero, decisively lost. Thiers stood for "peace at any price," and the first mission of his new assembly was to set terms with the enemy.

Opposition papers called him the "Laughing Man" and printed political cartoons showing the voluptuous body of France, sacks of coins spilling around her; caricatures of Thiers sniggering while he severed France's limbs, the provinces of Alsace and Lorraine. The Kaiser hauled these territories off as the urchins had lopped branches from the trees during the siege.

The Prussian army made a triumphal march through Paris, and all of the statues in the capital were shrouded in black. German soldiers lounged in the streets and gathered at the few cafés that would serve them, and they appeared very round, thick, and healthily pink like the pork sausages they munched while we wraiths looked on. We were told that they had relinquished their arms, but who was going to believe that? We had swallowed so many lies. And now we were sure we'd be shot in our beds, but not before the rent was paid.

What the government termed peace, others called capitulation — that was the word whispered or angrily hissed. But capitulate to whom? *Better Bismarck than Blanqui*, said the Thiers faction — which included Stephan, and Francisque, and La Tigre; Amélie held out firmly for Gambetta; Jolie and Henri were thick with the Commune in Belleville. There was no doubt that our governors had blundered, betrayed the trust of the population, and were poised to visit further calamities upon us. But if I stood with anyone it would have been Chasseloup, doubting all sides.

"Mademoiselle Eugénie, a guest for you," called La Tigre from the landing. "A handsome one in a gunner's coat." Taking the stairs two at a time, coat flaring behind him.

"Where is Jolie, is she all right?"

"She's up on the hill, practicing breech-loading and learning to wind up the *mitrailleuse*. Come for a ride."

"There's not a spare horse in the capital!"

Henri laughed. (He was politer than I remembered.) And the man did have a horse, a fine, sleek animal. It was all I could do not to throw my arms around its head and press my cheek to its glossy neck. I climbed up sidesaddle in front of Henri while a tribe of urchins gawked as if they'd never seen such an animal.

The streets were eerie, quiet, and strange . . . Blindfolded windows, covered statues. Somber streets, doors locked and double-locked. Quiet gray skies over a march of Prussians, an array of giant cannon lining up at the place de la Concorde, wheels higher than a man's shoulder. German soldiers posed for photographs in front of monuments, or all in a line, wearing their pointed helmets. Photographers hunched under their cloaks, black-shrouded like the statues. The whistling and explosion of shells from outside the walls had stopped, but the city made a sorry sight, with trees felled, gardens bare. Here and there people gathered in small groups to stare at the enemy. Every so often, the horse's movement jostled me against Henri, and his clean chin grazed the top of my head.

We angled away from the center, climbed higher through the streets, up to the buttes, and stopped at a point where we could see the capital spread below. On Montmartre's flat plain, where we now stood, cannon were set in neat rows. A few days earlier, before the Germans were scheduled to march through, members of the National Guard from the working-class districts had dragged this artillery from various parts of the city and up the side of the hill. They did it themselves — without aid of horses — in order to keep the guns from falling into enemy hands, and to preserve some vestige of their honor. These guardsmen had banded together and named themselves the Fédérés.

Henri said, close to my ear, "These guns belong to the people. Each and every one bought and paid for by subscription, by the sweat of the brow, by brothers and sisters in every *quartier*, to defend Paris. By right they belong to us."

"To be pointed at whom? The Germans?"

"We want our city back — every wall, every cesspool, every cobblestone. Every blade of grass in the Luxembourg and every branch left on every tree. How long were we robbed under the empire? Our streets redrawn for the cannon to roll down; our friends and neighbors driven like animals from their homes? The autocrats wanted to turn Paris into a factory, a living machine to churn out profits for them. When they failed, they staged a corrupt tourney with the Prussians, then betrayed us with a general who never had a plan to defend his country. And now they want the working people, who built this city — and to whom they turned for their defense — to buy them a rancid, fraudulent peace. Five hundred million francs — to be paid, by whom? And how?" The sinews tightened in his neck; he looked off into the distance. On the plain beneath us, guardsmen pulled up their hoods, adjusted the straps on their rifles, prepared to change shifts for evening. "What can we do but refuse?" Henri was windblown, clear-eyed. Dark, flickering like a banked hearth. A map in his hand, with positions on it. I looked over his shoulder.

"No, we are not going to fire upon the Germans. But upon the standing government, and drive them out — the bloodsucking traitors and their hangers-on, their *cocottes* and their police and their bankers with them. And we are going to turn Paris back over to the working man and woman. The teachers and artists, the families and children and plenty more than that. But the Commune is for order. I wanted you to see for yourself."

And then he kissed me.

. . . *Nous sommes trahis.* We are all betrayed. We betray one another.

Be more generous with yourself, Louise had said to me, long ago. *If you will not, who will be for you?* Up on Montmartre, with the Germans strolling on the boulevards below, I crossed a line within. Perhaps to join the banquet of life at last. I kissed the Communard up on that hill. Kissed him back. Several times.

When we got back to the rue du Mail, later that evening, La Tigre had apparently considered the possibility of a banquet as well—a fire was lit in the grate; my good bed linens refreshed and turned back.

"We don't sleep with our feet to the fire here, as in a Prussian camp," I said—only a little apprehensive, because the man had clearly done a few things other than thieve, protect, and fight—his lips told me that much.

"I've seen bed linens," he said, bemused.

"Oh? How is that?"

"A certain Russian . . . a countess. A dacha outside Moscow. I was there with the old man—Blanqui. My first experience of bed linens." Henri was standing with his back to the fire, his tall shadow leaning into the room. He smelled of gunpowder and iron; and I wanted the taste of wine in my mouth but recalled he didn't drink it. I also wanted to ask him questions, but he didn't answer many. Henri was tight-lipped and silent as the grave about his affiliations.

"Thank goodness. So you don't choose your bed companions by their politics?"

"Not generally. Nor by their linens."

Still shivering from the raw weather, we warmed our hands in front of the fire.

"Henri, do you think there is something—larger than the Commune, the assembly, all of these politics, these—arguments swirling around our heads?"

"Larger? Of course. God is . . . Love is larger."

"I thought the Commune had taken against God."

"No, only the atrocities committed by the church in the name of God. The abuse of the people's trust—"

"Yes, yes. But to many people it is the same thing, when they see you turning churches into podiums and shouting that nuns should be put in Saint-Lazare, and worse for the priests. They feel you are using their cherished beliefs against them — denying them hope and putting yourselves in its place."

"Probably love and God are one and the same, but neither science nor philosophy will prove it, and men have little vocabulary for it, so we stick to what we know. Some stick to the past. Others try to set up structures of society that can allow the larger matters to take root. The generations will follow what is right. That is our true hope, justice embedded in the structure of society, not promised after death by a God for whom only the archbishop can speak. To carry on what others began."

"So — your duty as a soldier of this army is to die for that?"

"Women bear children, and men must die in numbers to make a better world . . . Oh, perhaps not! Perhaps some will live to see it. I am not intent on dying."

"I'm glad, Henri. Enough death."

"Indeed."

He shed his gunner's coat; washed his blackened hands in the basin. Held them out, laughing, because he hesitated to sully my white damask. I took them, wet, and examined them, turned them over. His palms were callused from the guns. I dried his hands, finger by finger.

"You are a working man, Henri. I can see it in your palms."

He laughed. Poured a glass of water from the pitcher, and drank.

Later I would dream of that night. His body, the shock of recognition; how we desired each other and suddenly were together, tangled in sheets, twilight pouring through the balcony window. Henri a rare lover, his hard edges melting in my soft . . . And afterward we lay together, bodies floating and content.

Slowly then, in my dream, he pulls himself up, out of my arms. Crosses the room, pours water into a glass, drinks again, deeply. Next he must reach for his shirt, shoes, trousers, move to the door. But he does not. He stands, glass in hand, looking out the window. What does he intend? Then comes another shock, the realization. Not words, but something else; some foreign gesture, a language

I recognize as if it were my own, but it is not. This place where he stands, he is entirely present. When he drinks water it satisfies his thirst. When he makes love, he loves. His love is not complicated.

But this is alien territory, too soon entered: this game laid out on the table is not one I know, and the stakes, I fear, are high. I have lived in a world I cannot describe to him. A nomad well adjusted to desert life, happening upon an oasis long forgotten.

28

BETWEEN PARIS AND VERSAILLES

T HE STANDING GOVERNMENT, it was learned, would not wait it out with the Paris rabble but instead decamp to Versailles (recently vacated by the occupying German commanders) and take much of high society with it. For that reason, and because it was announced that rent was due, with arrears for the entire period of the siege, the rue du Mail corridors filled with packing trunks. Their lids gaped open, as did the tops of the dress boxes, lined up in the halls like coffins; and round hatboxes and a rainbow of textiles: watered silks, lace, cashmere. Sylvie (who had managed to sit out the siege in Vienna, having quite a high time of it) and Francisque were up to their elbows in panniers and dresses, guessing as to what migh next transpire.

"I've been promised a *laissez-passer*," said Francisque, who was hedging her bets and trying to keep up her residence in both locations. All things considered, she had fared better than many — pale and fine-boned to begin with, her porcelain beauty had taken on an ethereal quality; her skin was almost translucent. Sylvie, fattened on sausages and sacher torte all winter, was plump and ruddy by comparison, even though she always watched her figure.

"It's that moiré from last season that's passé. I hope you're not planning to break hearts in Versailles wearing that."

"Certainly the French army has had nothing to do but recall every flounce of my dress."

"If you greet them with shouts of 'July 1870!' they will remember it," said Amélie, who was looking on.

"July 1870 has been ripped apart for bandages."

"The Prussian army is there as well," said Sylvie. "You'll find them politer, at least in the streets." She had had her piano tuned and begun practicing scales again, her voice bent flat in the upper ranges, groping against the chords. Out of practice. "They say the opera will begin again, at Versailles."

"With a lot of German music? . . . They say a lot of things," said Amélie. "*Manille, manille.* Twenty-four ways of playing it and it's all the same game."

"Working at the balloon factory has changed *your* tune, my girl," I said. Amélie had not lifted a finger to pack.

"That, and watching the world unravel."

Francisque said, "I don't have much patience for Versailles, either — I suspect it will be boorish and dull, with everyone's nerves on edge, all wishing they were back in Paris. But how else will I manage two thousand francs to the landlord for not having starved to death?" Her beau, de Ligneville, was still a prisoner of war at Sedan, along with the former emperor.

Amé said, "I read in *Le Rappel* that there are no lodgings to be had; even ministers are sleeping in chairs in the Hall of Mirrors, using the drapes to cover themselves. Or paying ten francs a night to sleep on straw in a cellar."

"I'm not a minister, darling!" said Francisque. "La Tigre knows a woman there. But I will be dancing, not sleeping. How are *you* paying the rent?"

"I'm not planning to," retorted Amé. "Let them try to throw me out."

Sylvie added, "Besides, the Commune will have us all sewing uniforms and filling sandbags any day now."

Amé said, "You should all stay and join the Women's Union. I am going to stand, for once, not follow the rats."

"We've eaten the rats," snapped Francisque, edgy with nerves.

"Well. You don't want the ones that are left to eat you."

Sylvie said, "I've been to the Women's Union. The agenda never ends until you are falling asleep in your seat. Should we form work cooperatives, or plan to march on Versailles with kitchen knives like the Bread March in 1789; or is it better to march peacefully? No, we must take up arms, make cartridges on the avenue Rapp, threaten to leave our husbands if they refuse to join the National Guard. As for divorce, we wanted it once, got it, lost it again. What now? The fine men on the Left have rejected divorce. So, no divorce. Now it is down to whether or not to wear the red sash. But no! We must get rid of silly fashions, of fashion entirely. But. That would put the seamstresses out of work, the one profession we can stick to! At any rate, we must prepare to fight and die for justice. And then, everything is tabled until the next time."

"It's always suspicious when they ask us to die for justice, if you ask me," said Francisque, shaking out a length of berry-colored cashmere. "What do you think — too Red?"

"I think it is a breath of fresh air, hearing what everyone has to say. You can't be so impatient. I can tell you that women would have cast their votes for Gambetta, not that old toad Thiers. Think of our daughters and their daughters!"

"I didn't know you had a daughter, Amé," said Sylvie drily.

"It's a manner of speaking."

"And if everyone speaks and no one listens, what then?" said Francisque.

There was a brief silence. Then Sylvie said, "What about you, Eugénie?"

"I haven't the stomach for Versailles, at the moment."

"More for a bite of a Communard, I'd say," said Francisque. "But what about Monsieur de Chaveignes? *He* must be going. I'll never forget how he looked in that uniform, the day of the *sortie torrentielle.*"

"Has anyone seen Finette? I'm dying for some hot water," I said, ignoring the question, but not without a pang . . . Stephan bending down in military colors, pressing his cheek against my hand while I was delirious with fever before the Great Sortie. Promising that he would bring us Prussian souvenirs. And freedom.

"Oh, that's the other thing," said Francisque. "The girl has vanished. My guess is up the hill." Whatever else was going on, a few dance halls had opened on Montmartre, alongside the cannon.

In March, just after the gates opened, another late snow and a blast of icy cold arrived. Gas was a flicker, coal still a luxury; and the demands had now been levied. The new assembly needed to pay the first sums due to Germany under the peace agreement; and Paris must be put back on its feet — but how? The vast numbers of pawned items at the Mont de Piété were the tools of the citizens' trades — from spades to sewing machines; and the government decreed that all of them were to be sold instead of returned, or made redeemable to, their original owners. It was all put up for sale, down to the last chamber pot.

Placards went up, exhorting Parisians to return to regular work, but for most it was impossible — we lacked shoes, cooking pots — furnishings, which had been burned for fuel — all the essentials for living. But any civil "disturbances" would be put down, the walls proclaimed. THERE WILL BE NO COUP D'ÉTAT. No more pictures of Thiers as the "Laughing Man" appeared; the assembly had called back the censors to suppress dissenting papers, which gave the new-minted assembly a stale, empire stink. People gathered on street corners, whispered. In droves, by the dozen and the horde, they made any plan they could to leave Paris; waiting in endless lines for the few trains out.

Near the rue Montmartre a pile of paving stones dug up from the street stood in a tumbled pyramid. A tattered red strip tied to a stick had been stuck in the top of the pile, fluttering in the bare breath of spring. I climbed down from the cab because we were not able to pass. The driver gestured to it; he growled through his pipe.

"That's right," he said. "We were not beaten; we were sold."

And Paris could not accept the terms imposed, negotiated by Thiers, a man most of Paris had not elected. It was the provinces that had gone for Thiers. A people's army; walking ghosts of the capital, those who had starved on behalf of their country now refused the proposition of the failed Government of National Defense, and the newly constituted assembly. Ranks of fathers and mothers, battalions of daughters and sons, nurses and cooks, gardeners and children—an army of the hungry, of gray beards and no-beards, furies of the siege clubs and barricades and taverns lined up behind the sons of the "true Paris" to throw themselves upon the enemy and their own false protectors. Their ranks were swelling, quietly and after dark.

It began to feel as though not only the Communards were the Commune. The landlord's demand was a rallying cry, as were the officious clerks at the Mont; and the neighborhood boys who guarded the cannon, who patrolled the neighborhoods and gathered in certain cafés, defying the occupiers with their looks, seemed our defenders. We who had lived through the siege, who had seen the bodies floating down the Seine after the first sortie and then read with incredulity what the papers said about victory, felt a collective shudder of fury. We looked around and saw what propped up the Versailles government—from the banks and the Bourse to the *tolérances*. We remembered the ways so many of us had to scrabble for a living under the empire; what it had been like to do what survival required—coerce acts from our most cynical selves. Under direct Prussian fire we had come together at last, opening our doors to one another as the shells fell. I understood the revulsion and contempt for the profiteers; for the government that turned its back on us and then with relish served up our thin bodies and souls to the enemy. Then grabbed their hats and coattails and mistresses and fled to Versailles so as not to suffer the consequences. But we could be more fiery and harrowing than they understood.

This was an old anger. Fathomless, tribal. *Order without bloodshed is possible*, said the Commune. But at night we heard the roll of cannon down the cobbles; in the morning, fresh barricades and knots of whisperers on the corners.

It was early spring. The melting of the snow; a few brave buds appeared on the few remaining trees; one or two cautious birds sang in the upper branches. The German soldiers had retreated from sight, after a two-day occupation agreed upon by the governments. When they left, people scrubbed the pavements. Removing the Germans from our minds was more difficult: Prussian troops were stationed outside the *enceinte,* occasionally making their presence known with volleys of gunshots. Daily more provisions appeared in the shop windows and on the shelves. The post was delivered: bags of letters from the outside world, dating back to October. One of these was a letter from Rome, from Sidonie, Giulia's Paris maid who had gone back with her to Italy. At my little desk, my eyes blurred with tears. Giulia had died of consumption shortly after the siege began; that is, very soon after I had seen her last, shivering under a torrent of ice and champagne. And her little girl had wanted to take care of her mother better than Giulia wanted to care for herself.

I drove across town. The boulevards were in an upheaval again, and my driver did not know the reason — some kind of hubbub, a flurry of running boys and mobs on the corners. Some sort of altercation up on the Montmartre buttes, but we did not stop because I was in a hurry to pound on the door of my sometime lover . . . My foul-weather friend who arrived when things turned bad and Giulia was put in mind to kill herself for Russian gold. I had not heard a word from him — no thanks for the supplies, no indication of his plans, given the reconfiguration of Paris. On the other hand, my own thoughts strayed more and more to Henri.

After banging at the door I heard Mitra's voice; then the boy unlocking many locks and opening it on creaking hinges. Now that the shelling was past, and Germans in the streets vivid in our minds, doors were locked again. In his bedchamber Stephan was flopped down in his sandbagged fortress, asleep. Mitra stood to the side, alert and guardlike, looking more like a man than his father did at that moment.

"Stephan, wake up! *Monsieur le comte,* it's nearly noon!" Stephan groaned and flung an arm over his eyes. I turned up Stephan's palm and tickled it, a most unpleasant sensation for a sleeping person. Palm of narrow escapes, indeed.

A pile of mail lay scattered to the side; thin envelopes with foreign postmarks. Indian letters, and thicker ones with seals. Stephan stirred and hoisted himself up on a sandbag.

"Mitra, coffee!" Glanced at me, sullen. I knew that look. I had brought apples with me, and tossed one at him now.

"Your post has come, I see. Mine came. Giulia is dead of the grippe."

"I'm sorry. Truly," muttered Stephan. "And Paris gossip has traveled quickly as ever, so you may as well hear it from me. My family intends to press forward with the lawsuit. They are sending their man to me today."

I stared at him, not quite in surprise. "Your actions toward me haven't made their claim any easier to prove, monsieur."

"But lent it urgency, I'm afraid."

"And where do you stand?"

"I am not standing, at the moment. I am lying down in bed, about to expire for want of a decent cup of coffee. Mitra!"

"Stephan. Are you going to Versailles?"

"I don't know. But you should, if you want to. Your business affairs will have moved there, I daresay." It took me a moment to think of what he meant.

"I have not come to ask your permission! But I am not in spirit for Versailles."

"So much the worse. But. Eugénie, you and I must communicate through intermediaries now—otherwise it will simply be a wreck. I will mediate with the family, I promise you." He sighed. "My mother is not well. My sister is not married. I have been hunting neither Bengal tigers—nor heiresses, as is my filial duty—"

"No heiresses! And why might that be?"

He sent me a cryptic glance. I sat back, stared at him. Could I possibly still love this man? Something in me had changed; it had begun on those dark nights of the siege. A silent passage, laid stone by stone. My "business affairs" indeed. How dare he.

I said, "Your family can act as they like. But their suit is useless, as will soon be proved in a republican court—or perhaps they would prefer a judge under the auspices of the Commune. Which will have been advised by the Women's Union."

"The Commune! Now you are ridiculous."

"And one day — quite soon — I intend to retrieve Berthe and help her as best I can. I am not going to throw her away because of them. Or because you are a coward."

"The suit happens to be based in the law, which is on the side of my family's interests and its honor."

"Bah! And it is a convenient sandbag for you, monsieur."

"Eugénie, there is no winning this argument. Even if you had the girl — if she is alive — "

"She is alive."

"How, under what circumstances, would you intend to raise her? As Giulia brought up her daughter?"

"Please. Giulia died trying to cover Giulietta's school fees."

"You see? It's preposterous."

"Own up to the situation you helped to create, Stephan."

"In another world I'd marry you, Eugénie." The man looked miserable. "But I cannot abandon my mother and Sophia, or divide myself from my family in that way — don't you see that I am trapped as well? And besides, you would not understand India."

And I would not have a "dictionary of the bed" to explain it to me, I thought, but I said only, "Very well. My lawyers will take it from here."

"All right — all right. Perhaps I have not entirely thought it through; I need more time."

"What else have you had to do these past three months?"

"Perhaps I can break with the family, with indigo and all the rest of it. Perhaps I do want the girl. Perhaps I do want us to — I don't know. What the hell would we do? Go to America? Australia?"

I turned impatiently, went to his window, and looked out at the rooftops, at the place de l'Étoile — down at the avenue d'Eylau, where Haussmann's construction remained incomplete even now. The avenue was divided, with half of it twenty feet above the new street level. Residents had to climb stairways, built along a "temporary" retaining wall, to get to their doors. There it had been left when the empire fell; and so it remained.

"Do you love me, Stephan? Do I love you? What obligation do we have, not under the Code, but between ourselves? I don't have the answer; I have not asked you for a wedding ring, but why is it that we can never speak of—of what is important?"

The question went unanswered, for at that moment Mitra stepped into the room, turbanless and barefoot, balancing a tray with a silver pot on it, cups and spoons; he was wide-eyed, looking as though he was about to jump out of his skin. A sheaf of paper under his arm.

"Ah, Mitra. Coffee, thank you. And the papers; you are a prince among young men . . . Good Lord. What is happening out there this morning?" I peered over his shoulder—not at a newspaper, but at a hastily printed broadsheet. For a few moments, not a breath between us; just the rustling of the page.

Free of the tray and unable to contain himself any longer, Mitra hopped on one foot and shouted gleefully, "The government's army has surrendered to the Commune!"

Stephan was pale, as if he had seen a ghost. "Mitra, do you know what that means?"

"Yes!"

"Then you are the only one in the capital who does."

I said, "I may not understand India, but Mitra understands France."

Early that morning of March 18, 1871, two brigades of the Eighty-eighth Regiment of the regular army had been sent up to the buttes, where Henri and I had kissed, to retrieve the cannon held by the the Fédérés, the so-called insurgents—or the Commune, depending on how you saw it. In advance of the move to Versailles, Thiers and the assembly wanted assurances that Paris was under control; that it was not a powder keg controlled by the Reds and the rabble. They roused the troops at three in the morning and, in a chilly rain, without coffee or breakfast, sent them to retrieve the cannon. But there were not enough horses in harness to pull down the guns, and the troops of the Eighty-eighth had to wait while runners were sent back down to get them. Another runner went down the hill as well, I would later learn. Louise Michel, our former companion of the supper table and woman of no second thoughts (would she have had them if she had known what was to come?) bolted down from Montmartre with a gun on her back, rallying half of Paris to support the Fédérés.

Dawn was breaking just then, and up on the buttes only the milk-maids and a few guardsmen were out. Some of the women walked in front of the cannon and offered the soldiers of the Eigthy-eighth Regiment fresh milk; a few café girls from the dance halls stood by and flirted. More women and children came out to see what was happening; there was a lull, a suspension. The general in charge gave an order to fire, but the stars and planets changed position, perhaps; the first brigade turned up the butts of the guns, and refused.

"We don't have to kill one another!" someone shouted, and the second brigade too turned its guns butt-up. No one let off a shot, but rather everyone put down their arms and began drinking milk, the troops of the Eighty-eighth and the National Guard together. It was a bloodless coup up on the buttes on a quiet morning in March, where Henri and I had been — the place Chasseloup used to stare at, brooding, from his atelier. (*Almost* bloodless. But all details of the event did not come out until later.) The broadsheets that Mitra brought told the story their own way.

We might be "thin as keys," as someone later wrote, but our keys had unlocked a door and on that fine March morning we walked through it. By evening, the troops of the regular army had surrendered, deserted, or disintegrated, unwilling to rally on behalf of their generals and the assembly. The red flag flew over the great clock at the Hôtel de Ville. The next day, the weather turned bright, and everyone came out onto the boulevards, promenading in their best clothes as if it was a holiday. Henri, exhilarated and wearing a new and spotless National Guard coat, came to gather me up at the rue du Mail; and we rode through Paris together, to the roll of drums of the Fédérés, before he had to go back on duty. Finette stopped by, after work at the *café chantant* where she was employed — to tell us with shining eyes how it had been, up on Montmartre that morning, how the girls had moved through the ranks of soldiers with flowers and cups of milk, "not at all afraid even though there were guns!" It had already become a myth, a beautiful story people wanted to believe. Over the next few days — which were quiet — the streets were swept clean for the first time since the empire had ended, and flags sprang up like fields of poppies.

29

CORRESPONDENCE

WHEN DO THE EDDIES separate ship from shore; when do you notice, with a hole in your heart, the widening distance between what you have been and what you will become? You might be able to string act to event, cause to consequence, but still you search for the moment when one substance becomes another. When color becomes image, or clay, flesh. Field corn is transformed to foie gras; the red dress becomes the red flag; an empress becomes a commoner, leaving behind her boiled egg. The awl slips and shatters the ivory, the paper is torn into shreds; love is broken like a crystal bowl. A woman's body, once beloved, becomes a draining trough, a gutter. She has taken a turn in her life from found to lost. Or from lost to found again.

A singular moment, at the corner of the rue Montmartre and the rue du Mail. A plain moment, when one thinks, *Someday I will look back at that street corner, at that woman in the green dress, with the umbrella: very ordinary except for the fact that there is a war on — but who was she, and what is she to become? Is there any hope for her?* Moments ago she exited the corner building, a structure like many others, with shallow balconies onto the street. The sort of building where the mattress men stopped to drop and collect their rentals during the empire. It was the first thing she noticed about the place. She walks down the rue du Mail to the rue Montmartre. Above the Bakery Saint-Claude is a bold sign: SALONS, CABINETS. PRIVATE ROOMS. Over the entrance, marble cupids tease one another with garlands. And a round lozenge says GAZ: a restaurant's proud advertisement of illumination within. All signs, now, of an era past . . . Something about the desultory tilt of her umbrella and the way she blinks in the weak April sun. But she is not headed for the teahouse that, during the siege, was known for black-market items other than tea; nor to the *boulangerie* that only intermittently displayed round loaves and long *ficelles* and braids of bread; and for some time, only ship's biscuit. No, she is ringing the bell, then opening the door, for Maison Gellé at number 4, Impasse Saint-Sauveur: DYES, CLEANING, AND FINISHING. SPECIALITÉ: BLACK FOR MOURNING. The clock's hands stand at ten before ten. Because of a shortage of German clock winders, the clocks have not been reset, and all over the city, their hands remain askew.

I was at my desk again, sorting mail. More of it trickling in, months old. Solicitations, invitations, events from another time and a different world. Among them was one envelope of heavy paper; brown ink. Angular, pointy, old-fashioned script I had not seen often, and not in a very long time. A postmark from Auch. My stomach knotted, but before I had a chance to break the seal, Amélie, still in a morning dress and half-corset, appeared at my door.

"There is fighting in the place Vendôme. A group calling itself the Friends of Order has marched down the rue de la Paix in their top hats and canes, but shots were fired and the National Guard on the *place* has responded — or — "

"Who are these Friends of Order?"

"They marched yesterday, unarmed — today they are back. They want some kind of treaty with Versailles, or some further assurances from the Commune."

"The chief of police has just been slapping too many rich men in jail . . . I just heard cannonade from the forts."

"They say the Prussians are firing blanks to celebrate some kind

of anniversary. But I don't think I'll go out. Are you seeing the
Communard tonight? Or is something else up your sleeve?"

"Henri is a revolutionary. He doesn't make firm plans. If there is
fighting on the place Vendôme I hardly think he'll be taking me to
dinner."

"Hard to keep up with you these days, Rigault. And *are* you related to the chief of police? Everyone is asking. I'd like to know
which way the wind's going to blow next." She sighed.

The new chief under the Commune had long been an agitator
on the Left; he had achieved his greatest fame by using a spyglass
from the Seine bookstalls to look in on the former empire's Préfecture—at all of the Noëls and Coués and their henchmen and su-
periors—then publishing his scandalous findings. Long before the
coup of March 18, he had dubbed the police the Ex-Préfecture. So
it was still called the Ex-Préfecture, although he was now the head
of it. He was also a rake, notorious for believing that female favors
should be granted for free; and he had no fond eye for priests. With
his coarse black beard and cynical eye, he seemed to be trusted by
no one. Oddly, I shared his name—Rigault.

"I can't help you there. I may need to change my name. Everyone
seems to hate the man."

The letter was from my Uncle Charles. My mother's brother had
always prided himself on a dispassionate, full, and objective setting out of facts, and his crabbed and pointy script covered several
pages. The letter recalled his voice, flowing with precision—dull
to an impatient child; but now I devoured every word like the produce that had rolled in from the countryside, though I wasn't sure
it wouldn't make me just as bilious. I looked up from the page to
the ticking clock on my desk, the little porcelain-and-gilt one with
filigree hands, a gift from Beausoleil. Its hands told the hour because
I wound it myself, with a small gold key.

The occasion of his writing was to inform me about Berthe: my
mother. She had been ill for some time, he wrote. She was confined
to bed and in and out of consciousness; the medical men had given
up bleeding her. Weak and jaundiced, she could not stand any cov-

erings on her feet. *"To a man, not one of the doctors has seen such feet . . . You will recall her willfulness."* Several times she had been near death, and Charles had gone through papers to settle personal matters while she was able to state her preferences. It was in these papers that my uncle had located my present address. All of my previous residences had been struck off, save the last, he wrote. A meticulous record keeper, my mother. She had kept track of it: through the Auch Préfecture. Reading that, I felt ill and stopped to take some bismuth and quince.

> Berthe had never spoken about the documents that she received during the winter of 1861; and it was since that date that she refused to hear your name spoken in our home. But it is these documents that I have found among her papers.
> . . . Her very great unhappiness, and blaming of herself for your situation, I believe, caused her to descend to her current state. It is the case that over a course of years under these conditions the feminine liver will collapse.
> If history permits it, consider traveling to see her.

The letter closed with my uncle's certainty of the victory of France in battle. I glanced again at the date: December — around the time true hunger began, with famine not far off.

Berthe. She had made only perfect things. Loved what was unsullied and beautiful: dowry sheets kept folded in the chest; china never used. Tiny, exact miniature portraits; the first immaculate radishes in the spring, rinsed of garden dirt, ruby-throated, white-tipped, arranged in a wooden bowl for her to paint. She was an artist, a creator of the unblemished surface. Except, of course — for her daughter, whom she had had to trace through the Préfecture, that pustulent wart on the rue des Fèves.

Bad currents in the air that night; a chunk of moon like a moldy Camembert. It had been more than a bit of trouble at the place Vendôme — it had been an outright and brutal massacre of the unarmed or barely armed. There had been a pistol or two among the banners of the peaceful "friends" that afternoon, and no one knew who fired the first shot—but sentiment went against the Commune. The boulevards filled with anxious faces, then emptied, so the capital looked once again like it had during the siege; and for the first time since the coup, we felt the heaviness of dread.

Under the Commune's administration, the streets were clean. Water played in the fountains. The Communards had cleaned up the boulevards, abolished petty fines, remitted rents, allowed reclamations of the tools and cherished items that had been pawned at the Mont. (Even at the rate of thousands of items returned each day, this would take a year, we were told.) They had opened the question of women working for fair wages in the professions, and with these acts they had captured a degree of popular support. Not a murder had been committed in the capital since March 18; and citizens were permitted to walk in the Tuileries.

But. A great deal of fresh air was wanted, to blow out the ghastly memories of winter; and we had only a gust of spring. People felt they were too quick on the trigger, hotheaded, these Communards. As gluttonous for retribution as the empire had been for stuffing itself on foreign wars and the working man's labor. Public opinion went against them on the darker matters of March 18: the execution of two government generals up on Montmartre. To govern, to win over public sentiment, required reason, nuance, the ability to become attuned to the body politic; to speak with an undivided voice and yet to mediate, to compromise, to negotiate—the Commune faltered here; and a few of them were outlaws or worse. Meanwhile, the assembly at Versailles consorted with the Prussians (so it was said); for them, the menace in Paris was kept at a distance.

But between Paris and Versailles, how was the thing to be settled? . . . When would life as usual resume? What *was* life as usual; for whom was it usual? So the arguments circled, turned back on themselves, as the cannonade rumbled ominously from the ring of fortifications outside the capital, just beyond the Paris walls.

In my own case, if the Versailles-based government came back to power, I supposed they would reestablish Regulation; the Préfecture would reconstitute itself and my desk would again be covered with offers and enticements, solicitations to business. It seemed as odious as drinking rum or eating horseflesh: a retreat to an impossible past. At present, Chief of Police Rigault's tolerance of unregulated debauchery was at odds with the Commune's principled stand against it. The upper echelons of the business had left town and the tolerated houses were officially closed. Stray boulevard girls were periodically rounded up and sent to sew sandbags or pack cartridges, as Sylvie had predicted.

A shifting uneasiness hung over the city like a fog. Day by day, the circle tightened; and once again we lined up to stock our larders. Similarly, people waited for hours at the Préfecture to apply for the *laissez-passer*—though not males between the ages of seventeen and forty, who were ripe for conscription into the National Guard.

Word came down that the Commune particularly welcomed issuing the exit paper to any girl who carried a *carte* from the empire's Préfecture. They did not know what to do with us—never mind that it had been *les inscrits* who had defended the cannon on Montmartre on March 18 and initiated the mood of "fraternization" with the army. No language existed to credit such girls and women for any of the events that transpired that day.

Henri believed that the Commune's battle with the Versailles army would be efficient and decisive. He sketched a picture of columns of citizens, a *levée en masse,* marching out to the fortifications to confront weak and depleted battalions; he was confident in a general who had fought in the American Civil War, for the Union side. Cluseret.

"And Jolie goes to the barricades too?" I asked him.

"Dissuade her if you can. She wants to fight." He sighed. "For Louise."

Increasingly militant since Strasbourg, and a Commune hero for rousing Paris at the crucial hour, Louise had practically marshaled a battalion of her own. She went to the former fairgrounds for target practice and made fierce anti-Versailles speeches. Jolie was among her closest allies.

Henri wanted me to obtain the *laissez-passer,* however, and to leave Paris when the battle began—not to go to the barricades with a rifle. Henri, I was learning, was a man of some principled contradictions.

I did not know what kind of reception I might receive at the Préfecture but took a place in line and toiled my way to the front. The officer issuing the document took one look at the name Rigault, assumed I was some relative of his new chief, and stamped the papers in a hurry, without even checking the Register or asking me to produce my *carte*. I had to laugh in spite of myself at the look on the poor man's face as he slid me the *laissez-passer*. Rigault must be terrible indeed.

"*Manille, manille,*" chuckled Amélie, when I told her about it later. "Are you going to leave?"

"No, it's just a precaution, and to stop Henri from worrying. What about you, Amé?

"The women are going—some hundred of us—to the Hôtel de Ville to request protection; then we are going to Versailles to demand a peaceful resolution between the Commune and the assembly. These men must begin to speak sense to one another." Her eyes shone as she described the delegation of siege housewives from the ration lines, balloon workers, laundresses, factory workers, café keepers. "Our captain is a lacemaker and café singer. Why don't you come?"

"Maybe I will."

"If Versailles prevails, they will clap us back into Regulation so they can pay the reparations to Germany off our backs. Or the Commune will take what they want and claim to be pure as Spartans. These men have got to compromise with one another, and we women need to stand our ground. They have made a hash of this; for once, it would do them good to listen."

Palm Sunday dawned dull and gray as though forces had amassed against spring. Under our windows, little girls were calling up, trying to sell sprigs of boxwood for a sou; but the cannonade boomed out at ten o'clock from the direction of Courbevoie: an utterance so

profound it rattled the teacups, or maybe it was my shaking hand
that set them shuddering.

"It sounds like thunder," said Amé shakily.

"It is not thunder; it is civil war," said La Tigre, who had rushed
in, and over to the windows to peer out. "Your ladies' march will be
shipped back through the walls by the cartload to be buried like the
casualties," said our fierce concierge, no sentimentalist. La Tigre
had no traffic with the Versaillais, but she was not Communard either. She thought they were rabble, although she liked Henri.

"I've got to go out," I said.

"Now? Are you out of your head? Wait until order is restored, at
least," said La Tigre.

"Order restored by whom?"

No one had an answer.

A ragged energy swelled and gusted, thick in the air, like a cloud of
soot, heavy and stinging, as my cab zigzagged through the streets.
The soldiers at the checkpoints all wore coats and insignia of the
National Guard; they motioned — with the points, not the butts, of
their guns — for me to step down. "Stop, in the name of the Commune!" Ragged urchins begged from the passing conveyances during these forced halts. Everywhere, paving stones were piled up, as
were barrels, ladders, ropes, carts . . . Posters plastered on any available wall — white, as the Commune had declared it would print
now only on white; the older red ones hung in strips underneath.
An omnibus had been upended at one corner and become part of a
barricade. "Drive on," a guardsman said, once I showed my *laissez-
passer*, signed by Rigault.

The sky had dulled; it was beginning to rain. We stopped again;
my cab's horses shied this time at the line of cannon pointing outward, and as many mortars, behind piles of cobbles and rubble, and
two more soldiers with their *tabatières*.

"How do you feel toward the Commune?" asked an awkward
boy, stepping up and peering into the window, which I had pulled
down. He was pale, with a two-day beard and weather-roughened
skin. Squared shoulders and a cutaway coat with a belt, his *tabatière*

strapped over his shoulder. Scuffed boots that had walked a thousand miles.

"I support the Commune." I showed my *laissez-passer*.

"Very well, but—madame—I say only for your well-being, do not go into the center unaccompanied."

And so we turned around before reaching the Seine. However, my foray had served its purpose. I could see how to do it, now.

After the first assault, a reprieve. We learned that the Versailles troops had pushed into the Neuilly suburbs on the western edge of the city, defeated the National Guard, and taken the bridge. A funeral procession to Père Lachaise was held. Commune caskets were draped in black, with red flags at each corner; drums were muffled and sounded very grave and the marchers kept faces cast down. Relatives and friends of the dead formed a long tail to the procession, and crowds lined the boulevards as they passed. Many shops were closed. At Neuilly the fighting continued, but the Versailles troops did not breach the *enceinte*.

What we did not know was that the quiet was one of retrenchment. That what would come to be called the second siege would begin, and it would be worse, much worse, than the first.

30

RUE D'ENFER

TWO DAYS AFTER my first attempt, with a deft driver and a red ribbon around my wrist, I made my way again past stripped trees, army canteens, and bivouacs; through interminable traffic and delay and the barricades at Montparnasse. I was clad from heel to crown in widow's black, an acceptable camouflage these days. Veiled I had entered the capital, and so I would leave it, I thought, fastening the gauzy thing. If it came to that. My stays and the lining of my brocade going-away coat were sewn tight with bills, more fortifying than baleine. A good half of Paris was walking around with their money stuffed and stitched into their clothes.

At the mouth of the rue d'Enfer, fresh cobbles had been pulled up for a barricade, with ranks of sandbags and holes for the muzzles of cannon. Pockmarks, scars, and powder burn from the earlier Prussian assaults showed on the buildings' stone walls. At the hospice's entrance, a long line of gray-and-white-clad *nourrices* twisted up from the steps and around the drive. Some just in from the countryside; others showing siege pallor and thin as rails. A fleet of wagons waited, staves resting on the ground, and as a few straggling old mares were let through the barricade, the women began to organize the children and infants, hitching up their skirts and climbing into the wagons. Inside I could see narrow benches and hammocks, and children, each one in uniform, with a shorn head, teetering like birds on a wire. The air was filled with wails.

The director and his wife had been hailed for staying in Paris through the siege, but now an evacuation was underway. A National Guard on a black horse, uniformed in a blue Zouave jacket belted with the red sash and tall well-shined Hessian boots, inspected the barricade and barked orders. It was Lisbonne, the actor-turned-soldier, the Commune's brash "d'Artagnan" whom I'd met up on Montmartre with Henri; the two of them had saluted each other. If names were portents, this street might yet justify its designation as the street of hell. But Lisbonne was among the most bold of the Commune's warriors, Henri said — so perhaps he would save it.

A plain-skirted woman answered the hospice's private-entrance bell. Her neck was bare of any crucifix and her hair bundled into a swatch of crochet; she hurried ahead on floors that today were less than polished. She knew me as a "friend of the widow Chateaubriand." She had accepted the friends' packets during the siege; our blankets and food supplies and little bundles of sticks, what kindling we could find. Over the course of those bitter months, this emissary and I had come to know each other a little. I did not tell her the nature of my mission; she knew enough to hold up her hand when I began to speak of it.

Conditions at the hospice were much changed from before the siege. The Commune had removed the religious from their positions in the hospitals, but here, unlike the military hospitals, few replacements had come. The director was now negotiating with the Commune about the barricades on the rue d'Enfer, as he wanted to ensure the transport of all of his charges to an orphanage outside the enceinte before the fighting began in earnest. The daily running of the place had fallen to madame.

From a ring of keys, my friend lifted one and unlocked the door of the hospice archives; allowed my entrance and hurried off to more pressing concerns. From within, the musty scent of old paper and mildew mingled with the sour metallic and sulfurous odors of the corridor, and my eyes adjusted to the dimness enough to descry banks of wooden cabinets with drawers. My heart began to pound; my palms perspired inside my gloves. But otherwise it was drafty and cold, and my time limited, so I set aside gloves and veil but did not take off my coat.

The files were arranged by year and catalogued by number. The first bank held the hospice's massive leather-bound record books, marked by the year. Each was lined with entries, one for each child left in its care. The first admitted on New Year's Day of any given year was given the number one; the year and number also were inscribed on the medallion each child wore from the date of abandonment to that of majority, at age twenty-one. Within this lined record was listed too the name at entry and the new name provided, first and last.

Further on in the archive stood rows of shelves and cabinets. Banks of files and within them, black file boxes and mud-color ones. Jammed together, glued with some unknown substance; some thin and seemingly not touched for years. These, I discovered, contained birth certificates and identifying articles left at the time of abandonment—scraps of linen; misspelled notes and small charms: a thimble, a ring, glass baubles bound with thread. A lock of hair in an embroidered pouch. A tiny padlock with a key; a brass label from a café bottle marked simply VIN. Original birth certificates, copies, or nothing; pleading letters. Requests for children to be taken in and cared for; to be returned to a mother, "made legal," or simply—stories.

Too much life had been pushed helter-skelter into these files. And all of it retained; locked away, never passed on to the children. These vestiges of their history were, for them, erased. As they themselves were. It was too much to take in, to know; and certainly—too much to sort through in the time I had. I sighed, then breathed in dust. And returned to the ledgers, which appeared to be in some kind of order. From the shelves I selected the record book of 1861.

I understood now that in my earlier ignorance and rage, I had misjudged the directors to some extent. I may not have agreed with their principles, but at least they had applied them with constancy, laboring under every condition of war and peace, strained funds, understaffing, and an overload of cases to record assiduously the abandoned of Paris. The sheer weight of their conviction was impressive. At administration, that strange human ability, they excelled. I could only hope that genuine care for newborn persons had not lagged behind too far.

Even before entering this archive I knew that if abandoned infants survived the hospice and its poxy wet nurses; its filthy *biberons,* the communal wheat-paste sucking cloths; its stagnant air and close-packed cribs — if they passed through these walls intact, they often perished on the journey to the countryside. Once there, some suffocated by smoke or on smoldering straw mattresses; were burned by a hot brick in a cradle; or wandered too close to a fire. Unwatched and ignored, they fell into rivers and streams; succumbed to diseases of the gut and the lungs; and though precautions were taken against it — the syphilis passed on by their nurses. Inspectors skipped visits due to bad roads and weather and overlooked breaches of conduct; in the worst cases, they trafficked in their own charges. *Nourrices,* even the honest ones, stretched layettes to cover their own children's needs; favored home remedies and postponed doctors' visits for fear of penalties for neglect. The *abandonnés* were often transferred, and with each move came a new set of hazards. I had read about all of it in newspaper accounts and from documents to which my solicitors had gained access. Over the course of my years of hospice visits, I had spoken to midwives like Mathilde, wet nurses who worked for the state, knowledgeable mothers, and anyone else who would talk. Thus I had traced many of the possibilities for Berthe's fate. I was in some way resigned to them.

I paged through 1861 to June, to July. Mortality rates had not been too bad at that time, though the drop-offs at the *tour* had been high, and turnover to the *nourrices* rapid. Inspection visits, at least on paper, seemed to be in order. My heart beat faster and my stomach clenched as I paged past August, then September. Impatient, but reluctant too; once this page was turned I would know what I had never known. Even if no entry existed — which seemed possible — this too would alter my course. But at last I did turn to October, and there it was, in a crabbed and faded brownish script, a careful ledger-book hand.

Ledger No. 3568. October 10, 1861.
Mother: *Eugénie Louise Rigault.*
Father:

The identity of the father had been struck out; written above it, the word *Inconnu.* But unlike the illegibility of the birth certificate shown to me by the director of L'Assistance Publique, on this document Stephan's name could still be made out; some administrative hand had failed to efface it entirely.

Name Given: *Berthe Sophia Louise Rigault.*
Health at Arrival: *Fevered but otherwise good.*

Two days after her admittance, the record had been marked, "Fever abated. Taking nourishment." On the fifteenth Berthe was transferred to Avallon, in Yonne, and again the recording hand had noted that she had survived the two-day journey by train and post wagon, "despite rains."

So there it was. But of course it was; this was France, and this keeping of records had been in place since Napoleon I. I myself had set the system in motion on Berthe's behalf. Still, it was a revelation to see the document in black and white.

Yonne was one of the better places; the area's wet nurses, even the poorest ones who worked for the state, were better fed and healthier than most. I did not have time to linger over this scant record, however. If I had any hope of learning more, I must confront other files.

The hospice records dated back to 1801, and though they represented a valiant attempt to catalogue more than half a century of abandoned children, they showed signs of age and entropy. The files were sticky; massive piles of "undetermineds" were stained with grease and water; caches of documents had been left unfiled by some harried or lazy clerk. I began with a warped wooden drawer marked 1860; it squeaked under the weight of its contents. I culled through small abandoned lives, file upon file of them. But I was hundreds of lives too early; then another thousand too late. I sifted through the mess, records with cross-filed papers, missing documents, half-lives. Beginnings with no endings, middles with no start or finish — the scars and gaps on these pages not even beginning to tell the tales to which they referred: histories of children scattered to the winds as the force of administration marched on. Mildew tickled my nose, and I began to feel overwhelmed by the gloom and sadness of the place; the hopelessness of this quest. My time here was short; the Commune had imposed a curfew for the general safety of the citizenry; very soon it would be unwise to travel the streets.

Once, idly at cards on the rue du Mail, Lili had explained the principles of clairvoyance, the trade she had briefly and unsuccessfully practiced — or too successfully, as she said wryly, because the information she conveyed, while accurate, had often discomfited her clients.

"In addition to the clairvoyant information, one must accurately read the human nature and communicate with it, and that was the difficulty," she had said, shaking her head. "Teeth are easier."

"But the information, Lili, how did you obtain it?"

"Follow a thread," she had said. "Use your mind like a dart; focus as though an invisible filament exists between you and what you want to know. Pass by everything else — all distractions." As a game, we had practiced on hidden objects — rings and cards and teaspoons (with limited success). Lacking any better method now, I closed my eyes and thought of Berthe, of the umbilicus that had bound her to my womb; surely a stronger connection than a mere teaspoon. I allowed my mind to gather in the many steps taken and the invincible desire that had brought me, despite every obstacle, to this mortuary of information, where some fragment of my daughter and of my former self surely lay. Some clue to the present; some stitch to the future.

"Become idle," said Lili's voice, in my mind. "Fool your thoughts, as though you are blindfolding them, and use only your senses." When I opened my eyes, I felt very tired and realized that my mind had drifted to the letter from my Uncle Charles, as yet unanswered;

to Berthe, my mother. Something painful, like the dart Lili had wanted my thoughts to become, stung my chest. With effort, I returned to the drawer for 1861. Perhaps I had missed something.

And then—it was there. Intact between two sets of files in disarray—a jewel in the rubble. Marked in old, faded ink: case number 3568.

Opening it, a mild scent—what? Absinthe, ashes, rain, tears? In front of my eyes was a mold-speckled sheet, creased and torn; in fact, several sheets of records, stuck together with age and grit.

Her name is Berthe Sophia Louise. She is my only star in a dark sky. And I simply sat on the floor, in my going-away coat in mourning black, and wept.

Berthe's first wardrobe consisted of six diapers; four sets of swaddling clothes, two in wool and two in cotton; undershirts in wool and cotton; four *béquins,* or hoods, and two bonnets, calico; two shawls. For bedding she was given a wool blanket, two pillowcases, two straw mattresses, and a cradle cover. Provided at the end of her first year, in addition to reinvestments of swaddling and shirts, were two dresses and two pairs of stockings, one each in cotton and wool, and a pair of shoes. Her Yonne *nourrice* had received the administration's one-year bonus, disbursed to those who had managed to keep their foundlings alive for the first twelve months. It was rare enough and I thanked this *nourrice,* whose name I would never know.

None of the other common fates I had so often imagined and feared had befallen Berthe, either. For six years, meticulously noted allotments of clothing and regular payments had been disbursed. On the health record, no illness or infirmity was mentioned—no gibbosity, scrofula, rickets, or incontinence; no maladies of the eyes or the lungs, nor any other of the numerous disorders of the abandoned. In these pages, if they were accurate, my daughter's early history was an advertisement for the orderliness of the system of state care. What was not noted could not be known. But what struck me most was that my worry and guilt, and even the dire statistics that I had learned, had not been indicators of the truth in Berthe's case. Though her odds of surviving were fifty-fifty at best—in fact, my decision (if you could call it a decision) to entrust Berthe to the state's care had improved her situation materially.

At age six, she was transferred out of Avallon, to Aveyron. In the company of a sub-inspector and—I surmised—a group of other children, she had traveled south from the forests and *abéqueuses* of the Marne to a region of thinner soil, a harsh climate, and stubborn, independent people. To a place of tripe eating and wild rivers. Her foster parents were identified as agricultural laborers. With them she would have heard a patois similar to the one I had grown up with. For her care they received six francs a month. My thumb flew down these records, month by month, though the entries ran fewer as the years went on, often skipping one entirely. Lost years. The last entry was for a disbursement for school fees in 1869. Then a document from the department of Aveyron, dated in July of that same year, indicated that she was to be transferred again.

This appeared to be the end of her record.

Behind this page in the file was a sheet that gave a sobering account of the dates I had appeared at the hospice. In a spidery hand, the word *inscrit*, a knife edge of blame and insufficiency cutting me off from Berthe, appeared after each entry. Every date permitted, for almost nine years, I visited but had not managed to shake off that *inscrit*. Nine years in that dank, vitriol-washed, nun-tended corridor; years of useless pleas. My actual written petitions, if they had ever been placed in this file, were now absent, as was any mention of the legal proceedings plaguing my case.

Many records of the abandoned, I knew, fell off as the children became older. State payments decreased (it was assumed that by then, the orphans were able to work and contribute to their own support), and inspection and supervision lagged. Boys were placed in workshops, worked in factories or the fields; girls went into domestic service or factories as well. But unless the file went on to document court records and delinquency, or, in happier situations, marriage (a dowry of one hundred francs might be provided by L'Assistance Publique, at its discretion), often a child's life simply seemed to fall off the edge of the world. That seemed to be the case here. Until I found, clipped to the back of the file, one final note, written in the director's hand.

Received: ƒ300 for transport and other reimbursements re No. 3568; July 15, 1870. Age: 8 yrs 11 mos. Health: Good.
Transferred at rqt of S. de Chaveignes.
Terminé

I stared hard; startled, jarred. At the notation; then at the date. Just this past July — *before the siege.* And before I had seen him at the dinner at Giulia's. His hooded, speculative, questioning glance at Giulietta. (Ah! He must have been flummoxed indeed.) Tears welled up — anger, confusion, bewilderment, the echo of Stephan's voice. *Perhaps I do want the girl!* And with the stroke of a pen — *one stroke —*
. . . But what did Stephan intend? To take her into his own care? Had he seen her, met her in July before arriving in Paris? What had happened during the siege — was his family involved, was his threat of prosecution a lie, or — was he deceiving them as well, and why? Did he actually have a plan? And where was Berthe now? And then, by the fading light, numbly staring at the documents, I turned over the paper and read, from its reverse side, the final note by some fact-loving, documenting hand, one demanding accuracy in a file, the end of the hospice's story.

Transfer to Lourdes convent, Aug. 8, 1870.

Hours had passed. Outside the grimy windows, it was near dusk. I must hurry, lock up this place, and leave it as a thief. So I took the brittle, stained pages, including my original letter on behalf of Berthe. Slipped them between my bodice and my stays. Who would notice now — who would care? With the barricade so near, and Lisbonne dashing about on his horse, the entire place could go up in flames.

The door of the archive swung closed behind me. After a few turns to the central corridor, the hall led once and for all to those big hospice doors, which brushed closed as well. As always, the cries of infants from the Green Room, where the little blind ones with infected eyes stayed behind dull shades, a treatment based on the latest medical thinking. Were they too to be evacuated? At least my fruitless visits were now finished. I passed through the courtyard, now empty of wagons, and finally to the barricade at the place d'Enfer, in front of which a single old woman sat in a dark cloak and bonnet with folded hands, as if she personally would stave off the encroaching Versaillais. The mother of a guardsman, sitting at his post while he ate his supper, probably. She allowed me passage without a murmur; I moved toward a taxi stand, and questionable safety.

Stephan's address—near l'Étoile in the sixteenth arrondissement. I ordered the driver to go there. And quickly! . . . Impossible, he said. There was no traveling to the west because of the barricades in that direction; and hadn't I heard about the shelling already, over there? I climbed in regardless; needing to close any door, however flimsy, between the hospice and me.

Should I attempt a possibly futile chase across the barricaded city, which was armed to the teeth, about to flare up? Stephan might have found a way to depart the capital, even with the Commune ready to slap a gun on him and march him to the fortifications. And what if I did find him? Perhaps I should leave, myself. From here, I might be able to board a train at the Embarcadero near the place d'Enfer, exit the capital to the south. Though you didn't see much evidence of it in Paris, it was Holy Week; certainly conveyance to Lourdes could be found. To Lourdes! Without even a change of clothes? Well, others were doing with even less.

The driver was taking up the horses, now nervously pawing the ground. These new horses were not used to Paris driving; they went badly in traffic and shied at the barricades. I tapped the roof of the cab with the handle of my black umbrella.

"To the Embarcadero, then. Sceaux Railway."

"You'll get nowhere from there, madame. Had a passenger just tried this morning. Eager to go south, he was, the fine gentleman, but threw himself right back on me. Only way to leave is the Gare du Nord to Saint-Denis, or the Saint-Lazare."

"What kind of gentleman?" I asked wildly. "Did he have a boy with him? An Indian boy, wearing a turban? You'd remember."

"Not that I recall. Fifty thousand passengers a day leaving Paris, madame! Where is it you want to go?"

"To Lourdes. Do you have any idea what route I could take out?"

"Lourdes? Why, my wife and I went just last year, Holy Week. Kept us alive, she did — our Lady and Saint Bernadette. Right down through the siege. Don't get me wrong, I'm for the Commune. But a man needs something other than bread and guns to keep him alive. I'm sorry to say it, seeing you're a widow. Well, I'll show you how you might go . . ." The man thrust his pipe-stained, leathery fingers through the window, explaining, and drew a map in the air.

"But I'd have to go north to go south!"

"Exactly what I told the gent earlier. North to go south. If this poor nag can hurry her legs, I might get you to the Nord. You'll have to be ready to face up to the Prussians, though — they are holding on to it for Versailles, you know."

He peered in, his face not unkind; cracked like the leather of his cushions. He waited for me to speak, but I was not ready. Not prepared to face the Prussians or anyone else. Still weak from the siege; and the revelations in the hospice archive still lay on the surface of my mind, unabsorbed. I felt as if I needed to go to bed for about three weeks. And I wanted to see Henri, if possible. God only knew what would happen to him, once it all began in earnest.

As if he read my mind, the cab driver said, "But if I were you, madame — widow like yourself — I wouldn't go traveling anywhere tonight. It's a bad moon up there, a pull-down moon, my grandmother would call it. Wait for a better one; build up your strength meanwhile . . . A bad business today, madame, for these young hotheads."

"It went badly for the Commune, did it?"

"Versailles took a load of prisoners to the west and south, where

you want to pass. Bad fighting out of Issy and Vanves, and Courbevoie we know was a disaster. This Cluseret's reorganizing the
whole army now. Put out the call for every able man below forty.
I've dodged that one by a few years." He chuckled.

"But — do I have time?"

"Oh, it'll hold on for a bit, madame. We're besieged but not invested; these Versaillais boys don't half know what they're about.
Plenty of them have brothers and sisters and cousins with the Commune; they don't want to fight hard. Versailles is still waiting for the
prisoners of war to be released, to put them back into battle; and the
Commune is fiddling with words. I've heard old Badinguet himself
is plotting . . . Where to then, madame? We'll have a few humps and
bumps to cross no matter what, that I promise." He winked.

What makes the moment in a woman's life when her story breaks,
splits down the middle? When nothing is retrievable, to hand? What
then does she do? To whom does she turn? And if she tires of turning, always turning? I did not, in fact, travel that night, but returned
to the rue du Mail. I had no more will for headlong journeys.

Later I was glad not to have left, because there was, in fact, a reprieve in the hostilities. Again, we did not know — but hoped — it
meant reconciliation, even though huge earthworks were being
thrown up in the rue Royale and the place de la Concorde; and it
was rumored that trenches of gunpowder had been laid on either
side of many of the barricades. It was said that the Commune would
ignite them rather than concede.

Henri — and Jolie — came by the rue du Mail that night, and
I threw my arms around them both. Two powder-stained, tensile
warriors in high spirits; their mood of tuned exuberance. We had
a picnic on the floor and talked over the news of the day: a guillotine chopped apart and symbolically burned at the feet of Voltaire.
The Commune Is for Order. Henri spoke of Blanqui, still a prisoner,
as though his return was imminent; he hinted that the police chief,
Rigault, had a foolproof plot to spring the Old Man at last — to swap
him for the Commune's highest-value prisoner, the archbishop of

Paris. We cut into *saucissons* and cheese and pulled purple grapes from their stems, relishing every luxurious bite while we could, and Jolie said that she'd walked down the rue du Temple, and Deux Soeurs was boarded up and padlocked.

"Is there anywhere for the girls to work besides the avenue Rapp?" I said. The Commune's ammunition factory was a firetrap and it hardly seemed better to send them there.

Jolie rolled her eyes and lit a cigarette. I asked Henri about the powder trenches and why there had been a standoff with Versailles. He shook his head.

"This fight is about who is allowed to live and why we live at all. Where are the Commune's compromises to be made?"

"Perhaps on the ground of pragmatism? Even Blanqui is only one man; Thiers keeps him under lock and key. A cabman today told me that 400,000 prisoners of war are returning to fortify the Versaillais." Henri's jaw set; he rose abruptly and went to the window to roll a cigarette. He did not, just now, look like a man to be kissed—though I had done so, and recently.

"I hope you have become good at target practice," I said to Jolie.

"I have aced the *tabatière*. If I run into any of my old friends, I'll show them what I really think!"

These two did not know doubt; neither ever had. Doubt was my province. So I uncorked the wine and while Henri was moodily staring out at the street, told Jolie about the hospice archives and finding Berthe's records. Stephan having transferred Berthe to Lourdes. And even she gasped in incredulity.

"Oh, Eugénie! It would have to be something with that man—but this trumps it."

"I want to go and find her, but perhaps that is what he intends as well—or maybe he just felt guilty and transferred her to a convent," I said in a low voice. "But it seems he has had something in mind since July."

"He let on nothing?"

"No."

"Do you think you should—confront him directly?"

"Jolie, he was my lover for three months——"

"Wartime lover, oldest trick in the book."

"I know, I know."

Henri turned back to us, saying that he needed to go on patrol. Jolie said, "Henri, do you think an able-bodied aristocrat of thirty-two can leave the capital? Get past the checkpoints, onto a train? *Monsieur le comte* is up to his old tricks. Maybe you could battalion the man."

"I'd be delighted to. I shall head over to the sixteenth and conscript him myself. But what now is the crime?"

"Never mind that. Do you really want to go all the way to Lourdes, Eugénie?"

"It is the only thing I want."

Henri stared, apparently finding me inscrutable.

"Then, *chouette*—you must," said Jolie.

"Lourdes?" asked Henri.

"Eugénie has family there."

"Well, don't go for the claptrap miracles. But you will be safer out of the capital."

"Could you really detain de Chaveignes?"

"With pleasure. Time enough that he should pay his debt to the working man."

" And woman, and child," added Jolie, full of mischief.

Henri was fixed on my traveling with a companion, suggesting everyone from Finette (if she could be tracked down) to La Tigre. I insisted that I had entered Paris alone and would navigate this exit in the same manner. I would travel as a widow; and be safe. He finally settled for giving me his knife and a lesson on how to use it, resting his hand on my own as he did. I looked up into his eyes. So much about the man I did not know. Then over to Jolie, on the balcony, peering out at the street. I had loved her; and had come close—so close—to loving him. Would I see either of them again? . . . Another time. Another place, another lifetime—I might know Henri better; and he me. I'd heard of such things. Other lives, lived long ago. And lives to be lived, future lives. Better ones, perhaps. Mitra and I discussed such things during the long nights of the siege. After the strangeness of the idea wore off, I found curious comfort in it.

Then we took out the maps and he sketched out a possible route—a long one that embarked from Saint-Lazare; passed through Courbevoie near the forts and the Commune's terrible battle; and traveled west past Versailles before curving south.

It was not for another two weeks that circumstances permitted exit. Fighting was heavy in the ring around the capital, with casualties coming into our reopened, now undersupplied *ambulance* at the rue du Mail. Francisque and Sylvie were still at Versailles with their past-season dresses, so it was left to La Tigre, Amé, and me to nurse and tend to the men as best we could. From them we heard of the increasing despair and disorganization of the Commune's forces; of the loss of morale following the defection of the once-heralded Cluseret to the side of Versailles and the assembly. They were angered by the current attitude of the leaders of the Commune, who favored appeasing the Prussians, still installed menacingly around the eastern perimeter. Some of these men had joined up to avenge the honor of France; others were true-blooded for the Commune; no faction had been presented with an effective leader or the desired enemy. The plan to free Blanqui was a failure; Thiers held fast to his prisoner and would accept no terms.

Although the air was full of betrayals, the gaiety of spring nonetheless strangely infused a city longing for reprieve, and Parisians rallied around a new project: tearing down the enormous Vendôme column, erected by Napoleon I and the icon of his departed nephew. This effectively shut down traffic, as did the razing of Premier Thiers's mansion in the place Saint-Georges—with great fanfare its artworks were shuttled off to the museums; its linens were sent to the hospitals. And the true life of Paris went on. Gardeners gardened; spring flowers came up and consoled us for the lack of trees. Fishermen fished the Seine and street hawkers came out with their chestnuts, bouquets, birdcages, and window glass. Theaters were lit; the Salon of 1871 was announced, and Parisians promenaded in Sunday attire even as wagons of corpses rattled by. Amid this hub-bub and chaos, Finette came down from the Red Cat with a sprained ankle, begging to be taken back.

And so it was the middle of May, during a brief cease-fire lasting only a few hours, that I boarded the train, alone, out of Paris. The *Aurore,* the night train, headed south-southwest.

31

GROTTO

MAKE WAY FOR the *malades*!" the porter called, and at that, the railway men took off their hats and stood still. Limoges station was bright and sunny—an echo of Paris, without the surrounding ring of Prussians. "The Red City of France," Henri had called it, because its porcelain workers had pushed for recognition of the Commune. This had plunged the city into a maelstrom of civil strife; soldiers who had been marshaled to support Versailles refused to board the trains to travel to the capital. Some stacked their rifles at the station; others, when the train was stopped some distance outside the city, disembarked and marched back home, singing "La Marseillaise." On Henri's railway map, a firm, blue-inked artery flowed with confidence to Limoges.

After that, it was crossed with hatch marks. At Agen, a pale green thread indicated a change to a line that continued on to Auch, but in the station key there was no mention of Auch as a stop. The map may have been one of railway optimism rather than actuality—at any rate, it was printed before the war.

Thus I was uncertain what I would find by way of rail accommodation to Lourdes; and I wondered if the anticlerical sentiments of the Commune had penetrated its sister city and the way to the shrine of Our Lady would be barred. However, the reverse was true—at Limoges I was issued a ticket without question. In a city of divided sentiments, the law of contraries was in force. At the rail station, piety prevailed: for what soldier would prevent the dying one last chance at a miracle?

When I stepped aboard the train, there were no compartments, no superior classes of service, no baggage racks, and no seats. Only stretchers, nuns, rosaries, and raised hands; keening wails and sights better left undescribed. It was the White Train, the train of pilgrimage. And as was obligatory for ambulatory passengers, I accepted a smock, a tin cup, and a water pitcher. Began with the first stretcher in front of me, and looked, dismayed, down the long carriage.

"Everything is for the best; we are praying," a nun said to me, seeing the look on my face. "There are no more remedies here."

Lourdes was not far from the place of my birth, but then, roads hardly went directly from one place to the next and never when the terrain was as difficult as this passage toward the Pyrenees. Those mountains were our distant watchers; portents of weather, of the local mood—loftily unapproachable. After Bernadette had her visions at the Grotto Massabielle, Lourdes had gone from stone to gold, and not by plowing and planting, or mining, or any other recognized means of human progress: but for miracles.

I assumed that Berthe had been sent to Lourdes for pragmatic reasons, though; because it was the nearest large convent that would take her after her transfer out of the hospice system. As to why Stephan would have wanted it and what exactly he intended—that I could not know.

I filled my cup with water and turned to the first cot.

It was morning when we arrived, and as the train dropped down into the valley, I could see the processions, the long winding lines of pilgrims. As the White Train disgorged, and one by one, my fellow passengers fell to their knees or their stomachs, or raised their hands in the air if they were on their stretchers—as they wailed and shouted and prayed, called out for hands to carry them, the porters and lay brothers and sisters prepared for the passage, joining the thousands already converged. Lourdes, during pilgrimage season, is not a place to search for someone you have never seen.

Walking uphill from the station and into the center of town, my head went light and dizzy; my limbs ached, and my lungs and chest, as though my entire being was attempting to expel a vicious poison but was too weak to do it. It was the altitude, but more than that. I shouldered past the stretchers and wheeled chairs and carts; swept along in the crowd but solitary. How was I ever to find Berthe here? I felt entirely alone, and resentful. I was not ill or dying and had limited curiosity about the miracles of Lourdes. After all that we had witnessed during the siege, I did not want to confront more piteous sights of illness and death. Was humanity never to be healed? Was it never to fight? But they were fighting in Paris, brother against brother, and what good was it doing? Piteous we were, with every form of human malady on full display under the beating Pyrenees sun. No remedies, indeed.

It was a southern sun, and too hot for the uphill trudge to the center of Lourdes, which was a humble sort of place like a thousand others, except for its gigantic fairground of promised miracles. I kicked at my long, full skirts; tugged askew the lace and embroidery going-away cape in black silk; ruffled across its hem, its small criss-cross embroidered buttons undone in this heat — the cape was meant to cross in front and required the hands of a maid to tie properly, but I was not traveling with a maid. The view-obscuring veil and kid gloves tightened around my heat-swollen fingers. And here I was, in a place very similar to the one in which I had once worn a skirt and chemise as simple as Bernadette's. My old wooden sabots would have been superior to the Paris ladies' boots manacling my feet, mincing between the gaps in the cobbles. I picked up a religious flyer that stuck to one of my heels, tossed it aside. The Grotto was not my goal nor my intention. My pilgrimage was of a different kind.

The streets of Lourdes were clogged. At cafés, crutches were propped against the walls. Jugglers and fire eaters gathered in the square; hawkers offered tours and sold souvenirs: plaster virgins and medallions, water bottles and everything Bernadette. I waited in a long line for a café table, and when finally blessed by a chair, ordered *vin ordinaire*. My eyes had begun to blur, to search, to well with tears. Tears began to stream amid the cacophony of the marketplace of saints' bones, splinters of the True Cross, vessels for holy water. I was more tired than I knew. Out of place, left out of the general miracle seeking — and yet I wanted a miracle too, just not the sort advertised.

My eyes followed a girl across the square; swept her for signs, marks of the abandoned — *you will see Berthes everywhere* — stooped shoulders, a limp, a lead medallion — any of a thousand consequences of neglect. Did this one look like my mother when she was young, or like me? But it was merely a girl's body; hips just beginning to curve out below the drawn-in waist; a face that could be lovely, or dull as lead; one of those faces that changed with the weather. A girl's body, before she has lived in it many years. *What is my fate today? Which clouds will tumble across my sky?* And would she be overcome, one day — wake like a sudden storm — to that roaring in the ears that led to leaving everything behind to follow her desires to the nethermost; would she find herself gripped by the passions of her foremothers?

I pushed aside the wineglass; the liquid tasted cheap and bitter; then changed my mind, drank the dregs, and worried about my soul. I did not consider myself hardhearted; so why did the sights and sounds around me not arouse compassion? *Must my hand be worn and callused in order to appear innocent? Must I brandish my wound to feel it . . .* Who were they, the religious, the authorities — to judge my own harm? How long had my own wounds been effaced, silenced; never touched, never seen? For as long as ever was. As long as Eve's day, after the serpent slid away. A day that lasted forever. These and other inchoate ideas occupied me as I made my way over the bridge, toward the convent. The way was not difficult; all roads ended at the hospice, and at the Grotto.

"Yes, it was a gentleman who came for her," said the sister to me, the one I found nearly without looking. Her skin luminous as parchment, her voice low. "Accompanied by a dark-skinned boy, a servant. He prayed at the Grotto and then he came here to speak to us. He presented papers attesting to his name and estate; apologized for the unholy chaos in Paris and for his boy, who he said was Hindoo but studying the Bible." The sister paused and almost smiled. "He came by permission of the director of the Hospice des Enfants Assistés in Paris. The girl was his daughter, he said."

"Of course we hesitated. Berthe Sophia was very special to us; she had been with us such a short while. But she worked right along with us, from the first. So old for her years, that girl. No matter how hard or difficult the chore, she never flinched; whether she was attending us at the baths or meeting the White Trains. She had the mark of the abandoned on her, but she hid it very well . . . Oh, no, my dear — not last August. It was only last week!"

I gasped. My heart dropped to my feet; my head into my hands.

"I called her to my office, that day he arrived. I didn't want to let her go, but he insisted; he had the papers. A father. Oh, I did hesitate. We loved her, our little daughter. Whatever she had been through; we didn't know what it was. When she saw him, she went to him as though she had known him all her life. She went right to him and held out her hand.

"'Mother, I feel I know him,' she said. I did not know whether it was right, my dear. I prayed about it that night. While the gentleman was here taking the waters, attending the masses, I met with him again; I felt that he was not the most abject of sinners; he had a heart in him, this man. He had been in India, had started a school there for the poor. He also wanted to speak to us about transporting French Bibles there."

"I don't think —" I began, but stopped.

"It was not that, that moved me. But when he was to leave, he asked her if she wanted to go with him. He gave her the choice and I knew in my heart she would go. I was torn, you see — I did not understand. I believe she was perplexed herself, at first. I went to pray with her and when we were finished she spoke. She did not — she did not want to become a nun, she said. It nearly broke my heart; and I knew that I was too attached to her. It was a caution to me, that bond.

"Do not blame yourself, my dear. She was to be found one way or another. You missed them only by a matter of days." She was quiet for a moment, then dropped her head as if in prayer. "I have been in this order all my life. The world—it still astonishes me. That little girl—Berthe Sophia—so many wanting her after she was so long abandoned. All of our sisters here, this father, you. It is the work of the Holies, it is a mystery. But there are many orphans here. Children and the grown, as well. Your daughter will have what is needed, I think. But you must look to your own soul, Eugénie. Lourdes is a place of miracles; and one may be hovering over us even now. Do not travel from here as you came: in anger, in recrimination."

"I do not—I am sorry, Mother. Faith is not to me what it is to you. I don't say I have none—but . . ." I stopped, tried to breathe deeply into my constricted lungs.

"Go to the Grotto, my dear. Pray there. Do not go with the crowds. If you go now," she glanced at the clock, "you will be there when most of the others are at Mass. It is a good time. Quiet. Allow yourself some healing, after what you have been through in Paris." She bowed her head, then raised it, smiling.

And so, helpless and exhausted; my tears now a dried, poisonlike fury on my cheeks, I followed the parade of push chairs, nuns, and pilgrims; stretchers with those unable even to stand, who wanted to die in front of a rock. As the sister had promised, they broke off and filed up to the church, where the bells were ringing. And I carried on to the Grotto. An attendant was removing spent tapers and replacing them with fresh ones on an enormous standing candelabra.

The attendant paid no attention and in a few steps I walked up inside the Grotto, the very place where Bernadette had scraped in the dirt and found a miracle. Rules and restrictions, at least, seemed to have fallen away; I did not even need a ticket to enter. It was cool and damp, at least; the interior itself a comfort after the sunny heat. *The place of the mothers,* the sister had said. I glanced over my shoulder. Still no one interfered, nor seemed to care at all what I might be doing. I had the instinct to unclasp my boots and slip them off, to stand on the Grotto's bare earth. Undid the traveling cape; and since it did not seem to matter, shed the coat as well, placing it over a shelf of rock. I shivered, slightly, in the cool; a Pyrenees breeze came through — a small gust like those I remembered from my own province — and all around was quiet but for the sound of trickling water; rivulets running down the side of the cavern. Near me, by the Grotto's opposite wall, a well-dressed man dabbed his handkerchief on one of the rivulets and pressed the dampened cloth to his brow. Like mine, his trouble, whatever it was, was not apparent.

A strange feeling stole over me, a relief from thoughts because it was different, other. I would put words to it if I could; but I cannot. The sensation, a slight tremulous feeling, whether from the rock or from my own body, passed through me as I touched the mottled, damp surface, ran my palm over the cavern's craggy, damp interior. A humble place, similar to dozens of others, it reminded me of the springs of my childhood, those places of wishes and rags, where my aunt had mumbled and the village had strung up their tokens and supplicated the spirits. It was that feeling, that kind of place; and very strong. My aunt would not have been amazed at all. *The more you listen, the more you shall hear,* she used to say — and perhaps it was true.

I was not ready to cast my lot with the hordes and masses, but had a feeling in this place connected with something in the past — like two bells rung together, one distant, the other near. I stood in the interior of that rocky outcropping and experienced peace, for the first time that day; the first for a very long time.

I sensed that I had passed through a long struggle . . . Could that be? *Passed through* — when such fresh hurt as the sister's words had caused — had hardly even begun? I stood, rock-still, for a long time. *Not wanting to move from there.*

But then the masses were over; the throng began to trickle along the path, first two or three, then hundreds behind them. The tower of candles was lit for the procession then, sparkling in the midday sunlight. They came and kneeled; they filled their bottles and jars and vessels from the Grotto's spring. And I passed out of the cavern. No longer angry; no longer blinking with tears.

32

AUCH

Must every tale have its villain, or are we all of us, from salt spoon to carving knife, complicit in the evil of our own lives? Was this to be a journey of retrieval, then—a restitution not of what I most desired but what I wished to deny—a full serving of life's heartbreak? Berthe, my mother, casts a long shadow. She always did.

The Hôtel de Gascogne's terrace was decorated with flower boxes; the petals protected by a fine mesh screen, not bee-stung to death. Tomorrow there was to be a tasting of the local foie gras. Tonight, it seemed, beds were at a premium, the hotelier harried as he served a portly woman in a silk bonnet with a shrill, trumpeting voice. Another customer stood at the desk, his voice the edge of a whine. He wanted many beds—two beds, three beds, one bed additional. At Lourdes, the hospital beds were made ready for as many as came. Nor did the dying demand or rush, though they may have traveled a thousand miles for a cup of water. And yet I was more attached to this world than that other.

I came away altered from Lourdes, and not just because of what I had learned. Indeed—Stephan had so long played the villain, it would be easy to continue to cast him in that role. But much of the

news, as I now reflected, was good. Berthe was alive; she had been
brought up in some way that had made her kind and civilized. Even
hard truths could be faced, at least in my little whitewashed room
near the Grotto; and in quiet conversation with the sister, who had
embraced me as we parted, told me to be of good courage. I did not
bathe nor go to mass, visit the stations of the cross, nor did I have
the strength to push the sick and suffering up the hill. Yet it was
enough. Lourdes gave what was needed and offered no reproach. It
was a rare place on earth, for that. But the Grotto was the Grotto;
and Auch was Auch. My boots were back on; and on my ring finger lay a gold band from a Limoges pawnshop; it gleamed palely,
strange and heavy. My trunk, left in Limoges with instructions to be
sent on, had arrived, disgorging every trapping of conventionality
I could drape over myself. Boots, crinoline, gloves, hat, and veil.
My umbrella—a good one from Lafarge, in the Galerie Feydeau
on the Passage des Panoramas in Paris. A man's umbrella, not a
flimsy woman's parasol. Black, with a silver head. I wrapped my
hand around it.

My grandfather's house, which now belonged to Uncle Charles,
was off the place Salinis in the shadow of the pale stone Tour
d'Armagnac, not far from the center of the upper part of the town.
High and lower Auch were linked by a network of steep, narrow alley stepways, the *poustrelles.* Poustrelle de las Houmettos, Poustrelle
des Couloumats. The names still had a ghostly magic; I had made
many trips up and down them during my school days, studies forgotten; counting the moments until I was able to get back home to
the finches and linnets and fields, the gusts of perfumed wind.

"Madame Auguste Maillard." I announced myself to the maid at
the door. Her face was impassive as a plank.

Uncle Charles rubbed his shiny-pated head, now fringed with gray;
he wore small, rounded, gold-framed spectacles. His young, second
wife was called Christiane, and they had two small daughters, Susanne and Sabine. After they had gone to bed, and Christiane retired
to instruct the cook and housekeepers, we sat alone in front of the

fire, my uncle and I, with a bottle of his good *vieille resérve* Armagnac. Fiery stuff, liquid gold, fragrant with oak and sun on the vineyards. My uncle, a capable and optimistic man, owned vineyards around Auch and a good part of the town. For him, to build was to invest and what was broken merely waited for repair—he was less certain when confronted with the vagaries and contradictions of women. And war.

I had been telling him, as neutrally as possible, of the events in Paris during the siege; how the capital had felt in March, after the army surrendered to the Commune. Charles had been to Paris as a young man; now he pushed the flat of his hand against his scalp, as if to press it in place, and sighed. He was silent for a moment, and rested the heavy glass in his hand; the conversation turned back to Berthe.

"We believed for a long time that you had died. Your mother had a slab of marble put up at Sainte-Marie's, with an epitaph. It was not until recently that I began to doubt. And then I found the papers." I must have turned quite white, for he said, after a pause, "Of course it has always been difficult. With my sister Berthe." He sighed again and reached for the bottle.

"Are you familiar with the works of Augustin Benedict Morel?" he resumed. "The belief is very deep with your mother that a man, or a woman, can fall from the pure, original nature into a state of degeneration, and that these characteristics or qualities may be passed down from parent to child. Your mother believes that it was a very great sin of her own—that she was responsible for what happened to you—and that this is a part of a—*spiraling downward*—of society as a whole, to which she has contributed. Of course, science and medicine and even philosophy have come some distance since Morel, but she holds by her own thinking."

"What—what sin does she believe she committed, Uncle Charles?"

A cloud crossed his face; he shook his head. "My sister has not risen from bed in weeks. We have run through all of the domestic help in town; Christiane has been a merciful angel, but it is perhaps you that she needs. I am glad you've come, Eugénie."

"It may be the final straw to put her under," I said wryly.

"According to the doctors, she could have been buried a year ago; the last six months beat the miracles at Lourdes. She'll have a crisis, but pull back. She's had last rites"—he counted on his fingers—"*eight* times. Every priest in the department has been here."

"She may not let me in the door, Uncle."

"Nonsense. You are a respectable married woman now. And priests—well, she tosses them on their ear, anyway."

Later Uncle Charles walked me across the square and kissed me on both cheeks in front of the Hôtel de Gascogne. If he disapproved of a woman staying alone at a hotel, he never said as much, merely invited me to dine the next evening. After all, I was a respectable married woman; for some inexplicable reason traveling without her maid.

"And you will see Jean-Louis," he said, with his gloved hand on my elbow. "Your brother . . . Oh, he hasn't answered to 'Charles' in years. Now, get some rest."

Tall tapers flickered in their holders on Christiane's table. Two table maids, a pair of clear-eyed, tight-lipped girls, both the very stamp of the older woman who had answered the door, moved on cat's paws in and out of the swinging door, with stacks of snowy folded napkins, wine and water glasses of cut crystal sparkling in their pale hands. The soup bowls had been set out. Gold-banded, white and ruby; their creamy interiors set off the rich gold of a translucent broth. A filigreed fuss of salvers and spoon holders, napkin rings and silver carafes. The damask was well-known to my fingertips; the fleur-de-lis pattern, hemstitches thin as threads of frost. My fingers had rubbed that silver until it shone; it was Berthe's dowry silver.

"It is a lovely table, Christiane."

She was bare-shouldered and glowing—fashionably dressed, for a provincial wife—but Charles was wealthy and I should know better than to hold such prejudices. *Les auscitaines* had always been stylish, and Christiane's smile was warm and genuine.

The two girls, blonde-headed, hair tied up in ribbons, sat wide-eyed and bolt upright. Because of their new Paris relative and their—apparently—badly mannered cousin Jean-Louis, they were allowed to sit at the dining table with the adults. Sabine, the older of the two, had confided in me, earlier, in the drawing room.

"What is so impolite about your cousin, Sabine?" I had asked earlier; and she looked carefully around the room before answering. "Well, he is always late, with muddy shoes and no handkerchief, and he says terrible things out loud!" At table, she held her sister's hand, and they both barely controlled their giggles. The gold band on my third finger lay heavily against the damask, clicked softly against the wineglass. Our silver spoons had been set down, and the tureens and the ruby bowls cleared, when from the outer hall, my younger brother's arrival was announced.

"Jean-Louis," said my uncle, before I could speak, "Your sister, Madame Maillard."

"Eugénie, of course," I said, rising to meet him.

The boy was tall and graceful for his thirteen and a half years, with a shock of silky hair falling over his face. As a male of the Daudet line, he was set to lose it in about three more years, but he seemed quite vain of it now. And Jean-Louis was the very mark of my mother's spirit; he wore her like his unnecessarily ragged coat. He had Berthe's eyes, and my own.

"You are here to see Maman," he said. "But you are supposed to be dead."

Susanne and Sabine were quiet and round-eyed; Christiane held herself very still, at an artificial angle, at Charles's side.

"As you can see, I am not. Just living in Paris."

"Do you know artists there?" he said, somewhat in spite of himself. "I am an artist." Uncle Charles sighed and Susanne suppressed a giggle.

"You take after our mother, then."

"Monsieur Maillard, your sister's husband, is an engineer," said Charles. I swallowed.

"Monsieur Maillard's first patent was for a table extender," I said, with a silent apology to the man. "That is for when a table must be more generous than was previously planned. As this one has been to me; and I thank you, Christiane."

"Maman has told me about you," Jean-Louis said. He and I were alone, walking back to the Hôtel de Gascogne. Past the old narrow, blackened *poustrelle*. One could get lost among them, even though by Paris standards, the area was small. Poustrelle de las Houmettos. It sounded like a place the ghosts would live, and I thought they did.

"Has she? Other than my death, that is?"

Jean-Louis made an unintelligible scoffing sound. "I knew you weren't dead. Only that you had shamed the family. Are you a thief?"

"No, Jean-Louis. And what does our mother think of your artistic ambitions?"

"She has always said we were alike, and I will do what she could not. When she dies, I will go to Paris, to the Beaux-Arts," he added. "In Paris, you were inside, during the siege?" His eyes round.

"Yes."

"They say you ate rats; is it true? How?"

"How would you eat them if you had to?"

"With a lot of sauce!"

"Indeed. And the brewery ones were much tastier than those from the sewers."

"Did you kill them yourself?"

"No, we bought them at the butcher." Tales of the siege were made for such boys.

"What about the zoo animals? Camels and bears and monkeys?"

"I saw them in the butcher's window, just like chickens and ducks. But you know—it was a serious business, Jean-Louis."

The Basilique Sainte-Marie was made of pale stone blocks, like the Préfecture in Paris; only it had huge windows and a garnished gothic entry, below which we stood.

"Do you want to see your epitaph? I can get inside."

Beyond the archways, an arcaded porch, two strong square towers. Jean-Louis led me past carved oak choir stalls (like caskets for the seated), then to a small chapel, tucked under a stone carving and hidden behind a stack of old chairs. All of the dust and mildew tickled my nose, and I began to sneeze. Affixed to the wall was the usual plastering of plaques, emblazoned with commemorative platitudes.

JEAN-JACQUES RIGAULT, 1818–1860. IN LOVING MEMORY.
EUGÉNIE LOUISE RIGAULT, 1845–1861. MAY MERCIFUL GOD FIND AND WALK WITH HER.

"She blames herself for your life," said Jean-Louis. And suddenly he was half an orphan, a boy whose mother was ill and dying and had been bitter for as long as he could remember. He did not remember her when she was young, when she was an artist herself.

The false gold band pressed against my finger; my heart snagged. Because of it, I would vanish from here like a ghost. Sometime in the future, Jean-Louis would remember, perhaps, and wonder if our meeting had happened at all . . . Madame Maillard? Why, no such person exists . . . or she does, but she is someone very different.

"Do you remember our father?" asked Jean-Louis sadly.

"Of course," I said. "I have an idea. Let's go taste the foie gras they are offering at the hotel, and I'll tell you about him. To begin with, he didn't like the stuff, said it tasted like geese smelled . . ."

By the time I sent Jean-Louis back across the square, the last of the foie gras tasters had left, the staff were clearing champagne glasses and sweeping up the leavings. Toast crumbs. Empty bottles. A rind of cheese. Slipped under my door was a note from my uncle. I was to come to the place Salinis at three the next day to see my mother.

"I will let you be; ring if you require anything," Charles said to me, and gestured to a bell pull to the side of the hearth. He softly departed and the room narrowed; darkened. We stood, facing each other, my mother and I; because she refused to seat herself even though she was hardly able to stand. Her penumbral cloud had descended; settled and spread in the room like an infection; and indeed, she was like the *malades* at Lourdes: suffused with illness. The table on which her hand rested had a marble surface and dark, whorled legs. On it were her miniatures, made so long ago—small painted jewels in their gilt frames, the ivory now as sallow as the whites of her eyes. There was my father, my uncles, my grandparents; the baby Charles. My own small portrait had once stood among them.

I felt dizzy and needed to touch something solid. On my finger, the Limoges wedding band felt cold and heavy. Oh, Maman. *So proud, lovely*—but the face in front of me could hardly be translated from the original. Her thin-lipped mouth was set above a heavy neck; her wrists and ankles, once so beautifully turned, were creased with the bloat of flesh on bone. There was a sickly sweet smell that was vaguely familiar—medicine and eau de vie? My mother's fingers, once slim and tapered, with strong, perfectly oval nails, were discolored; swollen. Her old wedding band could never have fit on these hands; the one she wore was larger, and plain. My grandmother's ring. I recognized it.

The tip of her tongue, caught by her teeth from long habit, protruded just slightly. And her eyes, their whites yellow-tinged, glittered like jet; the licking flame, faint, veiled; a sly, hungry fire. Her step forward was a laborious, burdened movement, the flesh of another woman heaped upon her once-graceful form. Her hands groped for a support. That much, at least—stubborn pride—was Berthe all over. She must usually rely on a cane, one that she had refused today.

"Maman—let me help you."

She stared at me, up and down. Her glance rested, solid as a rock, on my left hand. White lies, black magic; broken crockery; a boy's kisses still warm on my lips . . . nothing could touch what she knew. I was sixteen again, and transparent to her.

"You have no right to that word in this house," she said, at last. Her voice issued from a ravaged throat, but it was the same voice. My heart, that absurd, hopeful instrument, turned to stone, and the sick and queasy nausea of a lifetime welled up. I groped behind me and sat down; which I immediately realized was a mistake, on this battlefield. A cunning, satisfied expression traced my mother's face as she stared at me.

"I wore black for five years. The first and second for your father. The third and fourth for your grandfather; the fifth for you."

She stared back, her eyes cold, and the room was silent, but for the heavy wheeze of her breath. It was cold, but there was no fire, nor hope of one, it seemed. She shifted slightly; continued to look at me with the same glittering stare.

"You didn't think you would just be permitted to run off? A Rigault daughter? A Daudet granddaughter? With that—criminal who stole the harvest, bought it cheap, starved out your aunt and cousin and half the village, if it weren't for Besson to lend?" I closed my eyes. *Blink*, and let Berthe tell the story her way. *Blink*, and it is true. *Blink*, and you believe what she says, for half a lifetime. What she says bends lives; contours them to her meaning. It was always this way. It is no different now. "Yes. A fine business for *you* to be mixed up with."

"You left," I said, quietly, helplessly.

"Your grandfather and I searched every town from here to Rouen."

I looked up.

"We would have taken you back—even so. We investigated the matter thoroughly. My father tracked you down in Paris, through the police. We did not want to give you up, *I* did not want to give you up. But it was definitive. It was too late." Her voice dropped from a throaty whisper to a scratch. "How dare you come to this house." Scratch like rat's feet; like the nib of a pen . . . Sickness engulfed me, rising from my gut, that dizziness—the old feeling—that had followed me everywhere, everywhere, since Tillac, or even before . . . when had it begun? Perhaps it had always been there. Perhaps it had begun with her.

"The authorities in Paris wrote you off for a thief and a whore. My own daughter." She spat the words. "I doubted at first, how could I not? I would not believe it until I saw it with my own eyes. And so they finally sent it to me, a copy of the police register that bore your name. Your name, and mine — I tore out my own heart to think of what you had done. I refused to sign the paper. A notary had to do it for me. Then his silence was bought."

"Maman — " I whispered. *Why did you not help me — ?*

"You were dead to me after that. I mourned for a year and then put it away. Life — such as it was — went on. And now that I've had a good look at you — " Her voice changed, became a whine. High-pitched, out of body, like an insect's scream. "Do you know what I am? What you made me into? I will tell you. Oh, I'll go on — "

"I think you have said enough, Maman."

"You did not write, you never came. Just walked away, with that man who ruined you, and even when you were dead you never came back. I ordered a crate from Condòm every few months. *Eau-de-vie de vin.* That is what your leaving did to me." She steadied herself against the doorframe, gnarled old hands trembling. She was the very node of turmoil; a trouble inseparable from me, that webbed my life. She was every part of me; the knife edge of my own contamination. I didn't need Paris to find corruption.

"I'm sorry," said my uncle, later. "I had hoped for a better outcome." One of the maids brought tea, but I was too spent to pour.

"She was very beautiful once, your mother. You must remember her that way."

"Yes."

"Did you ever meet him, the man for whom she left Rigault?"

I looked up. Had my uncle abandoned his senses?

"Maman — "

"Petite salope," she hissed.

Berthe had a lover in Auch . . . The old voices, faint.

Berthe turned her head when Uncle Charles asked me to return to the house on the place Salinis. Her hands lay blue-veined and swollen on the covers; her feet on a cushion, the toes blue-black and yellow with the gout. She sat, propped up on pillows, eyes fixed, until her head fell to the side, and she breathed the even breath of sleep. The cloying, fetid smell saturated the room.

My Uncle Louis came. Elderly and mustached, watch chain straining across his paunch. Still tall as a tower, but stooped, now.

"She was the most beautiful girl in Auch," he said, and his dim blue eyes had a faraway look. "She made you think that she would do something extraordinary one day, our Berthe."

The doctor passed in and out in his dark suit, carrying his black bag. For him, she lifted her head, thrust her neck from the pillows, smiled a little girl's supplication in a bloated death mask. Eyes darting for the dropper, the rubber-capped bottle he drew from his bag. After he tended her, the man drew me aside in the hall outside her door, spoke in a low voice. He did not feel that my presence was helping Berthe.

"Are you telling me that I should leave, Doctor?"

"You mother is not a forgiving woman."

"Uncle Charles, the doctor feels I am having a bad effect," I said, later that evening.

"Ridiculous. He may think he understands Berthe; these medical men all have their notions—but all she wants from him is the rubber bulb. I believe it is good for her to have you here."

"She will not speak to me. I make her angrier, remind her of the past."

Charles sighed. "Very well. Jean-Louis will make the decision. He is the one who has her confidence."

And so my brother was brought to the bedside. Moodily he glanced from her face to mine. He didn't say much, Jean-Louis. Unlike everyone else, he did not doctor, soothe, feed, or fuss. He just sat, holding her hands by the hour, with a kind of gentleness not often seen in attendants of the dying, although I had seen it at Lourdes. His presence seemed to calm her. The maids passed in and out, with their sickroom routines. And we sat, and listened to the *tick-tick* of the clock.

The next day, quietly, clearly, and without her querulous sickbed manner, Berthe pulled herself up to sit, and in the way she had once peered through her magnifier, fixed her eyes to a mid-distant point on the wall. She took Jean-Louis's hand and spoke as though she was resuming a story. And maybe she was; one that had played long in her mind.

"My mother was just a country girl, the eldest of a big family. She had beautiful hair, and all the girls would cut their hair when it got long enough, send it off to the summer fair at Limoges where the wig makers from Paris came. That is how they got their dowries. But then the Revolution and no one in Paris wanted wigs anymore.

"She was thirteen when she left. All the little ones in the house were quiet by then, too hungry to cry. It was the silence in the house that let her know she had to go. All the way to Auch with hair to her waist, and when she arrived she saw the guillotine set up right in the place Salinis. But there was no work because the families were afraid to hire a servant, for fear their neighbors would think they were rich. But Maman had a bright, strong spirit and she found work at the hotel as a serving girl. Many were not as lucky.

"My papa was traveling in the region, he saw her—noticed her at once, she was so much prettier, with her long hair. Your grandfather, Jean-Louis, was a monsieur himself, one of the bourgeoisie, but he had buried his fortune in the ground and they married because it was a good Revolutionary act for him to marry a peasant girl. They settled at Auch in a hovel in the lower city as if they were poor, and my two brothers were born, Louis and Charles. Their third child was a girl. Not me. She fell all the way to the bottom of the Poustrelle des Houmettos, split her skull, and died.

"By the time I came they had moved to the upper city. Oh, my mother loved me too when I was born, but it was never the same. My sister had been pale, like a fairy, but I had red cheeks and strong legs and liked to run with the boys! But that was not allowed, lest I fall like she had. Maman didn't let me out of the house and I watched my brothers come and go. We used to visit the country, the old farm. I climbed the apple trees, followed my brothers wherever they'd let me.

"Happiness, all that happiness, ended—when did it end? I wanted to traipse the countryside with my books and paints—but they had in the gentlemen, one after another. I made sure not to like any of them, and finally they agreed to send me to the country for the summer, to Maman's people — to help out picking apples for the eau de vie.

"My mother became ill while I was gone. A disease of the brain, from a bump on the head. It was a box of my dead sister's things from the top of the armoire. They never let me know how ill she was, and I never forgave them. Oh, she was all love, all made of love — my mother. She had especially loved Rigault, the one who was to become my husband. With all his big ideas he reminded her of the real revolutionaries, the ones who wanted to do good for the people, before they set up the guillotine and beheaded anyone with an education. Rigault was from the country too. They understood each other, they used to laugh together at your stern *grandpère*. And then, my father was onto a mistress of his own. In Toulouse. That far! And so when she died, I married Rigault. I loved him, yes — I loved him then. Even though my idea of salting a goose was to use the salt meant for the whole winter, and in Tillac no one treated me like a little princess. It wasn't the life I'd been meant for. I wanted to go to Paris to paint.

"Then came the troubles in 'forty-eight. When 'forty-eight roared in like a storm, you didn't know who to bar your door against. We were considered rich by someone's standards, and a band of them climbed on the roof, pulled down the weathervane, and waved firebrands around that straw. That's why we eventually put tiles up there. Oh, they were silly, not serious like the first time, but I didn't know that. Eugénie was just three years old, she held on to my hands and cried. I'd heard my *maman*'s stories, I thought they were going to murder us. We went down to the root cellar and waited with the vinegar.

"I was young. And it changed for me, the countryside. Always afraid after 'forty-eight. No matter what Rigault said, I had nightmares that they would come for me, for my little girl. I began to make trips back to Auch, to Papa and my brothers. Rigault would take me there and one of my brothers would bring me back. I stayed longer and longer.

"A married woman without a husband along — only your uncles — it was quite unusual. No one knew what to make of it. I caught on to that, quickly enough; felt like I'd fallen out of a tree! I realized that being married, but not with my husband, was to be at liberty. Just free enough to do what I wished." She glanced at me; her sly madwoman's smile; she knew. Saw right through me, Berthe.

Christiane came into the room, rustling in her voluminous starched skirts.

"Berthe, it's enough talking now. Don't you want some *soupe*, and some of the drops; the doctor left a bottle of your special drops." She glanced at Jean-Louis. "Jean, will you go down? . . . She rambles," said Christiane to me, apologetically. "She makes up nonsense."

But I leaned forward, and Jean-Louis stayed where he was; and Christiane sighed and left the room and Berthe continued as if there had been no interruption.

" . . . Oh, I made the devil's bargain. I pleaded with my angels — just a tiny swallow, I said — just a small crumb of happiness after all of that fear. I'd met someone, you see. A devil who gave me all the excitement I had missed, riding in carriages late at night — secrets and tricks, whatever was needed to pull the wool over Papa's eyes, or my brothers' — Rigault never knew. To think of him, back in that stone house, laying in the tiles for the roof, shoring up the foundation — with Daudet money, of course. I was revenging myself on my father, for his trips to Toulouse; and showing my brothers *la petite*. Getting back at them because they had never let me be as they were." She paused. Jean-Louis poured some water. I could not tell if he was interested, had heard this tale before. Unlike him I had been a naive witness to these events.

"It ended," she said. "Two years after it began. He arrived at our meeting point, in his carriage — the Poustrelle des Houmettos, the same place my sister fell down. He told me that our *affaire de coeur* was over — that I should go back to my husband and become a good wife . . . Oh, I shed my tears — plenty of them — but in the end I did just as he said.

"I don't know when I first had the thought. Terrible, joining in with all those other fears. I no longer loved my husband and I had harmed my daughter in sinning. She was so pure, so innocent, and I had shamed myself and my marriage; it was nothing I could confess to any priest. I sent Eugénie to school, finally, and prayed she would be good.

"And then, what was worse yet—I went back to him. I knew how to find him and I did. I pretended I was coming to visit my old nuns and my daughter, coming for painting lessons. I cared even less than before. Oh, I found him, and I debased myself for him to love me again. He had business in Nérac and I met him there. Threw caution to the winds! But someone in Tillac had a long nose and sent Rigault after us.

"I thought Rigault would die of a broken heart; in the end I suppose he did. He came after the devil with a pistol. And by then, I was glad! I goaded him on. Painted a black picture of what had occurred—and Rigault, who was always such a peaceful, quiet man, who would have brought down the moon for me if I'd asked it—shot him in the leg. And so the devil had to stay in Nérac to heal. I always thought that the Nérac fire started from that devil's pipe, ember to the straw. He was very careless with a pipe, that man."

Careless with a pipe? So is that what had set the fires?

" . . . When they found Jean-Jacques's body on the Nérac road, I never knew—I still do not know. Had the two of them met? Or was it something else." Something else—that had taken Papa—brought Stephan—driven me to Paris? I glanced over at Jean-Louis. He did not know those things; knew less of life than he pretended. Who was his father? Our mother had stopped short of that subject. Telling her story to her own satisfaction, but with an ear to the audience. Artist to the end.

"You," she said, twisting her head toward me, her poor swollen face on a neck once so long and white, that had bent over a magnifier to perfect the smallest detail. Her eyes were unfocused, soft. She now seemed to address Christiane, who had come back to the sickroom with a tureen and was making movements to end Berthe's monologue.

"This is my daughter, Eugénie Louise," she said. "I don't care what she calls herself. She is a woman now. All grown! An independent woman, just like Madame Sand, the writer. I met her once, you know? *Aurore.* She called herself Aurore . . . So my daughter can call herself Madame–anything she likes." Her voice momentarily so bright and strong that Christiane dropped the napkin she was unfolding, took her hand, and stared up; Jean-Louis leaned in, concerned. Berthe looked up, suddenly, as though a ghost had passed.

"The way I loved that little girl, you know. I used to watch her. She amazed me, every day. Nothing else on earth—*nothing.* And Charles Jean-Louis, you must *paint.*" Then she closed her own eyes, as if to sleep.

And that is how my mother died. Passed out of this life telling her story; finessing the details. Maybe forgiving herself a little? Maybe forgiving me.

To wear mourning is not necessarily to mourn. To walk at the head of the procession, to bow one's head over the grave is not necessarily to understand the weight and change of death. Silk or crepe, leather or kid gloves, paste or true jewels . . . a mix of gray and lavender in half a year, or scarlet in a week, whatever the latest fashion codes dictated—none of it is to mourn; for me, it was a reawakening. At the Basilique Sainte-Marie, the priest swung the censer over my mother's casketed body—frankincense, the scent that made you remember too much—and intoned the liturgy; the choirboys opened their mouths in great O's of song, and we rose from our seats at the blessing. Out of the corner of my eye I glimpsed my own epitaph. No one had taken it down; and indeed, explanations would have been awkward . . . So give the old black hoods something to gossip about. Uncle Charles would have it removed later, quietly.

After the funeral I spoke to Jean-Louis. Told him to write, to come to Paris when he was ready. I found my uncles; kissed their bald heads; said my goodbyes to Christiane and Susanne and Sabine. And then returned to the Hôtel de Gascogne for my trunk and a driver to take me to the coach station. Jingling a small ring of keys, feeling for my uncle's letter to the caretaker. My father's house had not been sold; Berthe had never agreed to sell it. It had stood empty these past few years.

As I was leaving, passing from the upper to the lower city of Auch, an old woman was stretched against the brick of a narrow passage, dressed in bottle-fly green. She was old, so rouged and painted, there were cracks in her cheeks, but she still looked up from the *ville basse* as from some great height of her own, full of *amour-propre*.

I slipped off my Limoges band, Madame Maillard's counterfeit identity. Enough of *her*. I caught the eye of the old woman. Tossed the ring from the cab's window; watched it arc through the air and land at her feet. She stooped to pick it up; bit the gold, tipped up her head, and gave me a wave; and I felt freer than in all my life. The driver could think I was mad, for all I cared.

But when we arrived at the coach station I saw a newspaper — not from Paris, but with an account of the events in Paris. And everything else turned to dust.

33

INDEMNITY

PARIS, 1873

The rooms on the rue du Mail have a slightly musty smell. Of closed windows, the stiff strangeness of other peoples' lives, the contours of their difference in a place that is familiar. The flat had been let to a young couple, a professor and his wife who had lost everything. I had been able to arrange it when the dust settled and there were letters from Paris again. In a cupboard, now, tinned cherries and the remains of some Belgian chocolate folded in its paper. A scrap of foreign soap, a bottle of bitters. An empty feeling, of the hasty wiping of surfaces. An old pen, unmarked keys; wineglasses with lip prints. The drinks drunk; the selves, mingled in the sheets, sloughing, building, sleeping, waking—day after day, night after night, and what collects around them.

On the veranda the old persimmon has become a wicket of brown husks with one pale green shoot. The rugs feel thinner over the floorboards, faded by another season of sun pouring in through the tall windows. The walnut desk and tabletops are dry under my palm, needing wax and oil, and close brushing on the grain. My old bed linens, hastily bundled into a drawstring bag, are still tumbled on a high shelf. La Tigre is still here—she stayed through it all—but everyone else left in a hurry, and I don't recognize my neighbors.

Smooth sheets on a strange-but-familiar bed. *The unfolding of present time and the sense of not knowing what the next moment will bring.* The sketch Pierre did on our last day together, with a nub of charcoal during the bombardment. Clasped hands reaching up to a blank sky.

. . . It is summer again. Warm. I hear the sound of horses clopping, from below, in the street. And heat rises, not from the earth, but the tar-dripped macadam. Bodies are buried under those new-paved streets and the city reconstitutes itself above them. At sunset, now, it is not the birds and night creatures that I hear, but shouts and bells and city sounds. A man strolls at midnight as though it was full daylight, newspaper tucked under his arm. Two girls, dressed in all their finery, giggling and bright-eyed, sway their hips on their way up the hill. What about Finette? I wonder.

When I left, I wished for the luck of the dead: to leave it all behind — the tired silks, bent-toed shoes, and overtaxed chemises; gray-edged corsets and tired stays. A cherry waist; fifty francs' worth of India silk from Stephan (never worn); a ticket stub in a pocket, to Trouville, the beach. A white silk scarf forgotten. The weather had been warm when I wore it — brilliant in the morning; the scrap of fabric exhausted, damp, and gritty by day's end. These skirts, waists, dresses smell of must and need an airing; I hang them by the balcony window . . . Another box, lace collars. What is not discarded, apparently, remains — even though you have long forgotten it. Appointment books, bills, ledgers, notes piled in drawers. Letters, tied with a piece of string; ragged edges of torn envelopes. A wild, freakish wind, gusting like a dervish, comes twisting off the streets, whips at the balcony, and sends the dresses swinging. One crumples all the way down like a deflated balloon.

The wind does not stop but whirls up to the peak of Montmartre, all through the evening while I lean over the balcony and watch the flicker of the gas lamps. To return to a known place, when one has changed — and all has changed.

My life inside these walls was made of knocks and bells and women calling to one another; of guests wanting tea and brandy and a smooth caress; of young beauties wanting jobs or to get rich. Of vexed uncertainties, small giddy victories, and a vague feeling of always being a hostage regardless; La Tigre calling up from the stairs. Teaching Finette how to serve coffee. Later, Francisque, eating boxes of hoarded chocolates during the siege, Amélie coming home exuberant from the balloon factory — learning to uncivilize herself, by some standards. Sylvie, practicing scales. Always the same sequence, broken off after a quarter hour; resumed. Once I heard her sing an entire melody in her own voice, sweet and viola-pitched, but that was not what was wanted on the opera stage. For that, she toiled for the high notes; and dressed like the angel she pretended to be, while she might have sung like the women of Carpeaux.

I collect news, sort it as I am able. Some is happy: Beausoleil (who excels at avoiding actual battlefronts) plans a visit to Paris. And Odette writes from London: the French courts under the reinstated republic finally ruled against her. But it does not matter; she prefers London and she is in love. Surprise! It is Maxime Lisbonne, the Commune fighter and Henri's friend, whom I saw two years ago on the rue d'Enfer. He escaped the massacre and deportations — the shape-shifting devil — dressed in disguise, carrying a trunk of his old actor's costumes. I remembered his soft-looking mustache, his clear eyes, and my heart lifted for my old friend. So he and Odette go out in style, dressed as whomever they please.

I will write to her soon. Lisbonne will have information.

. . . The rising, falling, unsteadiness of one's spirit. A sudden desire to eat and drink with abandon; make lists of what to buy and to do — a new restaurant open around the corner; friends to call upon (as soon as one finds out if they are alive) — even with bags still unpacked, by the door. Then a new ingress of information, and the need to crawl between the sheets.

Francisque, ambitions rewarded, arrived one afternoon on a reinstated government arm; sat on the bergère chair, looking pinched despite her fashionable trappings. A year ago she had seen Amélie behind a prison fence at Satory, near Versailles. Arrested with others in the Women's Union, penned in like an animal, her gown in tatters. Our old comrade of the card table made a bitter sound. The fashionable set at Versailles had gone on "outings" to see the Commune prisoners.

"You cannot imagine," said Francisque. "It is beyond describing, Eugénie. If we had said anything we would have been arrested ourselves. Even to speak about it, now." She fell silent, than added, "You know, she had lovely patrician features, Amélie. She did not look like 'a proletarian.' There was a lot of talk in the papers about who looked degenerate, ferocious. And that is how the guards decided who the Commune had 'conscripted against their will.' And you know Amé. She never gave up her manicures, even when she worked at the balloon factory. Her hands and feet were smooth; she would have buffed them at Satory if she could. So she went to trial. Some in the military believed that women should not . . . have received such treatment. In the end she was among the deportees. They say there will be an amnesty, eventually. They say."

"And you, Francisque?"

But Francisque must not stop long; her "arm" was waiting; his elbow not a patient one.

Along the main "boulevard" in Tillac — the village in which I was born, and where I returned to my father's house after my mother's death — lay a pathway of pounded red earth. On a bench under the trees, the old ones sat, jowls and chins sunk to their chests, shaking their heads at the events in Paris. Ah, these times, and what things are possible. I walked through the center of town, touching the old walls. Found the bench, sat at twilight with the evening air soft against my skin. At first tensed for the weight of a hand, a shadow creeping up behind. But there were no police, no prowling hopefuls there. You might think one would forget, with the passing of years, but the body remembers every touch, the sensation of a falling shadow. I am black with handprints. They haunt me in dreams, or when I am traveling from one place to another.

The first night in Tillac, a ghost came to my room. The door stood open by a breath. It entered, pushed it open as only a lover would, came and kneeled down by my bed. I wasn't afraid. Laid fingertips against my temples, brushing my hot eyelids. Cool fingers.

For a moment neither of us breathed and I felt my heart move. Deep in the buried place where it lives.

People talked. They asked questions. Became less shy, as they saw me putting things to right in the empty place, and when they heard that my tongue remembered their patois. They asked, in disbelief: Has all of Paris burned — the Louvre, the Hôtel de Ville, the Tuileries, all ashes? Had the Seine become a bloody streak of red, were the rumors true — twenty, thirty thousand killed? Gunned down by firing squad, buried in trenches — such numbers, to a tiny village, were impossible to comprehend. Was it true that women joined the fighting with the men? Why had they not stayed with the children? Did girls carry kerosene in milk cans to and from building to building, setting fires like harpies, witches? (I said I did not think so.) Had prisoners lined up in the Luxembourg Garden to be shot? I had not been in Paris then, I tried to explain; had left before the capital became a battleground, before it was engulfed in flames. I could only tell them what I knew. But it did not matter. To them, I *was* Paris.

A few nights after I arrived the sky was purple dusk; little birds were dipping and scooping down toward the marshes; the scent of wild thyme. A lifetime apart from the Paris I left, with the milky night air soft; green ridges of vines fading into the twilight and stretching forward. The promise of rest tonight and fruit tomorrow, and the cold sweet water that comes up from deep in the ground. I had forgotten, living in the city for so long, that figs and flowers come up from the earth, grow for nothing. From here the world seems lit with possibility, not yet ruined. Possibility. A breath of it . . . Or God's deception come again?

Afternoons, the skies could turn blue-black as midnight, and the storms moved in from the mountains. Thunder crashed, lightning branched across the sky, and I rushed to gather up my cups and bowls and ink pens; ran back inside to bolt the shutters. The storms lasted half an hour, and after, the sky was clear blue again, with white wisps of cloud. The slates on the terrace, which had sizzled hot earlier, were cool and wet; covered with leaves that had dropped from the trees. A violet, rain-cleared evening sky, and the field poppies on the other side of the wall were bright crimson.

No matter that I dream that my hair is falling out. Tufts of it, wisps, were left, and the sores on my scalp, once hidden, were red and angry. The tide had gone out, leaving the scarred beach of my skull. I feared that I would die poor yet, of some wasting disease.

After the rain I went out in the garden to cut lavender, rosemary, fennel. Metal rang against pots and bowls; from the neighbors' hearths, wood smoke from a kitchen fire drifted out over the terrace. Small birds from the marshes were roasted over vine shoots. The locals ate them whole, making a crunching mouthful of the heads. I never touched them for fear of bones stuck in my throat.

Down the terrace steps a path led to a shaded grove with a stream running past. The village was out of sight up the hill; the trees slender-trunked, silver-skinned sentinels. The rush of water over stones drowned the swimming of my thoughts, settled and calmed the terrible clanging of the head. Breathing the icy cold of the stream, quiet came for whole minutes at a time. It was the edge of something not-known, the old magic fountains. Breath of wind against my cheek, a tingling feeling from the crown of my head, brushing.

But after a few moments, this was no refuge because the insects made themselves known and drove me back up the path. Small and large, winged and crawling; humming, buzzing, beating their way into the thick of the wildflowers. After the bees, with their dark, greasy wings and obscene pulsing bodies, come the hummingbirds, insectlike, with their green-slicked backs and needle bills; then the black-and-yellows again. They were at it before the sun rose; still there well after the terrace was too dark for reading, their dark anxious legs clambering from bloom to bloom. In the dark of night, the lesser mouths of the moths attached themselves to the blossoms with dusty wings fluttering; finally the stems hung down exhausted, bits of blossom scattered on the ground. Like dragging lace, ruffled skirts, and soiled crinolines, a last breath of perfume when evening

falls. The pots of lavender on the terrace were mercilessly distressed
at night until I wanted them to dispense venom instead of sweetness,
just like the earth shoots up poisonous plants when it has been disturbed . . . a beautiful, deadly blossom can repel all that touches it.

The villagers remembered quite well my having left with Stephan
after the Nérac fires. "Ah, he was handsome, and you were young,"
they said. "What do you expect?"

Writing is a loathsome task. If I had any talent for it I would paint,
or sculpt, or compose music. With words, you try to say a thing,
if you can convince yourself it is worth setting down, find the beginning of it at all; if, once you begin, you can follow the thread.
To write at all one must feel something other than deadened by the
press of human events, the terrible flat uselessness of the world. To
turn its broken fragments this way and that, make sense of the thing,
create logic, sequence, in the midst of shattering. What is the way
to look at it; what is the vindication? Why can a woman not answer
a single question about her own life? . . . My own siege was fought
from invisible barricades; and in some ways, the world that had betrayed me made more sense when it too was gone. And still it is that
one must live not only in the midst of one's times, but despite them;
all at once —

I buried my heart, after leaving Berthe. There was a night — in our
quarters on the rue Serpente, on the old pink velvet chaise — when
I felt my heart in my chest — the heart that *loves, therefore it is* — my
poor heart, so insufficient to what it desired. I took it in my hands
and wrapped it, as we used to wrap smoldering irons to warm the
featherbeds in Tillac. It was so hot that it scorched the inner layers
of the muslin. But I wrapped it in more layers, and when it was a
white bundle, carried it south. Flew with it over the Loire Valley,
swinging past the Dordogne. Carried it over the furrowed, rutted
roads and past the far fields, to the tree where I'd once lain — mostly
innocent, as it was. A tall pine, branches sweeping the ground like
skirts. A known tree; a place understood. And so I dug a hole where

its roots were coming up, knobby, out of the ground, and buried my heart among those roots. Heal, here. Draw sustenance, grow stronger. And I left my heart, and traveled on my road, and whenever I thought of it again, I said, It is safe. Safer than it would be with me.

Ah, but I was wrong.

In Paris, it's hard to come by good information, because people want to forget. Someone says that during that time in May known as Bloody Week, Henri was a hero, putting up a stiff fight against the government troops at a stronghold on the Left Bank. And that Jolie was firing at the rue Blanche barricade, shoulder-to-shoulder with Louise. Do I want to learn the truth, if it is even possible; replace the stories, gossip, noble lies, terrible speculations? Write to Lisbonne, look into the court records? Because the facts might be worse even than I imagine. For Jolie, I can still hope that if she died at the barricades it was swift, with Henri or Louise at her side, and that there was some glory in it — though I do not believe in martyrs nor, I think, did she. But Jolie had seen prisons enough for one lifetime, and dying of the pox would hardly suit her. It has been two years, but I hear her voice every day, see her cigarette waving in the air. Questions — the unresolved, unanswered, the unknown — tug at corners of my heart. Henri? A born warrior, without the privileges of a Lisbonne. Had Henri a chance of escaping the Versaillais death march, the broom that swept the capital clean?

I pull out my stationery box. *Dear Odette,* I begin. But my pen falters.

Amidst the pile on my desk, a note from Auguste Maillard: Chasseloup's painting, *An Unknown Girl,* was lost in the bombardment at Neuilly. Would I be willing to sit for another? If so, to contact Gustav Vollard, who was in touch with several artists.

My lawyer sends a large invoice and writes that the case for *recherche de la paternité* brought by the de Chaveigneses is to be dismissed. I almost laugh.

There is a small stack of my own letters, addressed to Berthe because at almost thirteen, she would be able to read them. I still do not know where she is. With the assistance of this same lawyer, I engaged a man in Calcutta to investigate Stephan's whereabouts. That was six months ago, and the effort and expense was not offering much reward.

I begin to shift things into piles.

The dress is green, a good polished linen, with white lace at the neck; the umbrella is black. The hat is a *galette*, a flat black cake. It is a sultry summer day; threatening skies, dust rising from the street. Men are rebuilding the city with enormous efficiency. All around me is a rainbow of stone, the insides of stone, all shades of blue-to-gray. New foundations, doors and windows and roofs.

Within my lifetime the old walls were brought down. Under the empire, boys earned enough in seven months to support their families the year round. Heaps of dirt and brick and stone, mounds of clean earth were pulled out from under tumbledown houses and the poor were pushed out of the center to the perimeters. Now the French people — my people — are raising the indemnity owed for the war. They are determined; already astonishing the world. I am stopped, now, in a sudden glare of sun through the clouds; dust and tears burn my eyes.

An omnibus careens down from the top of the rue du Mail, heading away from Montmartre to the Great Cross, the wide expanse of intersection where Saint-Germain meets Saint-Michel. Near where Henri may have fought. The Salamandre on Gay-Lussac is open for business; a girl at the bar — a new sight all over Paris — wipes down the zinc with a cloth. At the Luxembourg gates, women steer baby carriages toward tranquil, buzzing comfort, as though it had not, so recently, been a place to line up and be shot. Couples walk arm and arm and a kiosk offers glasses of beer; pressed lemon and water. I turn onto the boulevard Saint-Jacques. I had meant to veer toward Val de Grace, but now, instead, I am on the rue d'Enfer. Gas lamps and trees in full leaf, exposed brick and crumbling plaster walls, a wooden fence and spiked iron gates; the afternoon sun pounding

down, hot sweat running down under my arms and breasts, trickling down into my stays. Skirts—all bustles, now—and top hats
mingle down the block. A crowd gathers for an exhibition of some
kind, and a cool dark place out of the sun.

The pictures are lined up on the walls and divided by *quartier*. They
are photographs, some of the first ever taken in Paris. Each section
begins with a map; the monument, building, or street labeled in
sharp black script, homage to the known city: ÉCOLE DE MEDICINE.
HÔPITAL HOMMES VÉNÉRIENS. My heart slows and my blood cools
amid the murmur of voices and a swish of skirts. The light in the
pictures like the brightness of midday diffused though a sudden rain.
The sun comes out again, dazzling through the clouds. Just for a
few moments, the street glistens, wet and empty; but everyone has
rushed indoors.

The streets in these pictures are not lifelike, but empty. Shops
without customers, as they were during the first siege and in anticipation of the second. The very kiosk I had just passed, the one by
the Luxembourg gates, is shown with windows open for business,
but the little round cork mats on the counter have no beer glasses
upon them. Even the *pissoirs* are empty; no one fumbles with trouser buttons. In the Opéra-Madeleine section, on one corner stands
a flower shop with roses standing in pails; on another, a china shop
with white bowls in the window; opposite, a poster offering trans-
lations of documents and letters. Behind these, at the top of the
street, peculiarly angled is a seven-story building with its gabled
roof, spots in windows high enough to receive afternoon light. The
windows of the lower flats are shuttered; eggs and butter are for sale
in a shop on the ground level. These pictures could not have been
taken during the emptiness of the siege, then, because there would
have been no eggs. My heart begins to pound and my breath comes
faster; my stomach, calm just a few moments ago, lurches.
  Someone behind me is explaining the camera's mechanism. These
streets were full of people, he explains, but because of the swiftness

of their movements and the length of time needed to burn the image onto the plate, only the standing structures, radiant with light, remain. He is pointing at something that looks like a misty smudge on the surface, and I place my face very close, straining to see what has vanished.

And indeed, to look closely is to see light smears resolve into eerie silhouettes: a nipped-in waistline, the flare of crinoline; the round shape of a stovepipe hat. At a theater at matinee time, a crowd entering in a great rush of movement. What appear to be clouds of smoke occluding the photograph resolve, at a closer look, into umbrellas. A mist is two heads leaning together, a couple walking arm in arm; and here is a single, spinning, silver-spoked carriage wheel — captured without axles, horse, or driver; hovering above the cobbles . . . the luminosity of these pictures is not rain but light diffused through vanished movement. In a picture of a junk shop, a jumble of chipped cups and plates, tables without a leg, chairs without backs . . . a cloudy smear at head level. Whose, and on what errand? While the exposure was taken, shop doors swung open and closed; lemonade was paid for and drunk, carriages wheeled in and out of the frame . . . Every picture packed with the living, with the motion of life both evident and evanesced at once. I go back to the beginning and look at every picture again. On one map I find the Royal Observatory, a block marked ENFANTS ASSISTÉS. No camera could have captured the swift, furtive movements there. But the *tour* was long closed, anyway. The new authorities thought better of it.

But it is late in the day, and the *patronne* gives a sigh and pulls a black curtain across one end of the gallery. Another woman at the end of the hall has been looking as intently as I, making marks on a small tablet. I had to blink; her outline reminded me of Mlle. C.

Back outside, I blink again in the sunlight and find the café; order a lemonade, which warms quickly in the heat. Bits of pulp floating on top, turning from pale yellow to grayish while the boulevard fills and empties.

I have two letters with me, and I open the first now. Its postmarks and many stamps tell me that it is from Chandannagar, West Bengal.

It is not from the man I hired; but the black ink has a familiar slant. There is a name, and an address, of another lawyer's office — this one in Paris. Tickets are waiting, writes Stephan. Two, because I will need to employ a companion for this journey. The ship is the *India Queen* and it sails for Calcutta in September.

I pause, take a breath, consult my heart; and my heart demurs to answer. But it is a woman's heart now — not a girl's; not unknown. And with me for good.

Berthe is with him, he writes. She is well. Determined, he says, upon knowing her mother.

The second letter is from Odette and encloses a note from Maxime Lisbonne. Henri Duport, he writes, was not executed, but deported to New Caledonia, along with Louise Michel and certain others. Blanqui, the old prisoner, intervened on his behalf. And there is a movement afoot for amnesty, repatriation of the exiled Communards. It will take a long time, he writes. But hope is alive. And Henri is alive.

It is not a sound that awakens me; not a bell or a clap of thunder; perhaps it is the movement of a hand, an arm flung open, the arc of a gesture to throw open the shutters and let in some air. But perhaps not. Perhaps it is just time to lift my eyes. To be flooded with vision. In the end, no one could walk these streets and remain blind.

I am more a seeker of beginnings, than ends. Beginnings are sweeter, after all. An encounter on a bridge over the Seine; finding a friend over the *fripier*'s cart at the Temple; sharing a *pichet* in a seedy café or the bite of absinthe on the tongue at a long zinc bar. Although once you look closely, endings are deceptive. Once you do not turn the eyes away.

FRANCE, 1848–1871

Rise of the Second Empire, 1848–1869

February 1848 — King Louis Philippe abdicates, dissolving the "July Monarchy" of 1830 in favor of a provisional government.

March 1848 — The working day is limited to ten hours in Paris, eleven in the provinces.

June 1848 — Louis Napoleon Bonaparte is elected to the Constituent Assembly (along with Victor Hugo) but remains in exile in England until August.

December 1851 — Louis Napoleon Bonaparte stages a coup d'état. Despite demonstrations of resistance, the coup is ratified by plebiscite.

December 1852 — Empire is proclaimed, with Louis Napoleon Bonaparte at its head as Napoleon III.

January 1853 — Napoleon III marries Eugénie de Montijo, age twenty-eight, of the Spanish nobility.

July 1853 — Georges Haussmann becomes prefect of the Seine, charged with the rebuilding of Paris.

1856 — Birth and baptism of the prince imperial; Flaubert publishes *Madame Bovary;* photographer Charles Marville begins documenting Paris streets.

1857 — Flaubert is prosecuted for "offense of public morals."

February 1858 — First of Bernadette Soubirous's visions at a grotto near Lourdes.

January 1860 — Paris city limits are extended.

April 1861 — American Civil War commences.

January 1862 — France invades Mexico.

September 1862 — Construction begins for reservoir and aqueduct to ensure water supply in Paris.

November 1862 — Victor Hugo publishes *Les Misérables*.

1863 — Napoleon III suggests that France, Britain, and Russia intervene in the American Civil War; Russia and Britain decline.

January 1863 — Lincoln issues the Emancipation Proclamation.

May 1863 — Salon des Refusés launches the Impressionist painters.

1864 — International Working Men's Association founded in London.

April 1864 — The Austrian archduke and prince Ferdinand Maximilian, of the house of Hapsburg, is crowned Maximilian I of Mexico, with support from Mexican aristocrats and France.

April 1865 — Robert E. Lee surrenders to Ulysses S. Grant at Appomattox.

April 1865 — Lincoln is assassinated.

July 1866 — Prussian army conquers and annexes Austria, France's ally, at Sadowa, in a move toward German unification and expansion.

1867 — Karl Marx publishes *Das Kapital*.

April 1867 — The Great Exhibition opens in Paris, including "model workers' dwellings" and the Krupp cannon.

June 1867 — Maximilian I is abandoned by French protectors and shot at Querétaro by Mexican nationalists.

May 1868 — First issue of the leftist, empire-critical newspaper *La Lanterne* is published, becoming a bestseller among workers; its publisher is subsequently arrested.

May 1869 — French elections result in defeats of pro-empire candidates.

July 12, 1869 — Napoleon III announces liberalizing reforms, including freedom of the press.

August 1869 — The Carpeaux sculpture *La Danse,* in front of the Opéra Garnier, is defaced for being too realistic.

November 28, 1869 — At the last imperial ball at the Tuileries palace, Empress Eugénie dresses as Marie Antoinette.

The Empire's Collapse, 1870–1871

January 1870 — The republican journalist Victor Noir is murdered by Prince Pierre Bonaparte, great-nephew of Napoleon I and Napoleon III's cousin.

July 1870 — Otto von Bismarck advances the Hohenzollern prince Leopold of Sigmaringen for the vacant throne of Spain.

July 13, 1870 — King Wilhelm of Prussia receives the French ambassador at Bad Ems, but refuses terms that no Hohenzollern candidates be proposed for the Spanish throne.

July 19, 1870 — The French Empire declares war on Prussia.

July 28, 1870 — Napoleon III and his fifteen-year-old son, the prince imperial, embark from Saint-Cloud for the front.

August 3, 1870 — A successful French attack near Saarbrücken; newspapers hail the "invasion of Germany." Over the following few days, battles are fought at Wissemberg, Froeschwiller, Spicheren, Forbach, and Woerth.

August 15, 1870 — The Prussians surround Strasbourg, France, the start of a fifty-day siege.

September 3, 1870 — Napoleon III's armies are defeated at the Battle of Sedan on the Belgian border, and he is taken prisoner.

September 4, 1870 — The French Empire is overthrown. A republic is proclaimed by the provisional Government of National Defense.

September 19, 1870 — Siege of Paris by the Prussian army begins.

September 28, 1870 — Strasbourg capitulates and rations begin in Paris.

October 3, 1870 — The newspaper *La Liberté* suggests a women's army, the "Amazons of the Seine," be funded by the jewels of wealthy ladies. Trochu vetoes the project.

October 7, 1870 — Léon Gambetta leaves Paris in a balloon, to raise an army. The first major defeat of the Prussians follows at Coulmiers.

October 27, 1870 — Metz capitulates, leaving behind supplies and arms for the Prussians' use.

October 31, 1870 — A demonstration by 150,000 members of the National Guard of Belleville takes place at the Hôtel de Ville.

November 26, 1870 — The Great Sortie results in 12,000 French dead in three days.

January 1871 — Prussians bombard Paris for three weeks.

January 18, 1871 — Wilhelm I pronounced Kaiser of the Germans and the Emperor of Unified Germany at Versailles.

January 20, 1871 — No rations are left in Paris.

January 22, 1871 — Protest at the Hôtel de Ville is put down by Trochu's army, the Breton Mobiles.

January 28, 1871 — Armistice and capitulation of Paris.

February 8, 1871 — The National Assembly convenes in Bordeaux.

February 17, 1871 — Adolphe Thiers wins a vote of confidence and is appointed to lead the French Republic and to negotiate the terms of the Treaty of Frankfurt.

February 26, 1871 — During preliminary peace talks, the Prussians demand five billion gold francs in reparations within five years, as well as territories in the provinces of Alsace and Lorraine. Working-class Parisians drag cannon, which they have purchased by subscription, to Montmartre.

March 1, 1871 — Prussians march through Paris. The National Assembly moves to Versailles; the Central Committee of the National Guard (the Commune) forms in Paris.

March 18, 1871 — Government soldiers refuse to retrieve cannon from Montmartre, turning their rifles butt-up; the Commune begins a "bloodless revolution."

March 22, 1871 — A massacre takes place on the rue de la Paix, sparked by protests from the Friends of Order.

March 26, 1871 — The Commune and Municipal Council elected at the Hôtel de Ville.

April 1871 — Gustave Courbet calls for a federation of artists organized on democratic principles.

April 2, 1871 — Versailles troops push into Paris's suburbs, defeating the Commune's National Guard.

April 3–5, 1871 — Women march to Versailles to demand reconciliation.

April 5, 1871 — The Commune takes priests hostage.

April 6, 1871 — Thiers bombards western Paris, trapping residents.

April 11, 1871 — Women's section of the International is formed.

April 29, 1871 — Versailles troops victorious at Issy-les-Moulineaux after a strong Commune defense.

May 6, 1871 — Elizabeth Dmitrieff publishes the manifesto of the Union des Femmes, the Women's Union.

May 10, 1871 — The Treaty of Frankfurt ratifies the peace terms and cedes Alsace-Lorraine to Prussia.

May 17, 1871 — A cartridge factory on the avenue Rapp explodes, killing female workers.

May 18–21, 1871 — Meetings of working women on the reorganization of labor take place.

May 21–28, 1871 — Semaine Sanglante (Bloody Week).

May 21, 1871 — Versailles troops enter Paris, retaking the Champs-Élysées.

May 22, 1871 — Executions at the Parc Monceau. The Communards set fire to a number of buildings as they retreat.

May 24, 1871 — Death of Raoul Rigault on the rue Guy-Lussac and execution of the Archbishop of Paris by the Commune.

May 27, 1871 — Communards are executed at Père Lachaise Cemetery; large numbers are imprisoned or deported to New Caledonia in the South Pacific.

May 28, 1871 — Last battles in Belleville.

June 2, 1871 — The rebuilding of Paris begins.

GLOSSARY

Abandonné — abandoned infant; orphan

Abéqueuse — wet nurse

Académie — erotic photograph

Affair de coeur — love affair

Ambulance — hospital, or makeshift emergency center during the siege of Paris

Ami-coeur — term for partner in an intimate relationship

Amour-propre — self-respect

Assistance publique — welfare

Auch — ancient city founded by the Romans; the departmental seat of the province of Gers

Aurore — dawn

Auscitain — having an ancestry from Auch

Badinguet — nickname for Napoleon III, who borrowed the clothes of a mason of this name in order to enter Paris incognito

Balthazar's Feast — a lavish feast

Bar à vin — wine bar

Bibard — drunkard

Biberons — baby bottles

Billets-doux — love notes

Blanqui — Auguste Blanqui, revolutionary leader, writer, and philosopher of the Left; spent much of his life in prison

Blanquiste — partisan of the Left; supporter of the exiled leader

Bloc — short for *bloc de foie gras*

Bonne — housemaid

Bouilli — soup

Brigade des Moeurs — Morals Brigade; vice squad

Caleu — rustic oil lamp

Camélia — kept woman

Carte — mandatory identity card for registered prostitutes, marked with the dates of their health checks

Carte de brème — slang for the *carte,* named after the bream, a flat white fish

Carte de visite — photo post card

La Case de l'Oncle Tom — the novel *Uncle Tom's Cabin* by Harriet Beecher Stowe, a bestseller in France

Charenton — lunatic asylum

Chassepot — army-issued rifle

Chasseur — division of the French army, on foot or horse-mounted

Chauffe-pieds — braziers used as foot warmers

Chouette — slang for cute, great, nice

Chou-fleur — cauliflower

Cocotte — high-class prostitute cultivating a wealthy clientele

Code Napoleon — Napoleonic Code, from which the French Civil Code was derived

Comme il faut — accepted behavior in good society

Cora Pearl — a notorious Second Empire courtesan, rumored to be a mistress of Napoleon III; born Emma Crouch in England

Cotte — worker's blue canvas overall

Courte — slang for virile member, not necessarily large

Curé — priest, especially in rural areas

Dab — slang for doctors who inspected prostitutes; also, for the speculum

La Dame aux Camélias — the famous courtesan in the novel of the same name, by Alexandre Dumas *fils*

D'Artagnan — character in Dumas's *The Three Musketeers*, based on an actual man who rose from an aristocratic Auch lineage

Demimonde — fashionable society

Enceinte — pregnant; also, term for the walled perimeter of Paris

En cheveux — hatless; literally, clad only in her hair; a state denoting poverty, wantonness, bad taste, or all three

Enfant trouvé — orphan; a term used to refer to the individual throughout life

Estaminet — café or bar

Faiblard — weakling; a small-membered man

Fédérés — National Guard battalions that formed the core of the Commune fighters

La fée verte — the green fairy, meaning absinthe

Ficelle — thin baguette

Filles en carte — registered prostitutes who work on the street rather than in a brothel

Flâneur — boulevardier

Fouille merde — sewer scavenger

Fournisseur de l'empereur — furnisher to the emperor

Foie de canard — preserved duck liver

Foie d'oie — preserved goose liver

Fripier — seller of used clothing

Frisson — sudden feeling of excitement or fear

Frotteur — man who harasses women in public places

Gants d'amour — literally, gloves of love; a term for any kind of gift to a kept woman or prostitute

Garni — cheap furnished room

Gaveuse — goose-girl, named for the implement used to force-feed fowl, the *gavé*

Gers — province in southwest France

Grande horizontale — upscale prostitute, courtesan

La Grande Puttana — the great whore (Italian)

Grippe — flu

Grisette — young woman of bohemian tastes, often the lover of an artist or poet, and generally of the working class

Hospice des Enfants Trouvés — hospital for abandoned infants; commonly known as Enfants Trouvés and the same as the Hospice des Enfants Assistés

Hôpital de Lourcine — hospital where women who were not prostitutes were treated for syphilis

Hôpital Hommes Vénériens — men's venereal hospital

Hôtel de passe — cheap hotel for venal liaisons

"Il ne faut rien brusquer" — "One must never act rashly," a maxim of Napoleon III

Impasse de la Bouteille — street name, meaning "dead end of the bottle"

Inscrit — registered prostitute under the control of the police

Insoumise — a woman presumed to be working unregistered; a rather broad term also alluding to defiance, insubordination

Laissez-passer — document allowing travel into and out of Paris

La Lanterne — left-wing newspaper

Levée en masse — general uprising and rally to defeat the enemy

La lune — the moon

Mairie — city or town hall

Maison de rendezvous — hotel for assignations, but for the better-heeled, higher-paying customers

Maison de tolérance — tolerated house, meaning a high-class brothel

Malade — ill

Les Malheurs de Sophie — popular children's book by the Comtesse de Ségur, published in 1859

Marchande d'habits — wardrobe merchant who offered clothing on loan and for rent

"La Marseillaise" — French national anthem

Matefaim — kind of doughnut or fried dough

La Maternité — maternity hospital for poor or working-class women

Miché — john who patronizes prostitutes

Mitrailleuse — a rapid-firing wheel-mounted cannon used by the French in the Franco-Prussian War

Mogador — Céleste Mogador, a writer, performer, and at one time an inscribed prostitute; later Comtesse de Chabrillon

"Monsieur fils" — literally, "Mr. Son," meaning Louis Napoleon's son and heir

Mont de Piété — a pawnshop system run by the city of Paris

La morte — death

Muffe — rich old man who patronizes prostitutes

Non-inscrit — a clandestine, meaning unregistered, prostitute; see *insoumise*

Nourrice — wet nurse

Nouveau Plan de la Ville de Paris 1860 — street maps of Paris, by arrondissemont, bound as a small book

Paff — shot of brandy

Paris Illustré — popular illustrated periodical

Passe — brothel term for the period of a prostitute's engagement with a client

Patronne — woman manager of a shop, or similar

Père inconnu—father unknown, the term typically used on the birth certificate filed by an unwed mother

La petite—gesture of defiance

Petite salope—little slut

Petroleuse—female incendiary, mythical or real, during the siege of Paris

Pichet—measure of wine, in a carafe

Pissoir—public urinal

Poissonnière—fishmonger

Poulet rôti—roast chicken

Préservatif—condom

Prince Leopold—Leopold of Sigmaringen, from a branch of the dynastic Hohenzollern family; advanced as a candidate for the Spanish throne by Bismarck in 1870

Rebouiseur—fabric worker who restores old cloth

Recherche de la paternité—an unwed woman's claim that a particular man is the father of her child

Red Virgin—nickname for the leading Communard Louise Michel

Revanche—rematch, as in a duel

Rue d'Enfer—street name, meaning "street of hell"

Rue des Vertus—street name, meaning "street of virtues"

Quartier—quarter; area of the city

Quibus—slang for derrière

Sain et sauf—safe and sound

Saint-Lazare—both a prison and an infirmary for prostitutes with venereal disease; opened in 1836

Saint Martin's Day—a saint's day in November

Salope—slut; a term of contempt

La Salpêtrière—lunatic asylum famous for Charcot's investigations of female hysteria

Sanguettes — local treat of the slaughtering season, made of the blood of the fowl

Sans-culotte — working-class revolutionary of 1789

Sortie — the launching of an attack

Sortie torrentielle — large-scale attack launched from Paris to ward off Prussian forces

Sou — small coin worth about half a penny

Soupe du jour — soup of the day

Souteneur — pimp

Suiveur — lecher who follows women in the street

Tabatière — rifle used by the Communards

Tolérance — tolerated house, meaning an upscale brothel

Tour — a guard tower

Tour d'abandon — place for women to abandon infants anonymously, located at the Hospice des Enfants Assistés

Tricoteuse — one of the women who sat knitting while watching the public executions at the guillotine during the French Revolution

Tripes à la mode de Caen — a famous dish made from the four stomachs of a cow, cider, Calvados, and vegetables

Tripière — the covered pot in which tripe is served; can be heated over a small brazier at the table

Triqueur — rag picker

Vieille réserve — old, specially reserved, the finest

Ville basse — lower area of the city of Auch, linked by narrow stone stepways, the *poustrelles,* and steeply winding streets

Vin ordinaire — table wine

Visite sanitaire — mandatory health check for prostitutes

Acknowledgments

This novel has had a long coming-of-age, and many friends and supporters contributed to its making. The photographs and paintings, diaries, court records, letters, journals, memoirs, and artifacts consulted, and the historical commentary on them, were found over the course of my many visits to the British Library and the Cambridge University Library; the Musée Carnavelet (where an original loaf of *pain de Ferry* is available for study), the Musée de l'Assistance Publique, and the Musée de la Préfecture de Police in Paris; and the Musée des Jacobins in Auch. Many booksellers, museum curators, and casual archivists and documentarians, especially in Paris and Auch, unknowingly placed exactly what was needed on a shelf or wall or in a case.

My admiration and appreciation goes out to the historians whose work grounded this story and inspired it again and again. Most especially, I owe a great debt to Alain Corbin and Jill Harsin for their in-depth studies of nineteenth-century prostitution in France; and to Rachel Fuchs, for her insightful writing about pregnancy, poverty, motherhood, and child abandonment during the period. To better understand the era's upheavals, I relied particularly on the work of Alistair Horne, Gay L. Gullickson, John Milner, David H. Pinkney, and Rupert Christiansen. Elizabeth Anne McCauley wonderfully illuminated the history of photography in Paris. The work of many nineteenth-century writers sustained this project, especially that of Yves Guyot, who wrote vividly and courageously about (and against) the system of prostitution in his own day. Céleste Mogador has been this book's great-godmother; I first found her in passing anecdotes and scattered, but always pithy, fragments of writing. Monique Fleury Nagem's translation of Mogador's memoirs (2001) was highly appreciated and most welcome. And no acknowledgment and certainly no novel can do justice to Eugen Weber's landmark and fearsomely illuminating *Peasants into Frenchmen*.

I am extraordinarily grateful for early support from the Five College Women's Studies Research Center, and deepest thanks go to Susan Petersen Kennedy and Clare Ferraro at the Penguin Group for allowing me to structure my time to take advantage of the center's fellowship. Writing does not always fit easily or comfortably into a book editor's life, and my publishing colleagues have been patient, forgiving, and kind. I have had the honor of working with many authors at the Penguin Group, and they have taught me a great deal — especially about grace under pressure and sustaining faith in one's work despite the vicissitudes of life and the publishing environment. I draw constantly on their example and thank them from the bottom of my heart.

My gratitude goes to Susan Fox Rogers for her original introduction to the beauty of the Gers as well as its goose-women; to Arthur Levine-Ferrante, Ruth Ozeki Lounsbury, Ann Imbrie, and Carol Houck Smith for their creative support early in the novel's development and our many wonderful conversations about writing. Ann Rosalind Jones has been my teacher in so many ways. Lisa Holton, Karen Magee, and Peggy Pyle have made "dinner parties" a sustaining force. Andrew DeSanti's gifts over the years, not least of which is the example of his own tenacity, have encouraged me to persist. Betsy Lerner was an early ally and friend of this project; Rosemary Ahern's knowing editorial hand led me out of the woods of several drafts of the manuscript; and Robin Straus took on the book with conviction and confidence.

At Houghton Mifflin Harcourt, Adrienne Brodeur's formidable advocacy, her sharp and fearless insights, her generosity, and her rigor have taught me a great deal about a job I thought I knew.

For the manuscript's final polish, wholehearted thanks to Susanna Brougham's excellent eye, and to Lisa Glover. Also, my appreciation goes to Michaela Sullivan, Hannah Harlow, and Michelle Bonanno for the presention of the novel.

Above all, to my partner and *amie-coeur* in the truest sense, Gail Hornstein, gratitude for her sustaining and wide-ranging mind, her intrepid companionship, her listening heart, and her unflagging faith. Both Eugénie and I owe her more than I can ever express.